"*The Captivating Lady Charlotte*, Carolyn Miller's second Regency novel, surprised me. I was expecting a sweet romance and adventure, but I got so much more. The hero's story is touching, truly heartbreaking, and I loved seeing the heroine learn what true love really is. Well done! More please!"

—JULIANNA DEERING, author of the Drew Farthering Mysteries

"Carolyn Miller brings a story of high hopes, deep forgiveness, and a quiet kind of love that rings with truth. Drama and high society combine in a tale Regency lovers won't want to miss!"

—ROSEANNA M. WHITE, best-selling author of the
Ladies of the Manor series

Praise for *The Elusive Miss Ellison*
Regency Brides: A Legacy of Grace #1

"Displaying a flair for comedy and witty dialog, Miller is clearly an author to watch. Her debut Regency rockets off the page with clever, snappy repartee, creating an exciting and fast-paced read. Fans of Georgette Heyer and Julie Klassen will love this romance."

—LIBRARY JOURNAL, starred review

"This romantic story is reminiscent of Jane Austen: finding love despite the societal norms of the day while adding the spiritual elements of extending God's grace and forgiveness."

—CHRISTIAN MARKET

"*The Elusive Miss Ellison* will delight the hearts of Regency romance lovers with its poetic narrative, witty verbal swordplay, strict social constructs, and intriguing touch of mystery. Carolyn Miller is a bright new voice in the Regency genre."

—LOUISE M. GOUGE, award-winning author

"Fans of historical romance will love Carolyn Miller's debut novel. Nicholas's journey from proud, self-centered man to caring and devoted suitor will capture the reader's heart as it did Lavinia's. With just the right touch of inspiration and interesting historical detail, Carolyn transports you back to Regency England."

—CARRIE TURANSKY, award-winning author of *A Refuge at Highland Hall* and *Shine Like the Dawn*

"Lovers of Jane Austen will be enchanted by Carolyn Miller's debut novel. . . . This beautifully written book is definitely worth reading!"

—DAWN CRANDALL, award-winning author of The Everstone Chronicles

"*The Elusive Miss Ellison* is a delightful romp. Light and enjoyable, but also rich with the theme of forgiveness. A lovely read."

—ANGELA BREIDENBACH, Christian Authors Network president and best-selling historical romance author

"In *The Elusive Miss Ellison*, Carolyn Miller has created a heroine who will steal your heart and a hero who is as frustrating as he is charming. . . . Will capture the imagination of those who love the Regency period and win over those who are experiencing the era for the first time."

—MARTHA ROGERS, author of *Christmas at Holly Hill* and *Christmas at Stoney Creek*

"From the moment I cracked the pages I was transported to another era with a heroine as compelling as Lizzie Bennet and a Darcy-esque hero."

—LISA RICHARDSON, author of *The Peacock Throne*

"Carolyn Miller's writing style is reminiscent of Jane Austen, with a modern sense of wit and spunk. . . . You'll be swept into a story of God's amazing grace and the slow unfolding of a love that overcomes even the greatest opposition."

—AMBER STOCKTON, author of more than twenty novels, including the best-selling *Liberty's Promise*

The
CAPTIVATING
Lady
*C*HARLOTTE

REGENCY BRIDES
A LEGACY *of* GRACE

CAROLYN MILLER

Kregel
Publications

The Captivating Lady Charlotte
© 2017 by Carolyn Miller

Published by Kregel Publications, a division of Kregel, Inc., 2450 Oak Industrial Dr. NE, Grand Rapids, MI 49505.

Scripture quotations are from the King James Version.

The persons and events portrayed in this work are the creations of the author, and any resemblance to persons living or dead is purely coincidental.

ISBN 978-0-8254-4451-7

Printed in the United States of America
17 18 19 20 21 22 23 24 25 26 / 5 4 3 2 1

For my parents,
David & Kay Weaver.

Thank you.

❧ CHAPTER ONE

St. James's Palace, London
April 1814

THE ROOM GLIMMERED with a thousand points of sparkling light, the bright glow from the enormous crystal-dropped chandelier glinting off heavily beaded gowns, ornate mirrors, and the desperation shining in dozens of pairs of eyes.

Lady Charlotte Featherington glanced at her mother and smiled. "Truly, Mama, there is no need to look anxious. We shall not disgrace you."

Her mother drew herself up, as if the very idea of even appearing concerned was an affront. "I am not concerned about you, dear girl, but . . ." She made a helpless gesture with her hands and glanced at the young lady accompanying them.

"I assure you, Aunt Constance, I have no intention of disgracing you, either," said Lavinia Stamford, Charlotte's cousin and recent bride of the seventh Earl of Hawkesbury.

"You remember everything I told you?" Mama said worriedly.

"I cannot promise to have remembered everything, Aunt Constance, but I have no wish to embarrass you—or my husband." This was said with a sidelong glance at the earl, Nicholas Stamford, that caused a pang in Charlotte's chest. How lucky Lavinia was to have found such a perfect match.

Charlotte smiled as her mother bit her lip, no doubt torn between sharing her oft-stated opinion about the Stamfords and not wishing to offend Lavinia on such an important day.

She turned her attention to the front of the room, as the Lord Chamberlain called the name of the next young lady to make her presentation. Butterflies danced haphazardly in her stomach. Only two to go, then it was her turn. Pushing to her toes, she peered around the rather large pink-swathed matron in front, whose ridiculous confection of a headpiece held no less than eight—or was it nine?—ostrich feathers. She reached up a hand to pat her own far more modest hairstyle, with the obligatory five white ostrich feathers.

"Charlotte!"

"Yes, Mama." Charlotte fought a sigh and assumed the more correct stance of a gently bred young lady.

"I will rejoin you shortly, my dear." With a press of his lips to Lavinia's cheek, and a bow and good wishes for Charlotte, the earl exited, doubtless to join the other new husbands and fathers waiting in the chamber next door.

Charlotte followed Lavinia's gaze as she watched him leave. Such a handsome man, who wore so well the embroidered velvet coat and silk knee breeches demanded by court. She nodded to herself, heart dancing. She would marry a man who looked so well—perhaps even this year! For as Mama had said so often, after Charlotte's presentation the doors of every noble house would be open to her, and the offers to her father for her hand would pour in. Drawing in a breath, she braced her shoulders. If only she could find love among the eligible—

"Lady Anne Pennicooke," the Lord Chamberlain called, before gesturing forward the next young lady.

"Amelia has done well enough for the girl," Mama said with a sniff. "Though I do think the size of those diamonds veers toward the vulgar. One should hint at one's wealth, not trumpet it like the king's herald."

"Very poetic, Aunt Constance," Lavinia said, a smile lurking in her eyes as she glanced at Charlotte.

Mama sniffed again. "I'm pleased to see you took my advice about wearing the coronet, Lavinia. Your grandmother would be pleased to know it was getting some use again. It's such an elegant piece."

"Oh, I agree. It is very elegant," Lavinia said, touching the pearl- and diamond-encrusted band across her copper-blond waves. "But this is the Hawkesbury coronet."

"Are you sure?" Mama said, brows lowered, peering with an expression of suspicion.

"It appears very similar, but yes, I am sure. Nicholas assures me this is the coronet each new countess has worn."

"Last worn by your mother-in-law?" Charlotte murmured.

Something flickered in Lavinia's eyes, but her tranquil expression did not change. "Yes."

Charlotte inwardly applauded her cousin's fortitude. Her marriage had come with a very high price—that of a meddling older woman whose love for her son had been soured by his insistence on marrying a woman she despised. It must be so hard, Charlotte thought, to be at the receiving end of constant sniping and bitterness, but Lavinia bore it well. She possessed a measure of grace that seemed to permit her to smile and turn the other cheek, even as she must surely writhe inside.

Charlotte smoothed down her elbow-length gloves, surreptitiously watching her cousin as she continued waiting patiently. Why the dowager countess felt entitled to be so rude was a mystery, especially when her eldest son had proved responsible for the death of Lavinia's mother, the Aunt Grace whom Charlotte had never known. But fault seemed of little consequence. Probably it was the Duchess of Salisbury, Charlotte's grandmother, and her frequent avowals of the Stamford family's decidedly inferior connections—and cutting them in public—that had fed such bitterness.

Of course, Lavinia had never shared any of this, but it was there, evidenced by the dowager countess's not-so-discreet comments and the flushed cheeks and angry-looking flash in her eyes whenever Lavinia entered the room. The fact Lavinia had to rely upon her aunt for sponsoring her presentation to the Queen, and not her mother-in-law as other new brides might expect, said enough. No, while Charlotte might envy her cousin's good fortune in marrying such a handsome man, she did not envy her the cost. A family who could not esteem the son's chosen bride would be anathema to her—and yet another thing of which to be aware as her father presented young men as potential suitors.

"Miss Emma Hammerson."

The large lady in pink urged her sweet-faced charge forward, leaving Charlotte at the head of the line. Now she could see the royals, the Prince

Regent and his sisters standing either side of the elderly Queen. The butterflies grew tumultuous.

She turned to Lavinia. "Are you sure you do not want to go first?"

"And precede your mother's moment of triumph in her beautiful daughter?" Her cousin smiled. "I am happy to wait."

"She does look beautiful, doesn't she?"

Mama's rare compliment pricked warmth in Charlotte's eyes, the fond expression one she had not seen terribly often of late. Perhaps it was the pressure of organizing so many things for her court presentation and upcoming ball. She eyed Lavinia's gown, so similar to hers, save it was a pretty peach color, unlike Charlotte's white. But the hoops, the large bell sleeves, the requisite ostrich feathers were the same as those worn by the other ladies present. During their shopping expeditions to acquire such necessities, she'd often heard Lavinia's disapproval about the folly of hundreds of pounds spent for a gown worn only once. But then, Lavinia had grown up in rural Gloucestershire and had, until recently, little idea as to how things were done in society.

"I believe you the prettiest lady here today," her cousin continued.

"You exaggerate," Charlotte said, never too sure in her appearance.

"Not at all. You are quite in your best looks."

At Lavinia's comment, Mama assumed a look of complacency, nodding to the dark-haired Lord Chamberlain, as if expecting him to agree.

From the image greeting her in the mirrored door Charlotte thought she looked well, despite the ridiculous hooped petticoats doing nothing for anyone's figure. Her dark blond hair had been expertly styled by Ellen, Mama's lady's maid, whose skill in dressing hair far surpassed that of Sarah, Charlotte's own maid. The diamond drops in her ears, an early birthday present from Father, were of a beautiful cut and brilliancy; the pearl necklet everything expensive yet modest.

The dress itself, though of a style fashionable half a century ago, did suit her curves and tiny waist a *little* more than some others. Elegant silver embroidery embellished a petticoat of crêpe, trimmed with wreaths of white roses, with a double flounce at the bottom, fringed with silver. The train and body were of white crêpe and silver tissue, the short sleeves trimmed with blond lace and pearls, tied in two parts with a silver band. A laurel tippet, silver girdle, and white kid shoes topped with tiny rosettes completed her *grande toilette*, although standing for so long had made the ensemble weigh far more than one expected. But everything was in order, and enough—she hoped—to make her acceptable to the Queen.

"Lady Charlotte Featherington," the Lord Chamberlain called, unnecessarily loudly, considering they were standing so close.

Charlotte bit back a grin as Mama mumbled something about not being deaf, and returned the gentle pressure in Lavinia's clasped hand before moving forward, careful not to step on the lacy flounces of her bulky petticoats.

"Come."

Mama's grasp held nothing of gentleness, rather a feeling of determination. Charlotte kept her smile fixed in place as she walked to where the elderly Queen Charlotte sat, surrounded by the prince and princesses, with various attendants standing just beyond. Moisture lined her hands. She wished she could wipe them; thank goodness she wore gloves. "Glide like a swan," Lady Rosemond, the specialist on court etiquette, had cautioned. Since her lessons on gliding and curtsying appropriately, Charlotte had practiced studiously. Today would *not* be the day for any form of inelegance.

As she drew closer, she saw the lines marking the Queen's face, which elicited a pang of sympathy. She appeared very weary, which was not a surprise considering how many young ladies had been presented already today. Plus, the burden of her son's antics, which filled so many a hushed conversation, must prove a trial. Heart soft, she drew close, stopped at the marked spot, and inclined her head.

"My daughter, Lady Charlotte Featherington," Mama intoned.

Now was her moment. Lifting her gaze, she met the pale blue eyes gazing steadily in her direction. She smiled wider, and then bent her right leg behind her left before slowly, carefully, bending her left leg as far as she could, until her right knee almost touched the floor. Holding her upper body as straight as possible, she then forced herself to slowly rise, before finally, finally, she was fully upright again.

"Exeter's daughter?"

"Yes, Your Majesty."

The Queen nodded before shifting in her seat slightly. "Come here, child."

Charlotte moved closer and knelt. Lady Rosemond had instructed her for this next stage, too. Leaning forward, she bent her head, and felt the cool lips of the Queen press her forehead.

A kiss on the forehead for the daughters of nobility; an outstretched hand to be kissed by anyone else.

After what she judged a sufficient amount of time had passed, Charlotte pulled back, and resumed the posture Lady Rosemond had insisted upon. Straight back, chest out, chin up, but not looking like a soldier standing on parade.

"Charlotte." The Queen's gaze connected with hers, her stilted voice betraying her Germanic ancestry. "Such a pretty name, do you not agree?"

"Yes, ma'am." Stiff cheeks relaxed at the twinkle she saw in the blue eyes.

"Your namesake, your majesty," Mama asserted.

"I rather believe I am hers."

Charlotte swallowed the giggle at the chagrined look on Mama's face.

"Only daughter of the marquess?"

"Yes, ma'am."

"Very pretty."

Charlotte could almost feel Mama's relief at such queenly approval. The tightness encasing her chest eased a fraction. She hadn't failed. She hadn't disappointed—

Oh, but wait. Now to exit according to tradition.

Taking the tiny nod to be the sign of dismissal, Charlotte executed another heart-pounding deep curtsy, then backed away from the throne. One tiny careful step after another, praying desperately that she'd not step on the ridiculously long train the dress contained. She could not look behind her; to turn one's back on the Queen was an act of such rudeness one might never live it down.

Another step, then another, and finally a page gestured to the door on the right. With an inner sigh of relief, Charlotte exited the drawing room to find herself facing another door. This one opened to a room filled with men.

Her heart thumped, and she smiled, imagining the prospective candidates.

Now that she was presented, it would only be a matter of time before she found her husband. Perhaps she might even find him at the ball tomorrow night!

And with a quick prayer—*let him be someone young and exciting, handsome and brave*—she stepped across the threshold.

⁂

Bishoplea Common, London

The evening air held a thousand tiny water droplets, a dankness that filled his lungs and beaded across his skin. The starkness of the barren field stretched before him, echoing the cold emptiness inside. He shouldn't be here. He knew better. Taking vengeance like this was wrong. The only solace was that the remote location meant discovery was unlikely. *Lord, keep us from discovery . . .*

"Gentlemen? Are we ready?"

"Yes," William Hartwell, ninth Duke of Hartington, muttered, though he felt far from prepared. Pride bade him stand straight, to remain expressionless, to not show fear, but already he could not but regret the folly that had led him here.

The madness of his vows four years ago rose again in all its ugly glory. Why hadn't he followed his head instead of his heart, instead of seeking approval from the dead? Such depths of stupidity, stupidity he now recognized as having been engendered by a heart made vulnerable by pain, when he'd exchanged the dignity of his parents for the sweet nothings of a jade. How could he have ever believed his wife's lies? His finger twitched on the trigger.

"One. Two . . ."

Jerked from his contemplation, William forced his legs to move, to pace accordingly.

"Four. Five . . ."

Fear churned inside. Peripheral vision found Lord Ware, his brother-in-law and reluctant second, looking anxiously on.

"Seven. Eight . . ."

He gritted his teeth. Honor demanded justice. His pride demanded the truth. But—

"Ten."

He stopped.

But what if he had made a mistake, after all?

Shaking off the disquieting thought, he turned and faced his foe.

Nausea slid through his belly. Tall, blond, blue-eyed Lord Wrotham owned a handsome mien *she* had preferred. Disgust mingled with outrage, swelling hotly within until his chest banded and he could barely see.

Slowly he lifted the gleaming pistol, a relic from his father's day, something he'd thought he'd never need. But then, he had a bad habit of being wrong about things. Wrong about others. Wrong about himself.

Regrets churned inside. He studied the other man's face. Too handsome, but now holding a trace of fear in the puckered, glistening brow. Too handsome, but forever filled with lies. He *still* denied things. But William had seen him, had seen his figure depart from his wife's bedroom at an hour that could only mean one thing.

The last of his hesitations fled.

And at the word, he fired.

 CHAPTER TWO

Exeter House
Grosvenor Square, London

"LADY CHARLOTTE, MAY I request the honor of dancing with—"
"Lady Charlotte, you look enchanting—"
"So beautiful tonight, my lady!"
"Lady Charlotte! Please leave me the quadrille!"

Charlotte laughed as the men standing two—no, three!—deep clamored and jostled for attention. Her heart filled with the delightful sensation of being sought and admired. With so many guests, the receiving line had taken over an hour before Mama had finally propelled her toward the ballroom. "For you know they cannot begin until you commence the first dance."

Papa had the opening dance, and Henry was obliged for one, too. And while Mama said those of higher rank must be accepted when they offered an invitation, so far she had not had to consent to dance with anyone monstrously ugly or old.

Viscount Carmichael stepped adroitly between two gentlemen who were glaring at each other. "I believe the cotillion is mine, my lady?"

She met his laughing hazel eyes and curtsied. "Of course."

He bowed before shooting a grin at the two men whose squabbling had rendered them unable to offer an invitation, as if to say, "There, that's how it should be done." She smiled to herself. To have one of London's most eligible bachelors request her hand; surely Mama would be pleased!

The strains of violin grew louder, and her father drew near, parting her suitors as if Moses himself walked through the Red Sea.

"My dear." He offered a hand, which she accepted, then drew her to the center of the room. What felt like a million eyes watched as he drew her to the top of the set for the first dance of her come-out ball.

"It would seem you are quite the success," Father said, when they finally had a moment to speak.

"Mama has not been backward in her issuing of invitations."

"Nor should she. Not when it is *my* daughter who is making her come out."

Her smile stiffened, as the long ago questions panged again. Why was it so hard for Father to show his affection? How simple would it be to say something of how pretty she looked, or how proud he was of her, especially tonight of all nights? But . . . no. In keeping with usual, her mother's call to admire her was met with his half glance and a dismissive "very nice," an indifference that echoed in the hollow spaces of her heart. She blinked, looked down. Perhaps Henry was right, and she wanted too much, yearning for affection from such a busy man. But ever since Lavinia's wedding, when she had seen the love with which Mr. Ellison treated her cousin, she had realized not every father was as distant as hers. She lifted her gaze as resolve firmed within. Another point to add to her list for eligible candidates. The man she married would need to be willing to show his affection and emotions as freely as she showed her own.

The opening dance gave way to a country dance, which was followed by the cotillion. Lord Carmichael, the heir to the Earl of Bevington, had her laughing almost as much as her feet danced, with his smooth patter of compliments and commentary on the other guests.

"Don't look now, but I see a dragon."

"A dragon, my lord?"

The muddy green eyes smiled. "While this one does not have a long tail, she's still well able to scorch with her tongue."

"And why should she scorch you, sir?"

"Oh, no. It isn't me she wishes at the bottom of the sea. It is every young lady I dance with tonight. She labors under the misapprehension that I will offer for her daughter, but that will never do."

"No?"

"Can you imagine such a dragon as a mother-in-law? I have no wish to."
He smiled. "I much prefer dancing with the loveliest creature here tonight,
even if her father warns me away."

"Has he?"

"Not yet, but I'm sure as soon as we finish he is about to. Heaven forbid
you are seen to enjoy *my* company, my lady."

The whirl of flattery and praise kept her spirits high, until it was time
for the supper dance. Lord Wilmington, a baron from Bedfordshire, whose
flattering admiration of her looks soon gave way to dull detailings of his
vast holdings and wealth, escorted her into the dining room, where she
encountered a vast array of treats. Monsieur Robard had certainly outdone
himself tonight.

Without waiting to learn her preference, Lord Wilmington hurried to
load up two plates, then offered her one, before inveigling Mama's permission for him to join them at the table.

Henry caught Charlotte's unspoken plea, rolled his eyes, and drew the
baron into conversation about Ascot and whether Pranks stood a chance
this year, a circumstance that allowed Charlotte to quietly shift places and
move closer to the far more handsome young men at that end of the table.
After a satisfying amount of admiration and laughter, there was another
exchange of seats, and Lavinia and Lord Hawkesbury joined them.

"Are you enjoying yourself, Charlotte?" her cousin asked.

"How can I not?" She waved a hand at the room. "Everything is perfect."

The dining room, like the ballroom, was filled with laughter and roses.
Her favorite flower adorned every available surface; tastefully so, her mother
insisted.

"It appears a veritable garden," Lavinia said. "You're very blessed."

"Much more appealing than the Egyptian-themed ball we went to last
week," the earl said, with a glance at his wife. "Remember the scimitars?"
He grinned. "Not precisely Egyptian to my way of thinking."

Her cousin laughed. "Nor was it appropriate for a young lady marking
her come out."

The tender look she shared with her husband prickled envy in Charlotte.
Oh, to be so adored . . .

Lavinia dragged her gaze back to Charlotte. "Nicholas and I were saying earlier we'd love for you to stay with us sometime soon."

"That would be wonderful! I've never been to Gloucestershire."

There was another exchange of glances. Then the earl shifted forward. "We were rather thinking Hawkesbury House in Lincolnshire."

"Oh! Well, that would be lovely, too. As long as Mama agrees," she added doubtfully.

Lavinia patted her hand. "I'll talk with Aunt Constance soon."

"Thank you."

A dark-haired young lady captured Lavinia's attention, and Charlotte turned her attention to her food, the ice confection garnered by Lord Wilmington now melted, puddling on her plate. She scooped a mouthful in. Nearly moaned. Still tasted as it ought.

She savored the moment, a bubble of quiet in the midst of so much noise. Lavinia's words had elicited more than just excitement at the promised visit. She *was* blessed, immeasurably so, with family, friends, her father's finances such as to be able to afford almost anything her heart desired. And now, with so many opportunities available to her . . .

"I lay you a pony it's a girl brat."

"Fifty pounds."

"One hundred pounds!"

Charlotte studied her plate, ears straining as the conversation continued at the table behind her. Who was laying bets here? She didn't recognize the voices. Such foolishness, gambling over the birth of a child. Did Papa know? He'd never minded a flutter.

"Hartington needs an heir."

Hartington? Did they refer to the Duke of Hartington?

"If indeed he claims it."

She frowned. Why would a father not claim his own child?

Apparently this was also a question from one of the unseen party as there was a laugh. "Haven't you heard?" There was a hush of voices followed by a chorus of sniggers.

For some reason the mean-spirited gossip threaded sadness through her chest. The poor duke. How horrid to be gossiped over, to have the truth about such intimate family matters be fought over like dogs scrapping over a tasty bone. She was half inclined to interrupt, even though she knew Mama would not approve—

"Lottie?"

She glanced up, met her brother's amused gaze.

"I did not think the delicacies warranted such rapt attention, but it appears you do."

"Forgive me. I was woolgathering."

"Really? Why does that not surprise me?"

She held her retort, still appreciative of his having drawn away the attention of her previous dance partner. "Thank you for . . . before."

"I suppose I should get used to it, now you're out." His eyes glinted. "I confess I had little idea how popular I'd suddenly become with so many gentlemen wanting introductions to my sister."

"Perhaps some of these gentlemen have sisters as well."

He grinned. "I certainly hope so."

She laughed, drawing the attention of several passing prospects, one of whom was bold enough to ask what she found so amusing. After successfully parrying him, she turned back to her brother, now eyeing her curiously.

"What is it, Henry?"

"It's funny to see my little sister so flirtatious."

"Flirtatious?"

"Careful." He inclined his head to their mother, seated a few chairs away. "I'm just not sure I'm ready to see the girl who used to play with her dolls toying so confidently with the hearts of so many young men."

"I'm *not* toying."

"Be careful tonight does not mark your come out as a flirt."

Her jaw dropped.

"Charlotte!"

She closed it hurriedly at her mother's urgent whisper and met her brother's laughter.

"Admit it. Tonight would not be complete without that familiar refrain."

A smile tugged at her lips. "Neither of us would know what to do."

"But you have enjoyed the evening?"

"You mean apart from my brother's insinuations?"

"Apart from those."

"Of course I have. Tonight has been a dream!" A giddy, wonderful, delightful dream.

"Mama seems to think so, too."

Charlotte followed his gaze to where Mama sat, loudly exulting over Charlotte's success yesterday at the Queen's drawing rooms. "Two minutes! I'm sure that is far longer than any other young lady presented this year."

Mama's expression looked remarkably smug as she continued on her theme to a group of dowagers who were hiding their boredom moderately well.

"Two minutes." Henry gave a low whistle. "I can't imagine what the old girl would want with you for that amount of time."

"Can't you?" Charlotte reached across and pinched his arm. "You shouldn't call her an old girl. That is disrespectful."

"I'm sure she's been called worse," her brother said, rubbing his arm before rising. "Are you ready to return? I believe the dancing has recommenced."

She nodded, pushing to her feet, and they moved to the balustrade overlooking the ballroom. Henry's gaze roved the masses. "Why'd you have to invite so many old biddies, Lottie?"

"Mama issued the invitations, as you well know."

"I feel as though I've invited my friends here tonight under false pretenses."

"What pretenses were they? You mean to say they did not involve dancing with your sister? How shocking!"

"I confess I didn't overly advertise such possibilities." He coughed. "Some of my friends are not the sort of fellows I wish to dance attendance upon my sister."

"Which makes one wonder why they are your friends." She raised her brows.

He flushed. "Perhaps Mama is right, and you do spend too much time with our fair cousin." He jerked a nod at Lavinia, whirling in her husband's arms in the ballroom below. "You seem to have a way of making a fellow uncomfortable. It won't do, you know. Not if you mean to snare a husband."

"Snare a husband? You don't really think I need to resort to entrapment, do you?"

He turned, looked her over, before a reluctant-looking tilt to his lips suggested his approval once more. "You'll do."

She chuckled, looping her arm through his as they walked down the grand staircase. "I do hope when you meet a young lady you wish to charm that you'll refrain from being *quite* so economical in your praise."

"And I hope the man you wish to charm will realize just how much of his life will be spent in flattery and cajolery in order for you to be happy."

"I don't *require* flattery, Henry," she murmured as the elegantly dressed Lord Fanshawe drew near. Tall, handsome, impeccably attired in a dark dress coat and white neckcloth with a diamond winking in its folds, he was worth seven thousand a year, and known to be on the lookout for a bride, or so Mama said.

He bowed. "Lady Charlotte, are you ready now for our dance?"

"I am, thank you." She released her brother's arm and grasped the viscount's outstretched hand.

"May I say you appear the epitome of springtime loveliness tonight?"

"You may." She smiled, before staying her brother with a white-gloved hand, and saying in an undertone, "I don't require compliments, but I certainly can appreciate them."

"Careful, else you'll be known as the biggest flirt this side of Paris."

He chuckled, bowing, as the viscount drew her into the dance.

Such a whirl, such a heady delight these past hours had been. Round she twirled, as the ballroom echoed with the thud of skipping feet, and the musicians played a merry song. Her heart lifted as jewels glistened and candlelight flickered from three enormous candelabrum overhead. How joyous she felt, almost like flying—

"And that is why I believe the pumpkin flavor is the best."

She blinked, slanting a glance at her partner, who smiled.

"I'm ashamed to discover my conversation about Gunter's ices lacks the power to engage my fair companion's attention."

"Oh, forgive me! My head is awhirl with so much tonight, I can scarcely take it all in."

"Then I shall not be so ashamed, and shall venture to say something more to your liking."

"You tease me."

"No." Blue-gray eyes sparkled. "I simply wish to say how beautiful you appear tonight."

She smiled, even as the cynical part of her, the part recently fostered by Lavinia, paused to wonder if he would say the same to a young lady who was not titled, nor known to have a dowry in excess of fifty thousand pounds. How would she know whether he was being genuine or not? How would she know if any man was being genuine or not? She bit her lip.

"Pardon me, my dear lady, but you seem displeased. I trust it is not your partner that concerns you?"

"No." She smiled widely. "I simply wonder if your conversation extends to anything beyond compliments."

He mock-gasped. "Such wounds from one so young!"

She raised her brows.

"Now I have offended you. A thousand apologies."

She dipped her head, and his smile stretched, causing a little jolt to her heart, before the dancing led him away, and his place was claimed by another young man, somewhat more rotund; a marquess, so thus more titled—and more acceptable to her mother, whose loudly voiced desire that Charlotte dance with him had been met with a swift request she'd been unable to refuse.

The nature of the dance meant there was far less opportunity for conversation, which she did not mind, as the marquess was not quite as adept as her previous dancing partners. A crony of her father's, he had little to offer in the way of conversation either, save more compliments, which, while nice to hear, offered little in the way of ingenuity.

She fought a wince as he stepped on her toe for the third time.

"So sorry."

"So am I," she muttered, as the music led him away, leaving her at the bottom of the set.

"Lady Charlotte?"

She glanced up.

Her breath caught. *Here* was the man of her dreams. Dark-haired, chiseled features, blue eyes piercing from under brows so smooth they looked painted on. So angelically lovely, so impossibly handsome—yet *not* so impossible, for he stood before her now.

"I . . . sir, we have not been introduced."

"I know Henry from university. Lord Markham at your service." He bowed, and her heart fluttered anew. "I have come to save you from your partner."

She glanced at the red-faced marquess, lumbering toward them. "Oh, but I cannot—"

"Cannot permit your toes to be crushed by such a bore as he, yes, you are right." He picked up her gloved hand. "Shall we?"

She barely heard her answer, barely heard the marquess's words of protest as she floated off into this new lord's arms. Was barely aware of anything save the way his dark blue eyes captured her, caressed her, made her feel like she was dancing on air.

"Who *are* you?"

"Besides a knight in shining armor?"

A chuckle escaped. "Besides that."

"Besides a man who wishes himself a poet to do justice to your eyes?"

She blinked.

"Would you permit I should steal words from a poet? 'Around her shone the nameless charms unmarked by her alone—the light of Love, the purity of Grace, the mind, the Music breathing from her face . . .'"

"Who wrote that?"

"Byron."

Her gaze lowered, her cheeks heating. "Mama does not permit me to read his work."

"I hope she won't mind you *hearing* his work."

"Why do you say that?"

"You will have to wait to find out, won't you?"

She glanced up. He smiled, blue eyes lighting, and her heart began beating rapidly. And as they danced, and chatted, and laughed—and he did not once step on her toes—she began to wonder if perhaps *this* was the man who would prove husband material. Markham. Why had that name not leapt from the pages of the copy of Debrett's *Peerage* Mama had forced her to memorize?

As the music swelled, she caught a glimpse of her father standing next to an indignant marquess, and felt a moment's regret.

Her companion leaned down and murmured, "The marquess will look a little more sharply the next time he chooses to dance with such a beauty, I'll wager."

Though she smiled, his words drew her mind back to what she'd overheard earlier—wagers over the new child of the Duke of Hartington. The violins seemed to play a sadder strain, and in the middle of the ballroom, in the middle of her glorious debut into society, she found a prayer rising from her heart that all would be well.

# Chapter Three

Hartwell House
Hanover Square, London

THE SCREAM RENT the night.

William, Duke of Hartington, pushed his head into his hands and slumped over his desk. A prayer half formed on his lips before the darkness took it away. He'd be hanged before he prayed for her. Hanged before he let his heart be touched again. Hadn't he prayed enough?

Heat banded his chest, constricting his lungs until he grew desperate for air. He drew in a deep gulp and, for a few minutes, forced himself to concentrate on breathing: inhale, long exhale. Inhale, long exhale.

The room was unlit, the only light coming from the crackling fireplace. Red light danced behind his closed eyelids, echoing the fire threatening to consume his soul. His fingers clenched. With a great force of effort, he managed to release them, to straighten them, only to clasp his hair like a madman.

A madman. Laughter sputtered, died. How ironic. Had the board at Bethlem Royal Hospital and Asylum known the absurdity of offering a trustee position to one such as he? Mad? The heat within grew. Surely an understatement. How long would it be until he did not feel this insane rage?

Lord . . .

He couldn't pray the rest, wasn't even sure if God was real anymore. He certainly hadn't made His presence felt the past few months.

A scratching came at the door. He lifted his head but said nothing, waiting for the door to open as it always did, regardless of whether he'd issued instructions about his wishes to be disturbed or not.

"Your Grace?"

Jensen's voice.

"Your Grace, please come."

His valet knew everything, yet still made this request? "Go away."

"But—"

"No."

"Your wife is calling for you. She needs—"

"My wife?" He almost spat the word. "She made it clear long ago she needs me for nothing."

Not his love, not his seed. Only his name.

"If you do not, you will live to regret—"

"Do you truly dare to presume to tell me what I shall feel?" He eyed the man silhouetted in the doorway. "You have *no* idea what I go through!"

His valet said nothing, light from the hall lamp revealing his steady gaze.

A pang struck. Actually, Jensen did know. He was the one person William had taken into his confidence, the one person who knew the devastation caused by the discovery of the affair. The one member of his household who knew about last night's affair of honor. Paid almost a king's ransom to keep his lips sealed, the only man he could trust.

That maniacal laugh came again. How had he come to this, where his only friend was a paid servant?

"Your Grace?"

At the worried note in his valet's voice he forced his whirling thoughts to slow, to focus; forced himself to take a deep breath. "Yes?"

"The doctor . . . the doctor thinks it won't be long now."

A spike of resentment shafted his heart. "Until the brat is born?"

"Until your—the duchess is no more."

"What?" He spun in his chair to fully face his valet.

"Dr. Metcalfe says it is a hard case, that she has lost a great deal of blood. He believes it only a matter of hours."

For once the usually expressionless features held a measure of emotion, something that looked like pity. Hardening his heart, William said roughly, "Why should I care?"

"Because, if I may say so—"

"Never stopped you before, has it?" he muttered.

"If you don't, there may always be a measure of regret that things were left unresolved."

Like with his parents. William's hands clenched. He did not want that again, did he?

No. He didn't.

He grunted, pushing to his feet to follow Jensen. The great hall's lights made him squint and gave him pause, as the faces of his footmen smoothed from ambivalence to something approximating their usual impassivity.

No doubt they all knew, would be busy gossiping about his misfortunes, if they hadn't been so already. Hypocritical gossips—as bad as any matron from society's scandal-breathing *ton*.

He trudged up the stairs, heart hammering as another cry of desperation sliced the air.

"Your Grace?" Maria, his wife's dresser, hurried toward him, eyes reddened. "Oh, sir, Madam needs you. She—"

He waved an impatient hand, cutting off her words as he strode to the main bedchamber. Bracing internally, he entered.

Something akin to a collective sigh filled the room. A half dozen people scurried around on the room's periphery, but his vision focused only on the figure writhing on the giant bed. Horror suffused his chest, chasing away all previous emotions.

The brunette gnashed her teeth as a violent trembling shook her distended belly, almost like an invisible giant shook her. Beside her, a gray-haired man held one arm, while a couple of housemaids prevented the other from flailing. Blood stained the nightdress, stained the bed linens; too much blood it seemed from one small person.

Another low moaning sound swelled into a scream, piercing his soul.

He yanked his gaze away to focus anywhere but her face, her once adored, once so beautiful face. He focused instead on the carved bedposts twisting upward to a labyrinth of intricate cavorting gargoyle-type creatures. He'd always hated this bed.

"Is he here?" The voice, a hoarse whimper, drew his attention again, stealing past his internal barricades.

"I'm here, Pamela."

"William?" Blue eyes he'd once described as moonlit turned to him, focused on him.

For a moment he was transported back in time, back to last summer, when she'd last looked at him with something approaching kindness in her eyes. That single night when he'd tried to convince her of his love, show her his love, had tried to put aside his wretchedness in a final desperate attempt for an heir. Back before she'd taken up with Lord Wrotham again.

His heart hardened. "What is it?"

She whimpered, her face tensing, squinting, lines of pain furrowing her forehead as her back arched once more. "Oh, dear God!"

Her desperation seized him, stirring long-depleted compassion. From somewhere deep within he found the rest of the prayer. *Lord, help her, heal her.*

She gasped, eyes closed, the pains finally releasing their hold, as the accoucheur looked up at him, beetling gray brows pushed together.

"The child?"

"We . . . cannot get it out," Dr. Metcalfe said in a low voice.

"But surely . . ." He gestured helplessly to the bloodstained medical instruments. "Perhaps someone else?"

"There's no time, sir." Maria gazed up from her mistress, eyes filled with accusation.

"I'm sorry, Your Grace."

The finality of those words pummeled within. No. *Lord, no!* If only his resentment had not precluded his appearance sooner. If only he—if only she . . .

"William, please." Pamela's hand strained toward him. "Please believe I am sor—" Her words ended in a scream, before she slumped back motionless.

He staggered back from the bed, out of the way of the rush of women.

No! It couldn't end like this. *God!*

Horror crawled across his soul as the limbs refused motion, as Metcalfe received no response to his frantic pleas.

Lord God!

"She's gone."

"No!" A terrible wailing sound emanated from the far side of the bed. "Not my lovely!"

The screams, the sobbing, the frantic ministrations of the doctor seemed to fade as weight clanged against his chest like Westminster's bells. Nausea heaved within. Emotion lined his eyes, clamped his throat. No . . .

"You! You did this to her!" Maria staggered to her feet, finger outstretched in accusation. "I will never forgive you for what you have done!" She spat.

He dodged, though not quickly enough, as some of her spittle landed on his coat. She lifted a hand as if to strike him, so he grabbed her arm, twisting her around until she faced away from him, panting foul curses as the room's inhabitants watched in horrified fascination.

"And I will never forgive your role in all this." Swallowing the shakiness, he murmured in her ear, "You let your mistress play the whore, then have the nerve to blame me? How dare you?"

"Your Grace—"

William ignored the doctor, thrusting the Frenchwoman to the door. "Get out. Leave my home immediately. Jensen!"

"Here, Your Grace."

"Please ensure this person never darkens our doors again."

"Of course, sir."

"Your Grace—"

"You'll be sorry, Duke of Hartington!" She spat another vile obscenity. "I'll make you sorry that you breathe!"

"I doubt it." How could she, when he already felt that way?

Jensen, now assisted by some of the footmen, dragged the screaming maid away, her curses mixed with vulgar French he had little desire to understand.

"Your Grace!"

He spun to face the doctor. "What?"

The elderly man held a small bundle in his hands. "It's a girl."

"What?"

Dr. Metcalfe moved closer, holding the child toward him.

The tiny face seemed too tiny, too red, too still. "Is she—?"

"Alive, yes. For how long, I can't say."

His throat clamped, as for a moment, something melted in his heart. He reached to touch the tiny fingers. "How? I thought—"

"Sometimes when a body relaxes . . ."

He shuddered. His wife was now but a body?

"And we can pull them more freely . . ."

Ignoring the gory details, he focused on the silent child, before the reason for her existence rose again. His wife. Wrotham. That night. He shuddered. "Take her away."

"But—"

"I said take her away!"

And before any of them could see the moisture leaking from his eyes, he strode away, slamming the door to his bedchamber, where he could weep in solitude.

For of course the babe would be a girl.

Not an heir.

Not even a child he could call his own.

 CHAPTER FOUR

Exeter House, Grosvenor Square
Three days later

"OF COURSE SHE must go."

"But Mama—"

"Charlotte, please do not interrupt. Your father and I agree it would be impolite not to attend."

Charlotte glanced at her father, whose face wore signs of impatience, not agreement.

"Oh, hurry up, child. We cannot be late. Half of London will be there."

"But why?"

"Because she is—I mean, was a duchess!"

"But why must I go? I've never even met either of them."

"Something to be thankful for, if the rumors are true," Henry murmured, adjusting his black gloves in the doorway.

"I beg your pardon?" At the shake of his head, she looked to her mother. "How do you know the duke will even be there?"

"Because he always attends services. Now, this is not the time for idle speculation, Charlotte. Get yourself ready, and be downstairs in ten minutes."

Charlotte bit back an unladylike retort sure to get her into more trouble and motioned to Ellen to continue her ministrations. Wiry strength lay in the older woman's hands.

Within minutes she was downstairs, dressed in black crêpe, a small veil on her head. A short time later they were travelling in the landau to St. George's, the site of today's service, the regular Sunday time of communion sure to be packed with those wishing to pay their respects. How terrible an event to have occurred, on the very night of her ball, to have such sadness so close to where she'd spent the happiest evening of her life.

She studied her black gloves. Why *did* Mama want her to attend today? Their church attendance was sporadic at best. And with Mama's insistence on Charlotte's appearance, then releasing Ellen to ensure Charlotte's best looks, it almost seemed as though she wished Charlotte to make a positive impression. Surely she did not wish Charlotte to secure a grieving widower, even if he were a duke. Mama wouldn't, would she?

"Charlotte? Stop frowning."

"Yes, Mama."

She exchanged glances with Henry, then turned her attention outside. Spring had brought a flush of flowers, and the bright green new leaves were very pretty. Her spirits surged. Lord Markham, so assiduous in his attentions since the ball three nights ago, calling every afternoon, might even be amenable to taking her on a drive. "Do you think we could soon go and see Richmond Park? I'm sure it would be quite lovely at this time of year."

Mama's brow puckered. "Why you must suggest such a thing on such a sad day I do not know."

"But it's not as though we're sad, is it? You yourself said only yesterday we scarcely knew—"

"Charlotte, that's enough!"

"Yes, Mama."

Charlotte returned her attention to outside the carriage, which even now was slowing, no doubt due to the crush of vehicles the closer they drew to Hanover Square.

Minutes later they were being escorted to their box near the front, a box for which Papa paid a large sum each year, even if he rarely attended, and when he did, always complained of the condescending attitude of the minister.

Charlotte looked around her. Whilst not strictly a funeral, the number of black bombazine adorned congregants gave heavy suggestion of mourners. She smiled at Lord Fanshawe, seated across the aisle, which he acknowledged with a nod and grin.

"Charlotte, it is impolitic to acknowledge a young man in church."

"Yes, Mama."

It seemed impolitic to acknowledge a young man anywhere. Mama had been less than pleased with the post-ball visits from so many gentlemen she deemed minor conquests. Approval for Saturday's visit to Hyde Park with Lord Markham had been hard won, granted only by Henry's reluctant attendance. Never mind. They'd had a wonderful hour, and getting to know her brother's friend a little more had only deepened her attraction. He was such a handsome, charming man, always so amusing. Conversation with him always left her thrilled, wanting more . . .

The murmur of the congregants suddenly hushed, broken by a whispered, "The duke!"

Charlotte carefully peeked over her shoulder, working to make her movements as discreet as possible and not draw Mama's ire, as the man walked slowly down the center aisle. She eyed him curiously. Thin, not above medium height nor particularly handsome, he was dressed smartly, though completely in black, right down to his black neckcloth. The most notable feature of his face were the dark, dark eyes above which rested thick dark brows, which seemed a little incongruous with the lighter brown hair. No, he would never be generally held attractive. His head was held stiffly, as if he were aware of the crowds watching him. He was stopped by someone—she squinted, the Duke of Sutherland?—before moving to enter the box across the aisle and one row in front.

From this position she could see him more clearly, see the shadows lining his eyes and jaw, even see the clench of his jaw as Lady Someone-or-other turned to pat his hand. Something twinged in her chest. How awful for him to have lost a beloved wife and much-wanted child. How awful to be forced to grieve so publicly. Moisture clogged her throat, filled her eyes.

"Charlotte! Stop staring!"

But Mama's whispered recrimination could not force her gaze away. Poor man. He wore almost a haunted look. Hunting through her reticule, she found the black-edged handkerchief and wiped her eyes.

At that moment, the duke shifted, head turning as if he finally deigned to acknowledge the watching crowd. Something cold stole through her soul at the expression his face wore, as if he knew the reason the church was packed today and was contemptuous of the sudden increase in congregants. Shame bade her to avert her eyes, when she realized his gaze had landed on her.

The darkness in his eyes sent coldness up her spine, yet heat to the back of her eyes. Poor, *poor* man. Caught between wondering whether to deflect her look and pretend she hadn't been staring, or whether to continue her perusal, she felt a tear trickle down her cheek.

The narrowed eyes widened, the heavy brows lifted.

"Charlotte!"

Mama's pinch on her arm snapped her attention away, as if a spell had broken. Feeling a little dazed, she returned to study the front of the church, forcing her heart and mind to steady, to still. Inhaling deeply, she focused on the altar, which lacked much of the ornamentation or the beautiful stained glass windows that made visiting Westminster Abbey preferable to this much smaller, newer church.

As the minister moved to the pulpit and praised the congregation for their attendance at such a difficult time, a quiver of embarrassment trembled through her. How sad to think people attended services more for gossip than for instruction. And she . . . was no better. An urgency to leave swelled within, to leave this farce of worship, even if Mama would have an apoplectic fit.

The organ began the first hymn, prompting the congregation to stand. As she mouthed the words the restlessness gradually abated. Just because Mama might insist they attend today from motives other than worshipping God did not mean Charlotte need follow. The minister prayed, and her heart rippled with something deep, and she resolved not to be like one of today's shallow spectators.

And she'd begin by praying for the man across the aisle whose soul seemed as dark as his clothes.

William barely heard a word intoned by the minister, so conscious was he of what was being left unsaid. He went through the motions mechanically: Stand. Sing. Sit. Kneel. Sit. Listen. Try not to yawn. Stand. Sing. Sit. Pray.

His skin prickled at the eyes of the *ton* staring at his back. He knew what they said. Knew their gossip. Knew he was being mocked in the clubs, the cuckolded Duke of Hartington with the baseborn child—gossip mitigated only by the fact that Wrotham had fled the country, as he'd promised.

His throat clamped. While he could barely stand to think of the misbegotten child's antecedents, justice demanded he not hold her parents' sins against her. That and Jensen's pleas had transformed his initial reaction to something less dramatic, permitting the child to stay in the room farthest from him, where he wouldn't hear it, wouldn't see it. The wet-nurse his wife had previously engaged had been installed there, too, and Jensen assured him all was well. But he had yet to see her. Couldn't *bear* to see her, reminder as she was of his wife's failings—and his own.

God?

Silence.

His lips twisted. Even here in church, God seemed so very far away.

As he mouthed along to the last hymn, William found himself bracing for the crush of people. He nearly hadn't come today, but the knowledge his absence would result in all the more gossip had kept him to his regular practice.

The minister prayed, then released the congregation with a blessing: "Go forth into the world in peace, holding fast to that which is good. Strengthen the fainthearted, support the weak, help the afflicted, honor everyone. Love and serve the Lord, rejoicing in the power of the Holy Spirit, and the blessing of the Lord be amongst you, both now and forevermore."

"Amen."

His voice agreed, even though his heart doubted. How could he hold to what was good, how could he rejoice in the power of the Holy Spirit, how could he help anyone?

He was the one needing strengthening; *he* was the one afflicted. The next few days would be torture; the last three had been hell. So many decisions to be made, decisions pertaining not just to the funeral of his wife, but also to closing up the London town house, travel arrangements for the procession back to Hartwell Abbey, let alone all the arrangements required for the child. And then there were the visits, visits from the well-meaning, from the undertakers, the reverend, even the occasional call from the few who considered themselves his friends.

He'd barely slept since Thursday, the fog menacing the corners of his mind gradually massing, until reason and clarity of thought, so long his friends, seemed impossibly far away. At times he felt nearly dizzy with the weight of it all. Jensen urged him to rest, but he could not. Too much churned inside, begging release.

"Hartington?"

He blinked. Forced the whirring thoughts to slow. Forced his head to turn.

"May I say how sorry we were to hear of your loss?"

William forced himself to nod. Who was that? Remembering names had always been Pamela's forte. He joined the recessional, following in the wake of the reverend. If he hurried his escape, there would be fewer people to talk to.

"Duke?"

Good manners halted his steps, bade him turn, stay.

"May we offer our condolences."

People could offer all the condolences they liked; it didn't mean he believed them. Their eyes were too hard, glinting with latent amusement as they stored up their encounter for the latest *on-dit*, their mouths speaking sympathetic nothings while he searched their faces for anything of true compassion.

Not that he deserved compassion. He'd never been able to effectively hide his hatred of his wife's affairs, never been able to shrug off infidelity as so many others seemed able. *His* marriage vows had meant something, hence his devastation when he'd realized how little they'd meant to the woman he'd promised his life to. Yet despite the pain she had put him through, in these darkest hours of the past few days, her death had made him realize that underneath his anger, he'd never really given up every vestige of hope.

Not really.

Yes, perhaps he'd treated her unwisely—some would say badly—and didn't deserve people's compassion. But some twisted, bitter corner of his heart desired pity anyway.

It seemed the only ones who truly showed sympathy were those he barely knew. Hawkesbury's new wife, accompanying the earl on his visit of condolence yesterday, had seemed to hold something like sympathy in her glistening-eyed expression and soft words, her husband's words seeming more heartfelt than trite . . .

"Hartington?"

His attention jerked back to the present, the jostling crowd, the slightly plump marquess standing before him. They exchanged bows. "Exeter."

"Dreadful business, this."

"Yes."

The marchioness stepped forward, her black bombazine marking her as in mourning, though her face wore no ravages of grief. "Pamela was *such* a beauty. I still remember her come-out . . ."

As she gabbled on in reminisces he did not share, he fought the curl of his lip. Yes, his wife had been a beauty, some would say a *nonpareil*, but that was the problem. If she hadn't been so lovely, men would have paid her less heed, her head would not have been so easily turned, her feet would not have strayed . . .

"I don't believe you have met our daughter." She drew forth a young lady, similarly dark clothed, who'd been laughing with a tall, handsome gentleman standing behind her mother.

Breath whooshed from his chest. *Her.*

"Charlotte, meet His Grace, the Duke of Hartington."

The light in the young face drained away, replaced by a startled look in those wide eyes. She curtsied.

"Lady Charlotte," he managed to rasp.

Her gaze connected with his, blue eyes, as clear as the spring sky, holding him prisoner.

Like *hers* had once done.

He schooled his expression to neutral, but perhaps hadn't successfully wiped away all thought of his wife, as he noticed the pink lips falling open a fraction. "Duke."

A shaft of sunlight highlighted the faintest trail of saltwater on her cheek. His heart thudded. She at least did not seem to find his situation pathetically amusing, seemed rather to regard him with sympathy, just as the Hawkesburys had done.

But . . . truly? Desiring pity from a schoolgirl? What measure of fool had he become?

He nodded, made his excuses before moving swiftly through the throng to where his recently promoted coachman, Barrack, waited with his carriage and matched grays. He hurried inside, the door was closed, and within seconds they were away.

He leaned back, sagging against the squabs, closing his eyes as hooves clattered on cobblestones. The dim interior gave him precious moments to think.

Still so much to do.

So much to arrange.

Thank God it was Sunday; the house might be a little quieter than usual.

But the day of rest would not prove a respite for the servants, many of whom would travel back to Northamptonshire with him tomorrow. His man of business would follow in a few days, once the banks had been sorted. But Hapgood was trustworthy, as faithful in his parents' day as he'd proved in William's own.

Another pang squeezed his heart. Thank God his parents hadn't lived to see the mess he'd made of their line. Hadn't seen the young lady they'd selected as his bride years ago become the talk of society, nor he become society's joke. Despite the thorny past, he missed them. Their deaths had come too soon, although he couldn't but be glad they'd been spared such opened eyes.

His thoughts turned to Hartwell Abbey. His home all his life. His haven. His escape.

Perhaps now, as they neared the end of this session of Parliament, he *could* escape. Now that he wasn't expected to grace social functions he had no care for, nor attend the events his wife had insisted they appear at which inevitably turned into a mockery of marriage, he could finally invest in what he'd always wanted: Hartwell's experimental farm.

Hope flickered in his heart, tempering the heaviness of past days. Yes, one day soon he could devote his full attention to something he'd always dreamed. Surely recent progress in agricultural practices that had transformed the countryside and villages could be helped by the methods he and his men had labored over. He drew in a deep breath. He'd always had money. Now he had time. The ability to focus.

"Your Grace?"

He shook off the reverie, descended the carriage's step, and eyed the hatchment on the door, the mourning wreath marking a death, then strode up the shallow steps and entered the house.

A thin wail came from upstairs.

His spirits sank again.

CHAPTER FIVE

Vauxhall Gardens, London
May

IT WAS ENTIRELY possible that the excitement of last month's come-out ball was about to be surpassed. Charlotte clutched Henry's arm as they slowly walked through the entryway. Ever since she'd woken this morning, through getting dressed, the trip across the Thames in a scull, then walking up the shallow steps to the entrance, she'd been awash with thrills. How delightful, how romantic tonight would be!

She smiled at her brother and squeezed his arm affectionately. "Thank you for convincing them. I cannot believe I'm finally here."

"Truth be told, neither can I. Father had his reservations, and Mama has never been particularly fond of the out-of-doors."

As if on cue, Mama's voice came behind them, "It is a little warm, is it not?"

Charlotte sighed. Henry grinned and turned. "It will cool, and we are near the river, so that will help."

"But there are such nasty odors," Mama complained, fluttering her chicken-skin fan.

"Don't know why you insisted on coming if you're just going to moan," Father grumbled, his expression hinting this evening's expedition would offer him little pleasure.

"Well, *I'm* pleased we're here," Charlotte said. "I think tonight will be wonderful!"

Henry gave Charlotte's hand a squeeze, saying in an undertone as they waited for the queue to clear, "Never mind her. You know she's always anxious about anything out of the ordinary."

"Henry?" Mama turned, eyeing them. "What are you saying?"

"Nothing of importance, Mama."

"Hmph. If it's of no importance, then why must it be said at all?"

"Believe me, Mama, I wish it did not."

She frowned as they finally moved forward, and Charlotte's stifled giggle escaped in a gasp. "Oh, how lovely!"

Before them stretched the pleasure gardens. A grand avenue, intersected at right angles by several other gravel walks, stretched toward a gilded statue. Lofty sycamores, limes, and elms lined the promenades. Exotic structures hinting of Arabia and the Orient competed for attention with lantern-draped trees, lamps that also festooned the cast-iron pillars of the colonnades. Fruit bushes and perfumed flowers tickled her senses, while the strains of music promised further delight. And everywhere, everywhere, beautifully dressed people strolled, their smiles suggesting she wasn't the only one finding enjoyment in a place she never thought she'd see—until Henry's support for her birthday plans.

"Come, we must find our box if we wish to eat something before the concert begins."

At Father's impatient gesture, they followed him down the gravel path. Minstrels drew near, a piper on a pan flute meeting Charlotte's gaze, seeming to take that as an invitation to follow their party.

"I see you've made another conquest," Henry murmured.

"Don't be silly."

"Whatever will Markham say, now that you're being pursued by such a fellow?"

Heat rose in her cheeks, even as her insides curled with joy. "Do you think he will come tonight?"

"I cannot tell if that is a serious question or not."

"Henry!"

"Do you really think he would dare miss such an evening?"

His words—though uttered in a wry tone—gave courage to her hopes. Ever since the magical night of her come-out ball, she had been the delighted recipient of Lord Markham's attention. Nothing ever overt, nothing to which Mama might take exception, but the "accidental" meetings had kept her in a delightful daze these past weeks, fueling hope his notice might be leading to something more permanent.

She studied the people strolling by: elegant lords and ladies dressed in the height of fashion, next to those whose clothes proclaimed them as having lesser means—but none so poor they could not afford the shilling entrance fee.

"It is as though half the world is here!"

Everywhere the eye turned was another delight: fountains, statues, elegant arches, temples, and Chinese-styled pagodas, golden orbs of light radiating in a twinkling spectacular. She glanced up at the large bouquets of red, blue, yellow, and violet flowers hanging in the trees. "Oh!" She peered more closely. "They're lamps!"

"Not everything is as it appears."

They continued their promenade along the main walk, which was bounded either side with small pavilions housing tables and chairs. Henry nudged her. "We'll have supper there soon."

They strolled toward a large octagonal rotunda in which an orchestra performed. Beyond, just in front of the southern row of supper boxes, stood a white marble statue of a seated man holding a lyre. The familiar melodies made Charlotte long to join the couples pirouetting. She smiled, stifling the inclination. Mama would never live *that* down.

Before too long a whistle was blown, and a waiter drew forward, bowing to her father before gesturing to a large box along one of the colonnades. "My lord, I trust you shall find everything as required."

"I hope so, too," he muttered, before escorting them inside.

The small enclosure afforded a commanding view across the principal grove. Paintings adorned three sides: scenes of musicians, elegant ladies dancing, and rural idyll. "How lovely!"

"Charlotte, sit here." Mama motioned to a seat at the small table. With space for twice as many as their family numbered, she hoped the extra places meant the guests she had suggested would arrive soon.

A waiter drew near, bowed, then offered the selections: chicken cooked in a chafing dish in front of them, wafer-thin slices of ham, salad, custards, cheese cakes, fresh fruits, and punch. As a concession to her birthday, a large cake was placed on the center of the table.

"Charlotte!"

She turned. "Lavinia! Lord Hawkesbury, you made it!"

After a round of bows, curtsies, and kissed cheeks, Lavinia said with an apologetic smile, "Forgive us, we were inadvertently delayed."

"We head north tomorrow," the earl said.

"To your estate?"

"Yes, but Lavinia was determined not to miss her favorite cousin's birthday."

"Favorite?" Henry said, with a mock glare at the countess. "You always told me *I* was your favorite."

"Not all is as it appears, brother dear."

He chuckled.

Lavinia and the earl were seated, the conversation soon picking up in pace and volume. Lavinia smiled across the table. "Does Vauxhall live up to your expectations?"

"It is like a dream!"

Lavinia laughed. "Have you seen the statue of Handel?"

"Trust my wife to notice the musicians." The earl kissed Lavinia's hand. "I'm afraid, Lady Charlotte, we shall be most fortunate if we can get her to leave, she loves her music so."

"I have only been here once before," Lavinia confided.

Sounds of merriment rippled from the boxes nearby, as waiters rushed from one party to the next. Beyond the supper box strolled a myriad of people, all intent on enjoying themselves, if their smiles and laughter were any indication. Charlotte soaked it in: so many different people from so many different walks of life. At a distance, the sounds of the orchestra continued, familiar English melodies such as "Sally in our Alley" and "Sweet Lass of Richmond Hill."

"I know another sweet lass who might be described as a rose without a thorn," a deep voice drawled.

Charlotte turned, joy coiling within. "Lord Markham!"

"The very same." He bowed to her parents, the earl, Lavinia, and Henry, before picking up her hand. "May I say how lovely you appear tonight?"

Heat shivered at his touch. Words refused to form. She hoped her smile said enough.

He chuckled. "Never tell me I have robbed the beautiful maiden of her tongue?"

"Markham, if you are joining us, sit down. If not, then please return my sister's vocal cords to their rightful owner."

Lord Markham sat beside her, then offered a small posy of pink roses. "I trust this offering will appease and return your powers of speech?"

She drank in the delicate scent. "They're beautiful."

"Which is why they are apropos for you."

Delight danced around her heart as the night progressed. This was excitement! This was glamour! Lord Markham was everything she'd ever dreamed: charming, romantic, exciting, and so, *so* handsome.

Partway through the meal, a whistle sounded.

"What is happening?"

Lord Markham leaned close, eyes glinting. "Wait a moment, dear heart."

Her heart fluttered. Dear heart! Oh!

A second whistle sounded, then, as if in a magical dream, all the lamps adorning trees and colonnades were set aglow, hundreds of red and green and golden sparkling stars. "Oh . . ."

"It is breathtaking, is it not?"

Lord Markham's voice behind her stirred her hair, sending another delightful shiver up her spine. Oh yes, her breath was well and truly taken, and not solely by the illuminations.

Not long after finishing their meal, a bell rang, and they followed the crowds to the Rotunda. The concert had concluded, and a dark curtain covered part of the structure. Around them, the cooling air and dusky shadows filled with whispers and soft laughter. Lord Markham stood nearby. Anticipation thrummed within. What other wonders could tonight possess?

The curtain lifted, revealing a miniature country tableau of waterfall, mill, and bridge. As various wagons and carriages passed across the stage, the cunning simulation of the sound of the wheels and rush of waters reinforced the appearance of veracity.

Charlotte was mesmerized. "It is all so marvelous!" She glanced over her shoulder. "Have you ever seen anything so pretty?"

Lord Markham smiled. "I believe so."

The look in his eyes sent fire rushing along her cheeks, and she quickly returned her gaze to the rural scene. Surely he must hold her in some regard to say such things, to look at her that way. Her heart thrilled. Was this feeling akin to the love Lavinia felt for the earl?

The curtain descended, and the music recommenced. Mama murmured something and exchanged positions with Lord Markham, before saying something about needing a stroll. Placing Charlotte's arm in hers, Mama led her along a path. "I trust you are enjoying your evening?"

"Oh, it has been everything wonderful!" Not just the spectacles she had witnessed, but this delightful, fluttery feeling—no, certainty!—that tonight would lead to something yet more magnificent.

Mama's brow puckered. "I'm glad. But I cannot help feel Lord Markham is being a trifle obvious in his attentions. Do not encourage him too much, my dear. We do not want people getting the wrong impression."

"What people?"

Her mother refused to meet her eyes, glancing away, her smile widening as she nodded to a small party approaching them. "Oh, hello Amelia! How is Lady Anne? I trust she's recovered from her cold? No? *Such* a shame it should happen during her first season. I've always been so fortunate to be in the pink of health myself, and as for dear sweet Charlotte here, I cannot remember the last time she was ill. Well, lovely chatting with you, as always."

Mama's clasp on her arm tightened, and her smile seemed brittle as they hastened decorously back to their party. Lord Markham glanced up from his conversation with Henry, offering a quick smile that she returned.

"Charlotte!" Mama whispered.

She fought a sigh, and moved to stand near where Father was speaking to the earl and Lavinia. Yes, she would heed Mama's advice, but surely it was only polite to acknowledge a friendly gesture!

"And if you would be so good as to pass on our good wishes to Hartington when you next see him."

Her attention snagged. The man with the black brows and darker soul?

"Of course, sir," Lord Hawkesbury was saying. "He seems improved in spirits of late."

"Well, of course. Without that treacherous millstone around his neck—"

"Ahem!" The earl raised his brows at Father before turning to her. "How are you, Lady Charlotte?"

Disquiet swirled within. What millstone did they refer to? Why did they hush when she drew near? What were they hiding? Oh, why did people think her such a child?

"Charlotte?" Lavinia placed a hand on her arm. "Are you quite well?"

Charlotte nodded, forcing her lips up. She would not let talk of that man spoil her evening. "Of course!"

"Then shall we see the fireworks?"

"Oh, yes!"

Within minutes they had moved to the part of the park offering the best vantage of the fireworks, so Henry assured. Here the trees were a little farther back, offering a clearer view, something the swelling crowds seemed aware of also, as they drew closer, their anticipation palpable.

Boom! Rockets soared skywards, bursting into golden stars.

She clapped her hands. "Oh, it is enchanting!"

Lord Markham, who had somehow managed to secure a position beside her, smiled down into her eyes. "I agree."

But his eyes were not on the sky show, being fixed on her instead. She was thankful for the darkness, as another blush heated her cheeks.

She forced her attention heavenward, as the yellow and orange starbursts continued to illuminate the sky, conscious of his nearness, of his delightful sandalwood aroma, of the delicious thrill to have a man she admired admire her in return.

"I wish you great joy for your birthday," he murmured, his breath tickling her ear. "And for the year ahead."

Shivers rippled up her spine, her heart swelling with thankfulness for this most wonderful evening—this most wonderful man!—and she pleaded for God to continue to open the doors that would bless her future.

Hartwell Abbey, Northamptonshire

William studied the fields of rippling green. "The barley held up well over winter."

"That it has, Your Grace. Not too many losses this year." Mr. Hapgood bobbed his head.

"So you think the new seeds worked?"

"That I do, sir. That, and the addition of the fertilizer you created."

A flicker of pride swelled in his chest. So perhaps he could get *some* things right.

"And the shallow drilling?"

"They be your fields, sir"—this was said with a sidelong glance at William—"but yes, best to be avoided from now on, I be thinking."

William nodded, thankful once again that this man, estate manager extraordinaire, held the practices of his father and grandfather loosely. While some might consider that gentlemen had no right to be farmers, he'd never understood how a landlord could be satisfied with owning farms that yielded less than maximum productivity. Increasing rent was one thing, but surely knowing the people dependent on the land—his tenants, his villagers—would not go hungry was of greater importance. And if it meant people scorned his "loss of gentility," as Pamela had so often derided his scientific and agricultural experiments, then so be it. Surely he should care more for his people's welfare than his reputation.

Further discussion between them ceased with the arrival of a servant. "Your Grace, you are needed back at the Abbey. Lord and Lady Clarkson have arrived."

Pamela's parents. His heart sank. Acknowledging his obligation to Hapgood he turned and strolled back to the house. It would not do to make the viscount and his wife wait too long, but neither would he hurry back like an errant schoolboy, for what would doubtless lead to another fiery encounter.

His thoughts turned to their last meeting, the day of Pamela's burial. Lady Clarkson's sobs had haunted him almost as much as his memories of that terrible night. His heart had grown cold toward his wife long ago, but something in the way her mother had carried on, careless of observers, had touched his soul and made him wish he'd been a better husband, so Pamela had not felt the need to stray. But regrets were like dead seeds: useless things.

When he entered the hall, Jensen hurried forward, eyeing his mud-spattered clothes. "Your Grace, perhaps you might wish to change?"

As his butler helped remove his coat, William said, "How long have they been waiting, Travers?"

"Not more than a half hour, sir."

"Perhaps if you send in tea, I will exchange this for something more fitting to her ladyship's taste."

"Very good, sir."

William hurried up the steps, and under Jensen's ministrations he'd soon been made presentable enough to satisfy even the highest stickler of Almack's patronesses—which *should* placate her ladyship. To give Pamela her due, she had ensured William's dress was up to a Brummel-like standard, her eye for fashion something she'd inherited from her mother. And he had no intention to further antagonize his mother-in-law by meeting her in anything but what she would approve.

He descended the steps and entered the Blue Drawing Room.

Two dark heads glanced up, the viscount's corpulent features twisting in dislike, which proved a mild expression compared to that of the viscountess, whose sneer was another, rather less beneficial quality Pamela had also inherited.

William bowed. "Good afternoon, my lord, my lady." He refrained from adding anything of welcome or pleasure in their visit. He would not lie.

"Hartington." There was the merest scraping of bows.

"You did not hurry to greet your guests, I see," the viscountess said.

"I was unaware I was to expect guests today," he offered mildly.

"Hmph!"

The viscount shifted his considerable weight. "A most disturbing report has reached our ears."

William maintained his cool look, only permitting himself the smallest rise of a brow. He was well aware of how his mildness had always irritated Pamela, and by default her parents, and saw no reason to change. His had never been a disposition given to histrionics—yet another fault of which Pamela had been wont to accuse him.

"I see you refuse to oblige us by sharing the truth, as usual." Lord Clarkson's brow lowered in a ferocious scowl. "I had hoped better of you by now."

Anger surged. How dare they accuse *him* of lying? He—who unlike their daughter—had never deceived a soul! "Surely your fixed belief in my supposed lack of scruples must have some bearing on your refusal to accept my veracity." He fought the curl of his lip. "I rather think you'd say I misspoke if I said the sky was blue."

The viscountess frowned, but then, unlike perfect dress sense, logic had never been her forte. "You . . . you . . ." Her fingers clenched like angry claws. "Is it true you engaged in a duel?"

He blinked. How had they heard? "I beg your pardon?"

"There are rumors flying all around London that the Duke of Hartington was engaged in a duel to avenge his wife's honor!"

Dear God, he hoped not! He hoped his mother-in-law's gift for exaggeration was in play as per usual. Aiming for nonchalance, he settled back in his seat, crossing his legs in a languid gesture. "Is that so?"

"Is that—? Is that all you will say of the matter?"

"What would you prefer me say, madam?"

She made a sound suspiciously like a snarl before gesturing for her husband to continue the inquisition.

"For goodness' sake, Hartington, is it true?" Clarkson cried. "Did you or did you not engage in a duel against Lord Wrotham?"

He paused. Swallowed bile. "I did."

Identical gasps were matched by two pairs of rapidly paling cheeks. The viscount swore softly. "I never would have imagined that *you* of all people would countenance such a thing!"

He wasn't the only one, William thought sourly.

"I can scarcely credit it." Lady Clarkson fanned herself. "To avenge poor Pamela's honor?"

"To avenge mine."

Conciliation disappeared in her twin orbs of steel. "Surely you are not suggesting our daughter was anything but virtuous?"

"Again, your refusal to believe anything but what you wish is most impressive."

"How *dare* you accuse her of such things?"

"I dare, madam, because I saw Lord Wrotham exiting her bedchamber at such an early hour and in such a state of *dishabille*, one can only assume they had not spent their time talking."

"No!"

"My thoughts exactly."

"You lie!"

"And why would I make up something of such sordid nature? It gives me no pleasure, I assure you. I wish your daughter had been faithful—"

"Don't be so ridiculous! Pamela was well aware of her obligations."

Disgust roared through him. "Forgive me. I did not realize marriage vows were but obligations."

She snorted. "You portray yourself as a man of sense, yet believe such things? I never took you for such a fool! Did you speak with her?"

"Of course I did, and of course she denied everything. But would you have me deny what I saw with my own eyes?" The anger surged anew. "Would you have me deny the fact she never once sought *my* company this past year? Instead, she had a veritable cavalcade of young men she was seen with." Army officers, marquesses, viscounts, all more handsome, all more charming and engaging than him. "Did the gossips tell you that?"

Their faces pinked. So perhaps whispers concerning their daughter had reached their ears.

"I paid no heed at first, but after I saw Wrotham that night, I confronted your daughter. Oh, yes, I did." Memories of that night arose. Her tearful denials, which quickly turned into violent rage, culminating in the later admission that the child she carried was not William's after all. A savage pang crossed his heart. "Choose to disbelieve me if you will, but my *wife* held no compunctions about such things."

"I refuse to believe this," Lord Clarkson muttered.

"I am sure you do."

Lady Clarkson continued shaking her head, as if such an action might ward off the loathsome truth. "No. No, Maria would have told us—"

"Maria?" His hands fisted. "You cannot believe anything that creature says."

His word seemed to galvanize the viscountess, for she drew herself up, eyeing him icily. "She was always an excellent lady's maid, with exquisite taste in clothes—"

"She is a liar."

"No! She came to see us, to beg us to speak with you about the night Pamela died." Her eyes filled. "I just wanted to know if your child—"

"*Her* child," he corrected.

"If . . . it were a boy or girl?"

A broken sob roused the ashes of compassion. He cleared his throat. "Pamela wanted her child," he finally admitted. "She just could not birth her."

"Pamela was always such a slight thing." She wiped her eyes, glanced up. "It was a girl?"

"Yes."

Her face crumpled, and she heaved in a great shuddering breath before pushing to her feet, fire rekindling her eyes. "I will never forgive you, Hartington. You used my daughter ill, besmirched her name, insulted us in ways I never thought possible. We will never darken the threshold of this . . . this cursed mausoleum again!"

"Never," the viscount echoed, adding an expletive. "You are a blackguard and a scoundrel! We wipe our hands of you."

Without further ado, they exited, their mutterings and black looks giving him no chance to say anything further.

William slumped in his seat, the past few hours having left him drained. Should he have admitted the baby still lived? But what was the point? The doctor said it was unlikely she would survive, sickly as she was. William hadn't named her, hadn't wanted anyone becoming attached to a child sure to die. His fingers clenched. If he'd admitted she lived, would his denials of paternity have led them to demand custody? While he might wish to be rid of the reminder of Pamela's sins, he could *not*, in all good conscience, leave an innocent to such care. Leave her with the people who had shaped Pamela's morals so poorly? He'd duel Satan himself before such a thing occurred!

No. Lord Clarkson's exiting epithets regarding William's own paternity only reinforced his gladness at denying them the tiny bundle upstairs.

His hands burrowed through his hair. *Heavenly Father, forgive me if I did wrong, but I couldn't let them know . . .*

A groan wrung from the depths of his being. If only he'd married some-one with as much character as beauty, who valued him even a tenth as much as she valued her own interests—who had a whit of compassion, even!

An image of compassion floated before him: golden-haired, blue-eyed, a tear trickling down her cheek.

He shook his head. No. Men like him, so wretched, cursed by foolish choices, deserved no second chances. Had he not once considered Pamela the image of everything good? How could he trust his own ability to assess a woman's character? How could he ever trust a woman?

No. This foolish fancy was precisely that: foolish. God would not want him wishing for dreams that could never come true.

❧ CHAPTER SIX

Richmond Park, London
Late May

BLOND CURLS WHIPPED into her face as Charlotte raced along the tree-lined avenue. Exhilaration thrilled her to the tips of her gloved fingers, her heart throbbing in time to the hooves pounding the ground. Overhead branches dappled pools of shadows, a charming enough scene if she were one of those content to sketch. But she had never been drawn to such sedentary pursuits. Dancing and riding provided far more pleasure—and opportunities to showcase her skill.

"Careful, Charlotte!"

Ignoring her brother—forever jealous of her speed—she leaned closer to the flapping mane of her hired hack. "Come on, boy. Let's show them."

With an answering nicker the horse surged forward, they were now neck and neck, no, they were passing, passing—

With a burst of speed, she overtook the other man, flashing him a smile as they finally crested the hill. "Yes!"

He chuckled, slowing his horse as she did hers, before offering a nod of acquiescence. "I concede, Lady Charlotte."

She laughed. "I like to ride fast."

"You are quite the valiant."

"Quite the hoyden," her brother grumbled from behind them.

Lord Markham dismounted before moving to assist her slide to the ground. At the touch of his hands, the sandalwood scenting his nearness, the warmth in his smile—just for her!—her heart thumped loudly again. Oh, Lord Markham was everything she had ever dreamed!

Charlotte hooked her train over one arm, and they led their horses to a spot slightly away from Henry, who still muttered nonsense about how such wild riding would never be countenanced in Hyde Park.

"Hyde Park is pretty enough, but here"—she gazed around the extensive parklands, the view stretching as far away as the dome of St. Paul's—"here one can breathe."

She glanced around. Yellow laburnum flowers hung in golden chains. In the distance she could see a group of fallow deer frolicking in the sunshine.

Lord Markham's colt nickered, regaining her attention. He tugged the reins. "Does this remind you of your home in Devon?"

"A little. But without the sea air, of course."

"Of course." His lips lifted in that easy way she'd come to know and love. "Shall your family spend time there again this year?"

"Probably. We usually go in September, but only for a month or so. Mama much prefers London."

"And you prefer Devon?"

"I . . ." His eyes watched her carefully, as if begging her to an answer he wished to hear, but what was it? "I . . . find things appealing about both parts of the world."

He nodded, taking a step toward her, the colt now obscuring them from Henry's view. "I wonder . . ."

"You wonder what, my lord?" She tilted her head to see him better. Up close, he was so much taller than she. And even more handsome, with sunlight dancing in his laughing eyes.

"I wonder, do you think your parents agreeable to a visit?"

Her heart bumped against her ribs. He wished to visit? Oh! She forced her answer, her demeanor to be all that was demure. "My parents enjoy visitors."

"I wonder if they'd mind a visit from a *particular* acquaintance."

"That may depend on just whom that *particular* acquaintance might be."

"As wonderful as they are, it was not your parents I would wish to see."

The intent look in his eyes chased away all coherent thought.

"Nor"—he drew nearer still—"your brother."

She felt heat fill her cheeks, a fluttering in her midsection.

"Do you think your parents might be amenable to my paying you a visit, *my* lady?"

His smile sent tendrils of happiness curling the edges of her heart. "They might well be. Mama seems far more . . ." Resigned? Accepting? "Happy at your visits now."

The thumping grew louder, as his smile widened. "You must know how much I enjoy your company."

"Oh, and I do yours!"

He sighed. "It relieves me to hear you say so, for at times . . ." His brow lifted.

"Surely you cannot doubt my regard?"

"I merely want to be certain." His gaze dipped to her lips, then he drew closer, closer. She closed her eyes, excitement fizzing through her veins—

"Lottie?"

Her eyes flew open. Henry. Holding the reins of his horse—and a frown in his eyes.

"Markham, if I didn't know better, it would seem you intend to kiss my sister."

Mortification heated her chest, her cheeks. "Henry!"

"Charlotte and I were only talking," Markham said with his disarming smile.

Which didn't appear to disarm Henry. His scowl only deepened. "Didn't look like that was all you wanted to do. And it's *Lady* Charlotte to you."

Now Lord Markham's cheeks mottled, prompting her to interject, "Henry! How dare you?"

"I dare because you know Mama would be cast into a swoon should she hear of such things."

"Then she best not hear of such things," she said, tossing her curls.

"Excuse us," Henry muttered, grasping Charlotte by the arm, pulling her out of Markham's earshot. "You forget yourself when you are around him."

"I've done nothing wrong. He is a perfect gentleman."

He snorted. "Might I remind you it takes very little for a lady's reputation to be harmed?"

"At the risk of repeating myself, I have done nothing wrong."

"Not yet," he muttered.

He released her arm, returning to Lord Markham, whose air of curiosity made her hurry forward with a smile. "Please excuse my brother. He is somewhat overprotective."

Blue eyes flicked to her brother, the sardonic gaze growing more pronounced. "I'm sure he's merely thinking of your best."

No, he was only thinking of how to spoil her hopes and dreams.

Nothing more was said of Devon or visits or anything really, the ride home rather too short and too silent. Lord Markham returned to his lodgings, making no promises about meeting tomorrow, despite the fact she'd sent him her best smile and most concentrated thoughts of such a plan in an effort to induce him. Once they had returned the horses to the mews and she had changed, Charlotte found her brother reading a book in his bedchamber and, coming in, sat on the edge of the coverlet.

"Please don't say anything to Mama."

"I cannot like it, Lottie. I see the way he looks at you—"

"How does he look at me?"

"Not like a gentleman should."

Oh. Oh! "How can you say such things? I thought he was your friend."

"I knew him at university, but we were never close."

"Well, I think you're grossly unkind. If Mama has no concern for me being with Lord Markham, I don't see why you should."

He shook his head. "You are aware that, for all these visits, Father will never countenance Markham as a potential son-in-law."

"What? Of course he will."

The frustration in his eyes now layered with something more like pity. "You're actually serious about him."

"Of course I am! He is kind, handsome, charming, *and* titled."

"He's also heavily mortgaged and, Lottie, I hate to say this, but Markham is hardly the type of man to refrain from enjoying the favors of other ladies."

She gasped.

"I'm sorry if I shock you, but you cannot be so naive as to think our parents would permit you to marry anyone less than an earl."

"But I don't want to marry an earl! I want to marry him!"

"Charlotte! Calm yourself."

"Now you sound like Mama."

He shook his head. "I'd be doing you a great disservice to allow you to continue in this infatuation."

"It's not an infatuation! He feels the same way, too."

His brows pushed together. "The same way as what, precisely?"

"He . . . he holds me in regard."

"He's said that?"

"Of course!" She frowned. Wait. Had he? Or had she said that? He must if he wanted to visit her in Devon! She shook away the uncertainty. "This is none of your business, anyway."

"Where the family reputation is concerned, it *is* my business, Charlotte."

"How dare you?"

"Keep your voice down, unless you want Mama in here." He leaned close. "Have you already forgotten the scandal surrounding Pamela Hartington? The duchess has been dead for weeks, but still the gossip doesn't die. I cannot allow my sister to conduct herself in a manner conducive to wagging tongues."

She bit back the anger, forced in a deep breath, let it out on a sigh. "Henry." Relief at her sufficiently calm tone helped her smile. "Truly, I appreciate your concern, but I *assure* you, I've done nothing improper." He opened his mouth to speak so she hurried on. "Neither has Lord Markham. He is a gentleman, someone I have come to admire, and yes, I enjoy his company very much. I wish you could trust me."

"I trust *you*."

"Just not him? Then we shall need to prove ourselves, won't we?" She hopped off the bed, moved to the door.

"Where are you going?"

"To see Mama."

"Why?"

"Because I want her to know how much of a gentleman he has been."

"I don't think that wise—"

"Thank you, brother dear, but you have shared enough of your opinions for the moment."

"This is a mistake!" he called, as she walked down the hall.

No, it wasn't, she thought. A mistake would be letting her parents continue in the misapprehension that she planned to give up her friendship with her handsome lord for a future with a man she had yet to meet.

Marry someone she did not love? Why, the idea was ludicrous!

❦

Hartwell Abbey

"And how are you keeping, sir?"

"Well, thank you, Lady Hawkesbury."

She nodded, the afternoon light streaming through the drawing-room window, the Gothic glass highlighting copper strands in her hair. "And how do you fill your days?"

William mentioned something of his agricultural and scientific interests and his hopes for the asylum at Bethlem before returning the question. As she and her husband answered, he thought on the past fortnight since his last visitors had left in such high dudgeon.

The days had slid past slowly, counted by sunrises, the exact measurements of barley, and the hushed murmurings of his servants whenever he passed. He'd never noticed just how cavernous the Abbey felt, how empty it seemed. During his brief, tumultuous marriage, Pamela had never been content with just his company, and the house had been filled with guests, some of whom he met for the first time on their arrival. He hadn't minded at first, had initially thought she too would see the Abbey's beautiful, historic features and grow to love Hartwell as he did. Just hadn't counted on her appreciating certain historic elements far more than others.

Lavinia glanced around at the pointed arches, ornate ceiling frescos, the aged tapestries lining the wall. "This is such a lovely building, with many ancient tales, I'm sure."

He told her something of the Abbey's history. Like many an abbey claimed by Henry VIII, Hartwell had its share of secrets: concealed passages, hidden rooms, tunnels that linked the cellars and stables. The medieval features of an age of hidden priests had fascinated him as a boy, had led to many a game of hiding with his sister.

He *didn't* tell his guests how the secret passages had apparently also held appeal to his wife, as a way of ensuring her exit from her bedchamber to that of her *paramour*. Jensen had first alerted him to his wife's indiscretions at William's ancestral home. He had not believed his ears, until one night's silent watching had given proof of her infidelity, and he'd been forced to believe his eyes. Then he'd been forced to dismiss his coachman Rogerson for helping the duchess in her immoral activities.

Strange. Remembering such things did not sting the same anymore. Perhaps he was growing too accustomed to the lifestyle of those who'd populated the Abbey hundreds of years ago. Surrounded by others, yet rarely talking, content instead to fill his days with nature, with contemplation—albeit of scientific pursuits—finding comfort for his sins from the Bible. He *was* content. Wasn't he? Or did God want something more from him? More *for* him? Hope flickered, dwindled.

Lord Hawkesbury spoke briefly about Hawkesbury House and his mother, the dowager countess, before saying, "Sometimes it is more conducive to marital harmony if we are not at home."

William uttered a rusty-sounding laugh, then stopped, surprised. What was it about this couple that made him feel at ease?

Returning his teacup to the low table between them, he said, "How do you find this part of the country, my lady? I understand you are originally from Gloucestershire."

"Yes. Northamptonshire is lovely, with so many ancient churches and grand houses, but I suspect one shall always prefer the scenery of one's childhood." She gave a sweet smile. "I lived quite close to the Cotswolds, you see."

"One of the prettiest corners of England. I can appreciate such partiality."

"Thank you. Not everyone would . . ." She glanced at her husband, and bit her lip.

"My mother has never been backward in expressing her opinions," Hawkesbury said drily.

"Hence the need for escape." William nodded. "I quite understand."

Regret gnawed again about the visit from Pamela's parents. Should he have told them of the baby? He had rejoiced at his promised escape from their interfering ways, but surely it was only right that they should know about their grandchild?

"Hartington?"

William collected himself. "I beg your pardon." He managed a thin smile. "The effect of recent dealings with one's in-laws."

The countess laughed, and he was brought to mind of a similarly shining face.

"Tell me, my lady—"

"Oh, Lavinia, please."

He slid a look at Hawkesbury, who appeared unperturbed by his wife's most unusual request. "Very well, Lavinia. Our discussion of extended family leads me to enquire about your association with the Marquess of Exeter. I understand you are connected?"

"Aunt Constance is, was"—a shadow passed over her face—"my mother's sister."

"Your mother being . . . ?"

"Grace, the eldest daughter of the Duchess of Salisbury."

"Salisbury?" He straightened. "Forgive me, I didn't realize."

"Neither did I until very recently." She sipped her tea. "Learning of my lineage proved quite a shock, I assure you."

"I can imagine."

"Though it did have one benefit, did it not, my dear?" Hawkesbury said, caressing her hand.

At the sight, William's heart caught with memories of foolish feelings of romance and love. If only Pamela had returned his affection . . .

"But you were asking about the Marquess of Exeter," the countess said.

"Yes. He . . . seems a good speaker."

"When he attends Parliament rather than the gaming house," Hawkesbury murmured.

"Poor Aunt Constance." Lavinia sighed. "Have you ever noticed how some people become so caught up in imagined dramas they scarcely notice the true ones?"

Oh yes, he knew.

"I'm afraid my aunt is one such person. I can only hope and pray that Charlotte does not turn out like that."

He strove for nonchalance. "Lady Charlotte is your cousin?"

"Yes." She shook her head. "Poor Charlotte."

He eyed her but could not say anything. Heaven forbid he made his interest plain.

"I'm afraid she has fallen for quite an unsuitable young man, and her parents have made something of a fuss. I'm hopeful the dowager will be amenable for my cousin to visit."

His heart pricked. "At your place in Lincolnshire?"

"Yes."

"Whatever Mother says about it need not alter your plans, my dear," Hawkesbury said in an aside.

"I'd still rather have her blessing."

Again a look was shared between them that made him envy them not a little.

William cleared his throat. "I hope for your sake she is agreeable."

"Thank you." Her smile seemed ripe with friendship. "But if not, perhaps we should return to Hampton Hall, and Charlotte could visit there."

"That reminds me, Hartington. Would you be willing to visit to look over my fields? I admit our excursion today has opened my eyes to a world of possibilities I'd not considered."

Perhaps escaping the memories enshrined in every corner of the Abbey would be helpful to his state of mind. And even though his in-laws had threatened never to darken his doorstep, he did not doubt their ability to alter their word. "I'd be delighted. Name the date."

They settled on a time for the following week, and soon his guests made their exit.

His heart lifted—from the soothing nature of his visitors or their overtures of friendship, he did not know—but their call seemed molded by the fingerprints of the Almighty.

A visit to the West Country could be exactly what God wanted.

❧ CHAPTER SEVEN

Grosvenor Square

"I DON'T WANT to go to Devon!"

"My dear, if you cannot control yourself in a seemly manner, you present all the more proof that you are quite too young to consider marriage."

"But I love him!"

Mama sniffed. "Love! What is love but an indistinct feeling that muddles a girl's heart and mind, only to grow cold soon after?"

Charlotte stared at her mother. "Did you not love Father when you married him?"

"Of course." Mama waved a hand. "But I soon came to see my mother was right to insist I marry someone of our rank and substance. If I had not listened and had married someone other than your father, then my life— and yours, too, I might add—would have been very different."

Despite Charlotte's outraged feelings, her mother's absurdity tickled her sense of humor. Did Mama ever hear her nonsense?

Mama sighed the sigh of the very aggrieved. "Very well then. If you refuse to visit Great-Aunt Violet, then I suppose the only other person is Lavinia, much as I despise that family she married into. She, at least, seems willing to take you."

The words pressed against her soul like a bruise. Did nobody want her?

"There is no need to come the tragedy with me, my girl. Such dramatic airs you take on! You would not need to remove from London if you had behaved with just a little more decorum. As it is, I've had more than one lady of my acquaintance whisper something of their concern for you. And you *cannot* know how unsettling all this is to my nerves."

"I've got some idea," she muttered.

"Charlotte! I might be nearly prostrate with worry, but I am not deaf! Your actions in walking off with Markham were unconscionable! How a daughter of mine could think such behavior appropriate I do not know."

"It was only for a few moments—"

"A few moments is all it takes for the whispers to begin, and then your chance at a splendid marriage is irretrievably lost!"

She lifted her chin. "Not if Lord Markham wishes to marry me."

"Oh, my dear, no!" Her mother's eyes nearly fell from her face. "You cannot be serious!"

"Why not?"

"Why not? The man has nothing! His title is but the veriest wisp, he has little in the way of finances, less in the way of estates. No, no, you cannot marry him." She frowned. "Never tell me he has made you an offer?"

Charlotte bit her lip.

"Charlotte? Good heavens, *has* he made you an offer? Oh!" She sagged against the settee. "The room is spinning."

"Mama?" Concern tugged at her. Perhaps this time she really *was* ill . . .

"Tell me," her mother continued, in a weak voice, "has he made you an offer?"

"He has not."

Her mother pushed herself upright, with strength surprising for one ostensibly weak. "Then I forbid you to marry him, do you hear me? Forbid it! He is *not* the man your father and I have picked for you. I will not have my daughter throwing herself away on such a man as he."

Heat pricked Charlotte's eyes. She clamped her lips. Protest was useless.

"Now, such talk is injurious to my health. Go fetch my smelling salts. All this talk of scandal is making me quite light-headed."

With a swish of skirts, Charlotte exited the room, stomping up the stairs until she found Ellen and passed along Mama's request. She hurried to her room, locked the door, then threw herself onto her bed. Fire danced through her chest. How dare Mama make such accusations? How could she think so low of her own daughter? Was smiling at a young man such a crime?

She swiped angrily at the tears leaking onto her cheeks. Staying with Lavinia was one good thing, but she could *never* like the separation from Lord Markham. Never! She released a shuddery breath, her mind ticking over the other thing Mama had said. Had Mama truly picked someone for her to marry? Why, the idea was positively medieval!

And just who might that someone be that Mama had selected instead?

※

Hampton Hall, Gloucestershire
Early June

Late-afternoon sun baked William's neck, the heat relieved a fraction by the light breeze eddying the scent and dust of earth. "So the addition of peat and lime should bring about decided improvement."

Hawkesbury crossed his arms. "Is it expensive?"

"The cost is high regardless. Would you prefer the price of diminished yields over upcoming years? If you do nothing, in ten or twenty years' time you will see the land fit for nothing but grazing."

"But if these Corn Laws take effect as I fear they will—"

"The price will matter not if the land cannot sustain crops."

The earl sighed. "I suppose it should not be terribly difficult to access lime, seeing as we have a lime works on the estate near Hawkesbury House."

"Transportation might prove the bigger expense," said the third man with them, Hawkesbury's estate manager, whose prim appearance belied his aptitude for the sciences of the land.

William studied the far blue hills as the others continued their quiet discussion. Well he could understand the countess's preference for this pocket of England. The advent of summer had sprinkled a gold-tinged beauty across the tranquil landscape, inducing a sense of calm he had not realized he'd needed until his arrival four days ago. Since then, his visits to the fields and farms of the Hawkesbury estate had been interspersed with convivial conversation and meals fit for a king. How long since he'd stayed with like-minded people who shared his faith along with his interest in bettering the lives of those dependent on their estates?

"I beg your pardon, Hartington. We seem to have become distracted. Shall we return? I'm sure Lavinia would have returned from her visit by now."

"Her father must miss her lively spirits." He'd met the reverend two days ago at services, followed by a meal, during which he'd come to appreciate where Lavinia got her intelligent humor.

"He's getting old. I do not know how she will cope when he passes."

"It is never easy to lose a parent."

William thought back to when his parents had died. He'd been partway through a lecture at Cambridge when his studies were interrupted by word they had been killed in a carriage accident. The news had instantly propelled him to the dukedom, his title inevitable, but the manner in which he received it still felt a heavy price to pay. So much to remain forever unresolved.

They returned to the Hall to see a carriage unloading.

Hawkesbury muttered beside him, "I didn't think they would come so soon." He glanced across, offering a half smile. "Forgive me. It seems the guests we expected next week have come rather earlier."

A footman helped a golden head alight. William's heart tingled. He peered more closely. "That is Lavinia's cousin?"

"Yes. And her aunt. Apparently soon was not soon enough to escape the season." Hawkesbury drew nearer as the marchioness exited the carriage. "Ah, Lady Exeter. How wonderful to see you again."

She permitted her cheek to be kissed, dark blue eyes flicking to William before returning to Hawkesbury. "I cannot admit the trip has been to my inclination—"

"And yet you're here so soon," the earl murmured.

"*Nor* has it been especially comfortable. I really must speak to Exeter about ordering a new conveyance. It is beyond time. Oh! Duke. What a surprise."

William offered a small bow. "Lady Exeter."

"You know my daughter, of course," she waved a hand at the young lady whose mulish expression suggested the trip had definitely not been to her liking, either.

"Lady Charlotte."

His bow was met with a small curtsy and muttered, "Duke."

"And how is it that we might be so fortunate as to be in your company, sir?"

"How indeed?" The earl smiled, as if through gritted teeth.

"I know we are a trifle earlier than planned, Hawkesbury, but we simply could *not* stay in London a moment longer. So hot, you know." She fanned herself vigorously, as if stranded in the deserts of Africa.

Her daughter's gaze narrowed.

"While it is indeed a delight to see you again, madam, forgive my assumption it was to Hawkesbury House we were to await you," the earl said, with a curving brow.

"Really?"

"Really."

"Oh. Well, you must know that for me to stay there when the dowager is at home is simply quite out of the question!" She smiled at William. "You might not be aware of a certain *strain* that exists between our family and that of Hawkesbury's."

"I prefer to avoid gossip, madam," he said quietly.

"Lady Exeter," the earl said, his look darkening.

She hurried on. "And Lavinia was *so* kind to invite us, and I just knew she would not mind us coming a few days in advance. So here we are. And how fortuitous to have the pleasure of your company, Duke!"

"Alas, my visit concludes tomorrow."

"So soon?"

"I have responsibilities in Bristol and at home."

"Of course." Disappointment ringed the marchioness's eyes, though he thought he detected an air of relief around her daughter's.

The thought that his departure might relieve the young lady brought a disconcerting twist to his heart. And fresh determination to stifle this ridiculous attraction.

Chapter Eight

Charlotte forked in another piece of delicious venison. If she ate, perhaps she wouldn't be required to talk. And apart from Lavinia, and possibly the earl, she had no desire to talk to anyone at the table.

Mama eyed her with an upraised brow, forcing her chewing to slow and her gaze to lower. She peeked underneath her lashes across the table to where the duke sat, bemusement on his face as he endeavored to answer the questions Mama thrust at him.

Now she could see him more closely, she noticed the shadows marking his grief from two months ago had lightened. Yet his eyes remained as disconcerting as ever, especially when accompanied by the twist to his lips, which made his expression seem wry and self-deprecating. No, she thought, sipping her lemonade, while holding a manner somewhat sardonic, he seemed rather mild for a duke of the king's empire, his voice and opinions everything unassuming. How absurd for anyone to believe such a meek man had engaged in a duel!

Her gaze found her mother's, whose less-than-subtle head jerks suggested she wanted Charlotte to converse with the duke. Her fingers clenched in her lap. She might feel sorry for him, but that didn't mean she wanted to speak with him!

Her gaze lowered to avoid any more of her mother's mute messages. How preposterous were Mama's machinations? Changing their plans to immediately vacate London upon receipt of Lavinia's letter, a letter containing the news of the duke's visit to Gloucestershire. What did Mama think would happen? That Charlotte would forget Lord Markham? That the duke would be enchanted by her less-than-sparkling conversation? She had no wish to speak with him; neither did he seem keen to speak with her. The one time he'd addressed her this evening was to say something about how well she looked after the long journey from London, which Mama had quickly responded to by commenting to the effect that Charlotte always travelled well.

The anger rose. She forced it down, along with a bite of ham. Surely Mama could see her efforts were for naught—that this ridiculous charade should stop. Nausea swirled in her stomach. Mama's intent had remained unclear until her confession in the carriage about Lavinia's other guest. Which could only mean Mama's plans for Charlotte included him!

She shuddered.

"Charlotte?" came Lavinia's anxious voice. "Are you cold?"

She met the duke's dark eyes and hastened her gaze away. "No, Cousin."

"I trust the turbot is to everyone's taste."

Charlotte joined in as a chorus of assent rang around the table, even though she hadn't tasted it.

She glanced up, met the duke's gaze, noticed the half smile as he glanced at the uneaten fish on her plate. Her cheeks heated.

"Charlotte, why don't you tell everyone about how much you love to ride?"

By "everyone," Mama apparently meant the duke, as the others already knew of her partiality for riding.

Very well. If Mama insisted on playing such a silly game . . .

"I love to ride," she said in as flat a voice as she could manage.

"Why, Charlotte!" Mama said with a warning frown for her and a laugh for the others, before smiling brightly at the duke. "When Lavinia was staying with us last year, Charlotte helped her with her riding."

"I thought Mr. Horrocks did that. Remember, Mama, my riding instructor?"

"Yes, well, ah . . . I understand *you* enjoy riding, sir?"

The duke inclined his head. "I enjoy it, yes, but I make no claims to great sportsmanship, unlike Hawkesbury here."

No, Charlotte thought, disregarding the rest of his words. He made no claims great anything. He was dull, so dull in fact she felt like falling asleep whenever he opened his mouth. At least Lord Markham could flutter a girl's heart, as well as being *so* handsome, and able to quote poetry, and—

"Do you agree, Charlotte?"

She blinked, trying to recall what had been said. "I beg your pardon?"

"The duke was telling us how he enjoys plants, and I was saying you do, too."

Plants? She fought the curl of her lip as she shifted her attention from her mother to the duke. "I like flowers."

He nodded. "Any particular favorites?"

She thought back to the bouquets she'd received after her ball, bouquets filled with roses and lilies, the bouquets Lord Markham had sent. Her eyes stung. "Roses."

Before she was forced to answer again she pushed in another mouthful and hid her gaze.

"I understand you have a lovely rose garden at Hartwell, sir," Mama continued.

"Yes."

Despite her loathing of both Mama's games and the duke's meekness, Charlotte had to admire his fortitude. He answered Mama's questions exactly as he ought: in monosyllables.

"Your principal estate is in a lovely part of England, is it not?" Mama persisted.

"It is."

"And do you prefer London or the countryside?"

"The country," he said.

"Aunt Constance—" Lavinia whispered.

"Charlotte loves the countryside," Mama said, in such a way it was obvious she would have said Charlotte preferred the city had the duke expressed such a preference. "You were saying that just today, weren't you, Charlotte? How much you love the country?"

Charlotte noticed the sympathy lining Lavinia's and the earl's faces. Shame at being so exposed mingled with perverseness, making her say loudly, "I'm afraid you misunderstood, Mama. I said how much I preferred London."

"Why Charlotte! I—"

"I have never understood the appeal of the countryside when there is so much more to do and see in town." She stabbed at her plate. Yes, she was behaving badly, but . . . "I like balls, and parties, and shopping, and outings with my *friends*." How could Mama make her forsake Lord Markham? It wasn't fair. It wasn't fair! "I'm sorry, Lavinia, but the countryside seems rather unexciting in comparison."

Lavinia met her look of apology with a smile. "I quite understand. Especially when one has grown up in London, it must be difficult to imagine the pleasures that can be found in country living, although they *can* be found."

"Especially if one truly does enjoy riding," murmured the duke.

Her gaze met his before the amusement there forced her attention to her plate again.

Was he laughing at her? How dare he!

"I do hope you'll enjoy your time with us, Cousin."

Lavinia's kind tone clogged moisture in Charlotte's throat, and she nodded, bitterly aware of how her ungracious comments would be fussed over later by Mama, most likely with accompanying smelling salts and threats of swoons.

Coupled with this was the even more bitter confirmation from the direction of her mother's conversation: Mama truly did intend the duke to be Charlotte's husband.

❦

Poor girl. William smiled to himself as the ladies departed. He had little doubt of what would constitute the ladies' conversation in the drawing room while he and Hawkesbury drank port.

"Please excuse my wife's aunt," Hawkesbury said, once the servants had left. "Constance is a little eager to see Charlotte situated well."

"Understandable."

"She's usually a good deal more subtle in her methods."

"Sometimes it is best to be aware of what the attack consists, would you not agree?" William hooked an eyebrow at the former soldier.

Hawkesbury chuckled. "I don't think she was counting on the change of tactics from her daughter."

"No." William studied the port swilling around in his glass.

"Poor Charlotte. I'm sure she's being made to rue her outburst, even as we speak."

"I much prefer honesty to dissembling."

"Of course."

As Hawkesbury retreated behind his glass, William's earlier amusement faded. He didn't mind her lack of enthusiasm toward the countryside, could only be glad she did not lie. It made him wish he'd taken time to know the character of his first wife a little more before she had proved her lack of principles so disastrously.

"Again, I feel it necessary to beg your pardon, Hartington. I assure you such events were definitely not on our agenda when we issued the invitation."

"I understand the arrival of the marchioness was as unexpected for you as for me. I assure you, no pardon is necessary." William sighed. "I just imagined it would be a little longer until I'd be forced to think on such things."

"Of course."

Silence filled the dining room, the warmth of the evening forbidding even the friendly crackle of a lit fire. How long *should* it be before he thought on such things? Polite society demanded a widow wait at least a year and a day until remarriage, but for a widower, especially one known to have endured a loveless marriage, there was no such compunction.

Next time, he would marry to please himself. He was no longer the young man seeking to carry out the plans of his father. And truth be told, he needed an heir. The only way that could happen was if he wed again. But who would have him? Despite his amusement, something hollow had clanged in his soul about the way the young lady seated opposite had eyed him so dismissively. As if she thought him old and boring. He swallowed the rest of his port, hiding his wince. To a girl ten years his junior, perhaps he *was* old and dull. It was just a shame he thought of her in quite the opposite way.

Stifling another sigh, he glanced around. The room held a warm and cheery feel, one he'd be hard-pressed to emulate at the Abbey, due to the larger scale of the rooms. But perhaps this feeling was not related strictly to the enjoyable satiation after a good meal, but was more to do with a sense of camaraderie. How long had it been since he'd had someone to stand as friend? For despite the unease wrought by today's arrivals, he felt like he'd finally gained such a thing in both Hawkesbury and his wife. A prayer of thanks bubbled from his heart.

"Hartington? Do you wish to join the ladies?"

He smiled. "I confess to lacking as much courage as you."

Hawkesbury laughed. "I'm content to stay longer, if you are, too." He drained his glass. "So, any further thoughts on our position here in Gloucestershire?"

Their conversation veered from field management to fertilizers to the benefits of sheep versus cattle, when Hawkesbury's laughing reference to the Farmer Duke gave him pause.

Was that truly how others saw him? No wonder young ladies held him in aversion, even if such nomenclature did not dissuade their parents.

Later that night, after eventually joining the ladies and enduring more of the marchioness's attack—thus deciding him on an even earlier departure the next day—William tossed and turned in his hitherto comfortable bed.

Marriage? Again?

Heavenly Father, what do You think?

He listened for that still small voice that so often led his steps.

Ancient words permeated his mind: "Trust in the Lord with all thine heart; and lean not unto thine own understanding. In all thy ways acknowledge Him, and He shall direct thy paths."

He exhaled. *Lord, give me wisdom.*

He felt his senses dulling as the promise of granted wisdom for those who ask washed certainty into his soul. He closed his eyes. Snapped them open.

"How would I ever know I could trust her?"

His voice echoed in the room, thankfully not loud enough to wake Jensen, asleep in the adjoining room. He waited, but there was nothing save the scrape of ivy against his window.

Troubled, he closed his eyes again and practiced exhaling long and deep until the sounds and worries faded, and fatigue dragged him into slumber.

❧ Chapter Nine

Charlotte studied her reflection as Sarah finished braiding her hair and tucked the ends into her topknot. Nothing fussy, but nothing to pique Mama, either. She did *not* want a repeat of last night's scoldings.

A knock came at the door. Sarah opened it to reveal her hostess. "How are you, this morning, Charlotte?"

"Well, thank you. Come in." Charlotte dismissed her maid and gestured for Lavinia to sit on the edge of the bed, her company soothing and welcome after the tumult of last night.

"I trust you slept well?"

"Thank you, yes." She studied her cousin, her features paler than normal. "Are *you* quite well, Lavinia? I remember you usually being so bright and cheerful at this time of day."

"I . . ." A faint rose flushed her cousin's cheek.

"You?" Charlotte put up her brows.

Lavinia laughed. "Oh, don't do that! You put me in mind of Grandmama, and I can never withhold anything from that lady when she looks at me so!"

"What do you wish to withhold?" Hurt throbbed within. "Why do people never think I'm old enough to know things?"

"Poor pet. I'll tell you, but it is a great secret, and I do not wish—" She bit her lip.

"You do not wish Mama to know? Of course not! I don't wish Mama to know many things, so you can be sure I'm well practiced in keeping my lips sealed."

73

For some reason this declaration creased Lavinia's brow. She finally sighed. "It is nothing bad. Instead"—her forehead smoothed as light filled her eyes—"it is all that is wonderful."

"Then tell me! Let me rejoice with you."

"I am, that is, Nicholas and I, we are . . . expecting."

"You are increasing?"

Lavinia nodded, brightness shining from her face.

"Oh! I'm so pleased!" Charlotte gathered her close for a hug. "Oh, how wonderful for you! I gather Lord Hawkesbury is pleased, too?"

"Walking on air."

"As well he should."

"Lucky man." Lavinia made a face. "Him walking around pleased as punch, while I cast up my accounts every morning."

"You poor thing. You need looking after—"

"I'm not an invalid," Lavinia said with another laugh. "But it is all so new. Dr. Hanbury only confirmed it yesterday. I do hope you see why I don't want everyone knowing just yet."

"There will be time enough. When will the happy event be?"

"We think around Christmas."

"What a lovely gift."

"Yes. We're very thankful."

Lavinia's luminous expression cramped envy across Charlotte's chest. Oh, to look forward to such a bright future! She fiddled with the appliqued flowers of the bedcovers. She had never been in want, and up until Lord Markham, she had usually managed to successfully wheedle whatever she liked from her parents. But if only she could marry a man she loved, who adored her in return. And have a baby, a gorgeous lovely baby . . . Producing a man's heir might be her duty in life, but oh, how she wanted the warm and loving family environment to go along with it.

She swallowed a sigh. Forced a smile. "I heard a carriage leave."

"Yes, the duke had to return early."

"Of course." He'd made his goodbyes last night, his farewell everything polite and distant. "I hope nobody was too offended by my remarks about the merits of the city last night."

Lavinia chuckled. "*Nobody* was upset, and neither were Nicholas or I."

She groaned. "Not you, too? Mama's behavior last night was downright embarrassing. Could her intentions be any more obvious?"

Lavinia's smile dimmed a little, as her expression grew thoughtful. "Do you find the duke so distasteful?"

"Did it seem I did?"

"You barely looked at him all night—"

"Only because of Mama's carryings on."

"Which I *quite* understand, but I wonder if he did."

"But you said he wasn't offended."

"I don't believe he was, but perhaps a little confused, or maybe disappointed, that an attractive young lady seated across from him could barely spare him the time of day."

Charlotte drew back. "I was not rude, was I? Besides, why should he mind? He's only just buried his wife."

"True. And I can't imagine him wishing to have another one soon. Not after . . ."

"Not after what? Her affairs?" At Lavinia's soft gasp, she hurried on. "Mama mentioned the duchess was known to be less than faithful."

"I wish you didn't know that."

"Why? Is it not better to know such things when Mama has made her intentions so very plain? Though why she wants me to, I don't know."

"I'm sure she only wants your best."

Charlotte shook her head. "How can she? He's old enough to be my father!"

"Hardly!" Lavinia laughed. "I understand he's not even thirty."

"He looks older."

"His life has not been easy."

"Well, he's nothing like my Lord Markham."

"Thank goodness," she thought she heard Lavinia murmur.

"He's not! I am sorry, but the duke is unattractive, with those bushy brows, and so boring. I can't understand how anyone could think *him* capable of dueling."

Lavinia shuddered.

"Do you know about the duel?" Charlotte asked. "Mama refused to tell me about that."

"I . . . I cannot say with any degree of certainty."

"You *will* not say, you mean."

"I do not like to engage in idle speculation, especially when it concerns someone for whom both Nicholas and I are swiftly gaining the highest regard."

"Hmph," Charlotte snorted, uncomfortably aware of just how much like her mother she sounded in that moment. "Well, I couldn't stand being married to someone like him."

"Someone like him?" Lavinia's eyes flashed. "My dear, I do wish you knew how childish you sound sometimes."

Charlotte drew back as if slapped. She lifted her chin, avoiding her cousin's eyes, her heart stinging like a salt-rubbed wound. She pressed her lips together to halt the tremor.

"Charlotte, I'm sorry if my words sound harsh, but His Grace is one of the kindest people I've ever met, and one of the most interesting. Did you know he has created a formula to make certain crops resist disease? He is known throughout England as being one of the most benevolent masters toward his tenants. He is a man of faith, and vision, and—"

"A perfect paragon of virtue," she muttered.

"Any lady he pays attention to should count herself very fortunate indeed."

"Now you sound like Mama."

"Now you sound like a petulant schoolgirl." Lavinia eased from the bed. "Don't waste your life on an unworthy dream."

"I suppose you mean Lord Markham."

Her cousin nodded. "I do mean Lord Markham. What do you truly know of his character?"

"He is kind." He paid her compliments. "He does good things, too." Like asking her to dance. Fetching her a glass of lemonade.

"I'm not saying he doesn't."

"Yet you warn me away from him. Why? I love him."

"Do you?" Her cousin moved to the window. "Do you know what love is?"

"Of course! It . . . it's the most wonderful feeling. I have never felt so alive!"

Lavinia's smile grew tender, and Charlotte could suddenly see the wonderful mother she would be. "Love is so much more than just a feeling."

Charlotte's brow furrowed. What secret did Lavinia know? How could love be anything greater than the slushy feeling in one's middle whenever the man she dreamed about smiled at her? Or the heated shiver whenever she felt his touch? Or the enormous sense of happiness that made her want to dance and spin around whenever he laughed with her? That had to be love. Didn't it?

Her chin lifted. "When I think on Lord Markham, my only desire is to be near him and hear his voice. Every activity provides more delight when he is in attendance. And when he is not—"

"Come. Let us not argue. We'll talk on this subject more later," Lavinia said.

With great effort, Charlotte shoved aside the offense, forced a smile to her lips. "I expect arguing wouldn't be good for the baby."

Lavinia laughed, placing a finger on her lips. "Remember, *nobody* knows."

"You mean the duke does?"

Her cousin blinked, then smiled, catching the reference to her earlier jest. "I don't think so."

"My lips shall remain sealed."

"Remain sealed about what?" came a querulous voice from beyond the partially opened door. Mama limped in, wearing a silken wrapper and a disconsolate expression. "I don't know what time you call this, but I could not stay in bed a moment longer while I could hear voices penetrating from next door." She frowned at Lavinia. "Such very thin walls you have here, my dear. Most unfortunate."

"I've never noticed," Lavinia said, smiling. "I'll be sure to mention something to Nicholas—"

"Don't bother. I will mention it to him myself. But one can hardly expect anything less when one considers it was built by Hawkesburys after all."

"Mama, I don't think it appropriate to cast aspersions against the family of your host—"

"Your opinion carries little weight with me, my girl, especially after your atrocious behavior last night."

Charlotte clamped her lips together, her heart writhing at the sympathy she saw in Lavinia's glance before her cousin's gaze returned to Mama, her expression cool.

"Aunt Constance, I must admit to feeling uncomfortable when you criticize my husband's family. I am doing my best to overlook the past, and when people make such accusations, it does nobody any good, least of all my or Nicholas's peace of mind."

Mama sniffed. "Be that as it may, it does not change the events of the past."

"Nothing can, Aunt Constance. The only thing that can change is our response to it. And I have determined to not hold bitterness against the Hawkesbury family in my heart."

"Even with such a mother-in-law?"

Lavinia smiled sweetly. "Please do not cause trouble, Aunt Constance, else I'll be forced to renege my invitation."

"Hmph. Very well. Now perhaps you will tell me when you're expecting Hawkesbury's whelp to be born?"

Near Ashton Common
Three days later

Jensen drew out his pocket watch and checked the time. "Only another hour to go, sir."

"Thank goodness." William stifled a yawn against the back of his hand. But his time in Bristol had been worthwhile, his conversation with Mr. McAdam concerning road design and construction instructive, to say the least. McAdam had made suggestions to help William's cause, believing road surfaces that used evenly spread smaller stones—no larger than what might fit into a man's mouth, as he'd startlingly explained—should ensure the vehicle wheels passed along well, while enabling water to drain away to ditches on either side. Without requiring heavy stones or arduous engineering work, roads could be built more easily, releasing men to work elsewhere. All in all a most productive time, time spent determining how best to employ a prototype of McAdam's ideas on William's estate, before eventually deciding that lining the road between the Abbey and the neighboring village of Hartwell would best serve his purpose.

William leaned back against the squabs and closed his eyes. Three days in four spent travelling gave new appreciation for the Marchioness of Exeter's complaints about coach travel. Three days of wincing over bone-jarring stretches of roads, roads that made an excellent case for Mr. McAdam's signature coating. Three days of travel interspersed with interminable waits at inns, before the longer break afforded by nights in Bristol and Oxford. Three days which, save for his valet, he'd passed almost alone, which meant hours spent thinking, planning, dreaming . . .

A myriad of images flicked through his mind. Road improvements. Pasture improvements. Blue hills. Hampton Hall. Sunny skies. A golden head. Blue eyes. Perfect pout. Candid tongue.

Amusement tugged the corners of his mouth. The images continued, chased by half-formed prayers.

A golden head. Hartwell Abbey. A darker head. A sleepless night. A crying infant . . .

He shifted position, working to get comfortable. What should he do about the child? Society, like Pamela's parents, seemed to suppose it had died at birth. His staff were paid enough not to talk, but was keeping such a secret wise? Surely acknowledging her birth would only expose her to scurrilous whispers all her days. But if he did not, what would happen? The Abbey might have its share of ghosts, but a living child shouldn't be one of them. Yet giving her into the care of others seemed heartless, and to give an innocent life into the care of Pamela's parents would be cruel. What should he do?

Heavenly Father?

The carriage jerked. His eyes flew open. The carriage jolted again before slowing. Jensen wore a frown as somber as his tailored coat.

"What's happened?"

"I'm not sure, sir."

A horse whinnied, followed by a second horse cry. His stomach clenched. Something was not right. "What—?"

The carriage suddenly swayed, and he grasped the leather strap, clinging tight as the horses suddenly took off at speed. Barrack, such an improvement on Rogerson, the ne'er-do-well coachman of his parents' time, never allowed such confusion.

Jensen muttered something, his face drawn in the carriage's dim lamplight.

"What did you say?"

"I'm not sure if Barrack is still driving, sir."

"You think him indisposed?"

"I think it important to check."

"Sit down. I'll look."

The carriage was careening wildly, forcing William to brace against the floor as he lowered the window sash. "Barrack!"

The wind stole his words away.

"Barrack!"

Through the darkness he could just make out the shapes of the fleeing horses, their sounds of fright cutting a fresh strain of fear through him. A tug on his coat and he was back inside, Jensen's frown more pronounced than ever. "Sir, you should be more careful."

"We have to stop them."

"Barrack?"

"No answer."

Jensen hissed a long sigh. "The horses know where to go."

True. The team picked up in Towcester was one they'd used before, but that was small comfort, especially if his coachman were ill.

"We need—"

The coach slowed, then drew to a standstill. William flung open the door and descended, hurrying to the front. "Barrack?"

Horror curdled inside. "Good God!"

He scrambled up alongside his bleeding coachman, pulled off his neck-cloth, wadding it to press against Barrack's forehead to staunch the flow. "What happened?"

Barrack muttered something incomprehensible, his posture slumping until his head rested heavily against William's shoulder. William looked about him. Fragments of rock lay on the coachman's seat, remnants of which were embedded in the side of Barrack's skull. A shiver dashed up his spine. Who could do something so despicable?

"Jensen!"

"Right here, sir."

"Give me another neckcloth. He's bleeding badly."

In answer, Jensen stripped his off and handed it over. William tossed away his bloodied one and pressed the new cloth firmly to the gaping wound.

"He needs a doctor."

"Ashton is not far, Your Grace," called the footman, who now held the lead horses.

"We need to go. Jensen, can you manage the reins?"

"Sir, I . . . I do not think that wise."

He bit back a word, recalling his valet had never any great love for—or skill with—animals.

"Very well, I will. Here, help me get him down and inside. You'll attend to him while I drive."

"But sir, what if the attacker comes for you?"

Then God help them all.

"Here, hold his legs." He gently maneuvered Barrack's heavy form, waiting until Jensen held him securely, before leaping down to assist. "Lift him slowly, slowly . . ."

Eventually they managed to get him lying on the cushioned seat where William had been ensconced for hours. "There." He heaved out a breath, rubbing his upper arms. "Keep up a steady pressure. I don't care how many neckcloths are used."

"Yes, sir."

Returning to the coachman's position, William picked up the reins and called for the footman to release the horses. "Go help Jensen!"

A slam of the carriage door suggested he was obeyed, and he slapped the reins. The horses soon picked up pace. Ashton lay only a couple of miles away, the Abbey another three beyond the small village. He wanted speed, but in this dim light, with only the faintest rays of sunset rimming the horizon behind, he couldn't afford further misadventure.

William maintained a taut hold, huddling into his coat, the evening air holding a chill that made him wish for the protection of his greatcoat. Within a mile of their unforeseen stop his teeth were chattering, his fingers so cold they could barely grasp the reins.

"Heavenly Father, guide us, protect us. Please protect Barrack . . ."

He slapped the reins and the horses found further momentum, as if sensing his desperation to find shelter and help. In the distance he could see a glimmering light.

"Thank You, God."

By the time they reached the village boundary, the horses had assumed a walking pace. By the time they reached the Old Crown, he'd managed to halt them.

"Hello there!"

The inn door opened, and a swarthy-faced man appeared. His jaw sagged. "Your Grace!"

"Send for the doctor." Shivers wracked his body. "We need him."

Within minutes Barrack was being tended in the inn's snug before a freshly lit fire—and a gaggle of interested spectators.

The villagers' commentary swirled around him: "Looking like demons were a-chasin' 'em. And 'im, a dook!"

"Never thought I'd see the day!"

"Aye, but there's something smoky 'bout this, mark my words."

William slumped in his chair, fingers wrapped around a mug of hot spiced ale, watching the doctor continue his ministrations. The villagers were right; something was suspicious. Who had done such a thing? Why?

His skin prickled. Was Jensen correct in assuming this attack was against him?

"Your Grace?"

William placed the mug down and pushed to his feet. "How is he?"

"Not good. He should be removed someplace where he can remain undisturbed for some time. I'm afraid it might be a very long time." Dr. Lansbury looked up sharply. "Has he family?"

"No. We at Hartwell are Barrack's family."

"Hmm."

"We will take care of him there." William scrubbed a hand over his weary face. "I gather he can stay here until you deem it safe for travel?"

"Of course." The doctor peered at him, frowned. "You look a trifle poorly yourself, sir."

"I feel a trifle poorly." William managed a hollow smile.

"Perhaps it might be best you should rest for a while. Stay the night also."

And miss his own comfortable lodgings? He fought a groan, the effort causing him to totter.

"Sir." Jensen cupped his elbow, leading him back to his chair, gently shoving him down. "The doctor is correct. You're in no fit state to return."

"I suppose if we stay then we'll remain best apprised on how Barrack fares." William glanced at the landlord. "I gather you've adequate space?"

"Of course, sir. And very nice accommodation it is, too, if I might say so. Just . . . how many more of you are there?"

"I travel light. Just us four." William motioned to Jensen and the footman.

The landlord beamed. "No trouble at all, then. You'll have the best rooms." He moved to the door, then paused. "I gather you'll be requiring a meal?"

William nodded, smiling inwardly at the way the man's eyes lit up, as if he had already started counting the coins soon coming his way.

That night, sleep took a long time coming, not least because the bed was the most uncomfortable he'd ever had the misfortune to lie upon. Dim light peeked around thin curtains, splintering up the wall to show the dusty lacework of ancient spiderwebs. He forced himself to relax in the method once taught him by Dr. Blakeney, physician to the royals and the very rich: clench his hands, shoulders, his back, legs, and feet, before slowly releasing the pressure, section by section, limb by limb, as he deliberately exhaled. Once he'd completed the routine, he intentionally forced his thoughts from the welter of confusion and thought on good things.

Good things, like the fact the doctor had been home and not out attending a birth in the rural byways of Northamptonshire. Good things, like the fact the meal tonight had at least been hot. Good things, like tomorrow they would be at home again at last. Good things . . .

He yawned, closed his eyes, and dreamed of a girl with compassion in her eyes, and candor on her lips.

❧ Chapter Ten

Hampton Hall
June 8

CHARLOTTE'S NOSE WRINKLED as the sound of retching reached through the closed door.

"Poor pet," Mrs. Florrick murmured, casting Charlotte a worried glance. "She's barely kept a bite down these past days."

The door opened, and Lavinia emerged, hair bedraggled, looking wan and thin. Her maid bustled past them, holding a chamber pot.

"Poor thing," Mrs. Florrick said again. "Come lie down, my lady. You really should—"

"I'm fine, Mrs. Florrick," Lavinia said, with a most unconvincing smile. "I would much prefer to return downstairs. If I stay here, I shall only mope, and feel even more wretched."

"Oh, but—"

"I will keep her company, Mrs. Florrick," Charlotte said firmly, at her cousin's look of entreaty. "She will not do anything strenuous, I assure you."

"But my lady—"

"Come," Charlotte said, throwing the housekeeper her sweetest smile, even as she guided Lavinia from the room.

"Thank you," Lavinia whispered. "I can't think where all my energy has gone."

"Can't you?" Charlotte said, with a none-too-subtle glance at her midsection.

Lavinia chuckled. "I didn't know increasing would make me feel so wretched. I don't know how women manage without such friendly faces and people so willing to help."

"Yet somehow those without servants still manage to survive, otherwise the population would be decreasing. Now, let's get you settled."

After ensuring her cousin was comfortably ensconced on the sofa, a pile of correspondence before her, Charlotte picked up her embroidery from earlier. Soon all thought of sickness faded as quiet calm filled the room.

The tall case clock near the door provided a reassuring tick. The crackle of flames gave heartening warmth. The yellow drawing room might not be as large as the one in the Grosvenor Square house, but the view, over fields and distant hills, was a much pleasanter prospect, and made the room seem more spacious.

Charlotte glanced back at the embroidery, stifling a sigh. Sewing had never held much pleasure. These past few days had only reinforced her fears about country living. When Mama had seen just how dull the earl and Lavinia lived, she had quickly relinquished her chaperonage to escape back to London. A niggle of resentment flared; subsided. She couldn't blame Mama for leaving, nor, she supposed, for carrying out her maternal duty. It wasn't like Charlotte could do anything about it, anyway. Wasn't like she could make choices about anything.

She stabbed at the scrap of silk. What if Henry—unfeeling, unreasonable Henry—had never said anything to Mama? Could Charlotte have said anything to change Mama's mind? Why did Father always follow Mama's lead? The heat spiking her chest suddenly turned to ice. What if Lord Markham had found a new lady interest?

No. No! Charlotte forced herself to breathe, to think on other things. Lavinia's challenge about childishness had sparked resolve to not live from her emotions *quite* so much. If she behaved with dignity and decorum, Mama might not think her so spoiled and silly. But it was very hard!

Smothering a yawn, she peeked up to meet Lavinia's smiling glance before her cousin resumed reading her letters. At least Charlotte's time here had proved of *some* benefit. Apart from comforting Lavinia, Charlotte had been forced to act as a kind of gatekeeper, doing her best to shield her cousin from the servants' fuss and worry, while secretly sharing Mrs. Florrick's concern about just how thin the countess was becoming. And Charlotte's presence meant the earl had felt easier about leaving his wife for a few days while he returned to London for some important parliamentary function to do with the peace.

"I hate leaving you, especially now, at such a time," he'd avowed yesterday, clasping Lavinia's hand, moments before he was due to drive away.

"I'll look after her," Charlotte had said. "Stop worrying."

"You remind me of your Aunt Patience," Lord Hawkesbury said, with his easy chuckle. "Thank you for staying, Charlotte."

"Where else would I go?"

Lavinia smiled. "You're a pearl amongst women, just like Aunt Patience."

The memory of the compliment drew heat to her cheeks again.

She'd rarely met the woman who had raised Lavinia from the age of nine, apart from that brief stay last November, when the discovery she possessed an aunt and cousin had transformed her world. Brusque, bluestocking Aunt Patience was like a force of nature, speeding headlong into situations and wreaking change—havoc, Mama would say—wherever she went. To be compared to such a capable, intelligent woman caused her heart to glow. She smiled, resuming her stitching. Her boring stitching. Her tedious, dull, and dreary—

"Good gracious!"

"Yes?" Charlotte glanced up eagerly. News, even of the "good gracious" kind, *had* to be better than this mind-numbing stupor. "What is it?"

"Nicholas writes . . . oh my!"

"Lavinia?"

"Oh, thank goodness!"

"Lavinia, stop being so cruel."

"Oh!" Her cousin glanced up from her letter, gray eyes wide. "I'm sorry. But it is just so dreadful."

"Really? I wouldn't know."

Lavinia's mouth pulled to one side. "Sarcasm does not become you, dear Charlotte."

"Neither does intentionally withholding exciting news, *dearest* Lavinia."

Lavinia's brow puckered. "I don't know if I would describe it as exciting."

"I wouldn't know how to describe it at all, seeing as I don't even know what 'it' is!"

"Oh! You don't, do you? I'm sorry. Read this." She handed over the letter, the firm bold scrawl denoting a masculine hand. "Second paragraph."

Charlotte read the missive, dated the day before:

> *I regret to inform you of a matter of a most alarming nature. Only days after leaving us, Hartington was involved in a terrible incident. A rock was thrown at his coach, injuring his coachman and causing the horses to run away. H. was fortunate (we would agree blessed) to find help at a nearby village, and it seems the coachman will make a slow recovery. I have this on the word of H. himself, whom I met at White's last night. Seems he has managed to keep much of this quiet (amazing what enough gold lining hands will do) and would prefer people not to know. Please pray for him, and for his household, who are understandably shocked and worried. Join me also in praying for H. whose matter-of-fact attitude toward it all concerns me not a little, as I cannot but wonder if this "accident" was more intentional than otherwise.*

Charlotte glanced up and met Lavinia's troubled eyes.

"We should pray," her cousin said.

"Er, yes?"

"Let's pray now." Lavinia bowed her head, and Charlotte followed suit. Such open prayer was a little extreme, but it couldn't do any harm—

"Dear Lord, we thank You for Your protection for the duke and his servant . . ."

As Lavinia continued, Charlotte forced herself to focus on the good intention, not the awkwardness of hearing something so personal expressed aloud. Wasn't praying supposed to be a private thing? Lavinia prayed like she was engaged in normal conversation. Charlotte shivered. She hoped her cousin wouldn't ask *her* to pray out loud!

"And, Lord, please bring whoever is responsible to justice, and help them see Your grace and understand they can live a better way. Amen."

"Amen," Charlotte echoed weakly.

"Poor man. I'm so glad he is safe."

"Yes."

"It must have been terrifying! The Lord really looked after them." Lavinia glanced over, as if she expected a response.

"Er, yes."

"The duke is a man of faith, which is good."

"Mmm."

"Forgive me, but you don't sound terribly convinced."

"I . . ." What was she supposed to say? Mama's mantra on the journey west from London rose again: "The most important things concerning a potential husband are his income, estate, and title. Attractiveness does not matter. Whether you consider yourself in love with him does not matter. Personal qualities such as faith are of little consequence."

"Charlotte?"

"I'm sorry. I was thinking of Mama."

Lavinia chuckled. "I can see why talk of the duke must immediately lead to thoughts of your parents."

"Please don't."

"Very well." But the disconcerting grin remained. "How thankful I am to know he's safe."

"It . . . it must have been quite the adventure."

"Perhaps the countryside is not so boring after all."

"Perhaps." Charlotte shrugged.

Lavinia's teasing smile faded. "But I do hope whoever was behind this will be soon discovered."

"Yes, indeed. What was it you prayed? Something about the perpetrator and grace? You did not mean your mother, did you?"

"No. Simply that it's one thing for a person to commit a crime and be found guilty, but quite another for them to realize their wrong and seek restoration."

"You don't honestly think the duke will wish to be restored to this person, do you? You've heard the rumors concerning how he treated his wife. I don't think he's the saint you make him out to be."

"I don't think he's a saint."

"No? You seem to be pushing him at me."

"Really? I did not think my dropping his name into conversation now and then constituted pushing, exactly. Are you perhaps misreading things? Why would that be, I wonder?"

"Careful, else you will sound too much like Mama."

"And we can't have that, can we?" Lavinia smiled, her expression one of warmth and affection. "Forgive me if I seemed too forward in my opinions. It was kindly meant."

Charlotte's brows rose.

"Truly. If you prefer me to not mention his intelligence, nor his wit, nor how very charming his smile is—"

"Lavinia!"

"Very well. I shall not mention him again. Today, anyway."

※

Hartwell Abbey
Two days later

The library's hush and gloom matched the doctor's demeanor perfectly. William gestured him to a seat, bracing internally for bad news.

"I'm terribly sorry, Your Grace, but there has been no change."

William's heart sank a little deeper. "I know Barrack has not woken, but you hold no hope?"

"He's not responded in the week since the incident and doesn't seem likely to waken. As I said, I'm sorry, sir."

"Perhaps a little more time—"

Dr. Lansbury shook his head. "I do not want to give false hope, sir. I don't believe anything is likely to change. Poor soul," he added, almost as an afterthought.

His dismissive attitude fired grit within. Well, prayer could change things. *God* could. William still believed it, even if some of the prayers he'd prayed in the past few months seemed to have fallen on deaf ears.

"If I may, sir, I would suggest you remove him to a more suitable environment."

"Such as?"

"The hospital of St. Luke."

His eyes narrowed. "The one for imbeciles?"

"It is a very good infirmary, and one that promises good care for its inmates—"

"Inmates? Good God, man! Barrack is injured, not a lunatic."

"And he needs proper medical care—"

"Which he is receiving here."

"Which he is *not* receiving here, sir, no matter how good your intentions."

He felt his choler rise. "I believe I shall seek another opinion."

"That is your prerogative, of course." The doctor bowed his head.

He left, and the room became silent again. Too quiet again. Thoughts clattered round his head.

Somehow he needed to find another doctor for Barrack; he refused to give up hope, no matter what Dr. Lansbury said. He'd rather swing than see poor Barrack placed in a mental asylum.

Somehow he still needed to decide what to do about the child upstairs. In the weeks since he'd been home, it had just felt wrong to send the mite away, his one visit to the nursery only deepening indecision. She'd looked so sweet, peacefully asleep, it had almost made him wish she was his. For all her faults, Pamela had managed to bestow something of her beauty on the child.

He rested his elbows on the desk, pushed his head into his hands. The girl didn't need him, but she would soon need a mother. And how could he possibly supply one of those?

"Heavenly Father. . . ?"

Almost as soon as the whisper filled the room, an image hovered, fragmented.

No. He could never do that. Never force motherhood on such a young lady. Besides, hadn't she made her feelings toward him perfectly obvious?

"Lord, no. It could never work."

A verse floated into memory: "I can do all things through Christ which strengtheneth me."

A desperate chuckle forced past his doubts. "She'd be the one needing strength, Lord."

He pressed his fingers into his forehead, as the other concerns of past weeks ate into his thoughts. The assailant, whose identity remained unknown. The experiment for Mr. McAdam, yet to be implemented. The battle for funding for Bethlem's Hospital for the Insane. His responsibilities in London, necessitating his fleeting visit three days ago. The usual issues of tenants and farmers, his myriad of other concerns. Everyone wanted something from him: ideas, the implementation of ideas, financial handouts, help of one sort or another. Everyone wanted something.

Even him.

Around him, the ancient house groaned and settled, its creaks familiar, yet seemingly louder tonight. A window ajar drew a mournful moan, the sound that used to make his sister believe in ghostly voices. Inside, his concerns swelled and subsided, like the deep rolling waves of the ocean, washing round his mind, sluicing away, leaving him with but one certainty.

He was lonely.

❦ Chapter Eleven

Grosvenor Square
June 15

"MAMA, PLEASE. I'D give anything—"

"No."

"Oh, but—"

"Charlotte, it is simply not appropriate for a girl your age to be interested in such things."

"Out of curiosity, Mama, just how old *should* a girl be before such things are of interest?"

"Henry!"

Charlotte shot her brother a thankful look and pleaded her case again. "Mama, truly, how many opportunities will there be to see such splendid sights?"

"When you are older, perhaps."

"Yes, but when she is older there won't be a parade celebrating such a glorious occasion. Surely, Mama, you do not think Napoleon makes a habit of gathering troops to fight again?"

Charlotte silently applauded her brother. It seemed Henry had felt more than a twinge of remorse at being the chief reason for Charlotte's expulsion from London society for a fortnight. Upon news of Lord Markham having quit the season to head north, Henry's arguments that Charlotte be brought back to London and under Mama's watchful eye had finally found a soft ear. But while glad her family had finally seen reason, the very fact she'd been sent away in the first place, courtesy of his interference, continued to rankle. Coupled with the news that Lord Markham had not even left her word but had gone meekly on his way, doubled her desire to see her brother make amends.

She eyed him again, raising her brows.

Henry sighed. "Mama, I cannot understand how you consider Charlotte old enough to wed and take on the responsibilities of managing a household, but cannot find her old enough to watch a simple parade."

"That is because you are not a mother," Mama said with a sniff.

Henry exchanged glances with Charlotte, as if to say he'd tried his best, but Charlotte wasn't ready to concede. "Mama, if the person of whom you disapprove is not there, then what can be the matter?"

"There might be others."

"Other young gentlemen, you mean?"

"Yes."

"Well of course there will be," Henry said. "I'll be in attendance, and I'm sure Fanshawe won't mind putting in an appearance."

"No Fanshawe," Mama snapped.

"But Freddy is as good a man as any. Mama, you're not still thinking of selling Charlotte off to the highest bidder?"

"Oh, I wish your father were here to stop this silly brangling!"

Charlotte wished that, too. But he was in Parliament—or so he said.

After another exchange of glances, Charlotte bit back the heated words and summoned up a smile. She would *try* to live higher than her emotions.

"Very well, Mama."

Her mother blinked. "Well! I'm pleased to see you have come to your senses."

"I understand you have no wish to be embarrassed by me, Mama."

"Oh, but—"

Charlotte kissed her mother on the cheek. She would behave with dignity and decorum. Even if she felt like she might explode from the tension coiled within.

She left the drawing room and forced herself to walk slowly up the stairs to her room.

Footsteps hurried behind her. "You're taking things awfully well, Lottie."

"I am not *quite* the child everyone thinks me, Henry."

"Decided not to go, eh?"

"My decisions count for naught anyway," she said, plastering on a smile. She paused. Except . . . her decision on how to respond to disappointment really was a choice. She did not *need* to react in the heat of the moment. What was that verse Lavinia had spoken of? Something suggesting that as far as it depended on her, she would live at peace with others. Surely this applied to forgiving her brother, too?

"What is it? Lottie"—Henry cocked his head, smiling, as if to pacify his use of the old name—"you're not planning anything underhand, are you?"

"I don't know what you mean. The only decision I've made is to trust that Mama will see reason."

"That's it?"

"Well, I might even pray about it."

"How very devious! I gather this is our cousin's doing?"

"Perhaps. I know this may surprise you, Henry, but I've no wish to be thought a child *all* my days."

He laughed, and the sound caught her heart.

Yes, she might not have many choices open to her, but she could make choices about what lived in her heart. And just as she'd tried to protect Lavinia from the excessive concern of Mrs. Florrick, perhaps Charlotte needed to make choices to protect her own heart from those emotions that begged to hold sway. Her choices could lead to bitterness or shared laughter.

Her smile grew genuine. Today, at least, in forgiving her brother, she'd made a better choice.

Two days later, Charlotte was requested to attend Mama in her bedchamber. After making her wait for what seemed an eternity while Ellen fussed with her hair, Mama finally pronounced herself satisfied and eyed Charlotte in the looking glass.

"I have decided, due to your good behavior, you shall attend the parade after all."

"Oh, Mama! Truly?"

"Truly." Her mother smiled. "I am not coldhearted after all, and I still recall my first season." She sighed. "I remember what it was to find a young man appealing. In fact . . ."

Charlotte clamped her lips as her mother continued her reminisces, espousing the merits of some army officer she'd found quite attractive, until her own mother had put an end to it.

Mama sighed. "After Grace, you know . . ."

She nodded. Lavinia's mother, eldest daughter of a duke, who'd chosen love over a title, a quiet country life over the one to which she'd been born.

"Mother insisted I marry befitting my rank, and George was all I could ever ask." She sighed, smiling. "I tell you this because I want you to marry appropriately, and not throw yourself away on someone unworthy."

Was she suggesting Grace had thrown herself away on Lavinia's father? Yet wasn't Lavinia one of the kindest, loveliest people she knew? How could such a thing be a mistake?

"Your father has arranged for a room along the parade route. We shall invite a few of our more intimate friends and make quite a merry party. After all, it's not every year we shall have opportunity to celebrate the peace. That little man will not run riot over Europe again."

"True." She fought a smile at such an idea.

"So it will behoove you to look your best, and to ensure these next few weeks are ones where not the smallest whisper of scandal can be heard. I hope I've made myself clear?"

"Clear as crystal, Mama."

"Good." Mama turned back to the looking glass. "Not too many young ladies are fortunate enough to receive such opportunities, let alone a second chance with such a man."

Her spirits dropped. "With what man?"

"Why, with the duke, of course!"

THE DAY OF the twentieth dawned clear and sunny, excitement at the forthcoming parade lending wings to everyone, as regular morning preparations requiring hours seemed to take only minutes. Even Mama was dressed and at the breakfast table before her usual time, submitting to Father and his constant demands to hurry.

Their meal finished, they left Grosvenor Square and joined the stream of carriages headed to the Strand. In addition to the vehicles, pedestrian numbers were increasing. The air of excitement that so filled the streets had Charlotte abuzz, too.

Finally, she would once more be part of the season. If today went well, Mama might even see fit to let her attend the dress party at Carlton House on the twenty-first of next month. Seeing the Queen again held less anticipation than the opportunity to dress up most magnificently. And if she could capture the heart of someone less stuffy than the old duke, then so much the better. For the sooner Mama put away all this nonsense about him, the happier everyone could be.

By the time they reached the rooms hired for their use, the streets were pressed tightly with sightseers. Anyone setting out now would no doubt be sorely disappointed.

"I hope Fanshawe makes it in time," Henry grumbled. "It would be just like him to arrive late and leave me stuck talking with ol' Hartington."

Hartington. Her spirits drooped. She would have to look like she was making something of an effort with him, otherwise Mama would surely suspend further excitements and attractions.

The upper-story room, whose large windows afforded an excellent view of proceedings, had a number of sofas positioned to capture the scenes below. To the back of the room, a long table held a variety of victuals, including savory and sweet pies, fruit, ices, and jellies.

"Well, you have done things in style, my dear," Mama said with a pleased look at Father.

He harrumphed, muttering something about not being willing to put their distinguished guest to the blush.

Henry filled a plate as if he hadn't eaten two hours ago, prompting Charlotte to steal a small pastry. Her mouth filled with an explosion of creamy sweetness mingled with the tart tang of berries. How delicious!

"The Duke of Hartington," the footman announced.

Charlotte quickly wiped her mouth, chewing hastily. Why did he have to be so punctual? She eyed his outfit, even as he made his bows to the room. Dressed soberly as always, he still presented a neat, elegant figure, which she could only approve.

The duke turned, forcing her to gulp a too-large mouthful. "Lady Charlotte."

Pain trembled down her throat at the pastry's slow descent. She curtsied, hoping that would suffice, but Mama's whispered, "Charlotte!" forced her to mumble around stubborn flaky flecks of pastry, "Duke."

A tiny piece flew from her mouth. Mortification heated her cheeks.

But rather than the disgust she felt sure to see, his eyes seemed to lighten with unholy amusement, as if he found her a particularly silly creature at the Royal Menagerie.

She swallowed, lifted her chin. Not that it mattered what he thought. She only had to behave respectfully enough to satisfy Mama; then she would be free to go on as before.

Finally released from Mama's rapid chatter, the duke moved forward. "I gather you would recommend the creamy buns?"

"How did you—?"

He motioned to the side of his mouth, and she mirrored his actions, as if she were in a trance. Removing her finger, she found a spot of cream on her glove's fingertip. Oh . . .

She turned hurriedly away, desperately wiping at her face before Mama's eagle eyes became aware of her *faux pas*.

The duke moved nearer, murmuring, "There is nothing more."

She nodded, his kind tone drawing moisture to her eyes. Offering him a tight smile but refusing to meet his gaze, she returned to the settee near the windows.

"Charlotte?" Mama said in a startled whisper. "What is the matter? Why are your cheeks flushed?"

"I—"

"You do not want to give the duke a bad impression, remember?"

Too late for that.

Fortunately, further enquiry was cut short by the footman's announcement of Lord Fanshawe.

"Fanshawe, at last. We had begun to give up hope that you'd make it," Henry said.

"It's busier than I anticipated," Lord Fanshawe said, his round of bows far more elegant than the previous arrival's. His eyes rested warmly on Charlotte. "But I would not have missed this opportunity for the world."

Her heart fluttered. Lord Fanshawe was *truly* a gentleman, suavely exchanging politenesses while moving to her side. He would never laugh at her!

"Dear Lady Charlotte! May I say, you look divine."

"Indeed, you may."

He smiled, bending over her hand, pressing a kiss, then looked up, his blue-gray eyes watching her carefully.

While no Lord Markham, Lord Fanshawe *was* eligible, and more importantly, available. Charlotte drew in a deep breath as she removed her hand, removing her gaze to see the duke avert his attention, a crease in his forehead suggesting he did not like what he saw.

She shrugged mentally. The sooner he knew he'd never hold her heart, the better. She drew closer to the window, watching the spectators below, working to ignore her inner unease.

The streets were crowded now, so crowded in fact it seemed impassable. She shuddered. How awful to be squeezed amongst so many strangers. Indeed, the press of bodies and the day's heat meant every so often a spectator collapsed. "Oh!"

"Lady Charlotte?" Lord Fanshawe moved to her side. "Is something the matter?"

"That lady, there"—she pointed—"she just fainted."

"Silly widgeon," Henry said with a laugh. "She won't be the last."

"How long do you think until the next swoon?" Lord Fanshawe said. "I'll lay you a pony it's not more than ten minutes."

"You're on."

Charlotte bit her lip. It seemed uncommonly cruel to be placing wagers on other people's misfortunes. She peeked across at the other guests. Father and Mama seemed indifferent, but the duke's frown had deepened. Rumor had it he disliked gambling, no doubt due to his wife's reputation for reckless deep play. But really, did he need to show such antipathy? Did he ever enjoy himself?

His gaze shifted, meeting hers. Her skin prickled. But now the dark eyes seemed almost sad.

She hastily returned her attention outside, where the hum from the crowd had intensified, along with the commentary from her brother and his guest.

"I think the procession will take awhile yet—oh, look! Another one down. You owe me twenty-five pounds, Feather."

As Henry grumbled something, Mama sighed, the disconsolate lines of her face smoothing as she smiled at the duke. "Well, if we must wait longer, I suppose we should do justice to some of Monsieur Robard's fare. I hope you like glazed ham, sir. One of Robard's special sauces which he refuses to share, even when I've had the likes of the Regent himself request the recipe."

"Thank you."

Why didn't the duke respond in kind? Mama was trying to make him feel welcome, but he seemed so aloof, so removed from anything like sociability. How dull could one man be?

Lord Fanshawe drew to her side. "Lady Charlotte, may I fill your plate?" He leaned closer. "I'm told I have excellent taste in knowing just what a young lady likes."

Charlotte blinked. Did he intimate something else? She shook her head. How ridiculous!

"No? I assure you, I seek only to be of assistance."

"Of course. Thank you."

"Anything you prefer?"

"I love peaches. They are my favorite fruit."

"It amazes me how many things we share in common."

For a few minutes the room was filled with the clatter and bustle of filling of plates, during which she noticed that despite Mama's insistence he go first, the duke had barely placed a thing on his plate. "Thank you, madam, but I ate earlier."

Charlotte glanced down at her plate, filled to overflowing with pies, small cakes, and fruit—but no more pastries. She wasn't exactly hungry either, but Robard cooked so exquisitely, it would be a shame to see his good efforts go to waste. She discreetly removed her gloves and placed them in her lap.

Henry and Fanshawe began a low-voiced conversation, leaving her to follow Mama's lead and begin eating.

"So, Hartington," Father said, his plate filled, "tell us what brings you to London."

The duke returned his forkful of food to his plate. "My coachman remains unwell, and I remain unconvinced the doctor attending him has explored every avenue for success."

"Ah, doctors." Father nodded, shoving in a large piece of ham. "Who'd you have?"

"Dr. Lansbury." The duke lifted his fork.

"Lansbury?"

At her father's question, he placed the fork down again.

"Never heard of him," continued Father.

A wisp of a smile crossed the duke's face. "He is a local man."

"Never trust local men. What would they know?"

"In my experience, I've found they usually know a great deal more than those from the city."

"Yet you're here now," Father said in a tone almost aggressive.

"Yes."

At the duke's bland look and quiet word, her father nodded, before finally returning his attention to his plate. Charlotte almost wanted to cheer as the duke finally lifted his fork and ate. His very mildness seemed to have a soothing effect on her father's sensibilities, and made her wonder how often he employed such meek strategies.

Mama placed her fork down. "Well, that was delicious, if I do say so myself."

Charlotte smiled inwardly. How typical of Mama to take credit when she hadn't lifted a finger.

"I cannot believe the poor princess has broken off her engagement. Can you, sir?"

"Constance, don't bother the man when he's eating," Father said, as if he had not done the very same.

"But the talk is all over town, isn't it, Charlotte?" Mama said, with inclined head.

"Yes, Mama," Charlotte said obediently.

"Poor thing. Not knowing her own mind. But there have been rumors, you know."

"I try not to pay attention to rumors," the duke said, without lifting his gaze from his plate.

"Oh! Well, yes, of course."

For a moment, the room filled with the unspoken, like a dozen crows circling the room, silently shrieking about the duke and his wife, and that ridiculous rumor about a duel. No wonder he didn't want to talk about the latest *on-dit*.

"Mother, don't tease our guest with thoughts on Slender Billy," said Henry. "Next you'll be saying again you'd prefer the princess marry Gloucester."

"Silly Billy," interjected Fanshawe, with a grin.

"I beg your pardon, Duke," Mama said with high dignity. "It is not my desire to make you feel uncomfortable."

"Thank you, ma'am, but your conversation does not discomfort *per se*. Truth be told, I find the situation rather sad."

Charlotte paused.

Yes. She'd never realized it before, but the princess's situation *was* sad. To be forced by one's father to live apart from one's mother. To have every move scrutinized and gossiped over in a thousand places. To have your choice sneered at by the very people who then curtsy and smile. She remembered back to her brief glimpse at the Queen's drawing rooms. The princess was pretty, and by all accounts warmhearted, too. How *sad* she could not find happiness . . .

Something whispered that Princess Charlotte's situation was not dissimilar to her own. That while she might live with her parents, their machinations meant happiness might forever elude her, too. She stifled the thought, lifting her chin, to see the duke's dark eyes on her again.

She shivered.

"Charlotte, are you finished?"

"Almost, Mama." Her mouth felt dry, like she needed something sweet, yet not the sickly flavor of the lemonade.

"Permit me."

Before she knew it, the duke had placed a perfectly peeled peach on her plate. Her mouth watered. She swallowed. Found a smile. "Thank you. It's just what I wanted."

He inclined his head, but not before she saw a trace of pleasure cross his features.

Her cheeks heated. Had he truly paid attention to her earlier words? Why? She focused on the globe of delicate sweetness, enjoying its perfect ripeness, firm, yet oh so tasty. She licked her lips. "It tastes like golden sunshine. The perfect way to finish a meal." She smiled fully this time at the duke. "Thank you."

He drew back a little and nodded. "I'm glad." And the most charming smile filled his face, transforming his features from darkness to light.

Her heart caught. Oh . . .

"Quick! I can hear cheering," Henry called.

Charlotte dragged her gaze away, wishing for water to cool her cheeks, for something to slow her rapid pulse. She glanced at her brother, precariously perched halfway out the window. "Be careful, Henry."

"Come on, Lottie!" He gestured her nearer. "I can see the head of the procession!"

She watched the parade, thankful for the distraction. The first to pass were the Light Dragoons, followed by the Eleventh Regiment. The uniforms of blue and buff looked most striking.

"I wonder if Hawkesbury's watching this somewhere," Henry mused. "He'd know most of them, wouldn't he?"

"He was in the Twelfth," the duke said from behind them.

Charlotte stole another glance at him. What was it about him? He stood behind the others, never jostling for position, or demanding that which his rank should afford. In his quiet, unobtrusive way, he seemed to notice quite a great deal, offering answers to Mama's questions as to which officers and generals rode in each carriage.

She returned her attention to the passing carriages: officers of the Regent's household followed by the foreign generals, state carriages bearing the royal dukes, the speaker's coach, the carriages bearing the members of cabinet. On and on it went. A troop of the Royal Horse Guards, the Regent's officers of state, the Regent's state carriage pulled by eight cream horses, then the czar.

Mama sniffed. "I cannot believe those persons dare hiss the Prince Regent when the king of Prussia passes by! Most uncouth. Well"—she settled back into her seat, fanning herself—"all this excitement finds me quite thirsty."

Lord Fanshawe drew near. "Shall I procure you a drink, Lady Exeter? And something for you also, Lady Charlotte?"

"Thank you."

A snap of fingers brought a footman, hurried orders, and soon, two glasses of champagne.

Charlotte tasted hers and grimaced. Champagne had never been to her liking, hence the ubiquitous lemonade at family meals, even despite Henry's teasing. She placed the glass down, swallowed a sigh.

"Here." The low, quiet voice accompanied another glass: lemonade.

"Oh!" She glanced up at her benefactor. "Thank you."

The duke bowed, and she sipped, enjoying the tang and sweetness, pretending to watch the conclusion of the parade as her thoughts chased each other.

Why did the duke notice such things? Surely he did not care for her? Had she been too kind, offering false hope? She had better take heed, lest her behavior gave rise to expectations she had no desire to fulfill. What could she do to make him understand?

❧ Chapter Twelve

Hartwell Abbey
Two days later

HE SHOULD NEVER have agreed.

William shut his eyes firmly, as if he could block the images tumbling through his head. Spending the day with the marquess and family had proved every bit as torturous as he'd imagined. As if it wasn't enough for him to be forced to politely fence with the marchioness over all manner of things, he'd also been forced to watch Fanshawe fawning over her daughter.

The very daughter who now haunted his dreams.

One smile was all it had taken. The first real smile she'd shown him, over a matter so ridiculously simple as a peach, had been enough to make him wish for his hothouses so he could feed her peaches every day.

Charlotte wore her beauty loosely, as if unaware. Her complexion was such that she would not need the pots and powders with which Pamela had crowded her dressing table. Instead, Charlotte glowed with natural vibrancy, her fairness and blushes a mirror to her emotions. Her lips—oh, her lips!—were berry red, her hair like tendrils of curly sunshine. And when her face lit, as it had with that smile, it seemed all the cold spaces of his heart thawed.

He'd tried to be more interesting, to not play the mute as was his wont. He believed he'd covered his amusement when he'd pointed out—kindly, he thought—the spot of cream beside her mouth. A spot of cream that, were he a romantic man, he would beg to kiss away.

His eyes flew open. "Heavenly Father, please take these desires away."

He shouldn't desire her; heaven knew she'd made it plain she did not desire him. But her vitality called to him, her lack of artifice as appealing as the kindness she'd shown in caring for Hawkesbury's wife as the earl had mentioned recently. He couldn't help longing for someone whose spirits boosted his, whose passions were harnessed by politeness, not harbored by lies . . .

His stomach tensed. Perhaps it would be best to escape and head farther north, to the border, like that Markham fellow had been rumored to have done. He *would* leave, except his presence was needed, poor Barrack finally having been seen by Dr. Blakeney, whose diagnosis and treatment concurred with William's own: rest.

"Removing him to a disease-riddled hospice will only exacerbate his condition and might, in fact, kill him," the doctor had affirmed.

And he could not permit the last member of a family who had served his for countless generations to be forced to suffer such an indignity. Following Blakeney's advice, he had instead sent Barrack to be looked after by a couple in Caister-on-Sea, whose coastal locale had helped many an injured man's recovery.

So William remained at Hartwell, wishing he could be back in London, wishing he could see her even as duty demanded his attention here.

Evening heat made him tug off the bedcovers. He stared at the shadows slowly marching across the walls. What was she doing? Who was she with? At whom did she smile?

Apprehension slithered through him. He guessed young Fanshawe would be her preference, with his elegant manners and ease of address. But he suspected the young viscount would not meet with the approval William's own suit would. Yet he had no wish to pursue the unwinnable. If her heart was given elsewhere, what was the point? His heart panged. If only she had not smiled at him and given wings to a hope that scarcely dared to breathe.

He rolled to his side. What was the point in even thinking such things? Until matters were resolved here, he should not indulge his dreams. His arrival back from London had been greeted with the news that a mysterious disease had claimed the seedlings he'd nurtured on the Home Farm for nearly two years. Hapgood insisted it was due to some kind of poison—which meant the soil would take even longer to recover. His estate manager had instigated a search in the nearby villages for any stranger, to no avail. Another pang of annoyance rose. Who would want to do such a thing? First Barrack, then the poison. It was almost enough to make him believe the old wives' tales about the mysterious cursed happenings at the Abbey.

A thin wail carried on the air.

On this hot night the windows of the baby's rooms must be open, too. The wail came again, longer this time. After a few long seconds he heard the window screech shut.

He closed his eyes, but like before, the crying started again, muffled but still audible. Every so often it would cease, and his body would relax, then the wails would resume. Poor mite. To be so warm without means to cool oneself must be a trial.

The wailing picked up again, louder and longer. Even longer. It was as if the child had found some new source of energy and was determined to keep crying until the matter was finally resolved. Previously dulled senses sharpened to a needlepoint, and he sighed. There'd be no returning to sleep now.

He got up, yawning as he moved to the window. From this position the Abbey's grounds extended as far as the horizon. Moonlight bathed trees in an unnatural glow, shadows stretching long into the night. A pretty, some would say haunting, setting. He rubbed a hand over his face, through his hair. Studied the serene scene, ripe for painting. It *was* beautiful. He *was* blessed. The myriad of responsibilities his title carried didn't make him feel terribly blessed at times, though. Perhaps he needed to focus more on the good things, like he'd read about in Philippians that morning—

He blinked. Was that a shadow moving? He peered again. Nothing. Was he going mad?

The wailing ceased. For a precious few seconds it seemed he might be able to resume his bed, but then it began again. Annoyance flickered, subsided. The nursemaids were doing their best. He didn't envy them their charge.

He groaned, and pulled on a heavily brocaded robe.

"Sir?" Jensen appeared, bleary-eyed. "I thought I heard something."

William pointed above. "I know I heard something."

His valet's grin flickered. "Would you like me to see if I can quiet—?"

"No, I'll go."

Doubtless the child had awoken the entire household, and whilst his staff might show his valet a level of respect, it would not silence the grumbles like his presence would.

He trudged up the steps, the noise growing louder, found the old nursery that used to be his world, and entered.

"Your Grace!" Martha's red face almost rivaled that of the screaming infant. "We did not mean to wake you!" she almost yelled to be heard above the sobbing girl.

"I'm sure you did not." He nodded to Meg, a maid, whose presence was no doubt requested by the older lady, before turning his attention to the child. "Come now, that's enough."

The little girl started, and ceased crying, as if the sound of his deeper voice was something new and peculiar and warranted attention.

"It is the height of bad manners to behave so."

She stared at him a moment, then the little face screwed up again and the high-pitched wail continued.

"She's been like this for weeks now."

"I know," he said grimly. "Give her to me."

"Oh, but sir—"

"Now, if you please."

The jiggling efforts stopped, and Martha handed him the pink-swathed bundle, in which instant he realized he'd never held an infant before.

"How do—?"

"Like this, sir." She guided his arms until he was supporting the head with the crook of his elbow, leaving him one hand free to tug at the blankets tucked up to her chin, the move instantly causing the crying to cease, to be replaced by a series of hiccups. He laid two fingers on her forehead. Frowned.

"No wonder she's crying. She's too warm."

"My mother said it was bad for children to get cold. Weakens their lungs, she said."

"I think we'd all agree this one's lungs are not suffering," he said wryly.

He examined the infant, the thatch of dark hair so like her mother's. Dark eyes studied him, even as the tiny pink lips puckered, unsure whether to cry or no.

"Come now—" Shock lined his heart. He glanced at Martha. "We have not named her?"

"No, sir."

"How appalling of me."

"You've been a little distracted, if I may say so."

He nodded, but there was only so much his busyness could pardon. How could this be only the second time he'd entered the nursery? He knew Martha was doing her best, but good God! He spent more time with his horses than he ever had with his wife's child.

And it wasn't the little mite's fault.

He studied the tiny face. Impossible to tell whom she resembled. The old hurt spurted. How could Pamela have betrayed him? Yet her features did not resemble Wrotham. A niggle of doubt stole inside. Wrotham had always protested his innocence . . .

He exhaled, refusing to entertain any possible injustice, murmuring instead to the tiny girl, "You have not had an easy time of it, have you?"

"No, sir."

As Martha expounded on the various trials her young charge had put her through, he bit back a smile. While he possessed some measure of sympathy for the nursemaid, she was paid exceedingly well for her job. No, his compassion was for the tiny girl he held. "Heavenly Father," he whispered, "bless this one."

The little lips puckered as if she would cry again.

"Please don't."

She gave a shuddery sigh, her eyes fixed on his.

"She knows your voice, sir."

He doubted it, but he allowed the nursemaid her delusion.

"I hope you will learn to mind your manners now, young lady."

The little girl blinked, and resumed her relentless dark stare.

He smiled, amazed at how long the infant could gaze without blinking. The act seemed to settle the child even more, her lips twitching as if to copy him.

Heart melting, he gently stroked her face. Such petallike softness, such pink sweetness.

"I trust you will sleep well now—" He paused.

What to name her? What she should have been named long ago.

"Rose."

HALF AN HOUR later, having ensured Rose was thoroughly asleep, William stumbled downstairs. His limbs felt like they'd been poured with lead. He reached his bedchamber to find Jensen still awake, trimming a candlestick.

"You seem to have the knack of things, sir."

"Perhaps." William yawned, casting off his dressing gown. "I just hope Rose manages to sleep the rest of the night."

"Rose, is it, sir?"

He eyed his valet. "Yes. The Lady Rose Pamela Hartwell."

"Very good, sir," Jensen said with a pleased smile.

William sat on the edge of the bed and closed his eyes. "Shut the window, would you, Jensen? I'm afraid if Lady Rose wakes again I do not want to hear her."

"Of course, sir."

He heard Jensen's footsteps move to the window, heard a sharp gasp. "Sir!"

His eyelids flicked open. "Yes?"

"The carriage house! It's on fire."

"What? How—?" William hastened to the window. His heart lurched. "Quick! Ring the bells!"

Jensen ran off, calling loudly to awaken the other servants. William struggled to button his dressing gown as he followed the thumping footsteps to the ground floor. Fear pummeled his insides. While the carriage house should lie far enough from the Abbey to preclude danger here, it stood too close to the stables. Even now he could hear panicked whinnying.

He rushed outside and stopped. Fire flickered through the carriage house windows, streams of smoke poured through the roof. A lost cause; it would only be a matter of time before the structure caved in. Thank God Barrack was safely away and nobody slept in the carriage house anymore.

Already the grooms and stable boys were leading horses away, but unless something was done, the structure would soon catch alight.

A well stood idle. He raced toward it. "Jensen! Buckets."

He started pumping furiously, up, down, water sloshing into the wooden pails with every squeaking thrust. A footman soon joined Jensen, and replaced the first container with another, while Jensen threw the contents of the first on the fire.

More pumping. More crackle of flames. The air was hot, weighty with smoke and cinders. He glanced at the Abbey. So far no embers had traveled there. *Dear God!*

"Rose! Where is Rose? Make sure she's safe!"

"They're over there!" Jensen shouted over the roaring flames.

He glanced across to where a few of the female staff clustered, watching anxiously. At the sight of a larger figure holding an unmistakable pink bundle, sweet relief filled him. *Thank God.*

William glanced back at his valet. "How are we—?"

"Horses all out," Jensen grunted, snatching away the next bucket.

He dragged in another breath. Regretted it, as he started coughing. A creaking sound preceded the splintering of the carriage house roof and then it finally collapsed.

Yells rent the air, but they could not stop. Another bucket filled, used to dampen blankets to beat down the flames.

William's arms were screaming by the time the eighth bucket filled.

"Sir! Allow me!"

Jensen almost shoved him from position, and he stumbled back, eyeing the scene desperately, as he fumbled prayers beneath his breath. *God, protect—God, help . . .*

The loss of the carriages he could bear.

The loss of something irreplaceable, like a life, he could not.

He jogged to the stables where smoke-grimed servants continued their desperate labors. He picked up a singed blanket and joined the frantic efforts.

Finally, finally, it seemed they were winning, as the flames shrank and sputtered, until at long last the remaining few embers were doused with water.

A tired cheer filled the night air, as his bedraggled staff collapsed around the terrace, gasping, ash-smudged, grateful for the cooling drinks being passed around.

Fighting exhaustion himself, William moved to the stairs leading to the side entrance. He pulled himself up on the plinth and clapped his hands.

"Oy! His Grace is speaking!"

William smiled wearily at the head groom. "Thank you, Evans." He turned to the waiting assembly. "And thank you all. Without your sterling efforts tonight, we would have lost a great deal more than just a few coaches. I . . ." His throat clamped, emotion clogged his chest. "I don't know why I'm so blessed to have such wonderful people working for me. From the bottom of my heart, thank you."

"Three cheers for His Grace!"

Heat filled his eyes as they cheered. He rubbed a hand over his face, fighting emotion. He didn't deserve cheers. He didn't deserve loyalty. But oh, he was so grateful . . .

An hour later, washed, in bed, willing himself to rest while the sun rose, he realized something else. If the cries of little Rose had not woken him, tonight's misdeed could have been so much worse.

And he fell asleep, praying blessings on the little child who had remained incongruously, blissfully asleep, through the remainder of the night.

❧ Chapter Thirteen

Carlton House, London
July 24

THE QUEEN'S FAMED gilt-and-mirrored ballroom was filled with guests whose accents tickled Charlotte's ears, teasing her to discover if the words were Prussian or Russian or German. The Allied sovereigns might have returned to their respective countries, but the number of handsome young officers still in town had added thrumming excitement to the procession of parties and dinners she'd attended since the parade a month ago.

She caught Henry's eye as she swirled in time to the music, and felt a fresh gush of gratitude. Without her brother's support, Mama would never have consented to Charlotte's attendance at such an evening, nor would she have discovered just how entertaining Lord Fanshawe's company could be.

That gentleman stood across from her in the dance line now, returning her look with a smile that bloomed anticipation within. Perhaps he might never fully capture her heart as Lord Markham had done, but he was very good company and knew a girl appreciated a compliment as well as a good jest. His handsome looks and manners could not contrast any greater than with the duke's staid ways. She could only pray Mama would let such foolishness go.

The flutes and strings led the music transition into the next part of the dance. Charlotte joined hands with Lord Fanshawe, who murmured in an undertone, "I do wish you'd let me speak with your father."

Her footsteps stumbled. Quickly recovering, she tightened her grip. "My lord, I think you are being a *little* precipitate."

"Who can think of caution when holding such beauty in his arms?"

Her heart glowed. Perhaps Papa would be amenable to having a viscount as a son-in-law. And Lord Fanshawe was Henry's friend, so that would be well. And she'd be mistress of a fine house in Cumberland. Yes, perhaps she *should* make a push for Father to find approval . . .

A turn to the outside, and she met her mother's frown. Charlotte averted her face, her spirits sinking. If only Mama would relinquish this ridiculous notion of Charlotte becoming a duchess. Until then, she would need to continue to tread a path of the strictest propriety.

The dance formation drew them together again, the viscount's gaze warm as he led her in the maneuvers. "Lady Charlotte," he said softly, "I am like a man dying in the desert. One sign, just one sign that you are not completely indifferent to me will give me hope."

"I would have thought the fact that I agreed to dance with you enough sign, my lord."

"Ah, but that sign loses potency when shared with so many others."

She smiled, joining the other ladies of their set in a small circle, before the music drew them together again, his continued compliments causing a flutter in her breast.

When the dance concluded, he escorted her back to Mama, but did not release her hand. "Lady Exeter, thank you for the honor of dancing with Lady Charlotte."

Mama murmured something inconsequential, bestowing him with a gracious nod before eyeing her. "Charlotte, I see Lord Broughton approaches. He is yours for the cotillion, I believe?"

"Yes." Charlotte plastered a smile on her face, working to feign enthusiasm for dancing with a man who truly *was* old enough to be her father. Was nearly old enough to be her father's father!

She kept the smile glued on as the dance progressed. Mama wanted her to dance with the Earl of Broughton simply because he was an earl—and perhaps because he was so old whoever married him would not be forced to be married for long. A twinge of conscience washed away as his corset creaked alarmingly. The man's figure rivaled the Regent's for corpulence, and he wasn't the only one using such aids. What would happen if his corsets failed? Would his coat buttons fly off? Possibly land in someone's glass of champagne? What if they landed in the Regent's glass of champagne? As her imagination conjured scenes of chaos, she fought laughter, glad to think on something other than his reeking breath and yellow teeth and asinine conversation that seemed to consist of nothing but skin-crawling observations about what a tidy armful she was. Why, even the duke was better than this!

As if summoned by her thoughts, she looked up and found him standing on the perimeter of the room, sober-faced yet elegantly dressed as always. He was talking to an equally serious Lavinia, who had chosen to sit out most of the evening.

Sympathy tugged. Poor man. His run of bad luck had not yet abated. The burning down of his carriage house had sent Mama into a spasm and provided the gossipmongers plenty to feed upon in the past days. For him to show his face here tonight was another surprise—and sure to provide yet more speculation as to his reasons.

She dropped her gaze. Heaven forbid she look too long and give the gossips further ammunition. His company at the parade had set tongues wagging, tongues sure to wag even faster were they to dance together tonight. Thank goodness all her dances had been spoken for so promptly, leaving no space for latecomers. Disobliging a gentleman for a dance already promised was a breach of propriety at which even Mama would balk.

"My dear, you are very quiet," Lord Broughton said when the music drew them together again.

"Yes." While her role was to be amusing, she would not give this man the slightest whiff of encouragement. In addition to his faults, which she did not desire to face every day, she had no desire to become stepmother to his three children—who all had children of their own!

"I trust the company is not too dull for one so young?"

She renewed her polite smile, but did not answer. If he thought her rude, so be it. This farce had gone on long enough.

As soon as the music ended, she extracted her hands from his, offered a curtsy, and hurried to where Mama sat talking with Lavinia. The duke was now half a room away, talking to a plain young lady and presumably the young lady's mother.

"How was your dance with the earl?"

She shuddered. "Mama, please do not make me dance with that man again, I beg of you."

"Very well." Her mother waved a carved ivory fan, eyes narrowing as she glanced past Charlotte. "Who is that creature to whom Hartington speaks? I trust there is nothing in that quarter for which we should be alarmed?"

Lavinia's chin rose. "That *creature* is one of my dearest friends, Aunt Constance. Catherine Winthrop, a baron's daughter. She's here from Gloucestershire to attend her grandfather's birthday."

Mama sniffed. "But why is he talking with a *baron's* daughter?"

"I do not know," Lavinia's eyes held a militant glint. "Perhaps you should ask him."

"Oh my dear, I would never presume to ask such a thing! It is of no matter to me whether he talks with one or twenty-one horse-faced girls."

"Mama!"

Her mother tossed her head. "My apologies, Lavinia, that she be one of your friends. Oh, look, there's that scandalous Lady Carlew! Did you hear about her?"

As Mama began to gossip with a nearby chaperone about a redheaded beauty, Charlotte turned to a stiff-faced Lavinia. "I think your friend looks very nice."

"Catherine *is* very nice."

"I . . . I am surprised to see the duke here."

"He said he's here to purchase a new carriage. Actually, several new vehicles, as they were all burned." Lavinia sighed. "We should continue to hold him in our prayers."

Guilt streaked through her. She hadn't prayed for him or anyone in recent days, the glamour of balls and parties offering too many diversions.

"I'm worried about him," Lavinia continued. "Do you not think he holds something of a lean look about him?"

Charlotte studied him. Now she paid attention she could see the shadows under his eyes, the way his coat hung slightly, like it was made for a bigger man. "He looks weighed down."

"I agree." Lavinia sighed. "I must speak to Nicholas. I sense he could do with a friend."

Charlotte could only nod as her next dance partner arrived, full of apologies for his tardiness. "But Prinny himself wanted a word, and I could not leave, even knowing I was possibly squandering my opportunity to dance with the prettiest young lady here."

Another two dances, then it was time for supper. Lord Fanshawe had secured her a place next to him and was busy plying her with sweet cakes and champagne, truffles and pastries sure to flake when she ate them—and risk social disgrace. While she appreciated his efforts, it would be nice to have his attention such that he remembered what she preferred—

"Lady Charlotte, is something not to your liking?" Lord Fanshawe's eyes looked into hers, concern touched with uncertainty. "I notice you have not touched your champagne."

"I . . . I find I do not care overly for it," she admitted.

"Then tell me at once what you do, and I shall get some." He bowed. "I'm at your command."

"I prefer lemonade, sir."

Surprise crossed his features, mingled with not a little amusement. "Then lemonade it shall be. I'll be but a moment." He disappeared in the crowd, his place taken by a clutch of young men, whose flatteries and flirting faded at the arrival of another, at first unseen, gentleman.

"Lady Charlotte." The gentle voice accompanied a glass of lemonade.

She looked up, strangely unsurprised to find the dark eyes watching her. "Th–thank you."

His lips curled to one side. "I'm always glad to render you a small service."

Confusion filled her. What should she say? She glanced across the table. Mama was watching, nodding approvingly. But if she was too appreciative, he might get the wrong idea. But if she simply accepted his help without offering any interest in his concerns, how selfish would she appear? She cringed. How selfish did *that* thought make her?

She swallowed. "I . . . I was sorry to hear about the fire."

"Thank you."

"But pleased to hear there was no loss of life."

"As was I."

Silence stretched into awkwardness. She glanced away. How could Mama wish her to marry a man of such stilted conversation? Surely it was his turn to ask a question. If nothing else, he could say how nice she looked!

She glanced back. Sure enough, the dark eyes still watched her. Fighting frustration, she asked desperately, "Have they discovered the cause?"

"Yes." His face clouded. "My servants discovered a pile of rags on fire in a corner."

"Rather careless of someone."

"Yes." His gaze touched hers, veered away. He shook his head. "Tell me"—he straightened, his smile wry, as if determined to throw off his worry—"are you enjoying being back amongst the social scene?"

"I am, sir. It is most diverting."

A trace of something like disappointment crossed his features before his face assumed its usual gravity. "I am . . . that is, I wish—"

"Hartington!" Charlotte turned to see a flash of annoyance fill Lord Fanshawe's eyes before he smiled thinly. "Imagine, seeing you here."

"Fanshawe." The bow the duke offered was small, even by his standards.

"Thank you for looking after Charlotte while I was engaged in important matters." He turned to her, holding out the glass. "Forgive me, it took an age—oh! I see my efforts have been supplanted."

"The duke was kind enough—"

"I bet he was." Lord Fanshawe's smile faded, his eyes glittering as he faced the duke. "You are such a helpful sort of person, aren't you, Hartington?"

"I try."

Charlotte swallowed a giggle at the uncharacteristic reply, noting with satisfaction Lord Fanshawe's discomfort at the dry response. How rude to speak so to someone who had shown her only kindness! She might not wish to become affianced to the duke, but neither did she desire to see him hurt by others. She smiled at the shorter man. "Thank you again, sir, for your kind attentions."

She didn't mean it for a dismissal, but he bowed and was soon swallowed up in the crowd.

"Kind attentions," Lord Fanshawe muttered. He shook his head, drawing near, saying in an undertone, "That man is always watching you. I confess I cannot like it."

So it wasn't just her imagination. "He watches me?"

"Yes." He drew nearer still. "I know such a man is not to your liking—"

"How do you know?" A spark of annoyance at his presumption bloomed. "You cannot know my feelings on the matter."

His eyebrows shot up. "Well! Perhaps I have mistaken things. I'm surprised you would entertain the suit of such a man."

"Such a man? You keep saying that, but what do you mean?"

"Surely you have heard the rumors. That he killed his wife's lover, and keeps the by-blow locked in an attic."

She laughed. "You really should leave off reading such Gothic tales, my lord."

He shook his head. "It is not fiction but fact. He is cursed."

"Cursed? Now you are being ridiculous."

"Am I? How else do you explain the runaway coach, and a fire that threatened the Abbey? And a wife, of whose actions I shall not sully your ears."

She ticked off her fingers. "Accident, accident, and poor judgment."

"Forgive me, Charlotte, but you are not experienced in the world."

His condescension heated her chest as much as his over-familiar use of her name. "And I suppose you are?"

He stared at her. "But of course. I am a man."

She drew in a breath. Exhaled slowly. "Forgive me, Lord Fanshawe, but I did not think being born female automatically precluded me from a measure of good sense."

"I beg your pardon?"

"Yes, you should! You *should* beg my pardon for casting slights upon my intelligence, and then you should plead for the duke's pardon for casting such aspersions against him! I did not think you so unkind."

"Lady Charlotte, forgive me! I have no wish to argue with you."

Heat still streamed through her chest, but aware their intense discussion was attracting attention, she fixed a smile on her face. "Nor I you."

He sighed, a little theatrically, she thought. "It is growing rather warm in here. Perhaps we should find someplace cooler."

"Perhaps."

He rose and offered his hand before addressing her mother. "Lady Exeter, might I return your daughter to the ballroom?"

"I suppose so." She frowned a warning at Charlotte. "I trust you remember you are promised to Lord Carmichael for the next dance. Remember, he is destined to be an earl one day . . ."

"Yes, Mama." She followed the silent tug as the viscount led her away. "I thought we were going to the ballroom?"

"I could not very well tell your dear Mama we were not, could I?" He smiled, his teeth gleaming. "We'll go there first, and then move someplace quieter."

"But what if Lord Carmichael sees me?"

"We shall take good care not to see him."

"Oh, but—"

Her protest was swallowed up in the hubbub of the ballroom, the laughter and music drowning out her concerns. Yes, she suspected Lord Carmichael would not miss her terribly, and people would probably assume she was still in the supper room, but still . . . why was Lord Fanshawe so keen to risk such a breach of propriety?

The sight of her brother brought a measure of relief. "Henry!"

"Charlotte, Freddy." He clapped Lord Fanshawe on the back. "I see you've been doing the pretty with my sister."

"Henry, have you seen Lord Carmichael anywhere? Mama says I must dance with him."

"Good heavens, why would you ever want to dance with a man like him? A complete and utter rake if you ask me."

Who was the next gentleman she was promised to? "How about Lord Bracewell?"

"Bracewell? Good gracious! Why does Mama fix you up to dance with such men? Bracewell is nothing but a windsucker. Always rattling on about things nobody has the slightest interest in."

"My thoughts exactly," Lord Fanshawe said, his hand tugging hers. "Come, my dear—"

"No, I really think—"

"Freddy, you really missed something in the card room just now. Ashbolt just dropped five thousand! I couldn't believe such deep play, but they say that hag he married is the reason he's playing so wildly tonight, that she's put the hard word on him, so—"

"Lord Fanshawe, please." Charlotte tugged at her hand, but the viscount's grip only tightened. She glanced over Henry's shoulder. Saw the duke speaking with her father; surely he would help her. Look up, she silently pleaded, look up! But for all his constant watching, he was not attending now.

There was a hush as the crowds parted for the Prince Regent and royal princesses. Charlotte scanned the room for a savior. Who could release her? Even the rakish Lord Carmichael would be preferable to this.

"Ah, Charlotte, there you are!" Lavinia approached, wearing a stiff smile. "Henry, Lord Fanshawe."

"Lady Hawkesbury."

"Lord Fanshawe, please excuse my cousin." She looked pointedly at his hand.

His grip loosed. "Oh, but—"

"Surely you do not wish my cousin to forget her obligations?" She eyed him like she espied a particularly nasty insect, before turning to Charlotte. "Your mother does not want you to forget your dance with Lord Carmichael."

Charlotte forced herself to smile brightly. "How could I forget? I cannot disappoint him. Please excuse me."

Lavinia turned to the others. "Good evening."

"Good evening," Henry and Lord Fanshawe echoed, the latter's reply sounding as if through gritted teeth.

A shiver rippled through her. Surely he had not intended something nefarious. But in such a setting, with so many witnesses, it would not take much at all for a lady's reputation to be ruined, or for a scandal—or the presumption of one—to force a couple to the altar.

"Thank you, Lavinia."

"I'm sorry if you do not like to hear this, but I do not trust that man. He smiles too quickly with his lips, but never with his eyes."

Charlotte nodded, unable to disagree.

Lavinia drew her to where the sets were forming. "I cannot see Lord Carmichael, can you?"

"No."

"Oh well. Ah, look. Here is my friend." Lavinia smiled at the plain girl Charlotte had noticed earlier. "Charlotte, please permit me to introduce my dear friend Catherine Winthrop to you. Catherine, this is my cousin, Lady Charlotte Featherington."

After an exchange of curtsies the older girl smiled, genuine warmth lighting the corners of her honey-brown eyes. "It is a pleasure to meet you, Lady Charlotte."

"And you, Miss Winthrop."

"I'm sure you don't remember, but I was at Lavinia's wedding last December."

"Oh! I'm afraid—"

"Charlotte!" Mama drew near, the frown in her eyes reserved for Lavinia's friend. "Excuse us, Lavinia, but I must steal Charlotte for a moment. Her dance partner is waiting."

Charlotte made her farewells and hastened after her mother.

"I'm sorry, Mama, but I could not find Lord Carmichael anywhere."

"No matter, we have found you a new partner." Her mother headed past a woman wearing bright red sateen and a majestic turban of orange silk, shot with purple. "My goodness," Mama murmured. "The things some people think fit to wear in public."

"Who wishes to dance with me, Mama?" *Please Lord, not Lord Fanshawe!* She held no wish to speak with him, let alone stand so close as a dance required.

"Someone who has been quite anxious for this opportunity, I believe."

Her mother drew her forward, then gently pushed her toward the man standing next to her father.

The man whose countenance lit at the sight of her. The man around whom circled so much gossip and speculation. The man whom she'd thought she would never see dance.

The Duke of Hartington.

Chapter Fourteen

CHARLOTTE'S LOOK OF SHOCK stripped away the courage William had felt earlier. A prize he was not, not to this young lady, however much he might be considered one by her parents. William swallowed a sigh, pushed his lips into a smile. "Lady Charlotte, I hope you will do me the honor of standing up with me for this dance."

Her eyes flashed, and he knew in that moment she did not feel like she would be bestowing an honor, rather succumbing to an obligation. She slid a look at her parents, which only confirmed his suspicions.

His heart sank. Despite her mother's assertions, clearly Charlotte had little desire to dance. Was he such a fool to persist in this ridiculous hope?

Lady Exeter seemed aware of this as she said, "Charlotte?"

Her daughter's posture straightened, her chin lifted, yet she looked no higher than his neckcloth. "Thank you, sir. I'd be delighted," she said in a flat voice that suggested anything but.

Fighting dismay, he held out his hand and led her to join the set that had already formed. Around them, dancers responded to the lilting melody with laughter and smiles, but she said nothing, her manner as uncompromising as her posture.

"Thank you for not embarrassing me with a refusal."

Now her gaze met his. "Sir, I—" Her lips parted, closed again.

The dance progression parted them, preventing conversation momentarily, before she returned to his side. "Are you enjoying your season?"

"You asked me that earlier."

"Forgive me. You said it proved most diverting?"

"Yes."

He cleared his throat. "Is time spent with Fanshawe so diverting?"

"I beg your pardon?"

"At supper before, I assumed . . ."

Her eyes flashed; she said nothing, but two bright spots of color suffused her upper cheeks.

He had offended her.

Censure twisted within as the music separated them again. What kind of fool was he? How could he hope to win her—with slights and offenses?

When the dance finally returned her to him, he could think of nothing more to say. Were his assumptions about Fanshawe incorrect? He had wondered earlier, her look of relief at her cousin's intervention enough to lend wings to his hope. He opened his mouth. Closed it. What could he say that had not been said to her enough already tonight? He'd heard the young bucks tonight, heard their compliments; he needed something more original than flattery. But charm had always proved elusive, and as much as he admired her openness, found her youthful presence refreshing to his soul, and her looks very diverting indeed, he could not help but be aware that she did not feel so about him.

He glanced down at her. The top of her head reached to his eyes, and from this vantage point he could see the lovely lines of her neck, the creaminess of her skin, catch the flash of diamond drops in her perfect little ears. What could he say but the truth?

"Lady Charlotte?"

She glanced up, and their gazes held.

His pulse throbbed. He could drown in those eyes: so clear, so entrancing, so beautiful. "You are most lovely."

A rosy pink suffused her features, and she glanced down modestly.

His heart tripped. *Heavenly Father?*

⁂

Charlotte barely knew if she was to move or stand still. This man kept her off-kilter with his awkwardness and admiration, with those deeply lashed, deeply dark eyes.

"You dance very well, Lady Charlotte."

"Thank you."

So she should. Mama had engaged the redoubtable Mr. Finetti, whose command of the elegancies of all the proper dances had given him the reputation of London's foremost dancing master. But she could not say this.

Neither could she look at his eyes, risk sinking into their fathomless depths. Up close, his eyes held a myriad of specks, as if a fairy from a French tale had scattered golden dust while he dreamed. She, who had never considered him attractive save when he smiled, had suddenly become captive to his eyes.

She ducked her head, unwilling to see the dowagers sitting on the room's perimeter. Her cheeks flamed. She knew what they were saying behind their painted fans and painted smiles. The duke's singling her out in such a manner, dancing with her when he'd not danced with any others, would only set tongues flapping, and—her spirits sank—no doubt a heavy exchange of wagers in the card room next door.

Was Father there? She nearly stumbled, but the duke held her safely. Of course he would be; he never danced anymore. What bets would he lay down? She nearly slipped again. Was Henry right? Wasn't this akin to selling her off to the highest bidder?

Tears rushed to fill her eyes, to fill her throat. She blinked them back, keeping her lips lifted in a stiff smile, only to meet the sardonic gaze of Lord Fanshawe. Upon noticing her attention, he swept her a bow. Her smile wavered, and she turned her head away. Of course Lord Fanshawe was displeased; he knew she was supposed to be partnering Lord Carmichael. He might smile easily, but Lavinia was right. Lord Fanshawe's smile lit neither his eyes nor his features. He might as well wear a mask.

She returned her attention to covertly study the man across from her. His chin was firm, his lips thin, tweaking to an occasional half smile, as if wryly amused. This man might not smile often, but when he did, it made her pulse skip a little. Unlike other gentlemen of smooth manners and smoother words, the duke's conversation, sparse as it might be, held purpose, and a dignity that lent an authenticity to his speech. He might rarely flatter, but in the absence of flattery his words felt more trustworthy. And his eschewing of the props of the fops and dandies—his only concession to jewels a signet ring and pocket watch—such lack of ornamentation was perhaps also indicative of his character, that he felt no need to try to impress those who required such aids to be impressed. Which was, somehow . . . impressive.

The dance drew to an end, the lines reformed, the music faded, the dancers bowed, curtsied, applauded.

"Shall we?"

The duke offered his arm and they wended their way through the ogling crowds, the stares and whispers behind fluttering fans making her feel hot and jittery. By the time they'd crossed the ballroom, it was a relief to finally sink into a chair beside Mama, and pretend her exhaustion necessitated the duke's fetching her a glass of lemonade.

Mama leaned near as he walked away. "You dance together very well."

"He is too short."

"Nonsense! He is taller than you. Indeed, he is just as he ought to be."

Charlotte snatched up a fan to wave her heated face. And to hide her lack of smile.

"I was just saying to dear Lady Castlereagh how wonderful it is to see the duke in good spirits again, and she agreed. And he is always so elegantly dressed, such a lovely gentleman—"

"Why don't *you* dance with him then, Mama?"

"Why, Charlotte! The very idea. A woman of my age?" Her mother gave a tittery laugh. "No, he would be far more interested in someone much younger."

Someone who might give him an heir, Charlotte thought miserably.

"Now, turn those lips into a smile, my dear. I have good news. Lady Castlereagh has decided to overlook the whispers and grant you vouchers at Almack's."

"Oh! That is good news." Her spirits lifted. Perhaps if she were to go to London's chief marriage mart she might be able to find someone *truly* eligible. Henry might decry the fare of stale cakes and sandwiches, and that nothing stronger was served than orgeat and lemonade, but to receive entrée to Almack's was cachet beyond almost anything else.

Mama nudged her. "Pin on a smile. The duke approaches, and we can't have you giving him the wrong impression."

"And what precisely is the right impression, Mama?"

"Why, that you enjoy his company, of course! Ah, Duke," Mama said, bonhomie oozing from every pore. "So thoughtful, so kind of you," she said accepting the cup of lemonade.

The duke cut Charlotte a look, amusement dancing in the dark depths of his eyes. "Lady Charlotte, would you wish for some lemonade, too?"

Appreciation at his forbearance with her mother's antics made her smile genuine. "Yes, please."

"Oh, is this lemonade?" Mama said, a look of disgust crossing her face. "I would much prefer champagne, if you'd be so kind."

"Mama," Charlotte said in an undertone, behind her fan. "You cannot send him off like a servant!"

"Perhaps, madam, if you were to pass your drink to your daughter, you might find she may be in need of it." This was said with a hooked brow, which brought a flush to Mama's cheeks and a hurried passing of the cup to Charlotte, who drank from it gratefully.

"I apologize, Duke. I did not mean—"

"It is of no consequence, madam. I shall seek out a glass of champagne immediately."

With a small bow he departed, threading through the crowds until he was lost from view.

"Such a kind man," Mama sighed. "If your father were here and asked to do such a small thing, he'd no doubt create such a fuss. And you know I cannot stand it when people create fuss."

Charlotte hid her smile in the bottom of her glass. Well she knew Mama could not stand for people other than herself to make a fuss . . .

"Ah! You're here." Henry slipped into the vacant chair beside her. "Freddy didn't like it by half seeing you dancing with ol' Hartington."

"He's not that old."

"No? Older than you'd want though, isn't he, Lottie? Though not older than what Father—"

"Henry!" Mama snapped. "Do not speak in such a vulgar manner."

"Mama, it is not vulgar to speak plainly. Besides, don't you wish for Lottie to be happy?"

"I wish for what is best for her! Whether that constitutes her happiness is a matter only she can decide."

"Happiness as decision?" Henry chuckled. "Well, that'll be something to think about, Lottie, especially when—"

"Henry!" her mother said warningly.

Charlotte frowned at the pitying expression she saw on her brother's face. "Henry? Is there something I should know?"

"Of course not, Charlotte," Mama said, patting her knee.

Henry's face only deepened in compassion, his lips flattening.

"Ah, here is the duke again. Oh, look! He's with your father." Mama's gift for the obvious remained as sharp as ever.

"So he is."

"Charlotte, Henry, please behave. It is very import—Oh, thank you, Duke. How kind you are," Mama said with a big smile and a sideways glance at Charlotte, as if wanting her to recognize his extreme magnanimity in procuring her a glass.

"Lady Charlotte, I trust you are feeling a little better?"

"Thank you, sir, I am." She glanced at her gloved hands, folded neatly in her lap, doing her best to look maidenly, and not like someone who indulged in sarcastic musings.

"Charlotte," her father's voice brought her attention up. "Who is your next partner?"

"I believe it is Lord Bracewell."

"Forget him. I want you to dance with Hartington here."

"Oh, but—" At her mother's elbow in her ribs she swallowed back the protest.

"Perhaps Lady Charlotte is still weary after our previous dance." The duke smiled at her, causing her heart to quiver a little. "And I would not wish to deprive another soul of such an excellent partner."

"Doing it rather too brown," she thought she heard Henry mutter.

"Well, I have no desire to see her dancing with anyone other than you, so I guess we've come to an impasse, sir."

Charlotte searched her father's face, then the duke's. Why did they appear to have some understanding? A creeping kind of dread crawled across her chest. She glanced at her mother, whose smirk of self-satisfaction was one Charlotte had witnessed a dozen times before, whenever Mama had beaten a rival and procured the latest French silk or been first to procure the services of an expert like Mr. Finetti. But what did she have to look so smug about now?

Beside her, she heard Henry's sigh, felt his pat on her shoulder before he stood, shook the duke's hand, and was soon lost in the sea of people. Why shake his hand? Oh, *why* did she not know what was going on?

"Charlotte?" Mama said, a softness in her voice as she offered her a smile every bit as wide as the one she'd offered the duke previously. "Seeing as you appear rather warm, perhaps you and the duke might like to take some air along the terrace?"

"I don't—"

"Madam, I would not wish to presume—"

"Nonsense. Charlotte seems in need of some air, and I'm sure she would only be too happy to further the acquaintance between you both, wouldn't you, Charlotte?"

This last was said with such a piercing look there could be only one reply. Charlotte gave it. "Of course."

She took the duke's proffered arm, and he led her through the crowd, out to the cooler night air.

❧ Chapter Fifteen

The terrace air held a chill, a cooling bite that sent a tremble through his spine. Or perhaps that was the effect of being with his companion. He glanced at her. Lights spilling from the upper rooms shafted illumination across her face, revealing the pensive brow, the bottom lip being bitten. She seemed as anxious as he.

He noticed her grasp tighten a little on his sleeve as they descended the steps, still in silence. It wasn't the done thing for a mother to release her daughter into the company of a young man, but perhaps, he thought wryly, a mother did not care for the niceties when the future of said daughter was so near to being finalized. They reached the gravel path, and her hand quickly released his sleeve, like she was afraid of contamination.

As if conscious he had noticed, she glanced at him, eyes wide in the moonlight, before she shivered.

"Lady Charlotte, are you too cool? Would you prefer to return inside?"

"I . . ." She licked her bottom lip, the sight entrancing. "We can if *you* prefer, sir."

"But that was not my question."

She blinked. A smile flitted across her features. "That would be a strange question to ask oneself, wouldn't it?"

Now was his turn to blink. And smile. "Especially aloud."

"One might have questions asked about one's sanity, and whether one would be better spent inside Bedlam."

"Nobody is better inside Bethlem's Asylum, I assure you."

"Have you been?"

"Not as a patient, I assure you," he ventured, gladness rising within as her smile peeked out again. "But neither have I visited as some do, laughing about the inmates as they might the antics of an animal at the Royal Menagerie."

"Then why?"

"I . . ." Was it time to share some of his secrets? Oh, what would it matter? "I am on the board of governors."

"You?"

He nodded. "It is a new appointment, of only a year's standing or so. But I hope that with time we can see the conditions inside improve for the poor souls who dwell there."

"But are they not dangerous? Should not such people be locked away?"

"They are no more dangerous than any creature that is forever chained and treated badly when others come near." Memories surged of his most recent visit. Slipshod walls and damp floors filled with crawling vermin, filthy naked patients chained by iron bars at the neck and feet, physicians and apothecaries in denial that such treatment was inhumane. God help them all. Shaking away the painful recollections, he led her to a garden bench, lit by several golden Chinese lanterns, where he extracted his pocket-handkerchief and laid it on the seat for her to sit upon. Heaven forbid her beautiful gown be soiled.

She sat, gazing up at him. Her brow still held a wrinkle. "Are you a social reformist, sir?"

"I would never advertise the fact—"

"Then it *is* a fact?"

Gladness warmed him to again see the sharp mind behind the pretty face. "I believe so."

"But you are a duke."

"And you are a marquess's daughter."

"Yes." Her lips curled to one side. "But I don't see why you would care for those not of your, not of our—"

"Our rank, you mean?" At her nod he felt a pang of disappointment. "Surely you do not think those unhinged of mind are only from the lower levels of society?"

"I . . . I confess I have not thought on it at all."

Of course she hadn't. What kind of fool was he to speak on such matters? Pamela had thought *him* mad for wishing to help the poor souls locked away in their torment. "Forgive me. I should not speak about such—"

"No, please tell me. I wish to know why you care. Please don't treat me as a child."

Her gown, whilst modest, revealed her form to be far from childlike. He swallowed.

"Sir?"

Dragging his thoughts back to the question, he said, "Are we not commanded by our Lord to love our neighbor as ourselves?"

"But they are hardly our neighbors."

"Do you think Jesus intended us to restrict the meaning to such a literal interpretation?"

She bit her lip, before eventually saying in a small voice, "No."

The night sounds sharpened, the soft splash of a fountain, the call of a night bird, the smell of roses tickling his senses. Far beyond them he could hear the low laughter of a man, followed by the higher tinkly giggle of a lady, making the most of this evening made for romance. His lips pushed to one side. And here he was, charming his companion with talk of insane asylums. He shook his head at himself.

"Does my father know?"

"I beg your pardon?"

"Does my father know about your social reformist views?"

"I wouldn't exactly call them reformist views."

"What would you call them?"

"Merely the views of every aware man and woman who call themselves Christian."

Her brows pushed together. "You sound like Lavinia and the earl."

He chuckled. "We share a number of values, yes."

She turned slightly, and he ventured to study her profile, the delicate sloping nose and firm chin, the golden curl kissing her cheek and the one springing behind her ear.

His words seemed to echo in the silence, making him wonder just how many values he might share with this young lady. Surely that was of importance, especially when he was considering—

"Do you think if someone does not care about such poor creatures then he or she is not Christian?"

He blinked. "I would hesitate to make such a claim."

"But you said before that all those who call themselves Christian should be aware of the plight of such people."

He thought back to what he'd said minutes earlier. What had he said? "I believe that I said every *aware* Christian."

"Meaning some are not."

"Yes."

Her brow puckered once more, as if she were engaging in heavy thought.

"I do not intend my words to distress you, Lady Charlotte."

"They have not. You have merely made me see how blind I've been. I believe, but have never really considered claims of faith requiring action."

His heart gave a little ping of gladness. She shared his faith, which was more than Pamela had. "I hope I've not made you feel uncomfortable?"

"No." She shivered.

"Would you like to return? I would not have you grow cool."

"Thank you, I am well. As much as I enjoy balls, I'm not especially fond of crowds and being jostled. Besides, if we were to return, Mama would simply plague me with what you said, and what I said, and I do not think she'd be enamored to know we talked of such things." She tilted her head up at him and smiled.

Her smile caught him by the heart and refused to let go, stealing his breath.

"Sir?"

He swallowed, willed himself to talk normally. "Forgive me. So you do not care for our conversation?"

"I did not say that. Only that Mama might not approve."

"So I must endeavor to speak on things that might win her favor. Let me see, do you believe stars might suffice? Flowers? Or is there another topic you would like to discuss?"

She bit her lip, as if worried.

"You do have something?"

"I . . . I have wondered something about you, sir."

Many had. But he'd never felt inclined to satisfy their curiosity the way he wished to satisfy this young lady's. "Ask, and I will do my best to answer."

"It isn't—that is, Mama might consider such a topic . . . indelicate."

"But she is not here, and unless you choose to tell her, she shall never know. I certainly have no intention to report the substance of my every conversation to your mother."

She laughed, shoulders unstiffening. "Something we share in common."

One thing, at least. "Go on."

"People say . . ." Her cheeks pinked.

"All sorts of things, but it doesn't mean they're all true, now does it?"

"No." As if gathering her courage, she drew herself up. "People say you have a child."

"Ah." The tension that had seemed to afflict her now enveloped him, banding his chest.

"Is it true?"

"Yes, that is true. A little girl."

"Oh." Her features seemed to deflate, as if disappointed with his answer.

For some reason, her response coiled shame within. How was this even a question? How could he have been so backward in his duty to not have publicly acknowledged the child? He cleared his throat. "I can see why your mama might find such a question to be a trifle forward."

She glanced up with wide, worried eyes. "Oh! I'm sorry I—"

"Please, no." He drew closer, placed a hand on her arm, felt her freeze. He dropped his hand. "I said to ask, and so you did."

"But it was improper of me."

"It is improper for us to sit out here unaccompanied, yet the impropriety did not seem to concern your mother terribly."

Her eyes widened even more, then she jumped up. "Oh! I should—we should return, before—"

"Before the gossips run out of speculation? I doubt we will ever see that day."

She nodded, but the smiles and confiding air of earlier had gone, leaving her with a troubled look. He drew her hand onto his arm, and patted it. "Pray do not concern yourself with tittle-tattle. If one always wonders what others are saying, one shall go mad."

"And be placed in Bedlam?" she said with a slanting look.

"Precisely. And we are agreed that conditions there are not what they should be."

"Not yet, perhaps."

Her quiet words heartened him, like she held confidence in his determination to change conditions there. Perhaps it was foolishness but he couldn't deny the lift in his spirits. Pamela had never believed in him.

They ascended the steps, and the music swelled.

When they had reached the top, she stilled, glancing up at him with those entrancing blue eyes. "What is her name?"

Whose name?

He must have looked confused, for she smiled and said, "The name of your daughter?"

His daughter? The words washed over him, anger mingling into guilt and regret, swirling into his heart, his resolve. "My daughter's name is Rose."

She nodded, and he felt the affirmation of something far deeper than mere approval of a name. Almost like the Lord Himself was shining approval from heaven that William had finally decided to confess young Rose as his own.

A fresh twist of shame pierced him. How could he profess to care about the well-being of strangers in an asylum when he barely acknowledged the young babe to whom his wife had given birth?

They stood on the threshold, and he heard her draw in a breath, as if she too were bracing for the social onslaught. "Ready?"

"Ready."

They reentered the ballroom, with all its glitter, clamor, and speculation.

<hr/>

She had lied. She wasn't ready. Wasn't ready to return from peace to uproar. Wasn't ready for her mother's knowing glances or satisfied smile. Wasn't ready to encounter the flashing eyes of Lord Fanshawe or the fans rising to hide forked tongues. She wasn't prepared to see the haunted gaze of Clara DeLancey standing quietly with her mother and the Dowager Countess Hawkesbury, staring after Lavinia's husband. Her heart twisted, remembering last year's scandal when Miss DeLancey's well-publicized near-engagement had ended in dust, as the earl's true feelings for Lavinia had become known.

She felt similarly exposed, as if everyone knew where she had been and with whom. It made her smile feel brittle, her facade fragile, a facade which might slip any moment and reveal her inner turmoil. Oh, if only they could return to that pocket of quietude again . . .

The duke murmured his farewell, promising to call on them soon, and Charlotte was quickly swept away by a plethora of partners, who insisted on dancing until the small hours. But even though her smile was firmly affixed, the troubling revelations from earlier continued to resound. Why was there such mystery over the duke's daughter? Rose. Such a pretty name, doubtless for a pretty girl. She bit the inside of her lip. And why had their discussion of social reform led her to feeling such unease? Was it his comment about Christians being aware?

She sensed something profound had happened in those quiet moments outside, something suggesting her life had been rather shortsighted in her awareness of others. So why should she care now? Her prayer from months ago—something about not being shallow?—wafted into memory. Oh, Mama would have a fit! She'd always protested whenever Lavinia mentioned things to do with faith, saying such matters were private and to speak of them most indecorous. But how could Mama hold such scruples when she'd agreed to such a scandal-worthy thing as to permit Charlotte to remain outside and unchaperoned with a young gentleman?

Queasiness roiled.

That question only had answers she did not wish to consider.

Finally, *finally*, when Charlotte's cheeks ached as much as her feet, the Regent and princesses departed, and they were freed to take their leave and return home. But the conversation in the carriage rekindled her concerns.

"And how was your chat with the duke?"

She sighed. "The same as the last time I answered, Mama. It was pleasant."

"He is *such* a personable gentleman."

Her brows rose. Personable was overstating things. "He was pleasant."

"Pleasant?" Her mother sniffed. "I should think so."

Father leaned forward. "And you like the young man?"

"The duke?"

"Which other young man is there?" her mother snapped.

"I like him well enough," she hurried to say, smiling brightly before Mama's glare demanded further explanations.

"Good, good."

Fortunately their curiosity seemed to subside, leaving Charlotte to retreat upstairs, succumb to the ministrations of a yawning Sarah, and finally retire to a deep, uneasy sleep.

Waking at noon, Charlotte was greeted by Sarah with a refreshing cup of chocolate and the news that Father wanted to see her. When finally deemed presentable by an exceedingly fussy Sarah, Charlotte moved downstairs to discover her parents in the study.

"I gather you had an enjoyable time with the duke last evening?"

"Yes?" she replied cautiously.

"Good, very good." Father coughed. Beside him, Mama was nodding, a pleased expression on her face for once.

The earlier unease grew. "Why is that so good?"

"Because I've had an interview with the man this morning."

No.

She studied the landscape on the opposite wall. Perhaps if she said nothing, the awful suspicion would not eventuate. Perhaps if she said nothing, she could go back to bed and this would have proved to be a *very* bad dream. Perhaps she could enter that painted woodland glade and hide behind that grove and nobody would ever—

"Charlotte?" Father's voice now held a frown.

Returning her attention, she discovered his face now matched his voice. "Yes, Father?"

"I said I had an interview with the duke this morning."

Please God, no. It could only mean one thing. "Really?"

"Yes, really."

His gaze softened a little, taking her back a dozen years ago, when she'd sometimes felt his approval, and yes, even his love, when she'd dared believe she'd been the apple of his eye. Even Mama in those days had been warmer . . .

He cleared his throat, a far more guttural expression than the duke's. "I understand this might come as a bit of a shock, but I think it only fair you know"—he hurried on, as if he knew the news would be unpleasant—"the duke has requested your hand in marriage, and I have accepted."

Chapter Sixteen

No! No, no, no.

"Why are you shaking your head, Charlotte?" Mama said peevishly. "It has been decided—"

"But not by me!"

Father had the grace to look a little ashamed. "Now I know he might seem a little old—"

"A little?"

"There is no need to take that tone, young lady!"

"I'm sorry. It . . . it is a shock." She bit her lip to stop the tremble.

Her father nodded. "I understand you might not wish to become a stepmother—"

Tears pricked at the back of her eyes, clogging her throat. Why hadn't she refused her mother's request last night? Why hadn't she said more of how she felt? How had she permitted this situation to turn so bad so quickly?

"But I truly believe this will be a splendid match for you."

"How can you think such a thing?" she rasped.

"He is a duke!" Mama snapped. "Any other young lady would be thrilled to be so honored. How you can sit there whimpering when you will be a duchess I cannot know."

"But I don't want to be a duchess!"

Mama blanched as if Charlotte had blasphemed. "How can you say such a thing?"

"What *do* you want?"

Her father's kind tone forced her to bite the inside of her wobbling bottom lip, but she could not answer his question. What did she want? To be married, certainly. One day. When she'd had the pleasure of a season. But to a man of her choosing. A man she *loved*. Helplessness muddled her words, clamped her throat. How could she explain this to her parents? She could only shrug hopelessly.

"See? She doesn't even know what she wants," Mama said with a sniff.

Her heart stung. Why did Mama have to be so dismissive? Couldn't she try to understand?

"And even if you did, well, we don't always get what we want in this world, do we?"

Charlotte dashed away the moisture flecking her lashes, to stare at her mother. Why was Mama so adamant? Why did she sound so bitter?

"Do you have some objection to the man?" Father asked, a query in his brow.

"How anyone can have any objection, I hardly know. Why, to think you'll get to live at Hartwell Abbey! It is said to have one of the finest staircases in all of England."

Staircases! Was Mama serious?

"Think of the jewels, of the clothes, of the carriages—well, perhaps not them, just yet. Forget any silly speculations. Why, just think, I will even be forced to curtsy to you!"

While that thought contained some merit, her mother's words about silly speculations had aroused a new fear. "Some . . . some say he is cursed."

"Cursed? Nonsense! Whoever got you believing such an outrageous notion?" Mama's eyes narrowed. "I bet it was that ridiculous Fanshawe creature. Jealousy makes people say the vilest things. He's never had a kind word to say about poor Hartington."

"But if you describe him as poor, why must I be forced to marry him?" Why could they not see this? Her chest constricted. Why were they so unreasonable?

"Why are you so opposed?"

"I do not love him."

Father looked at her, concern etched in his forehead, as Mama snorted. "Love? What does love have to do with marriage?"

Her father's lips tightened.

Sympathy for him hurried Charlotte into speech. "I . . . I always hoped to marry for love, like Lavinia."

"Lavinia?" Mama snorted. "Why she chose to marry *that* man I'll never know."

Heat coiled inside, begging release. "She chose Lord Hawkesbury because she loves him, and he loves her!"

"Charlotte, calm yourself please. Such outbursts are most unladylike."

She drew in a breath, praying for some measure of control over her temper. "Mama, this . . . this is a shock."

"A shock? What do you think we've been doing these past weeks? It certainly wasn't so you could throw over someone of the wealth and importance of a duke for a near nobody like that frippery Fanshawe."

Her shoulders grew suddenly heavy. Her mother was right. She had known, or at least suspected Mama's intentions. But to announce it in such a way, so suddenly . . .

"Now, go upstairs and mend your face. The duke is arriving shortly and wishes to speak with you. He shan't wish to speak with a miss with blotchy cheeks and a red nose."

She ducked her head and hurried from the room, happy to escape her mother's cutting observations and her father's compassionate look. She stumbled up to her bedchamber, where she succumbed to the mute ministrations of Mama's lady's maid, who nevertheless seemed to be quivering with excitement. Had Ellen been told? Of course she had. Mama had never been known for discretion. So if Ellen knew, then all the servants must know, which meant she had nobody who understood just how trapped she felt.

Charlotte kept her eyes on her lap as Ellen tweaked and pulled, and dabbed a hare's foot of powder across her face. Her future seemed to roll ahead of her, unknown and terrifying. Panic roiled across her, stealing her breath. She clenched her hands more tightly, forcing herself to breathe slowly. It would not do to show her fear to the servants.

When Ellen left, with a smile, a curtsy, and a murmured, "Congratulations, Lady Charlotte," she finally lifted her gaze to the mirror, only to look into the face of a stranger. Somehow she seemed older, the arrangement firmly pulling her hair back accentuated her face. Her cheekbones looked more prominent, and her eyes seemed less round. But this stranger was paler, too, with dulled eyes, as though the excitement others shared drained life from her.

A memory from last night surfaced: Clara, pale-faced, wan-looking, staring after the man she could not marry. Her heart wrenched again. Would she be forced to look at Lord Markham—oh, dear God, Lord Markham!—with the haunted eyes of Clara DeLancey? Be laughed at behind a thousand fluttering fans?

But what could she do? What could she *do*? Escape out the window? Rush onto the street? What choice did she have but to somehow put on dignity and comply with her parents' decree?

A knock at the door preceded her own maid's entrance. "Lady Charlotte? Your mother sent me to say they are awaiting you downstairs."

"Thank you, Sarah." But she did not move.

"Lady Charlotte?"

She met her maid's eyes in the looking glass.

"May I say how pleased we all are for your good news?"

"Thank you," she replied mechanically, forcing her lips to push up in the faintest semblance of a smile.

"Oh, but you do look nice. Ellen has such a way with hair, doesn't she? I wish I had half her skill."

From through the open window came the sound of a carriage slowing, stopping, the snort and stamp of a horse. Sarah rushed to the window. "Oh, he's here!"

Charlotte's fingers clenched.

"Oh, my lady, come and look!"

She couldn't move. Her limbs felt like liquid.

"Oh, but he is elegant! Always dresses to a nicety, but with nothing of the dandy. You'll make a handsome pair, if I might say so, my lady."

Moisture clogged her eyes, her throat. She blinked rapidly, dragged in another breath, relieved Sarah's spying gave her the chance to recover from her emotion.

Sarah finally left her position by the window to come to the dressing table. As she studied Charlotte, the light in her face dimmed. "My lady?"

Charlotte swallowed, willing her voice not to waver. "Please be so kind as to let Mama know I shall be down directly."

"Of course." Sarah bobbed a curtsy and moved to the door, where she hesitated.

"Yes?"

"If I might be so bold, my lady?"

Charlotte waited, bracing herself internally for whatever her sharp-eyed maid had to say.

"May I just say that while this is a new circumstance, which may seem a little daunting, marriage is something in which to rejoice, and the duke, well, he is not the tyrant some say."

She turned sharply. "Who says?"

Sarah blushed. "Some of the maids from the big houses get to talking sometimes, and I've heard it said he is a blackguard and a madman."

A blackguard and a madman? She swallowed. "But you don't believe it?"

"No more than I believe anything a bitter person might say."

"Who said?"

"I'm not rightly sure, but I think she was the maid to the late duchess."

Charlotte shivered.

"Now, don't you be worrying yourself, my lady. Her fate won't be your lot."

She grasped the small hope like a drowning person might a lifeline. "But how can you know?"

"Because I'll be praying for you."

Her words pierced the soul, forcing Charlotte to dash away an errant tear. "Please don't stop."

"Trust in the Lord, my lady. He's the One who gives us hope."

Hope.

The word wavered in the room, almost a tangible thing, as her maid curtsied and finally left the room. *Lord God,* Charlotte breathed, *please help me.*

She pushed to her feet, brushed down her skirts, glanced at the unfamiliar reflection one more time. Filled with trepidation, filled with regrets, countered only by the tiniest flicker of hope instilled by her maid's—her maid's!—words, she exited the room.

Bracing to meet her destiny.

William flicked at an imaginary piece of fluff in an effort to avoid meeting the gaze of his soon-to-be new mother-in-law. From the mantelpiece the Sèvres clock ticked resolutely.

"I don't know what is keeping her," the marchioness said, forcing his attention to return to her overly smiling face. "Charlotte was in such a tizzy at the thought of marrying you."

He nodded, hiding his frustration that her parents had broached the idea of his marriage to their daughter before he'd had the chance to say anything himself. He'd asked the marquess to pay his addresses to Charlotte, to get to know her in a formal way, until both he and she were certain, for he would not have her coerced into something she did not wish. Her parents seemed to have taken his request as certainty.

"She's terribly eager, you understand," Lady Exeter continued. "Very excited."

But the look the marquess slid his wife only fueled the uncertainty. Now the only thing of which he was truly certain was that the marchioness herself was terribly eager for the marriage to occur.

He supposed he could not blame her. His previous proposal, four years prior, had been met with rapturous enthusiasm from Pamela's mother that was nearly matched by her daughter, as if they could not believe their good fortune, that a duke would condescend to marry a mere viscount's daughter. To her credit, Pamela had maintained the facade for the first year at least, enough to make him think she at least liked him, but when he'd found faith, she seemed to find more interest elsewhere. While his conversation with Charlotte made him sure she possessed more faith than Pamela ever did, he was thankful she was blessed with a cousin whose faith shone in everything she said and whose influence he hoped and prayed would only deepen Charlotte's commitment to the Lord.

William glanced at the clock again. He was used to Pamela's lengthy toilettes, but this wait did not exactly scream eagerness. Fear pricked. She wouldn't have run away?

"Duke," the marchioness began, with another of those irritatingly high-pitched laughs, "please forgive—oh!" She turned as Charlotte entered, forcing him to his feet. "Ah, here she is at last," the marchioness said. "And doesn't she look beautiful?"

"Yes," he replied obediently, but it was true. Charlotte appeared older today, her hair more severe, her poise more restrained. He glimpsed the woman she would be in several decades, her aristocratic heritage evident in the line of her jaw, her cheeks, her thin nose. Beautiful. Elegant. His.

Please God.

He cleared his throat. "Good afternoon, Lady Charlotte."

"Good afternoon, Duke." Charlotte gave him one quick, troubled look, before lowering her head.

A pang shot through him. Was she frightened of him? Or was it marriage for which she was not so keen?

He glanced at the marquess and marchioness, eyebrows raised.

Exeter coughed. "Well, we best leave you both to become further acquainted." He rose, motioned to his wife. "Come, Constance."

"Oh! Of course." She smiled widely at William before murmuring to her daughter, "For goodness' sake, smile!"

His own smile faded, as the doubts crowded in anew. The young lady was not pleased, that was plain, but perhaps that was mere nerves. Heaven knew he felt nervous enough himself.

"Lady Charlotte?"

She jumped.

"Please, shall we sit?"

"Of c–course."

She chose a single seat, foiling his desire to sit beside her again, forcing him to claim the chair opposite. Her posture was upright, yet her eyes still refused to meet his.

He cleared his throat. "I understand this has been something of a surprise."

Her too-pale cheeks grew rosy. "I, er . . . yes."

"I hope you will forgive the seeming suddenness of my . . ." What could he say? How could he apologize for the proposal her parents assumed he had made? He could not embarrass either her or them by saying such a thing.

"Of your . . . ?"

Now he felt his cheeks heat. "Of my appearance here today."

She nodded, gaze still not touching his. But it seemed she relaxed a little.

"You understand why I am here?"

"Father said . . . you wished to marry. Me," she added, as if an afterthought.

Again he fought the spurt of resentment at having his proposal usurped. "I wish to know whether you wish such a thing."

Her gaze met his then, and again he was entranced by the clarity of the blue eyes. So innocent, so pure, yet he could see the trouble shading them.

"You do not, do you?" he said softly.

Pink lips parted, then closed, as her eyes widened. "I . . . I am conscious of the tremendous honor you do me."

"But you do not wish to marry me."

She frowned. "Why do you say this, sir? I thought *you* wished to marry me?"

His lips pursed, as he strove to hide a sigh. "I have no wish to marry someone who has little inclination to marry me."

"But I do!"

He leaned against the cushions, studying her. She seemed almost scared, as if should she fail to convince him, he would depart. He frowned. Was it fear of losing him or fear of something—or someone—else that had her so concerned?

"My dear, may I be completely open with you?"

She nodded.

"It is not, it has never been, my intention to alarm you. I wish for a wife, and I think you and I would suit. My intention today was merely to see if you would be amenable to considering an offer from me, not to force you into something for which you have no desire." He picked up his gloves from the table. "I do not make it my practice to intimidate young ladies into matrimony, neither do I wish them to feel obligated, simply because I should wish to pay my addresses to them. I am exceedingly sorry you have been placed in such an awkward position."

She stared at him, eyes wide. "Do you wish to leave?"

"I have no wish to stay where my presence is unwelcome."

She licked her bottom lip. Her hands were pressed together so tightly he could see the whitened knuckles. "I . . . I do not find your presence unwelcome, sir."

"No?" He raised a brow.

Charlotte blushed, but her eyes kept his steadily. "I appreciate your candor, sir."

"Truly?"

She nodded. "I . . . I confess to being somewhat surprised at the . . . the speed at which things have progressed. I am not used to such things."

He suppressed a smile. "Of course." He returned the gloves to their position. "May I say that it is also not my habit to propose to every beautiful young lady fresh on the social scene?"

Her smile peeked out. "I am glad for your sake, sir." At his raised brow, she continued. "For that would make you a veritable Lothario."

He chuckled. The tension in the room dropped a notch. "I confess to being anything but."

"I'm glad," she said simply, and his heart warmed.

Yes, despite the hesitancies, despite the fear, the situation still held an ember of hope.

"Sir, I . . . please forgive my parents for rushing to assume. It is . . ." Her gaze lowered. "It is my mother's dearest wish for me to be settled respectably, and she can get a trifle carried away. She meant no harm, I'm sure."

"No harm done. Lady Charlotte." He waited until her eyes crept to his again. "Would you permit me to pay my addresses to you?" He smiled. "We can wait to see if this will prove to be something to our mutual satisfaction if you like."

"Oh, but Mama—" She raised a hand to her mouth. "Whatever would we say to her?"

"Simply that. That we wish to get to know each other a little more before leaping into something as binding as an engagement."

"You would do that for me?"

"I would do that for both of us."

She laughed, as if in relief. "Oh, sir. You cannot know what trepidation I have felt."

He forced his smile to not waver. She was that worried about his suit? "As I said earlier, I would not have you feeling any sense of obligation or fear."

"Oh, I don't fear you," she said ingenuously.

Whom did she fear, then? Her mother?

"I shall speak to your father, and suggest that, given your youth and my recent bereavement, it may be precipitous to announce an engagement."

Her eyes shimmered. "You would do that for me, sir?"

"Again, I would do that for both of us."

She smiled, a smile that seemed to fill her face. "Oh, Sarah said you were kind, but I never expected you to show such forbearance."

Whoever Sarah was, it appeared he owed her a debt of gratitude. "It may interest you to know that I have no wish to repeat the mistakes of the past." He had no wish for a wife who would not keep her vows.

"I am sorry, sir, that your first marriage was not all it could be."

First marriage. While her pity panged him a little, her words evoked a frisson of anticipation. First marriage. She spoke as if she would be part of his second. His heart buoyed.

Until he saw her frown.

"Oh, I only hope Mama and Father will understand." She looked up with that confiding air again. "Mama will be disappointed to not have a wedding date to plan for."

Of course. "Perhaps . . . perhaps their disappointment might be mitigated by a stay in the country. Do you think they might like to visit Hartwell?"

She blinked. "I . . . I thank you, sir. But if we stay, surely that's tantamount to announcing a betrothal?"

She was right. He'd have to word things in such a way to still somehow give that impression, while keeping the options open for both Charlotte and himself. "Perhaps a larger party might be of benefit. I could invite other friends." Other friends? His words mocked him. What friends could he claim?

"You mean like Lavinia and the earl?"

"Exactly." He smiled.

The relief evident in her eyes changed into something warmer, more receptive. Still, he sensed that if he pressed his advantage her only response would be the return of the earlier fear, and he did not want that. He wanted her to trust him, to realize he was a man of his word, someone who would always keep his vow to love and honor, someone from whom she would never feel it necessary to turn away, to seek comfort in the arms of another man.

He moved to her seat, bowing, until she was at eye level. "I give you my word, Lady Charlotte, you will never have reason to fear me."

From here he could smell the sweet scent she used, see the flicker of an eyelash.

She nodded, and his gaze dropped to her lips. But it was too soon for that. He settled for picking up her hand. He rubbed a thumb over her palm; her skin felt smooth and warm.

Lifting her hand to his lips he pressed them in the most gentle of kisses. Heard her breath catch. "Oh . . ."

Before he could fall back, the doors opened hurriedly, admitting a keen-eyed marchioness, trailed by a shame-faced marquess.

"Well, I suppose congratulations are in order! You are the most fortunate of young ladies, dearest Charlotte, to receive such attentions from the duke here."

"Mama—"

"And may I felicitate you on the happy news, too, sir," she continued, as if her daughter hadn't spoken. "Now, have you fixed a date?"

William's gaze travelled from Lord Exeter to Charlotte, who seemed to be looking at him with pleading eyes, to finally meet Lady Exeter's expectant stare. "We have not."

"Oh? Forgive my surprise. I had wondered what you were doing in here for so long."

He fought the churn of indignation that rose at her tone—and insinuation. "We *have* decided something, my lady."

"Yes?"

"As neither your daughter nor I have any wish to be fuel for gossip-mongers"—nor to be maneuvered into matrimony, he added silently—"we have decided an announcement of any engagement must be postponed for a time longer, at least until six months of mourning have passed."

"What?"

He worked to keep his tone mild. "My dear Lady Exeter, I am sure you can understand my objections to being made fodder for tittle-tattle, and no doubt you share my reluctance to see your daughter exposed to society's rumormongers."

"Yes, but—"

"Madam, forgive my plain speaking, but surely you do not wish it to be said I killed my wife simply so I could marry Lady Charlotte?"

Lady Exeter's mouth fell open. He glanced at Charlotte, whose jaw closed with a snap.

"But, sir, you are still intending to marry her, are you not?" The marchioness's face clouded. "We should not wish you to be sued for breach of promise."

He swallowed the spurt of anger, staring at her steadily until an ugly red flush marked her skin.

"Hartington, please forgive my wife. She is apt to leap ahead of—"

Reality, William muttered inwardly.

"Circumstances," her husband said, far more diplomatically, casting his daughter a look that could almost pass as loving. "We would not want Charlotte to feel manipulated into something she would not wish for—"

"Manipulated!" his wife exclaimed.

"Nor would we wish to alienate the duke by bounding ahead into wrong assumptions." This was said with a meaningful look at his wife that quieted that lady, whilst earning a look of approval from his daughter.

Somewhat mollified, William tried to appease them with the suggestion of a house party in a couple of weeks.

"At Hartwell Abbey?" Lady Exeter's eyes shone. "Well, that would be good."

Her husband looked somewhat relieved. "It has some merit."

William glanced at Charlotte and stretched out a hand, relief filling him when she slipped her hand into his. "We have determined to conduct this relationship"—he inwardly cringed, the word too heavily laden with meaning—"with the dignity and respect it deserves, and as such, I will brook no interference from those wishing for more than what either of us can reasonably be expected to own or to give. I hope you take my meaning?"

The marchioness flushed, before saying stiffly, "Your meaning is very clear, sir."

"Good. For I would be loath to learn that undue pressure was being exacted upon my dear Charlotte here."

He watched the battle on her face between her wince at having her intentions exposed and delight at his last words. Delight won. "My dear sir"—she smiled brightly—"how can I possibly wish anything but the very best for both you and my dearest daughter? Her happiness is our only wish."

The hand in his tightened suddenly, as if its owner recoiled from her mother's words. He glanced down to meet Charlotte's wry expression. A sudden feeling of overwhelming protectiveness flooded his being. Sweet and innocent, Charlotte was hardly different from little Rose at home in Hartwell. Victim of circumstances beyond her control, subject to the whims and decisions of others, robbed of a voice of her own because of her birth.

He gently squeezed Charlotte's hand in return. He would do his utmost to see her protected, too.

❦ Chapter Seventeen

St. James Park, London
August 4

CHARLOTTE FELT TRAPPED in a haze of confusion. The crowd filling the park surged and pressed around her, her senses overwhelmed by the sights and sounds—and smells!—of Londoners readying for celebrations as her thoughts continued their frantic pace. She needed escape, needed to breathe! The past ten days had barely left her with a moment to herself, consisting of a welter of shopping and visitors, as somehow London learned of her upcoming betrothal.

Her lips twisted. Of course, she didn't have to look too far to discover the source of that particular rumor, Mama's ability to keep a confidence virtually nil. It seemed news of her good fortune had been whispered about in many a drawing room, Mama so keen to share her daughter's most marvelous expectations. Charlotte could barely move through London society without encountering a knowing smile. Nor could anyone reasonably expect the many mantua-makers and milliners visited in past days to keep their mouths closed when tasked with dressing the future Duchess of Hartington.

Sarah was in high ecstasy, knowing she would likely receive Charlotte's castoffs, and while Charlotte had always enjoyed obtaining new clothes, the sheer volume of new attire seemed excessive. And almost unimportant. Not when compared to the weight of responsibilities that would be demanded by her new role.

A hurried visit to Salisbury and her grandmother had been a respite of sorts, away from London's congratulatory tattle-mongers, even if it had brought home just what was expected of her. But her grandmother's sharp eyes and sharper tongue had always left her feeling intimidated. Lavinia had confided her own particular method for dealing with the grandmother she had first met less than a year ago: to remember just how lonely she must be and filter all her words through the ears of grace.

Grace hadn't helped her much, though. Instead it had proven rather hard to remember when Grandmama had gazed at her with those beady eyes.

"So, I hear you are to marry Hartington."

She'd forced herself to nod.

"Hmph. Suppose he'll do. Rich enough by all accounts. Bit of an odd fish if I recall, but that family always had a most peculiar interest in scientific rubbish."

Charlotte hadn't known what to say, her smile feeling like it might slip at any moment.

"Have a tongue?"

She'd blinked. "I beg your pardon?"

"So it *is* there." Her grandmother chortled. "Thought you might have lost it."

Charlotte had murmured something incoherent, her grandmother talking over the top in her usual indomitable style. "I don't suppose you're fool enough to imagine you love the man?" She snorted. "Not like that cousin of yours. Marrying such a man. Stupid girl. Well, at least you're not sinking that low."

This criticism of Lavinia placed words in her mouth. "She and Lord Hawkesbury are very happ—"

"I have no interest in hearing that person's name! Lavinia I will tolerate, but as for imagining herself in love with a member of such a family, well I—" She shook her head before gazing sharply at Charlotte. "You did not answer my question. You think you love him?"

She swallowed. "Mama says it is a splendid match."

"Well, it is. But you didn't say you did. Good." She sniffed. "Love is something for romantic simpletons. If you don't have money, or the connections a good match brings, then you are wasting your time."

Mama had nodded, like Grandmama's marionette bobbing on a string. Charlotte smiled internally. Really, it was most unreasonable to expect Mama to think anything but what Grandmama dictated. Hadn't Lavinia once said something about how Grandmama controlled the purse strings?

The older woman's brows pushed together. "But didn't I hear something rather disturbing about that gentleman? What was it?" Her expression cleared. "That's right. His wife was something of a trollop, wasn't she?"

"Mother!" Mama said in agonized tones, casting a pleading look at Charlotte.

"Good heavens, Constance. I didn't take you to be so prudish. Well, I can only hope your daughter won't cause such a scandal as his first wife did."

Charlotte had glared at her, which only seemed to make her grandmother to laugh.

"Well, well. Perfect that look, my dear, and we'll make a duchess of you yet! One requires something of a backbone and at least an ounce of spunk, in my experience."

That backbone was what was keeping her head high as the crowds filled St. James Park. Henry had wondered if the festivities at Green Park would be better, the talk of the balloon ascent and temple illuminations sounded all that was wonderful. But instead they were here, preparing to watch the reenactments on the canal. An exotic seven-story Chinese pagoda stood atop a picturesque yellow bridge, the pagoda and four bridge pavilions each topped with a bright blue roof.

"Is it true you have a Chinese pavilion at Hartwell?"

Charlotte glanced at the duke as he answered Mama. "Only a little one, I'm afraid. In my Oriental garden. Nothing of the height and substance of the one before us."

"Oh, how I'd love to see it. I've always said I love the Orient."

"Have you really, Mama? I cannot recall—"

"Of course, Charlotte! You must have forgotten," Mama vigorously asserted, cheeks pinking. "I assure you, Hartington, that I find such things *most* fascinating."

"You never cease to surprise me, madam," the duke said.

A giggle pushed past Charlotte's tension.

"Look!" Lavinia pointed to dozens of rowboats moving toward each other in mock battle, their colors signaling Lord Nelson and his opposition at the Battle of the Nile.

Charlotte watched for a while, but the tactics failed to engage her attention for long. She glanced away, hating the crowds, the stifling heat, the air of oppressiveness. She drew in a deep breath, caught a wisp of bergamot and musk, the duke's scent subtle and refined.

"May I get you a refreshment, Lady Charlotte?"

The quiet voice drew her attention. The duke's tone matched his attire, an understated elegance that stated he did not need to try as some might to garner attention.

She nodded, thankful for his offer, even as she found his solicitous nature perversely irritating. Why did he have to notice things all the time? Why couldn't he leave her be? The tension inside her mounted. He was too careful, too courteous. His very attentiveness fed remorse that she did not feel the same.

Her gaze slid past his shoulder, to where the earl had wrapped a protective arm around Lavinia, her cousin leaning back to smile adoringly into her husband's face. Her heart wrenched, as a desperate yearning took hold. If only she could marry someone whom she loved! If only she felt a tenth for the duke what Lavinia seemed to feel for her husband. Her fingers clenched, released.

Charlotte glanced to where the duke had remained, surprised to see him watching them, too. A look of something like regret crossed his features, before his face smoothed to its usual impassivity as he turned to her. "Forgive me. I shall attend to your drink immediately."

Irritation burned anew. Why did he have to be so polite? If only she could make him lose that genteel mask so she could learn what kind of man he truly was. "Please, do not trouble yourself."

His head inclined. "It is no trouble, I assure you."

A man, stinking of cheap alcohol, jostled her. She made a noise of disgust, inching away, only to step on the duke's foot.

Mortification heated her cheeks. "Sorry," she muttered.

"It is nothing. Perhaps"—his dark eyes studied her—"perhaps you might prefer to move away from these crowds. I recall you are not overly fond of such things."

Annoyance pricked again, irrational though it was. Why was he so considerate?

"Would you like to see if we can find a less crowded location?"

She looked at him in alarm. Surely he didn't mean to suggest . . .

He smiled, soothing away the annoyance from before. "I promise to take no liberties."

"No, of course not." Of course he wouldn't, passionless creature that he was. She lifted her chin. "Very well."

William murmured a brief explanation to the marchioness and, having secured her permission, offered his arm to Charlotte. She took it, her manner and posture as stiff with him as it had been all afternoon.

What had made her lose the confiding air? She was a mystery. At times she was so easy to read, her innocent blushes saying as much as her lips. Her artlessness enchanted, her frank—at times wry—remarks suggesting they might share a similar sense of humor. But at other times . . .

Somehow he managed to extract her from the throngs and draw her to a slightly more spacious section. He didn't blame the crowds for coming; each of London's major parks would be crowded with those wishing to celebrate the victories and see the Regent's overpriced spectaculars.

A horde of soldiers approached. William drew her to one side, noting the drunken widened eyes and muttered oaths as they spied his pretty companion. For her part, Charlotte seemed far less vain than a young lady of her good looks might normally be. Either she truly did not notice the attention or her good breeding demanded it remain unacknowledged.

He drew her toward a booth selling lemonade. "Two glasses please."

The woman's eyes widened. "Well, if ain't a fancy lordship."

"His Grace, actually," Charlotte corrected.

"A dook? Aw, go on wiv ye, luv. This ain't no dook, else I'm a monkey's uncle."

"Well, perhaps you're a monkey's—"

He bit back a smile, placed a hand on Charlotte's arm. "Surely it does not matter what others so completely unconnected to us might think."

She drew her arm away and turned back to the woman. "Why do you say he's not a duke?"

The woman cackled. "He ain't tall enough for one thing."

He fought the cringe, conscious Charlotte had straightened.

"Precisely how many dukes have you had the honor of meeting?"

"Me? Meet a dook? Oh, you're a saucy thing, ain't you?" The woman cackled again, handing him the refreshments he now wished he'd never bought.

He passed one glass to Charlotte then fished out a more than appropriate coin. "Thank you."

The woman looked at the coin, eyes nearly popping out of her head. "Is this wot I thinks it is?" She bit it, then turned to her husband. "I think he *is* a dook!"

William turned away, noting with a smile that Charlotte's glass was empty. He handed her the next.

"This is not for you?"

"I find I have no desire for lemonade this evening."

"Oh." She glanced at him doubtfully. "Are you sure? Despite that woman's rudeness, it *is* very good lemonade."

"I am glad." He drew her to one side as a drunken man chased another down the path. His pulse raced, at the feel of her so close, her scent—roses? lilies?—drifting to stir his senses wildly. Did she notice? She appeared unmoved.

He guided her back to her family, politely dismissing the marchioness's thanks. He did not wish for her gratitude. He wished only her daughter would not dismiss him quite so obviously. He glanced at Charlotte again. Even now she did not look at him, instead peering around behind him. He glanced over his shoulder, but saw nothing but a sea of faces. When she next met his gaze she shivered.

He wished, like Hawkesbury, that he had a husband's right to wrap his arm around her, but they were not yet betrothed, so any touch must be seen to be innocent. "What is it?"

"A woman was looking at you most peculiarly."

"Perhaps she wished to know who was so fortunate as to be escorting such a lovely young lady on such an evening." He smiled, thankful that for once he'd managed to say something that sounded complimentary, like what he imagined her many suitors would say.

Her smile peeked out, and she glanced behind him again, only to freeze once more.

He turned with the aim to identify the mysterious woman, but saw no woman staring their direction. Instead, his eyes fixed on a far more concerning sight.

A young gentleman, staring at Charlotte beside him.

Lord Markham.

CHAPTER EIGHTEEN

Hartwell, Northamptonshire
Four days later

THE CLATTER OF carriage wheels had long ago settled into a bumpy rhythm that echoed the jolting in her heart. Markham. Hartington. Which man? Markham! Hartington. Hartwell? Heartsick. Hartington . . .

Charlotte shifted her head, uneasiness sliding queasily within. Dreams of balloon ascents and Chinese pavilions, fireworks reflected in the Serpentine, pagodas on fire—on fire!—mingled with other, stranger dreams, ones scented with bergamot and wry humor that fueled security to her core . . .

Her eyelids drifted open to meet the same scene of the past three hours. Mama, seated opposite, a handkerchief covering her face, quivering with each breath. Father beside her reading, making occasional low-voiced conversation with Henry, who sprawled next to Charlotte. Unwilling to interrupt, she turned slightly to face the view outside.

Unlike the pretty hills of the Cotswolds, this area was much more flat, but its patchwork of fields and farms held a rustic simplicity she appreciated, despite her avowed preference for city life. The carriage slowed, turning to pass a large gatehouse before they rode along an avenue of trees. Thick woods bound the avenue, ancient tree branches intertwined overhead. What creatures lived there? Mama had talked about the duke's deer park, but it seemed a haven for fairy folk, too.

Finally, the carriage escaped the shadows and pulled into the afternoon sunlight. Mama stirred, and Charlotte sat up, her eyes widening, mouth drying. Grandmama's estate at Salisbury had forever been her touchstone for elegance, but this . . .

The Palladian-styled house rose majestically on the far side of a shining pond, its three stories gleaming white in the sun. A central bay possessed four Greek Ionic columns, which supported a handsome pediment and was flanked on either side by two wings stretching five windows deep, finished with handsome Venetian windows.

The road curved back, allowing a view of the triple-arched stone bridge before the carriage passed over it and drew closer. Her heart thumped. All this could be hers.

As if sensing her thoughts, Mama eyed her. "I trust you know what is expected of you."

"Yes, Mama."

But she hoped her mother remembered what was expected of *her*. For all his mildness, the duke had appeared surprisingly firm about Mama's need to desist from interference on that morning two weeks ago.

The carriage slowed, then stopped beside the steps, lined with a score of servants.

And the duke.

Her skin goose-fleshed.

Another moment later and the duke was handing them out, bowing to their curtsies, uttering a warm welcome in his quiet way. Her eyes met his before skittering away, nerves rising as they always did when they met after absence.

She passed inside, to find a great hall with checkerboard floor, sided by oak panels, protected by gleaming suits of armor in each corner. Large cabinets lined each wall like one might find in a museum, above which hung magnificent allegorical paintings. Her breath caught. "I thought this was an abbey. It seems more like a palace!"

The duke smiled his charming smile. "About seven hundred years ago, the original building was founded by Cistercian monks, and used as a place of worship, until the dissolution of the monasteries, when Henry VIII handed possession to the first Duke of Hartington in 1547."

She studied the decor. Already she could sense what was important to him: family, history, nature. She moved to study the contents of one of the glass cases lining the walls: animal specimens.

"What is this?" She pointed to a gray creature, smaller than a cat, with dark tabby-like stripes and a pointy face.

"That is a *merrnine*, a banded hare wallaby, brought back from the wilds of Western Australia."

"And why do you—?"

"Have a specimen? Because my father gave me it when I attained my majority." His lips turned wry. "I suspect it was something of a joke, seeing as our family emblem is a stag."

A hart. Yet the slight build of the duke could scarcely support a vision of that majestic beast. But to give a small, hopping creature instead . . . Sympathy panged. How unkind for the previous duke to mock his son that way!

As if sensing her pity, he turned away, gesturing to the staircase. "The Abbey contains many treasures, not least of which is the stairs."

Her head tilted. "They are . . . impressive."

"Among the first cantilevered staircases in England. If you move to here," he gestured her forward, "you will see they almost seem to float."

"Are they safe?"

He chuckled. "They have supported generations of Hartingtons, so yes, they are quite safe."

She stiffened, embarrassment washing over her. What a stupid question. As if she needed to be seen as naive.

As if to make up for his laughter, the duke drew closer. "I am glad to see you again."

Her gaze dropped. "And I you."

She swallowed a bubble of panic. She did not wish to lie, but neither could she look into his honest brown eyes and admit the truth: that time apart had made the absence sweeter and had not stirred her affections in any way. She *couldn't* admit such a thing, not when it might hurt him. Especially with her mother listening avidly, even while pretending she was not.

"You must all be weary," the duke said, as their trunks were brought inside. "Travers will show you to your rooms so you may rest. We shall be dining at six."

"Thank you, Hartington," Father said.

"Thank you," Charlotte managed to echo.

An hour later, freshly washed and dressed, she sat at the dressing table, waiting as Sarah fussed with her hair, remembering the events since the last time such a fuss had been made.

Two weeks since the duke's proposal. Two weeks of enduring society's knowing smiles and little jests. It was a strange position to be in. Few could express what was truly felt, knowing if they gave offense, she had every likelihood of one day being in such an exalted position she could afford to give the cut without fear of recrimination. On the other hand, whispers about her former dancing partners had never truly gone away. But how could they? Not when the feelings she had felt had never truly gone away, either.

She had seen Lord Markham again two days ago at Almack's. Had tried in vain not to watch him. But her traitorous heart had refused reason, impelling her to look over the duke's shoulder and meet the steady gaze. What she had seen had caused a shock that caused another shiver now.

Lord Markham had grown thin, nearly reed thin, and about him were the marks of dissipation. Henry had said of his friend that he spent too much time in gambling halls, had nearly been forced to seek the moneylenders, save for a lucky throw at hazard. He hadn't said any of this in a vindictive way, merely stated it as fact, but Charlotte couldn't help feeling it was her fault, that if only she'd been permitted to follow her inclination, his manner of life would have been spared, her dowry sufficient to preserve his remaining family fortune.

An unlucky chance had caused them to brush shoulders in the supper room. A startled glimpse and muttered oath from him, a wretched inner pang from her. Somehow in that too-brief moment of time he'd managed to say in a low voice, "Can you be serious? Marrying him?"

The haunted eyes had plagued her dreams, had caused her many a sleepless night. Oh, how unlucky was she, to have been forced to answer as she had. She cringed again, remembering her careless words: "I am not married yet."

His eyes had lit, igniting hope, before the flow of masses had forced them to move away. But later, when a dance had shifted partners, she'd encountered him once more. Just the act of standing up with him was agony—his scent, the way his eyes crinkled in the corners, as if delight at seeing her filled his being. Surely he loved her still . . .

"I cannot bear to see you with him," he'd whispered. "You cannot know what I feel, having lost you, knowing he has won."

How she regretted her next words. If only she had possessed an ounce of her cousin's fortitude and dismissed him, or better yet, ignored him. If only she'd not said what she had.

"He has not won my heart."

His eyes had lit again. "Tell me I'm not too late."

She could not answer, could hardly believe he would dare say such things.

"I understand," he'd said finally. "You cannot speak. It is not wise. Only know I will be looking for a way to help you, to hinder this . . . this God-forsaken match."

She should have told him no.

She should have told him to forget her.

She stared at her reflection.

But she had not.

※

The next day

It still seemed extraordinary to have Charlotte here. William glanced at his companion, glad to have finally escaped the rest of his guests for the chance to talk with the youngest—and prettiest. For while Charlotte's family, the Hawkesburys, his sister Cressinda, and her husband, the Earl of Ware, and several others could each be amusing in their ways, nobody compared to the vivid creature beside him whose freshness was balm to his heart.

She shifted the parasol to her other shoulder, allowing him a better chance to see her face. She held a thoughtful expression, like a scholar trying to memorize for an examination. "So you have a forcing garden, a medicinal garden, the Orient garden, and this—"

"The arboretum."

She nodded, repeating it softly, pausing to touch one specimen's feathery leaves. "What is this called?"

"This is an acacia. From southern Africa."

"It is very pretty."

"It is only a young specimen, but they are said to grow nearly thirty feet tall."

She nodded, wandering to the next tree. "And this?"

"A eucalyptus. From New South Wales." He plucked a leaf and rubbed it between his fingers, releasing the pungent oil. "What does this remind you of?"

She sniffed. "Lemon? Aniseed?"

"Very good. Did you know their seeds require fire to open? I find that most interesting."

"I think it quite marvelous how so many different varieties from so many parts of the world can grow in one place."

"I think so, too."

Charlotte's pensive expression disappeared in her wisp of a smile. The strain lifted a little more. He needed to remember she took a while to relax around him.

"I suppose it must be very pretty in autumn, with so many different trees changing colors at different times."

"I hope you will be here to see it."

"Oh! I . . . I thought this only a short visit."

"Perhaps next year, then."

Her shoulder drooped, and he fought the disappointment. What could he say, what should he say to make her realize this arrangement could work well?

"My sister enjoyed meeting you."

"Oh! Your sister seems charming."

She could be when she wanted. "I have told her to make a good impression."

"Why?"

"Because I have no wish for her to dissuade the young lady I hope to persuade."

Her cheeks pinked, and she ducked her head.

He truly wished his older sister would not give utterance to her doubts. Cressinda had been astounded at his decision. "I'll grant she's very pretty, but William, she's so young!" She'd shaken her head. "I cannot imagine such an innocent presiding over house parties and the like. She's too dominated by that awful mother of hers." She'd shuddered delicately. "I cannot think you employed any great manner of reason to reach such a decision, William, but were attracted to her less intellectual qualities, shall we say?"

Her smirk had heated his neck and brought a swift change in conversation. But he couldn't deny part of his fascination was Charlotte's fresh and incomparable beauty.

William pointed out the well, from which Hartwell was blessed by an underground spring, then rounded the corner, where workmen were putting the finishing touches on the carriage house.

Charlotte stopped. "I forgot to ask. Did you ever find out who was responsible for the fire? You mentioned something about rags catching fire. I imagine they didn't set fire to themselves."

"It appears an accident." Not strictly true, but he did not wish to be reminded of such unpleasantries, not on such a lovely day, with such convivial company.

"You seem to have had a spate of such accidents. I hope there are no more."

"As do I." *Heavenly Father, let there be no more such incidents.*

There had been another one a week ago, more annoying than dangerous. Paint had been spilled in the near-finished carriage house, spoiling the work of the men who had labored many a long hour to scrub soot and ash from the two walls that remained from the previous structure. Everything else had either been destroyed in the fire or deemed unsafe, necessitating demolishment. While the two new walls and roof were finished, the inside had been readied for painting, but the spill of paint had required buying new supplies, thus delaying what he'd hoped finished by his houseguests' arrival.

That "accident" had also necessitated employing an enquiry agent, to discern if Wrotham had indeed left the country as promised, as well as the posting of a guard: two men to walk the premises. He nodded to one of the men now, who waited for them to pass, hat doffed. William waited a moment for Charlotte to precede him, before murmuring, "Anything?"

"Nothing, Your Grace."

"Very good."

He caught up to his guest, who was eyeing the Abbey from the west side.

Whilst not designed to be quite as impressive as the approach from the south, the banks of windows were still imposing, as was the pediment hanging above.

"Does your Abbey hold any ghosts, sir?"

He smiled. So, she held a preference for things of a Gothic nature. "I don't believe so. However, my sister was once convinced there was a lady who walked the landings at night."

Her eyes widened. "Really?"

"Yes. That was until she learned it was our mother's maid. Cressinda was sorely disappointed."

Her laughter trickled joy into his heart. Finally he'd said something that amused. "I don't think Hartwell has ever had much in the way of clanking chains or headless specters. But we do have some secret passages."

"Really?" Her eyes lit.

Clearly he was in form. "I'm afraid the passages are blocked up now, but there are some sliding panels I can show you."

"That would be wonderful!"

So he'd finally learned one thing she enjoyed.

A whinnying sound drew her to a stop. "Oh, sir! Would you mind if we visit the stables?"

Make that two things. "I wouldn't mind at all."

Once inside, any other doubts about what harnessed her passion were extinguished. Light suffused her face, leading more than one stable hand to slow their work to gawk. Having no wish to draw further attention to his relationship to Charlotte by reprimanding such looks, he contented himself with pointing out the horses, to which she asked innumerable questions of both himself and Evans, the head groom. Finally they stopped outside the stall of his newest acquisition.

"Oh . . . she is beautiful."

"That she is, my lady. Not two years old, and as pretty a stepper as any I've seen in a long while."

Charlotte held out a hand with the carrot helpfully supplied by Evans. The gray filly tossed her white mane before moving closer, thick lips snuffling the treat. "What is her name?"

"She be a new 'un. We haven't got round to naming her yet."

"She was called *La Belle Princesse Magnifique*," William said.

"The beautiful, magnificent princess," Charlotte murmured, stroking the mane. "Most appropriate, but a bit of a mouthful."

"What would you see her called?"

"Me?" Charlotte looked up in surprise. "You mean she is not for your sister?"

"Cressinda has never had great inclination for horses."

"Like Lavinia." She shook her head. "I've never understood those who cannot appreciate how wonderful it is to ride." Her face grew wistful.

"Would you like to ride her, Lady Charlotte?"

"She looks just your height, if I may say so," Evans added helpfully, with a sidelong look at William.

He pretended not to notice, pretended that he hadn't asked his head groom to source a fine horse to meet the exact requirements of the young lady standing beside him.

"She is used to riders?"

"Of course. Her previous owner had to sell her, most reluctantly I might add. Debts."

"She looks so gentle. She is not too docile though, I hope?"

"Runs like the wind," Evans said confidently.

Her smile lit up her face. "Then I would love to ride. Would this afternoon be too soon?"

"Not at all, my lady," Evans said with a grin.

Pleasure filled him. The stiff asking price had been worth it for such a win.

"But I think we need to shorten your name, just a tad. Perhaps Bella might work?"

The horse nickered, tossing her head as if in agreement.

And the sound of Charlotte's laughter buoyed his heart—and his dreams.

CHAPTER NINETEEN

Three days later

"WELL DONE, MY lady," Evans said, as he helped her dismount. "You are quite the bruising rider, if I may say so."

"I gather the duke does not have too many ladies jump the fences," she said, patting the horse's nose gently.

"No. The previous duchess only liked a mild horse. One as spirited as your Bella there would never have done."

Her Bella? Surely he did not mean to imply the duke had bought the mare for her? She shook away the disquieting thought. "What was she like?" She didn't like gossiping with the servants, but Evans's open nature, and the fact he'd been in the duke's employ for many years, gave reason to suspect she might learn more about the goings on around the Abbey.

"The duchess?" His face closed. "She was a pretty, flighty thing."

Hardly a crime. Charlotte had been accused of much the same.

At her raised brow he hurried on. "I mean no disrespect, but she was not content, was always restless."

She nodded. Now she knew why the duke seemed so anxious to please. He would not want a repeat of his first wife's seeking contentment beyond her own hearth. She patted Bella one last time, giving her the sugar Evans had handed over, before thanking the head groom and moving back toward the house.

From this position, she could see the Abbey's original features, the narrow windows and ancient twisting chimney stacks, below which rested the fan-vaulted cloister that had once lined the Abbey chapel, long since demolished. The duke's tour of the house several days ago had provided a wealth of information, not just about the Abbey's architectural secrets, but also a little about the lives of those who served God here so many years ago.

The duke himself had also proved far more interesting than first impressions, and she felt the cords of fascination pulling more tightly around her heart. Was there anything this man did not know? Part scientist, part gentleman farmer, part researcher, everywhere he took their little party had revealed another facet of his eclectic interests. Whilst she cared little for road improvements or new farming methods, riding alongside Father, Henry, Lord Hawkesbury, and their host on these excursions allowed her to appreciate the depth and breadth of the duke's projects and his humble passion for improving the lot of humanity, as well as enjoy the fresh air and countryside, so pretty in late summer.

Other times she did not have to pretend interest. She was genuinely charmed by the gardens, particularly the assortment of trees he had imported, and found the collections of animals and art inside most fascinating. Many of the rooms, too, were decorated in a manner most intriguing, such as the beautiful morning room painted with flowers, butterflies, and birds. The duke had seemed quite pleased by her admiration, admitting it had been his mother's favorite room. And as for the secret passages . . . well, a girl would not have to read Gothic novels if she lived here. The walls very nearly hummed with ancient tales! The duke and his sister had taken great delight in showing her the priest hole in the dining room, and the entrance to a—thankfully blocked up—passage from the master bedroom to the stables. Indeed, his interests were so varied, it was enough to make her wonder why he took such interest in her.

She moved inside to the breakfast room, yet another of the Abbey's surprises, and studied the collection of works by Canaletto. The views of Venice were so realistic she could almost imagine she walked along the Great Canal or walked through the Piazza San Marco.

"Lady Charlotte." Travers interrupted her musings. "Do you wish for anything?"

"Thank you, no."

Nothing a butler could arrange, anyway. She returned her attention to the vivid paintings. What would Venice be like to visit? Upon seeing her absorption the other day, the duke had murmured of wishing to visit Italy again. Perhaps under all his solemnity lurked a romantic after all.

An opened window carried conversation from outside.

"I still think you a fool, William."

Charlotte frowned, having recognized Lady Ware's voice. "Of all the chits you could choose, why her?"

The duke made a low-voiced comment, too quiet for her to hear.

"I will admit she is pretty, but she doesn't seem to hold an original thought in her head. I'm sure she has no interest in anything beyond her next gown. Granted, her youth may make her easier to mold to your ways, but can you truly say you would be happy with someone so frivolous, so beneath your own intellect?"

Charlotte's chest tightened. Was that truly how others saw her? A pretty little half-wit? While she was the first to admit she had no desire for the intellectual pursuits that so consumed Lavinia, she wasn't quite the dunce people believed. She liked poetry. Even if she preferred words penned by Lord Byron to those of a long-dead John Donne.

She dashed at her cheeks, escaping the room, and the older woman's censure—the older sister whose affection the duke had clearly exaggerated, if not downright lied about.

"Charlotte?"

Lavinia's voice halted her steps.

She turned, facing her cousin, framed in the library door. Charlotte forced a smile to her lips, forced brightness to her voice. "Reading Shakespeare again?"

"I cannot believe Hartwell has a First Folio! So many treasures this house holds." The light in her cousin's face dimmed. "But you were rushing somewhere. Are you quite well?" This from Lavinia, who had rarely stirred from the Abbey due to tiredness. Her belly held a small bump now, a bump that drew tender looks and caresses from Lord Hawkesbury when he thought himself unobserved.

"I have been riding, and . . . and need a rest."

"Oh, I quite understand. The duke has been all solicitude, hasn't he? So many activities to keep one amused. I heard his sister say something about a game of pall-mall later."

Well, they could play that game without her, now she knew just how artificial were *that* lady's smiles. How stupid was she to have thought Cressinda liked her? "I would much prefer to read with you."

"Thank you, but I would not interrupt your time with the duke."

The duke. Whose sister thought Charlotte nothing but a simpleton. Her cheeks heated.

Lavinia's eyes sparked with something of their old mischief. "Forgive me. I should not tease."

"But it makes you happy." She studied her cousin, noting the drawn features. Compassion stirred. "Do you feel well? Truly, I am happy to spend time with you if you wish."

Lavinia both thanked and refused her, but her pale expression prompted Charlotte's prayers as she trudged up the stairs.

From somewhere came a baby's cry.

She glanced up. The cry came again. Her heart quickened. Another of the Abbey's secrets: the mysterious child. Why hadn't the duke introduced his guests to his daughter?

A sudden urge to see the little girl filled her. Lifting the long train of her riding habit over her arm, she hurried up the main staircase, escaping the principal rooms on the ground floor—and the drawing room so often claimed by Mama—without notice. Curiosity drew her on. What did the child look like? Dark like the duke? She hoped it didn't have his alarming eyebrows!

She moved past the next floor, which consisted chiefly of bedrooms, stopping at the landing above. From here she could see a long corridor devoid of servants. The crying sound made the nursery obvious, the door ajar. She peered in. A fat nurse rocked the child, but the infant's squalls suggested disinclination for such an activity.

"Can I help you, miss?"

Charlotte jumped. Glanced behind her to see a frowning maid. "I . . ."

"Who is it, Meg?"

"A young lady." The maid pushed the door open wider.

Charlotte stepped inside.

The nurse stopped rocking, a heavy crease pleating her forehead. "Can I help you?"

"Is this Rose?" The baby stopped crying, looking at her with tired eyes. "Yes."

She leaned forward. "Oh, but she's a pretty thing."

"She is that." The stern face seemed to soften fractionally.

The words popped out. "May I hold her?"

"You?" Graying brows shot to the ceiling. "Why would a young lady like you want to do such a thing?"

Charlotte couldn't explain. Something inside begged to show the child affection. "Please?"

"Oh, I suppose. What's it matter? It'll give me poor arms a chance for a break." The nurse rose, and Charlotte took her place in the rocking chair. "You know how to hold 'er?" the nurse asked suspiciously. "Be sure to support the neck."

"Of course."

The infant was placed in her arms. So light, so tiny, the sweetest face with the duke's dark eyes, and the most perfect little lashes.

"Hello, Lady Rose."

The tiny girl made a mewling noise.

"Shh." She brushed a finger down the soft cheek, watching the blinks lengthen, until sleep claimed her. Oh, how precious to be a mother. No wonder Lavinia was so excited. Her heart tugged.

"What are you doing?"

Charlotte jumped at the duke's voice, her startle causing the baby to awake. "Shh, sweetling. Please don't fret."

At her voice the child seemed to soothe, falling into sleep again.

Glancing at the duke's frowning brows, she handed the baby back to the nurse, and followed the duke from the room.

"Why are you up here?"

She swallowed. She had never seen him angry before, but there was no denying his displeasure. "I . . . I wanted to see little Rose."

"Why didn't you ask me?"

"I heard her crying, and I wanted to see if I could help."

"You do not trust my staff to see to such things?"

She blinked. Drew back. "Of course. But I was curious—"

"Please do not be too inquisitive. Too much curiosity in a lady is never a good thing."

Her mouth fell open. She stepped back a pace. Lifted her chin. "I was only trying to help. She should not be locked up here, never seen, getting but a whit of the affection your horses receive—"

"Thank you for your concern, but she is perfectly fine now."

Only because she'd helped settle her! Heat filled her chest as the words from earlier mingled with his present rudeness. "I understand, sir, that you might think young ladies should exhibit no curiosity in anything beyond the drawing room and prefer paying more attention to their appearance than to the needs of others, but I assure you, every daughter wishes for affection from her father!"

"She is not—"

"And although I enjoy wearing pretty clothes and reading novels, I am not *completely* frivolous—"

"No, you are wrong—"

"So you *do* think me completely frivolous?" Angry tears pricked. Frustration carried her on. "I have to wonder, sir, why you would wish to marry such a simpleton as you obviously think I am."

He blinked. "I do not think such—"

"Yes, you do. I heard you and your sister on the terrace just now. Your sister—the one who *so* enjoyed meeting me?—called me frivolous, with an intellect *far* inferior to your own. What else was it she said? Something about being so young I should be pliable enough for you? Do you truly think me so persuadable?" She stamped her foot. "I am not so very young!"

Amusement at the display of childish temper warred with the memory of other arguments, another woman . . . He fought the ice, fought the heated response, and stepped back. He would not let his past pain dictate his behavior now. "I beg your pardon."

Her glare softened, her shoulders slumped. "No, I'm sorry. It was presumptuous—"

"It was necessary. Thank you." He swallowed. Admitting he was wrong had never been easy, yet this "chit," as Cressinda referred to her, had managed it. "Please forgive my high-handedness."

"Oh, but—"

"Hartington, Charlotte!" He turned to see Lady Exeter stagger to the top step with panting breath. "Oh, Duke!"

"Lady Exeter, can I help you?"

She fanned herself with a hand, looking between them, reserving a frown for her daughter. "I heard raised voices. I trust Charlotte has not been obstreperous?"

"Your daughter has been everything she ought."

"But I heard the sounds of argument."

"And now you can hear the sound of concord." He turned to Charlotte, screening her from her mother's view, and grasped her hand. "Please forgive me. I should have recognized your interest for what it was. A desire to assist, nothing more."

She nodded, yet her eyes still held a trace of dread.

He smiled wryly at her. "My temper has always been the worst of my faults."

"You admit to others?"

"Slowness of wit is not one of yours, I see."

She stiffened, tried to pull her hand away.

What had he said wrong now? Even when he tried to compliment her she got upset. He studied her, as a vague memory of her earlier words firmed into uncomfortable certainty. Now he remembered the conversation to which Charlotte had been an unseen witness. He glanced at the marchioness. "Excuse us, please."

Without waiting for a response, he led Charlotte to the end of the corridor, where a window overlooked the front park. "You overheard a recent discussion between Cressinda and myself?"

Her head jerked a nod.

"But I gather you did not hear everything that was said?"

Her chin rose. "I did not wish to eavesdrop—"

"So you stayed long enough to think badly of me, but not long enough to hear it all."

"There was more?"

"Yes. I told my sister of your compassion, your intelligence and humor, and that while you might be young, your youthfulness makes me see things from a different perspective." He gave another wry smile. "I've been accused of being staid and boring, you know."

She shook her head. "Nobody could think that who truly knows you, sir. Why, I think you the most interesting person I have ever met!"

His heart glowed. "You think that of me?"

"Of course I do." Her brow knit. "So you don't think me too much a child?"

"Of course I don't."

She echoed his smile, and before he knew what had happened, she was hugging him.

Warmth exploded in his chest. After a moment's delighted wonder, he carefully wrapped his arms around her. So this was what affection felt like, this ease soothing the corners of his soul, chasing away the doubts and uncertainties. He drew in a breath, caught the scent of rose and lily. Perhaps his foolish dreams weren't so foolish after all . . .

"Charlotte!"

He lifted his head to meet the eye of the outraged marchioness.

"Release my daughter at once!" He pulled away reluctantly as she turned to her daughter. "One simply does not hug a duke."

Charlotte stepped from his embrace, cheeks scarlet. "I am sorry."

"You have nothing to apologize for," he assured her.

She peeked at him, before moving to gaze out the window, as if to remove herself from her mother's ire.

William eyed the marchioness. "Thank you, madam, but I do not appreciate your insinuations against my character."

Her eyes widened. "Forgive me. I meant no such thing."

"I'm sure you did not." He glanced at Charlotte, who now stood transfixed by the view outside. "Lady Charlotte?"

She glanced at him, brow creased. "I . . . I beg your pardon?"

"Thank you for giving me the chance to explain myself."

She ducked her head, her gaze slipping back to the window. The pucker in her brow deepened.

"Is something the matter?"

"I thought I saw a figure outside."

Lady Exeter gave a short laugh. "But of course you did. Such a vast estate as this has any number of people who may be outside."

"But—" Charlotte's cheeks tinged.

"But what, Lady Charlotte?" he asked.

She shook her head. "The person just seemed to disappear."

"Disappear? Don't be so foolish, Charlotte," her mother said.

Swallowing his irritation at Lady Exeter's condescension, he moved closer to the windows and scanned the grounds, could see nobody. "A servant, no doubt."

She nodded, though appeared unconvinced.

"Charlotte has always had a very good imagination, haven't you, dear? All those novels."

"I *did* see someone, Mama."

"Of course you did." The marchioness patted her daughter on the shoulder. "Well, I think we should permit the duke to resume his business affairs, don't you?"

"Of course," Charlotte murmured, not looking him in the eye.

He could not protest, could not do anything save watch the marchioness herd her daughter away, as a lioness might steer away a cub. His skin tingled, and he could still smell Charlotte's scent, could still feel how her curls had tickled his nose, could still feel the heat where her form nestled against his, her curves that made his breath catch and desire stir within.

All thought of business fled, as he fought not to imagine what it would be like to be married to her.

Chapter Twenty

That night a miracle occurred.

After dinner—an awkward affair Charlotte felt, with too much left unspoken, too many glances averted—the ladies retired to the drawing room as usual, leaving the gentlemen to their port. While Mama engaged Lavinia in conversation about Patience, Charlotte pretended to read, working to suppress the hurt from the duke's sister, who ignored her presence.

Before long the door opened, and all the men appeared, bar the duke. When he entered shortly afterward, he held a small pink bundle in his arms. He glanced at Charlotte, then his sister, then turned his attention to Lavinia and Mama. "I don't believe you've had the chance to meet Lady Rose."

"Oh, she is delightful!" Lavinia breathed. "May I hold her?"

"Of course."

The next minutes were spent watching her cousin coo over the tiny girl, watching Lord Hawkesbury cosset his wife, imagining their perfect little family with their new winter addition.

How blessed was Lavinia!

Charlotte studied the duke, also smiling at the scene, before his gaze lifted to connect with hers. A frisson of expectancy trembled through her, just as it had this afternoon when she'd hugged—Mama said later "thrown herself at"—him.

He moved to stand before her, tenderness in his eyes. "Thank you." He gestured to the scene of domestic tranquility. "I did not anticipate just how right this would feel."

"I am glad, sir. Rose is a dear sweet babe, who only wants to feel loved."

"Which is what we all want, is it not?" His dark eyes held a question.

She ducked her head, wishing away the fire in her cheeks.

There was an exchange of seats, and she was shocked to find that the Countess of Ware deigned to join her on the sateen-striped sofa.

"So he has you to thank for bringing the child down here. You have cast a spell on him, haven't you?"

What could she say? "I—"

"Poor William. He finds having Rose here such a burden."

"Why?"

"Because of Pamela, of course. You know the child is not his own."

"But she has his eyes."

"Hmph. I don't know about that. But I do know it is not easy for him to see her. Such a reminder, you know."

She did not know. But she could imagine. Fresh sorrow plowed her heart.

"My brother informs me I have been remiss in my comments concerning you, Lady Charlotte."

Charlotte studied her hands, neatly folded in her lap. Was an apology forthcoming? "People are entitled to their opinions," she said cautiously.

"Exactly."

Charlotte's head shot up. The countess's dark eyes studied her impassively. "I cannot like the fact that my brother has so foolishly entangled himself with a chit barely half his age."

"I am not so very young."

"You are seventeen, are you not?"

"Eighteen."

"It matters not. What does matter is the fact that you have allured him from his senses." This was said with a glance at Charlotte's low-necked gown. "I know what sort of girl you are. Your name was coupled with that Markham fellow, was it not?"

She blinked. Lord Markham? Why, she'd barely thought of him all week. The Abbey and the duke's attentions had stolen all thought of him. Indeed, this afternoon, when the duke had held her in his arms—her cheeks heated, had she really thrown herself at him?—all reason had fled. For the first time she'd known not only what it was to be sought and admired, but also to be appreciated and protected, leaving her with the feeling that perhaps, given enough time, this man might be someone she could love and esteem, even if he never stirred her to passion like Lord Markham did.

"Well! I see by that flush you have not forgotten him."

"Who?" Charlotte snapped from her reverie. "I beg your pardon?"

"You are just like her! Pamela broke his heart, just like I know you will."

Charlotte fought a wave of anger, praying for strength—and for the tears to stay away. When she finally managed to speak, she was relieved to hear her voice was steady. "As I said, people are entitled to their opinions"—she rose and smiled sweetly—"even if they are wrong."

And with dignity she envisaged fit for a queen, Charlotte moved to sit beside Lavinia.

❧

"Sir, I simply cannot see that such a proposition would be viable."

William eyed his estate manager, biting back the words that would only convince the older man that the Duke of Hartington had lost his mind. Of course Hapgood did not see it. The man might possess excellent organizational ability, but he lacked vision. Couldn't he see the potential that better roads could provide? Faster, safer travel meant improved communication, and more opportunities for farmers and those in business. Surely worth the investment.

As if sensing his displeasure, Hapgood pursed his lips, then sighed. "Perhaps if you were to concentrate on one task, rather than trying to achieve ten things at once, we might see something accomplished. Just why you need to be involved in the construction business, I do not know."

"It is not construction, precisely. More testing for McAdam."

"But still it eats up your time, and your resources." Hapgood shook his head. "I cannot like it."

"Surely we have enough funds to manage such a scheme."

"Yes, of course. But just because we have enough resources does not mean we need to spend them."

William forced himself to smile pleasantly and murmur something about getting on.

His estate manager walked from the room, leaving William to stare at the piles of paper cluttering his desk. It wasn't the first time Hapgood had begged him to relinquish some responsibility, but William knew that as soon as he lost control, he'd be forever behind. Besides, nobody could know all the ins and outs of his many interests as he did.

He shuffled a pile of papers to one side, quickly glancing through them. Perhaps he should get another secretary to assist with the filing. Things had become sorely disorganized of late. Another layer of weight settled on his shoulders.

Light shimmered from without, drawing his eyes to the window, through which he could see his houseguests playing a game of pall-mall.

His spirits lifted. At least one project held the tantalizing possibility of good news. Charlotte was coming around. She had even smiled at him this morning, such a happy smile it had kindled the corners of his heart. Surely it would not be long before his proposal would be met with an affirmative response. It could not come soon enough. Holding her in his arms, brief as it was, had been enough to plague his sleep again, hoping, praying, longing for her to finally let him love her as he dared in his dreams.

He pushed away from the desk and drew nearer the window to eye the young lady who consumed his thoughts. She stood beside her brother as he struck the ball with his mallet. The ball missed the iron ring, and she laughed. The tinkling sound warmed him inside. She was so pretty, with that golden hair and artless smile, so lighthearted, so vibrant, in every way the opposite of her predecessor. His pulse quickened. *Heavenly Father, help me be the man she could learn to love.*

She glanced at the window, spotting him, if the smile and tiny wave were any indication.

He lifted a hand. When young Featherington gestured he should join them, he shook his head and moved back to his desk, his spirits strangely unsettled. He probably should join them. Show them something of his willingness to enjoy life. He didn't want Charlotte to think him a misery. But if he abandoned duty to accompany her every time he wished, this work would never get done. With a sigh that wrenched from the very depths of his being, he forced his heart and his thoughts back to the layers of chaos and stress.

After an hour or so, a knock came at the door. He looked up. "Hawkesbury."

The earl moved inside at the gestured invitation. "I apologize for disturbing you, but I fear our pleasant interlude must conclude far sooner than I hoped."

William placed down his quill, fixed his full attention on his guest. "I'm sorry to hear so."

"It is Lavinia. She is not well, and at this time, well . . ."

"You want her somewhere where she can relax and feel comfortable. I understand."

"Hawkesbury House is not the environs either of us find truly comfortable, but travelling to Gloucestershire at this time is quite out of the question."

"Of course." A couple of hours travel was far preferable to a couple of days. "I hope she will feel easier there."

The earl gave a shadow of a smile. "My mother does not make it her aim to put one at ease, but I'm hopeful she is prepared to overlook her own desires in wishing to see the future heir's safe arrival."

"We all hope for that." He maintained the smile, though his spirits dipped. Would the departure of her favorite cousin lead to the loss of Charlotte's company, too? He shook his head at himself. How selfish to be thinking such things in this moment! *Lord, forgive me.*

"I am terribly sorry we shall be disturbing the house party, but I feel it's in Lavinia's best interest. You know what she is like, always thinking of others, but I'm afraid I cannot be so unselfish."

"Of course not."

William's heart ached. This is what he had missed out on, what his wife had deprived him—the ability not only to have a child, but then the chance to celebrate and protect them.

He fought the envy, found a smile, held out his hand, which the earl clasped warmly. "I trust you will stay for dinner?"

"Thank you. We shall leave tomorrow, if that is not inconvenient."

"Of course not."

With the departure of Lord Hawkesbury, William rang for his butler, informing him the dinner tonight should be extra special. He forced his thoughts to his work, and attempted to ignore the disquiet in his heart and soul.

❧ Chapter Twenty-One

Lavinia was not well.

Charlotte eyed her cousin across a dining table groaning with a veritable feast of delicacies, nearly none of which Lavinia had touched, let alone sampled as enthusiastically as Charlotte had managed. No, her cousin, she who never complained, had a distinct look of illness about her—something about the shadows underscoring her eyes, the cheekbones that had sharpened, the way she did not participate in conversation to her usual sociable standard.

She caught Lavinia's eye, raising her own brows in inquiry. Her cousin gave a half smile, a half shrug, which her husband seemed to notice, for he cleared his throat and eyed the table.

"I'm terribly sorry to cut our visit short, but we will be returning tomorrow to Hawkesbury House."

"Oh, must you?" Mama said plaintively. "Things won't be the same without you both."

"Mama, I am sure they would not be leaving without very good reason," Charlotte murmured in an undertone.

"But what possible reason could be more important than seeing you safely settled?" Mama hissed in reply. "I am sure," she said in a louder tone, "that it is something that could be altered, if one chose to."

"I am sure," he said with a tight smile, "it cannot be altered, Lady Exeter."

Ignoring her mother's small moue of protest, and having heard the edge in the earl's voice, Charlotte escaped the post-dinner chitchat as fast as she could to visit Lavinia in her room. She knocked on the door to be met by a maid, whose frowning refusal of admittance was cut short by a breathy voice.

"Who is it?"

"Lady Charlotte, my lady."

"Oh, she can come in."

She hurried in, saw her cousin lying in bed, her face as white as the pillow. "Oh Lavinia! What can I do?"

"Nothing." Lavinia patted the bed beside her. "I'm so dreadfully tired, that is all."

Charlotte hardly dared ask, but concern refused silence. "And the baby?"

Lavinia's lips tightened. "The doctor believes all should be well."

Should be.

The element of doubt in the answer struck a chord of fear within. Charlotte sought to hide it with a smile. "I'm sure he's right. And I will pray that God would make you feel better in the morning. And keep the babe well, too."

Lavinia's eyes shimmered. "Thank you."

Charlotte said her good-nights, before heading to her own room. She ignored Sarah's fussing as prayers filled her heart and lips: for Lavinia, for the earl, their child, their journey—even the dowager countess. She finally succumbed to the darkness, as hope battled fears too dreadful to contemplate.

THE PRAYERS DID not work.

When Sarah drew back the curtains the following morning, accompanying her chocolate and rolls was the news that Lavinia was feeling more poorly, and she and the Earl were leaving in an hour.

"An hour?" Charlotte pushed aside the pillows. "Who accompanies her besides the earl?"

"Oh, he is riding ahead to get the doctor. It will just be her maid with her."

"She goes by herself? She cannot possibly travel such a distance by herself in her condition."

"She will be well looked after. Lily is a good girl."

"I'm sure she is, but I would hate to be forced to travel in such a fashion, feeling unwell as she is." She frowned, thinking furiously. "Sarah, please pack a small case. I need to speak with Lavinia."

"A small case for you, my lady?"

"Yes. I'll need enough clothes for at least a few days."

"In a *small* case?"

"Yes," Charlotte said, ignoring her maid's skeptical tone. "But not a word to Mama, do you hear?" She eyed Sarah sternly.

"Yes, my lady."

Charlotte hurried from the room, down the hall to Lavinia's bedchamber. When the maid opened the door, she rushed past her to the bed. "Lavinia, I'm coming with you."

Her cousin pushed up to an elbow. A smile flickered across her face. "It is hardly a pleasure jaunt."

"Do you think I care only for my own pleasure?" Her eyes filled; she blinked the moisture back. "I cannot let you travel alone."

"I will not be alone. I'll have Lily for company."

"But it is not the same." Charlotte shook her head. "You need a friend."

Lavinia opened her mouth as if to protest, so Charlotte hurried on. "I mean a *real* friend, Livvie."

"But Aunt Constance—"

"Will have to cope. Besides, she cannot object to my wishing to be helpful."

Lavinia's lips pushed into something that could almost be called a doubting look. "What about the duke?"

Charlotte shrugged. "I'm sure he'll survive. Besides, coming here was never my idea."

"But it was arranged with you in mind."

"Perhaps. But I'm sure he won't miss me," she said, thinking of his many schemes and projects. "Regardless, his concerns are not mine right now. What does concern me is you." A knock on the door revealed Sarah, clutching two valises. "Ah, thank you, Sarah. But did I not say one?" She turned back to her cousin. "See? I am ready."

"But your mother—"

"Understands." Well, she would as soon as she read the note Charlotte planned to leave with Sarah. She hoped Mama would understand, any-way . . .

Lavinia gave a soft chuckle.

"What is it?"

"I'm put in mind of something our grandmother once said to me." Lavinia's brows lifted. "'You remind me of someone.'"

"Who?"

"Me."

⁂

Having farewelled Lord Hawkesbury immediately after an early breakfast, William made his way outside for the departure of the countess. As he neared the carriage he heard a higher-pitched voice, one he was not expect-ing. Spirits sinking, he drew near, only to have his fears confirmed. "Lady Charlotte! I . . . I did not expect you to be leaving us."

Her smile was small. "I am sorry, Duke, if it appears untoward, but I feel it is necessary for Lavinia to be accompanied home."

Emotions clashed within him. Relief that the countess would have a friend, mingled with admiration for Charlotte's kindness, and surprise at the marchioness's largesse—all underscored by the dismay he could feel permeating his soul. "I trust your trip goes well."

"Thank you," Lavinia said, heavy-eyed.

"You will be in my prayers," he said softly.

She nodded, eyes glimmering with tears.

His chest constricted, and he turned to her companion. "You are a good friend, Lady Charlotte."

Her cheeks pinked, and she ducked her gaze.

He silently pleaded for her to look at him, to give him a sign all was well. She denied him that reassurance.

Relief came with the arrival of a basket of food, carried by a servant. "Ah, here is a little something for your journey. I trust there are sufficient quantities."

"Thank you."

Seeing the weariness in Lavinia's eyes, he turned to the coachman, who had spent the past minutes trying to calm his ready-to-spring horses. "Travel safely, and Godspeed."

"Aye, sir."

William lifted a hand as the carriage pulled away. From her position by the window, Lady Charlotte turned, catching his eye, her manner all serious, without the hint of a smile.

Leaving him to fight the sense of loss and the disquieting certainty that, had her cousin not been ill, she would have soon found another way to leave Hartwell Abbey.

And him.

AN HOUR LATER, having decided to try drowning his unease with letters to Bethlem's chief physician and another to Barrack's caregivers, he heard a scream. He hurried from his study to see the marchioness on the landing.

"Madam?" He stopped at the base of the stairs. She appeared uninjured. "Are you quite well?"

"No, I am not." She lifted a hand to her forehead in a manner reminiscent of Mrs. Siddons at Covent Garden. "I have been most cruelly abused!"

What had happened now? "I beg your pardon?"

"Thankless vipers!"

He stared at her. "Madam?"

"Do you know what it is to raise a daughter and be treated in such a manner?"

He held his tongue. Raised his brows.

"No, I don't suppose you do. Silly girl."

He moved beside her, encouraging her to accompany him to the drawing room where they could speak without being overheard by the servants. When the doors were closed, he turned to his guest. "I presume you speak of Lady Charlotte?"

"She had the nerve to leave this!" She waved a note fiercely. "Begs my forgiveness but she simply *must* accompany poor Lavinia home." Lady Exeter sniffed. "Poor Lavinia, indeed."

"Begging your pardon, madam, but the countess *is* quite unwell."

"She has nothing but what countless other women have had. Simply because one is increasing is no reason to be sickly and demanding such attentions."

"I hardly think the countess could be accused of demanding attention, madam."

She sniffed. "Why else would Charlotte have thought it necessary to attend her?"

"From the goodness of her heart?" he suggested, putting up his brows. "Lady Hawkesbury is very unwell. I suspect her husband fears she may lose the child." And possibly his wife.

"What? No. That cannot be."

Apprehension tugged within. Losing Pamela had proved a grievous time, even when his love had long grown cold. For Hawkesbury to lose Lavinia in the first flush of love was unthinkable. He silently offered another prayer for their protection.

She flushed. "Well, of course, Charlotte is a good girl, Duke. I wouldn't want you to think otherwise."

"I'm sure you would not," he murmured.

"She's just a trifle impetuous, you see, running off like this. Of course, had she asked me in the usual manner, I would have ensured *you* did not mind before permitting Charlotte to accompany her cousin on such a trip."

Would you? He swallowed the sardonic response, settling for, "I think her cousin is appreciative of Lady Charlotte's company."

"You do?" Her pale brows knit. "How could you know? Surely you did not see them?"

He winced at his inadvertent slip. "I did. And I'm pleased that your daughter was assisting your niece—"

"And you did not think to tell me?"

He cleared his throat. "Forgive me, madam, but I was under the impression you already knew."

"Yes, but—"

"Perhaps, madam, instead of brangling over that which cannot be altered, our time would be better employed praying for that family."

Her cheeks flushed. "You are right, of course." Her eyes held a tinge of worry. "Hawkesbury really thinks the child's life in danger?"

"Yes."

"Is . . . is Lavinia's life in danger?"

Memories surged of another woman for whom childbirth had resulted in death. He thrust them away. "I pray not."

"Oh dear." She slumped in her seat. "I wonder . . . should I tell her father?"

"I believe the earl said he would write to let him know."

She nodded, clearly abstracted. "I should inform Patience. And Mama . . ."

"Please avail yourself of whatever writing materials you require."

"Thank you." She glanced up at him. "And you do not mind?"

Somehow he knew she did not refer to her use of paper. He managed a small smile. "I am sure Lady Charlotte's presence will prove to be a great boon to her cousin, and I trust a great boost to her spirits."

He bowed, exiting the room, calling for a footman to deliver a supply of necessary implements for the marchioness to begin her correspondence.

And tried to ignore his own niggling uncertainties by burying himself in work and exchanging his worries for prayers.

CHAPTER TWENTY-TWO

Hawkesbury House, Lincolnshire
Two days later

WAS IT POSSIBLE a heart could break?

Charlotte swiped away her tears, hoping against hope the dowager countess seated opposite had not noticed. But she rather doubted that; the earl's mother had a hawkeyed sense about everything that occurred under her son's roof.

She refocused her attention on the embroidery. Forced a shaking hand to weave the carmine-threaded needle in. Out. In. Out. Repetition calmed her scattering emotions, calming her breathing. In. Out. In. Out.

There was still hope. Nobody had descended to tell them otherwise. The doctor had been called early this morning, his carriage waking Charlotte from anxious slumber. She'd tried blocking the heavy foreboding with desperate prayers and even more desperate promises to God. But would God really be interested in her vow to marry the duke and never think on Lord Markham again, if only He preserved Lavinia's life and that of her babe?

She peeked again at the dowager, her face like flint, her eyes like blue ice. Not for her any pretense of industry. She sat motionless, as though carved in marble, the only sign of life the faintest flicker of an eyelash whenever a creaking movement came from upstairs.

Pity jostled with apprehension. The woman had barely acknowledged Charlotte's existence since their arrival two days ago, Charlotte's attempts to distract the dowager from attending Lavinia falling pitifully short.

Fortunately, the earl and doctor had been more successful in barring her from Lavinia's room, forcing her to rage around the house or sit remorselessly still.

A creak came on the stairs. Charlotte turned, the opened door revealing the doctor passing by.

"Jameson!" The dowager rose. "Jameson, what has happened?"

He did not pause, did not speak.

"Oh, dear God!" The dowager passed a hand over her face. "God could not be so cruel!"

Charlotte shuddered. "We . . . we do not know yet, my lady. Please do not give up hope."

She made a dismissive sound, reducing Charlotte and her opinions to dust.

There was another sound, and a tall form filled the doorway: the earl, with a pale face, unshaven jaw, and stricken eyes.

"Nicholas? What is it?"

He swallowed, his throat juddering in and out. "The . . . the baby died."

"Oh, Nicholas!" his mother cried.

Charlotte's breath caught on a sob.

"What was—?"

His shoulders slumped. "A boy."

"An heir," his mother moaned.

Charlotte bit her wobbling lip, the earl blurring as she blinked away tears. "I'm so sorry."

He nodded, turning, as if to leave.

"How is Lavinia?"

"Sleeping. The doctor gave her something to help her rest. He seems to think she will recover well enough."

"Too much gallivanting," his mother said. "She was always out and about—"

"Mother." His voice, his look was glacial.

She sniffed. "I know you will always prefer her to me, but the truth must be told. Lavinia did too much, and it is *her* fault you are without an heir—"

"Mother!"

"I never trusted that smiling facade. She is all that is wrong—"

"Charlotte, would you excuse us, please?"

Charlotte nodded, nearly running to escape the room, in which raised voices began as soon as the doors closed. Fighting to keep her expression calm, she hurried upstairs. Poor Lavinia. How could she live caught between her husband and a mother-in-law who despised her?

THE NEXT DAY, having eaten both yesterday's evening meal and then breakfast in her room after being informed the family would *not* be dining together, Charlotte found her courage and exited her bedchamber. She had no desire to meet the dowager, but her sleep had been broken with a multitude of prayers for her cousin and the earl, and when she heard his heavy tread go past her door, she judged now was as good a time as any to see how Lavinia fared.

Charlotte crept along the corridor, met a red-eyed maid, whose sorrow seemed more genuine than that of the dowager countess. "How is she today?"

"Poor thing." She shook her head. "His lordship is most concerned. She was crying her eyes out a while back, but is now in there, singing."

Singing?

Charlotte's look must have conveyed astonishment, for the maid nodded. "Aye. I don't think she's quite well."

She hurried to Lavinia's bedchamber. No wonder the earl had been concerned. If Lavinia was out of her mind . . .

As she neared, she heard the sound of Lavinia's beautiful singing voice from within. A sob filled her chest. Poor, *poor* thing. She tapped on the door. The singing ceased. "Lavinia?"

"Charlotte? Is that you?"

She gingerly turned the handle, only to have the door jerk open and be met by a visibly distraught Lily.

"Thank you, that will be all."

"Are you sure, my lady?"

"Quite sure." Despite her red eyes and ashen cheeks, Lavinia managed a small smile, which emboldened the maid to nod and leave.

Charlotte moved slowly toward the bedstead, where her cousin lay propped against a pile of pillows. "Lavinia, I . . . I cannot begin to express how sad I am." Tears pricked, fell. "I'm *so* desperately sorry."

"Thank you." Her cousin closed her eyes, bit her bottom lip.

Of course. No doubt Lavinia shared some of Charlotte's own sensibilities about sympathy. Sometimes sympathy did not soothe, but instead stirred grief. Charlotte sank onto the bed beside her, massaged a cold hand between both of hers. "How are you?"

Lavinia opened her eyes, gray eyes circled with sorrow. "I've been better."

Words failed her. What could she say that would not sound trite? Words were so empty, so futile. "Can I do anything?"

Lavinia shook her head. "Just be here."

Charlotte gently squeezed her hand and glanced around the room.

In direct contrast to the heartache and heavy atmosphere, the bedchamber was large and airy, possessing a sunny prospect from the large windows that overlooked the formal rose gardens below. The dark and ponderous furniture so prevalent in the rest of the house was conspicuously absent, replaced with honey-colored light-framed furnishings, and pale blue and gold fabric for the curtains and flooring, that seemed more indicative of Lavinia's usual ebullient nature. Doubtless the maids had cleared away all that remained of the miscarriage; there was no sign of anything to indicate the tragedy that had befallen the household. The only trace of dashed hopes was a tiny silver rattle on the dressing table.

Her heart panged. Had Charlotte done badly to insist on people seeing baby Rose? Had that evoked excessive dreams in Lavinia? Made things worse for her now? But surely Charlotte couldn't be responsible for how others felt. At least, she felt sure that was something like Aunt Patience would say. She patted Lavinia's hand and pushed to her feet, moving toward the window as if entranced by the view, but surreptitiously shifting the rattle to behind a vase of lilies, so it would not catch her cousin's eye and reinforce her sadness.

She met Lavinia's gaze in the looking glass, and turned, forcing her lips up. "Did I hear singing before?"

Her cousin nodded. Charlotte must have looked a question, for Lavinia murmured, "I . . . I am trying not to live in sorrow."

"But you can be sad." Charlotte glanced at the Bible on the bed, its pages spotted with moisture. She remembered a ponderous sermon on the raising of Lazarus. "Even Jesus wept."

"He did, that is true. And I am sad, Charlotte, so *desperately* sad."

Lavinia's voice shook, sending another wave of pain to Charlotte's heart. If her faith-filled cousin could falter, what hope was there for the rest of them?

"I wanted so much for Nicholas to have his son," Lavinia's voice cracked. "I hope he's not too disappointed with me."

Charlotte moved to hug her tightly. "He doesn't blame you." Unlike his mother.

"So he says." After a long moment, Lavinia's shudders eased. She pulled back, managed a watery smile. "I suppose I must believe him?"

"He's a good man who loves you."

"Then I cannot despair. He doesn't need a wife who despairs. That's too much of a burden for any man, even one as good as Nicholas."

Charlotte nodded. What could she say? No words seemed adequate for this strange conversation.

"Besides, to despair is to forget God's grace." Lavinia drew in a shaky breath. "I find myself in sore need of remembering His love and mercy at this time."

"Of course."

Lavinia winced and rubbed her forehead before accepting Charlotte's offer of a glass of water. "Thank you. I'm so weary."

"Of course you are. I should let you rest—"

"No, please stay." She clasped Charlotte's hand. "I want you to understand."

"Understand?"

"God's love doesn't change just because my circumstances do. While I know this, it is difficult to remember, so I . . . I am trying to sing to remind myself of God's love and faithfulness. I always remember things better when I sing them."

Charlotte stared at her. Her cousin's words made little sense. How could one expect singing to make any difference? She patted Lavinia's restless hand. Poor Lavinia . . .

Lavinia gave another half sob, before smearing away the trickling tears.

"Have you ever noticed how so many of David's psalms begin by him crying out to God in despair, then partway through his heart seems to change as he recalls God's goodness?"

No, she hadn't. Although she would pay closer attention in future. "But this isn't good."

"No. But do bad circumstances mean God is not good?"

The question seemed to hover in the air. Did God promise a life of roses? Or was faith more about remembering His presence and strength in the midst of suffering?

Charlotte tucked a stray strand of hair behind her ear. Why did it feel as though Lavinia was the one offering comfort to her when it should be the other way around?

"The Bible says that praise is like a garment we can put on. It is a choice I can make, just like I choose to love Nicholas when he's being stubborn"—a wisp of a smile crossed Lavinia's lips—"or he chooses to be patient with me when I'm being rather less than meek."

Something deep stirred within Charlotte's heart. This love Lavinia spoke of seemed grounded in faith, not based on feelings. *Lord, help me love like that.*

"Papa always says God's nature does not change just because our situation alters. I'm trying to remember what the Bible says, that nothing can separate us from God's love." Lavinia's smile faded as her voice shook on another muffled sob. "I am trying to sing, like David did, and declare God's truths over my circumstances, even though I don't feel like it."

Charlotte wrapped an arm around her, hugging her gently. "And is it working?"

Lavinia nodded, drawing in a deep breath. "I think so. God *is* faithful. He reminds me of that daily, through His many blessings, like Nicholas, and Lily, and you."

"Me?"

"Oh, I could not have borne this without you, dear Charlotte. Your company on the journey here, your kindness and sweet thoughtfulness, you've cheered my heart no end."

Moisture clogged her throat, her eyes. "I'm glad."

Charlotte drew her cousin close for another strong and tender hug. A moment longer and they drew apart, exchanging shaky exhales followed by tiny smiles.

"I must look a sight," Charlotte said, wiping her cheeks again.

"A sight for sore eyes. I'm certain I look far worse." Lavinia's smile peeped out again. "Thank goodness Nicholas doesn't seem to notice."

"He is a good man."

Lavinia eased back on her pillows. "It is such a blessing to have a husband who shares one's faith."

Charlotte dropped her gaze, working to ignore the niggle stirred by her cousin's implied approbation. The duke's faith was plain to see, evident in his words, his actions, his leading in prayers each day. He too was a good man . . .

She blinked rapidly, shifted from the bed. Pasted on a smile. "Shall I ring for tea?"

"Yes, please." Lavinia's eyes closed in weariness.

Charlotte pulled the heavy rope near Lavinia's bed, whose silent summons soon brought a maid, accompanied by the earl.

He glanced at his wife, then at Charlotte, his expression one of relief, as he murmured, "Your presence has helped, I see."

Charlotte matched his whispered tone. "Rather, her presence has helped me." At his raised brows she continued. "She chooses to remember God's love and faithfulness even when her heart breaks."

Something like a wince crossed his features. "She is too good for me."

"She fears that she has disappointed you, my lord."

He shook his head and turned away, dashing a hand over his eyes.

A maid appeared with a tea tray, releasing Charlotte from the need to stay longer. "If you'll excuse me, I have some things to attend to."

"Of course."

Charlotte hurried downstairs, glad to not encounter the dowager. Gladder still when she followed the footman's directions to the library to find it unoccupied. Searching through the shelves, she finally found what she required.

A Bible.

She flicked it open, and began to read.

❧ Chapter Twenty-Three

Charlotte peeked across the room as the dowager continued muttering under her breath, slashing at the thread with a pair of scissors. Sympathy swirled, no doubt cultivated by the psalms she'd read yesterday, which encouraged grace to be extended to even the most ungracious.

So she had tried to ignore her ladyship's venom. Any complaint against Lavinia heard by the earl he dismissed immediately. Any complaint she uttered in Charlotte's company and out of her son's was twice as poisonous, and often followed by a "still nothing to say for yourself?" Her refusal to respond seemed to have convinced the dowager of Charlotte's lack of wits, but that didn't matter. She wanted to be here for Lavinia's sake, even if the earl's mother cast aspersions against Charlotte for the rest of her days.

The lack of conversation provided plenty of time to think on the words spoken yesterday. Words about love. About good men. About faith.

She bit her lip. Seeing Lord Hawkesbury yesterday, remembering Lavinia's words about a husband who shared her faith, Charlotte couldn't help but compare his patience and selflessness with those of the duke and Lord Markham. One man compared favorably, the other . . .

Uneasiness stole through her. What she had thought love now seemed so superficial. Had Lord Markham ever acted selflessly? Had she? She winced.

That thought was only compounded by other words she'd read last night. Even in her convalescence, Lavinia was thinking of others besides herself. She had sent Lily to Charlotte's room with a journal which once belonged to Lavinia's mother, Charlotte's Aunt Grace whom she'd never met. "Her ladyship wants you to read this," Lily had said, tapping a page.

In it, Grandmama's eldest daughter had written about her impossible dream: to marry David Ellison, the handsome son of a Gloucestershire rector, even in the teeth of her parents' opposition.

> *I spoke to my parents yesterday and their bitter words sent me to my knees once more. David encourages me to remember God's grace, but at times I struggle to remain so sanguine. Yet he keeps gently reminding to keep seeking the One who is the Author of Life and of Love. And as I do, I sense His enabling in the kind of sacrificial love the apostle Paul writes about in First Corinthians. To be patient, to be kind, to keep no record of wrongs. To love the unlovely. I can love others truly, because my Heavenly Father loves me.*

Of course, that led to another bout of Bible reading, where the verses on love challenged. Beyond a mere feeling, it seemed true love involved choices: to practice patience instead of anger, to be kind to the undeserving, to persevere when wishing to give up, to be faithful, even in contrary circumstances. What contradictions a life of faith seemed to demand . . .

How could a person learn to love so deeply? Was it truly found—as Aunt Grace believed—in God?

She swallowed a sigh—best to not provoke the dowager into further interrogations—and refocused on her embroidery.

The door opened, admitting a footman, but before he spoke, in sailed another figure.

"Aunt Patience!"

"Why, Charlotte! I did not expect to see you here."

Charlotte hugged her, as the dowager muttered, "Patience. How unexpected."

Her aunt sniffed. "Hardly unexpected, I'd imagine, when both your son and my sister write to inform me about my poor niece. Where is she?"

"Upstairs," Charlotte said. "I'm sure she will be very pleased to see you."

"And the child?"

"Dead," the dowager said.

Aunt Patience's face seemed to age a dozen years. "No," she whispered. "A son, an heir for Nicholas, gone."

Her aunt's pained eyes slid back to Charlotte. "How is Lavinia?"

"Weak, but surprisingly strong in spirit."

"That's my girl." Aunt Patience nodded, then said in a louder voice. "Excuse us, Margaret."

The dowager waved a hand. "Of course. My house is yours."

Aunt Patience's eyes snapped, but she held her tongue until they headed up the stairs. "*Her* house? Her son's more like it, which she lives in like a leech. I don't know how Lavinia copes with her."

Probably with lots of singing, Charlotte thought with a wry smile.

Hartwell Abbey

The sun had gone.

As Hapgood kept talking, William stared out the library window at the clouded skies mirroring the gloom in his heart since the news arrived yesterday. He grieved for the Hawkesburys, for their lost child. Concern for Charlotte at this sorrowful time had him praying for her almost as frequently as for the earl and countess. Prayers for her health, for her faith, that she would not be overborne by sadness—nor by Hawkesbury's overbearing mother.

His estate manager coughed.

"I beg your pardon?"

Hapgood shifted slightly. "It is the new road. It appears someone has deliberately loosened the stones partway through, which meant the draper's cart wheels slid and broke."

His attention snapped back to Hapgood as a million questions raced through his mind. How could anyone do this? *Why* would anyone do such a thing? "How could this happen without anyone noticing?"

"It required only a few rocks to be loosed, then it was a matter of waiting until enough vehicles had passed over."

William shoved a hand through his hair. "Thank God it hadn't been a curricle going at speed. Someone might have died!"

Hapgood eyed him. "Yes."

"Wait—surely you don't think my life in danger?"

"You *are* known to drive at speed along that stretch, sir."

Fear trembled up his spine. He shook it away. He could not afford to think such things. He cleared his throat. "Please ensure the draper is fully recompensed."

"Of course, sir."

He rubbed his forehead. Thank God Lavinia had got away safely. Thank God the departure of Charlotte's family had not met with accident, either. Such a thing he could not have borne.

William glanced out the window again. "Did the flowers get through?"

"Yes, sir. They should arrive within the hour, barring any accidents."

"They were the best?"

"Of course. Callinan saw to them himself."

William nodded, Hapgood left, and he turned back to his piles of paper. They held no interest. His heart was snared by people and events two hours north. *Heavenly Father, please provide Your comfort, and Your healing . . .*

Emotion burned. He scrubbed a hand over his eyes and glanced out the window.

A figure ran behind a tree.

He blinked. Rubbed his eyes again. Had he just imagined that? He studied the space carefully, waiting for the person to reappear. Had Charlotte been right about seeing someone after all? Her mother might have scoffed, and truth be told, so had he, but was someone on the estate who had no right to be there? His heart thumped. His servants had no need to run and hide. Then who?

Unease slowly stirred within. *Did* someone have evil designs toward him? The fire, the paint, even the rock thrown at Barrack, could be counted as accidents or tomfoolery, but the deliberateness of rearranging a road to disguise a ditch spoke of something far more nefarious.

But who would wish to hurt him?

He pressed closer to the glass but could see no one. Perhaps if he hurried outside—

Walking as quickly as he could, he made his way to the tree. Nothing. No one. His hands clenched in annoyance. Of course. He should've known this was a fool's game. Unless . . .

Was Pamela right? Was he going mad after all?

❧ CHAPTER TWENTY-FOUR

Hawkesbury House

AUNT PATIENCE'S ARRIVAL was a godsend, her zest-filled presence adding color to Lavinia's cheeks, while providing Charlotte and the earl fresh diversion from their grief, particularly in her manner of dealing with the dowager countess. The dowager had only to open her mouth for Aunt Patience to object. So strident was their opposition, Charlotte was sure that if the dowager were to say the grass was green, Aunt Patience would say it was more yellow. Fortunately, their arguments never crossed into Lavinia's bedchamber. The earl had banned his mother from entering, which was just as well. After her challenging conversation with Charlotte, Lavinia's health had declined, and she remained too weak for anything but the most benign of conversation.

The doctor visited again, his words leaving Lord Hawkesbury even paler than previously. Upon his return to the drawing room, when questioned by Aunt Patience, he simply said, "Lavinia could have died."

"Don't be ridiculous, Son."

He cast his mother a weary glance before fixing his attention on Charlotte and her aunt. "The doctor said it was like the baby was poisoning her system. It is a miracle the child died when it did, as it could have been so much worse."

"How could it be any worse? She lost the heir to the Hawkesbury name."

He closed his eyes, as Aunt Patience snapped at the dowager.

Charlotte's heart wrenched. Poor man. Would this mean Lavinia might never be able to bear a child? She swallowed the rush of emotion, clearing her throat. "Thank God Lavinia lives."

The earl heaved in a breath, opening his eyes to give her a half smile. "Thank God."

A knock came at the door before admitting the butler, who bowed, then turned to the dowager. "The rooms are ready, my lady."

"What rooms?" the earl said, frowning.

His mother dismissed the servant, refusing to meet her son's gaze.

"*What* rooms, Mother?"

She sighed. "The rooms for our guests."

"Guests?" He looked thunderous. "Now is not the time for visitors."

"I am sorry that it does not convenience you, but this was decided long ago. Besides, how was I to know your wife would prove so sickly?"

Charlotte's breath caught.

"Who are these guests?" Aunt Patience asked.

"My oldest friend and her daughter." The dowager glanced at Charlotte. "It might do you some good to have someone more your own age to talk with."

Somehow Charlotte felt sure the earl would place as little credit to his mother's sudden magnanimity as she did.

"Who are these friends?" he said, a muscle ticking in his jaw.

"They're travelling north, visiting some friends in Yorkshire, I believe—"

"*Who* are these friends, Mother?"

Finally the countess looked at her son, snapping, "Lady Winpoole and Clara."

Charlotte gasped.

"How can you ask them to stay here at such a time?" Aunt Patience snapped. "Have you no consideration?"

The countess shrugged. "These are my friends, and this is my house—"

"It is *my* house," the earl said stiffly, before turning to Charlotte and her aunt, a tight smile on his lips. "I'm terribly sorry, but I must request another private word with my mother."

Charlotte and her aunt escaped to the library, shutting the door against the sounds of disharmony, which included the phrase *dower house*.

Charlotte shivered. Poor Lavinia. How could love win against the dowager's selfishness? "How could she do this?"

"Margaret is a very sad woman. I've no doubt she wants Hawkesbury to come to regret the choice he has made."

"But for what purpose? He will not divorce Lavinia. He loves her, and she loves him. What can she possibly hope to achieve?"

"It is a form of control. If one does not obey, one must be punished." Aunt Patience looked old. "You cannot pretend not to have noticed your grandmother employs the same tactics?"

Grandmama. The Dowager Duchess of Salisbury who had cast off two daughters for the one she could control: Mama. She winced. "Do you think he will permit them to stay?"

Aunt Patience sighed heavily. "I don't see that he has much choice. They have been invited and would be travelling already. The best we can hope for is that they will display some sensitivity and depart as soon as possible."

"If they are heading north, they should only stay a night or two anyway, shouldn't they?"

"That is *if* they are heading north."

Charlotte stared. "You mean—?"

"I mean I would not put it past the dowager to claim untruths for her own purposes. Did you see the look on Nicholas's face?"

"Poor Lavinia. She will not be pleased when she learns of the unexpected company."

"No." Aunt Patience looked grim. "Such news should be kept from her as long as possible."

"I somehow doubt that is the dowager's concern."

Her aunt chuckled. "Why Charlotte, what a cynic you have become."

"A cynic, or merely a realist?"

"Is this the influence of the Duke of Hartington I hear so much about?"

Heat filled her cheeks. "What have you heard?"

"Only that the good duke seems most enamored of my niece." She gave her a piercing look. "I hope he is worthy of you?"

He was worthy, most definitely. But was she worthy of him?

"The Farmer Duke, they call him," her aunt continued. "Well, a farmer's wife is certainly not what I expected of you, my dear. But he *is* a duke, and I suppose your Mama would countenance nothing less."

Fortunately she was prevented from answering by the earl's entrance. "Forgive me. I wish you did not have to witness such things."

Well did Charlotte know the strain of heated emotions. "Perhaps a ride might prove of benefit."

"Away from the hot air?" A smile ghosted his face.

Aunt Patience nodded. "Excellent idea. I will sit with Lavinia. Take a groom with you. I'm sure you will both appreciate the chance to escape."

Nearly two hours later, after a ride that blew away most of her internal cobwebs, the earl paused his black stallion atop a hillock overlooking the estate, turning to her with an expression that held none of the previous strain.

"Thank you, Charlotte. I did not realize I needed this." His hazel eyes glinted. "Such thoughtfulness means your husband will be a fortunate man."

She tried to smile, but it felt strained.

What would it be like to marry into a family who could not respect her? Cressinda certainly didn't. If Charlotte agreed to marry the duke, would she have to put up with her slurs and aspersions every time they met? Would the duke be forced to protect her, as the earl did Lavinia? She frowned. Or would he give up, as he'd given up on his first wife?

⁂

Hartwell Abbey

"Excuse me, Your Grace, but you have visitors."

William placed down the beaker gingerly. "I do not recall issuing any further invitations." The only guest he wanted was at Hawkesbury House, and as much as he might wish for her return, his wishes ran a very distant second to someone else's needs. "Who is it?"

The footman cleared his throat. "Lord and Lady Clarkson."

He stilled. There could only be one reason for their return. "Tell them I'll be there directly."

As the footman hurried away, William replaced the glass stoppers firmly, being careful not to inhale deeply. One didn't want poisonous vapors, even with such vile visitors awaiting him now.

His return to the Abbey was greeted by the sounds of raised voices in the drawing room. Cressinda, making her views heard again. Fighting a scowl, he entered the room. "Lord and Lady Clarkson"—he bowed—"what a surprise."

"Where is she?"

Confirmation. He turned to his sister. "Cressinda, would you please excuse us?"

For a moment, she did not move, until he raised a brow, which brought a flush to her cheeks, and an eventual flouncing from the room.

He turned back to his former in-laws. "I trust your journey was pleasant?"

"Would've been if we hadn't had to come down the servant's drive," the viscount muttered.

"Ah, yes. A thousand pities. The other road is being repaired—"

"Hartington!"

"Yes, my lady?"

"Where is my granddaughter?"

He bit down the bile, hoping for a neutral expression. "I presume she is in Bournemouth with your son and daughter-in-law."

"Not that one! Pamela's child. Where is she?"

"I imagine she is asleep upstairs. I cannot hear anything to suggest otherwise."

"You—! You let us believe she had died!"

"Yet here you are. After promising never to darken my doorstep again." He sighed. "If only people would keep their word."

"You blackguard! You villain!"

"Come, come. You said as much last time. Surely you've had time to develop your range of invective—"

"I wish Pamela had never met you!"

"For once, madam, we agree."

But it was not strictly true. For all the pain he'd gone through in the past few years, if he had not met Pamela, the little girl upstairs—fast twining tenderness around his heart—would not be here. Would not be *his*.

He eyed them. "What do you want?"

"Give us our grandchild," Lord Clarkson said.

Disbelief escaped in a laugh. "No."

"But you have said she's not your child."

"That may be so, but she is definitely *not* yours."

"But she was Pamela's."

"And Pamela bore my name, and bore a child with that same name. If the child had been birthed elsewhere, perhaps you might have grounds for argument, but she was born in my house, not a dozen rooms from me." Resentment hardened within. "You will *not* take her away."

"But you do not love her!"

"Do not dare presume to tell me whom I love, sir."

"But—"

"Please, Hartington," Lady Clarkson begged. "Please let me see her?"

William studied the woman's face, her eyes glimmering with tears. His annoyance subsided. A twist of compassion urged grace. He jerked a nod, pushed to his feet.

Ten minutes later he returned, the pink-swaddled child asleep in his arms. The older woman's face lit. "Oh, she is beautiful. Just like Pamela as a child." She glanced up. "What is her name?"

"Rose. Rose Pamela Hartwell."

She wiped her cheeks. "You named her after—?"

"Naturally."

She hiccuped out a breath. "We thought, I thought, she had died. At least that's what—" she stopped, giving him a scared glance.

"That's what Maria thought." At her nod he continued. "The doctor had said the baby could not live, but then . . ." He gently touched the rounded cheek. "She is a miracle."

"A miracle." She touched the tiny finger curled over the pink blanket. "Yes."

Compassion warred with the fast-draining dregs of bitterness. Should he? *Heavenly Father, what would—?* Oh, he didn't need to finish that prayer. "Would you like to hold her?"

His heart warmed as the little girl's grandmother cooed over the precious bundle for a few minutes. By the time she'd finished murmuring her thanks, he'd resolved on another act of grace. "I will not oppose another visit in the future, provided you write and request a time convenient for all. I—" His neck heated. "I suppose it only fair for you to know I intend the Marquess of Exeter's daughter to be my bride."

"So soon?"

"Pamela's love for me died long before mine did for her. Do not begrudge me happiness, and I will not refuse your visits to my daughter."

"*Your* daughter?"

William studied the downy head as a wave of tender affection rushed through him. Did it truly matter how little Rose came to be? Surely love was greater than any society gossip.

He lifted his gaze, met the faded blue eyes, and said firmly, "Yes. *My* daughter."

A sense of rightness, of gladness, overwhelmed him. And he smiled.

※

Hawkesbury House

Charlotte hurried down the steps, glad to finally escape the house. Relinquishing the bedside vigil to her aunt was no hardship; Lavinia had slept the entire time, her cheeks as pale as the pillow. Charlotte had returned the journal, but Grace's words haunted her still. Words about sacrificial love. Being patient, being kind. *Loving the unlovely.* It was easy to love people like Lavinia, so sweet and good-natured, but someone like the dowager countess—ugh!

Her skin prickled. She glanced over her shoulder, as if the flint-eyed woman saw her now. Perhaps it was easier to love from afar. No wonder Lavinia and Nicholas preferred the quiet elegance of Hampton Hall to the majestic pretensions of Hawkesbury House.

She stretched her fingers, caressing the velvety apricot roses that lined the steps down into a garden where a gaudy Italian marble fountain played softly in the midday sun. Her nose crinkled. Such a hideous monstrosity, fat cherubs gushing water with giant eel-like fish writhing around their legs. Somehow she did not think the earl or Lavinia responsible for such ugliness.

Turning away, she looked toward the east and drew in a deep breath. The scent of roses drifted on a warm breeze that seemed to hold the vaguest hint of sea salt. She smiled at herself. Probably mere ridiculousness—they were still many miles inland—and she pined for Devon. Would her family visit their estate this year?

A carriage pulled into view along the drive and then passed by on its way to the front of the house, a carriage with a familiar crest. Her heart sank. A few minutes later she was found by a footman requesting her attendance inside. Anxiety tinged her return. How would the earl regard *this* unexpected guest?

She found her mother in the drawing room with the dowager and Aunt Patience. Mama glanced at Charlotte and broke off mid conversation to accept a kiss on the cheek before continuing. "I see Hartington's flowers have arrived. I would recognize them anywhere. Such elegance, such uniqueness." She slid Charlotte a sly look. "Just like the man himself."

"Did he think we have no flowers here?" the dowager snapped.

Mama drew herself up. "I'm sure he was thinking more of what might please poor Lavinia than of what might displease you."

The countess hissed, turning on her heel and exiting the room.

"That woman has always given herself airs. When one thinks she was but a baronet's daughter, it's enough to make one long to smack her."

"Mama!"

Her mother shrugged. "Her vulgarity is something which we've always despaired."

"I don't understand why she does not remove to the Dower House."

"That woman? Remove to anywhere less than what she thinks her due?" Mama said, stripping off her gloves. "Come, Charlotte. Don't be naive."

"Naive?" Aunt Patience said. "You cannot be talking of your daughter here. I believe she has improved considerably in the past few months."

Why did that not sound terribly complimentary?

"Now, Constance, tell me more about this man who would take Charlotte as his wife."

As Mama swapped gossip with her sister, Charlotte roamed the room. After the Abbey's muted splendor, everything felt a little too heavy, a little too pompous, a little . . . ostentatious.

"And Charlotte, you do not mind such a match?"

"How could she?" Mama cried.

"I did not ask you, Constance, but your daughter."

Twin piercing stares demanded answer. "The duke is . . . quite amiable."

"Amiable? He is utterly charming!"

"Thank you, Constance. I believe we're all aware *you* would marry him if you could. Charlotte?"

"He is clever," she managed.

"One does not want a stupid husband," Aunt Patience said, with a sideways look at Mama. "And the previous wife, the one that ran off, that does not alarm you?"

"I . . . I don't believe she ran off. She died at Hartwell House in London."

"Hmm. There was always such a lot of silly speculation about that family."

Like the duel, Charlotte thought. One day she'd have to ask him about the duel.

"Wasn't there a child? How would you feel about becoming a stepmother?"

Charlotte's smile grew sincere. "Little Rose is the sweetest thing."

Aunt Patience eyed her, and then nodded, as if satisfied. The conversation changed to other things, such as Aunt Patience's time in Durham, before turning to the dowager once again. "Did you hear she has invited that poisonous DeLancey chit and her mother here?"

"What? Now?" Mama looked aghast.

"Poor girl." For a moment the two sisters seemed to droop, as if remembering why they were here in the first place. "However will Lavinia cope?"

NONE OF THEM could have anticipated just how Lavinia would deal with their unwanted guests when they finally arrived the next day. Charlotte, her mother, and her aunt were pretending not to notice how the dowager's conversation with Lady Winpoole and Clara excluded them, when the door opened. There was a collective gasp.

"Livvie!" Charlotte hurried to her side. "We were not expecting to see you."

Lavinia gave a wan smile. "I had to welcome our visitors." As she murmured greetings, Charlotte sent the dowager countess a narrow look. Her chin tilted and she looked away.

"Sit down, Livvie, do," Charlotte urged. "Before you collapse."

Lavinia obeyed, turning to Clara as the older ladies resumed their separate conversations. Her eyes, her smile appeared tired as she said, "And how are you, Miss DeLancey?"

"Well, thank you." There was an awkward silence.

Charlotte eyed the brunette, whose pale cheeks almost rivaled Lavinia's. Did she still hold a *tendre* for the earl? How could she be so bold-faced as to appear? Granted, they could not have known what sad circumstances would greet them, but still . . .

Clara glanced at her mother, before saying in a lowered voice, "I . . . I am very sorry for your loss."

The words, uttered in a kind tone, caused her cousin to wince. Lavinia managed to thank her, in a choking voice, before casting Charlotte a pleading look, which prompted her to engage Miss DeLancey in discussion of her trip north from their current abode, near Brighton.

Such innocuous conversation made Clara seem so ordinary, without the malice of her mother, who kept casting pitying looks at Lavinia. Perhaps Clara was a prisoner of circumstances as much as any daughter bound to her parents'—and society's—will.

Later, when the dowager escorted her guests to their rooms, Lavinia said much the same when her aunts questioned her concerning her fortitude with Clara and her mother.

"I do not think Clara vindictive, even if her mother might be. And even if she is, what better expression of grace than offering mercy to those who cannot appreciate it?"

"But they are using your good nature!"

She shook her head. "They are using God's good nature. For what is His mercy to us if we cannot extend that same mercy to others?"

"But what of the earl? Do you not worry about him and Clara?"

"Aunt Constance, I know Clara loved Nicholas, but she is only a threat if I allow her to be. I do not doubt my husband's love. I trust him."

Charlotte's eyes blurred. This was what love looked like: quiet confidence in another person, believing the best, looking for good, persevering in trials, trusting.

As Mama and Aunt Patience returned to discussing London, Lavinia turned to her. "Thank you for helping me earlier. I confess I found her sympathy a challenge. You're very good to me, Charlotte."

"Oh no." Charlotte shook her head, only too aware of her many faults, her vanity, her caprice, her resentments. "I'm not good at all."

"Then let us agree that God is good. He proves His goodness to me in so many ways."

"How can you say that, Livvie, when He took away your child?" She pressed a hand to her mouth, as Lavinia's eyes filled with tears. "I'm so sorry. I didn't mean . . ."

Lavinia shook her head. "I . . . struggle, but I still believe that our Lord is good and . . . somehow works all things together for our good."

Charlotte studied the floor. She needed to remember her cousin's example. She needed to remember that God loved her and His plans were for her good, also.

Chapter Twenty-Five

Any strain caused by unwanted visitors was resolved by the earl's declaration that he and Lavinia would remove to Gloucestershire the following day. His mother looked shocked, Lady Winpoole disappointed, but Charlotte thought she detected more than a mite of relief in Clara's demeanor. The earl had said Charlotte was welcome to join them, but because she suspected this was mere kindness on his part and that they would prefer to be by themselves at this time, she refused, much to her own mother's relief. "Good, for now we can return to Hartwell."

"But Mama," she said when they were alone, "have we not already outstayed our welcome?"

"Believe me, child, the duke is anxious for your return."

Anxious? She suspected it was her mother who was anxious for their return, but she did not comment, leaving Mama to write to Father and Henry in London, informing them of their new plans.

The next day saw a flurry of departures: the earl and Lavinia, Charlotte and Mama, Aunt Patience. It seemed that even Lady Winpoole was determined to travel farther north, not wishing to outstay the welcome offered by the dowager as originally announced.

The trip back to Hartwell passed without incident and was filled with Mama's warnings about Charlotte's conduct and what she must do to secure the duke's affections. "For I cannot like the fact you've been parted so many days. Although"—she brightened—"absence might encourage his affection. One can only hope."

Charlotte stared out the window. Had absence warmed the duke's heart?

Even if she had secured his affections, would his affections remain secured? Hadn't he despised his wife?

"Charlotte, I do wish you'd stop frowning. No man likes to see a lady with a scowl permanently etched between her brows."

Charlotte chewed her bottom lip as they passed through the tiny village of Hartwell. Farm laborers near stone houses eyed them as the carriage passed. How would they feel if they knew the potential next duchess was passing by? Had they respected the previous duchess? Would they—could they—respect her?

"Mama—" She glanced at where Ellen sat, apparently asleep, and lowered her voice. "Why did the duke forsake his wife?"

Mama shook her head, causing a tiny feather to escape her coiffure. "It was all a silly misunderstanding."

"Was it? I just do not understand how a man who seems so gentle could be accused of such wickedness."

"His was not the wicked act, my dear."

"You mean his wife—?"

"Played the harlot. Now, there's no need to look at me like that, Charlotte. It's a well-known fact that woman could bat her eyelashes at any man and have him come running."

"I don't understand. Why would the duke wish to marry a woman like that?"

Mama shrugged. "She was utterly beautiful. He is a man. What more needs to be said?"

But Charlotte knew that while others might commend her looks, nobody would ever accuse her of being this season's beauty. Is that why the duke seemed to prefer her? She would not be a threat and run away?

Her emotions were in a turmoil by the time they returned. Their arrival caused no small manner of surprise; it seemed Mama's note had arrived but an hour earlier, and their rooms were still being prepared. The duke's sister and her husband were still in residence, though on a visit to Northampton today; the duke himself was out inspecting a road, so the butler informed them.

Mama's look of distaste seemed to suggest she considered a road beneath the duke's attentions. "Then we shall wait."

"Very good, my lady," Travers said before withdrawing.

As they settled down to wait, Charlotte couldn't help but wonder what their host would think of their return, and whether their unlooked-for arrival would be greeted with more irritation than gratification.

Afternoon shadows stretched across the newly repaired road. A hush of breeze shivered through the branches of the nearby oaks and birch. William studied the road, then looked back at his foreman. "That should hold sufficiently, do you not agree, Wilkins?"

"Aye, sir," the foreman agreed, with a decided nod.

William noted the nod and wondered if it were perhaps just a little too determined. Did Wilkins have doubts, after all? "You know, if there is any concern I would prefer to be told sooner rather than later." He eyed the foreman carefully.

"No doubts, Your Grace. It's all as it should be."

"If you are quite certain?" Again the nod. "Then please continue. I would not have Mr. McAdam's project hindered any longer."

"Of course, sir." The foreman turned to shout orders to his team, a hefty-looking crew whose necks seemed wider than his thigh. No doubt any of these men would be more than capable of causing a great deal of damage to someone of his size.

He shook his head at himself. He was becoming fanatically mistrustful! How ludicrous to think his life might be in danger, simply because of a few odd occurrences. He really needed a firmer grasp on reality.

With a word of farewell, he turned Neptune back to the Abbey. A short ride, nothing more than a mile and a half, through the woods that formed this part of the Forest of Salcey, and he would be home.

Home.

Hartwell Abbey might be his primary dwelling, but surely a home was made of more than bricks and mortar. The Abbey felt too big these days, too cold, too lonely, even if Cressinda still insisted on inflicting him with her company.

Neptune jumped over a log, forcing him to catch his breath. He should probably pay closer attention, but his horse knew the trail, could probably ride it in pitch darkness, and really, he'd far rather muse on the young lady whose presence was never far from his mind, no matter how many miles lay between them.

Would Charlotte return? The days had seemed too long without her, his endeavors pointless. What did road repair matter when his heart felt sadly undone?

His sister's presence had not made matters easier, her oft-vocalized doubts about Charlotte's aptitude for the role of duchess fueling unease about his decisions. After all, his first bride had proved a grievous mistake. How could he be sure he would not make the same mistake again? Would Charlotte cope? He gritted his teeth. Of course the daughter of a marquess would cope. Would she stay? That was the real issue.

Heavenly Father, help me find strength and grace in You. Help Charlotte see—

Something whizzed cool air past his cheek, arcing into a tree with a bang.

Neptune reared, whinnying in fright, forcing William to dig his knees in and cling desperately to the reins, before the stallion took off at a fast gallop through the trees. Above, branches clung together, resisting light, while limbs and twigs variously slapped and clawed his cheeks. The stallion's hooves thundered, echoing the pulse racing in his ears.

The stallion continued frantically, as if being chased by a lurking monster. William glanced over his shoulder, but no figure appeared.

Suddenly there was another ping of branches. With a terrified neigh, Neptune plunged from the bridle path into the undergrowth.

"Whoa!" William tried in vain to wheel the horse around, but Neptune plunged on recklessly.

Blood rushed wildly through his ears as he sought to order his thoughts. The lack of an echoing ricochet suggested it was not a gunshot, as he'd first imagined, but a rock striking a tree that had so startled Neptune. But to what end? To instill fear—or something more sinister?

He peered over his shoulder again. Through the bouncing leaves he could see no one. But would they try again? Would they succeed?

He nudged the horse's flanks with his knees, urging Neptune onward, praying his hooves would not stumble on the uneven ground. Finally, the stallion resumed the path, and it wasn't long before they cleared the trees. Weight dropped away. Soon he would see the Abbey, and whoever was following would be—he hoped—reluctant to trespass any farther. He wheeled the horse around, searching the woods. Nobody would dare encroach the clearing. And whoever was hunting him, would soon be hunted.

He wheeled the horse around and galloped to the stables. "Hie, there!"

Evans appeared, brows raised. "Sir?"

"Get the men. There is someone in our woods who means me harm."

"What has happened?"

"Follow me."

William hurried Neptune back, gritting his teeth. He may never have been to war, but he felt like a field marshal now. Within minutes he had seven men with him and had divided them into pairs, readying to search the woods.

"Spread out. I want to know if someone is in our woods."

"A tramp?"

He shook his head. "A tramp does not throw rocks at a horse rider, not unless he is mad. And if he is, then all the better we flush him out. No, I strongly suspect that whoever did this also bears responsibility for the road destruction and for setting fire to the carriage house."

The mutters and nods indicated renewed determination, just as he'd thought mention of the carriage house fire might. If he mentioned poor Barrack, a long-popular member of staff, he was sure to have them helping with the search until nightfall.

He pushed into the woods, back to where he'd experienced the first encounter. Neptune resisted, ears flattened, obviously still terrified.

A twig cracked.

Evans gestured for William to stay back. He slid from his horse and crept noiselessly through the thicket. *Heavenly Father, protect him, protect us all, help us find who is responsible . . .*

A minute later the head groom reappeared, a sheepish smile on his face. "Nothing, sir, save a stray doe from the deer park."

William nodded, patting Neptune on the neck. "Frightened by a girl, were you? Never mind." In a louder voice he said, "Let's keep looking."

But two hours later, with no sign of anything, save a small rock that might have been the one that had nearly clipped his ear, William was forced to concede. Still, he warned the men, additional guards would need to be posted.

The Abbey had just emerged into view when Evans coughed. "Begging yer pardon, sir, but I forgot to mention earlier, you have visitors."

"What visitors?" Not Pamela's parents again. Hadn't he told them to write? "My sister has returned?"

"Not your sister, Your Grace." His groom grinned widely. "The pretty young lady and her mother."

He blinked. "Lady Featherington and the marchioness?"

"Aye. That be them. Glad I am she is back, too."

"Yes," he said, dazed. Why had they returned? His heart hammered. Surely it could only mean something good. He glanced back at his groom. "How long have they been here?"

"Oh, it must be nigh on four hours now."

"What?" Without waiting to hear apologies, he spurred Neptune to the house. Within minutes he was striding inside, only to be met by a wide-eyed butler.

"Your Grace, I'm terribly sorry, but you have visitors awaiting you in the drawing room. Lady Exeter's letter arrived this morning while you were out."

William nodded, eyeing his reflection in the hall mirror as he tried vainly to adjust his appearance into something less startling. At the gasp from the stairs, he saw Jensen rapidly descending.

"Sir! I cannot let you continue a moment longer—"

"You can, and you will. I have guests who need attention."

"They cannot require attention more than that neckcloth."

"Nevertheless, I shall attend to them. They have been kept waiting long enough."

Travers coughed. "I took the liberty of offering a light repast when you did not return for luncheon, Your Grace."

"Good." As if the mention of food was prompt enough, his stomach gave a growling protest.

"I shall tell Mrs. Bramford to prepare something for you, sir."

"And for the grooms. We have been out searching the woods."

"I had wondered," Jensen murmured, eyeing his dirty apparel with disfavor.

"It appears the woods hold a rock-wielding man, whose aim is either exceedingly poor, or exceedingly good, depending on whether he intended to wound me or simply cause poor Neptune a fright."

Both butler and valet gasped. He held up a hand to stem their questions. "I must greet our guests, change these clothes, then quickly eat something."

"Of course."

His servants hurried off, leaving a wide-eyed footman to open the door to the drawing room. William strode in, sweet pleasure stealing through him as the golden head lifted to greet him. "Good afternoon, ladies."

"Duke!" Two sets of rounded eyes met his gaze.

He bowed. "Please forgive my tardiness. I've only just returned from riding to learn I have the pleasure of such lovely guests."

He glanced at Lady Charlotte. Her cheeks were flushed, her gaze lowered, confirming his suspicions as to who had initiated their reappearance.

"Did my note not arrive?"

"This morning, it appears."

"Oh." The marchioness sat back in her seat, apparently perturbed. "I did not realize . . ."

"Merely thought me an inconsiderate host?" He raised a brow. Saw by her flush his hit had gone home. "I may allow myself to be called many things, madam, but an inconsiderate host is not one of them." He bowed. "Forgive me. I must exchange my riding dress for something more appropriate. I trust you shall be able to amuse yourselves for a few minutes more?"

"Of course, sir."

With another bow he escaped their speculative looks and raced up the stairs to change.

Jensen was waiting with a hot bath and fresh clothes, and a decidedly inquisitive manner. He answered as best he could but was unable to provide more detail than what he'd already shared.

No, he was not injured. Neither was poor Neptune. No, they had discovered nothing as to the identity of his assailant. Yes, they would be increasing nightly patrols. And no, he had no ideas as to either his unexpected guests' intentions on staying, or whom he suspected might be behind such an attack.

Nothing he was willing to admit aloud, anyway.

Less than half an hour after he'd last been in the drawing room, he returned, having wolfed down a plate of thickly sliced bread, cheese, and relish whilst scanning the letter the marchioness had written but a day previous.

"Good afternoon, again."

The marchioness nodded. "I'm pleased to see you dressed a trifle more appropriately."

"Mama!" her daughter whispered.

His smile grew fixed. "I am sorry if my manner displeased you, madam."

She seemed to consider how her words had been received, inclining her head. "Oh, what is a little dirt and dust between friends?"

"Indeed." He turned his attention to her daughter. "Lady Charlotte, I'm pleased to see you look well."

She murmured something noncommittal, any answer drowned out by her mother's voluble response. "Of course she looks well. Dear Charlotte has scarcely had a day's illness in her life."

It seemed the smile of "Dear Charlotte" grew strained.

"I'm pleased to hear it."

Her gaze touched his. "I apologize, sir, for leaving so abruptly before."

"I'm sure your poor cousin was grateful for your help. Tell me, how fares Hawkesbury and the countess?"

Her eyes filled with tears, telling him far more than her mother's convoluted chatter about the DeLancey chit, Patience, and the dowager countess.

He studied Charlotte, sorrow weaving between feelings of gladness at her return. Since the news, he'd barely stopped praying for his friends to find healing and comfort during this difficult time. But he could not help but be glad to have witnessed Charlotte's kind actions, which reflected a generous nature not evident in her parent.

The longer the marchioness chattered, the more edgy and restless he felt, the social niceties constraining him like a vise around his neck. Much as he longed to speak with Charlotte, he did not want to sit here parrying inanities from her mother while so much remained unknown. If they truly planned to stay here a few days as the marchioness's letter had proposed, was that wise? Would Charlotte be safe here? Was he safe here? Heaven forbid danger stray into her path.

"Duke?"

"I beg your pardon, madam. I was woolgathering."

"No doubt transfixed by the beauty of my dear daughter here."

He glanced at her dear daughter and smiled. "Charlotte is very beautiful," he said truthfully, his heart warming as the delicate blush filled those cheeks again.

He forced his hands to unclench, forced his whirling thoughts to focus. Here. Now. This was what was needed. To be still. To know. To hear God's voice.

What should he do?

"How is little Rose?" Charlotte asked.

He blinked. He'd scarcely thought about the child today. "She is well." He hoped.

"May I see her?"

"Of course." His spirits rose as Charlotte smiled her sweet smile at him. "Would you like to come see her with me now?"

"Yes, please." She glanced at her mother.

"Go, go. I declare all this travelling has made me quite long for a quiet rest."

As if she hadn't complained about enforced boredom only minutes ago. He swallowed a smile. Met an answering gleam in Charlotte's eyes.

"Then we shan't disturb you any longer." He turned to the younger lady, offering his arm. "My lady?"

The words seemed to echo around the room, resounding deep in his heart. How he longed for her to be *his* lady. How he wished she longed for that also.

She placed a hand on his arm, sending sweet fire through him. Good heavens, had it been so long? If such an innocent touch could affect him in such a way, what would Charlotte's kiss do to him?

As if sensing his thoughts, her pace quickened, and she hurried from the room, dropping his arm as they climbed the stairs. He tried to not let disappointment show. Forced his attention to the little girl above stairs. Why did Rose fascinate Charlotte so?

His companion stopped on the landing. "Sir?"

"I beg your pardon?"

Her smile was small. "You wanted to know why I care for little Rose?"

He'd said that aloud? His cheeks burned. What else had he unwittingly said?

She still studied him curiously, so he gathered he hadn't admitted anything about how tantalizing her touch was to him. Good thing, else she'd be running back to London with a scandalized Mama in tow. He forced himself to nod.

"I think she is sweet, so beautifully doll-like. And terribly sad that one so young should be forced to grow up motherless. And after seeing poor Lavinia . . ." She bit her lip.

Fresh guilt twisted his insides. Here he was neglecting a daughter when the Hawkesburys were mourning their childless state. How selfish, how unfeeling was he?

She stepped back. "Sir, I did not mean to upset you. I know you do not like references to your wife."

He frowned. "Who said so?"

"Your sister." She shook her head. "I'm sorry. I should return downstairs. We should not have returned, but Mama—" She twisted as if to leave.

"Please don't go." He stayed her with a hand.

She stilled.

In that moment, it felt as though the entire Abbey hushed, waiting with bated breath for his next words. He swallowed, feeling the moment to portend so much more. "I want you to stay."

Blue eyes met his, uncertainly.

"Please?"

How could one girl bring him to pleading? How could one young lady bring him, so powerful a personage that men of parliament and commerce sought his opinion on everything from Corn Laws to road development, nearly to his knees?

His heart thumped. He desired her. Wanted her to be his. But despite her mother's confidence, Charlotte was still too hesitant for words to be rashly spoken. He needed to guide her into trusting him, show her by his actions that he would be a faithful husband, cleaving only to her, should she do him the great honor and consent to be his wife.

She finally nodded.

His heart lifted, as once more the small hand rested on his forearm. Protectiveness surged. He would be hanged to see her hurt in any way. As they walked up the great stairs, he noted how she studied his painted ancestors, studied the frescoed ceilings. He longed to say, "All this can be yours, if you say the word."

He didn't.

Instead, he comforted himself with the knowledge that she fitted beside him wonderfully well, so much better than the taller Pamela, whose height seemed to have led her to look down on him in more ways than one. He led the way to the nursery and opened the door.

"Why, Lady Charlotte!" Martha said. "Oh, and Your Grace!"

He held a finger to his lips, hoping the nurse would not mention his sparse visits.

She nodded, clucking as Charlotte moved to the cradle to see the tiny girl.

"Hello, my sweet. How I have missed you."

And the tears on her cheeks turned his heart to slush, her soft compassion confirming what he had suspected long ago in London. Regardless of his sister's qualms, regardless of the assailant's threats, Lady Charlotte Featherington was indeed the only choice he could make.

Chapter Twenty-Six

THE NEXT MORNING, accompanied by nine chimes from the Great Hall's tall case clock, Charlotte hurried downstairs to the breakfast room. Sweet Rose wasn't the only part of the Abbey's heritage she had missed. But before gaining a chance to further examine the Canalettos, the duke entered. "Oh!"

"Good morning, Lady Charlotte. I trust you slept well."

"Oh, yes, thank you." Should she enquire about his sleep? Or was that too forward? Oh, that she could be natural with him, without all this awkwardness!

"I can recommend the ham."

She murmured thanks, moving to the sideboard laden with breakfast delicacies, conscious of his movements beside her.

"I thought Mama would be here."

The butler, up until now quiet in the corner, cleared his throat. "I believe Lady Exeter requested breakfast in her room."

"And my sister and Lord Ware are none too fond of early mornings."

"Early mornings?"

"Anything before noon."

She swallowed a smile, slipping into a seat not quite opposite the duke, so she need not face him and feel it necessary to hide from his too-discerning eyes.

Yesterday afternoon had been hard enough. She had detected a new warmth, a new tenderness, which only made her skittish, like a cat. What would she say when he made his offer? Though not quite three months, the time was drawing near, and still her heart remained unresolved. At times, like yesterday, when he seemed to have understood her eye roll at Mama's nonsense, she almost felt he was not all serious endeavor, was indeed someone she could learn to laugh with. Then there was that moment on the landing, when he'd looked at her with such tenderness, she had nearly expected him to suggest marriage then and there.

He filled her with confusion, not certainty, regardless of what Mama intended.

If she said yes, what would her life be like? Riding and admiring gardens were all very well, but could she really be happy being stuck in the country, as he seemed to prefer? What about her town friends, her visits to London's shops and amusements? But how could she ask about such things? She could not ask Mama; her answer was certain. And asking the duke would only reveal just how gauche she really was.

Charlotte swallowed. If she said no, what would happen then?

She peeked up and across at her dining companion. He seemed intently focused on his eggs. Morning light danced across his brows, revealing a strong nose and line of jaw similar to those exhibited in the paintings lining the halls. He would never be overly handsome, but his face held character.

She blinked. Perhaps the character he possessed was more important than his looks. Character, like his patience with Mama, his generous thoughtfulness to her. He might not have been a soldier, but she sensed he'd prove to be just as protective of her as Hawkesbury was of Lavinia.

Forcing her thoughts away from such disquieting ideas, she continued her surreptitious study. The morning sun burnished his hair with the slightest tinge of red, whilst revealing the shadows and lines of weariness marking his eyes. At once she knew that had she asked if he slept well, he would have replied in the affirmative, but been lying, not wishing to alarm her.

Her attention returned to her own plate. What had him so concerned? Was he worried about her, what she might say? She scolded herself. How self-centered was she to think his thoughts dwelled chiefly on her?

At the duke's clearing his throat she glanced up and met the warmth in his eyes, which brought heat to her cheeks. He smiled. "You seemed lost in thought."

"Oh! Ah . . ."

"Mrs. Bramford has a way with eggs, doesn't she?"

"I gathered from your earlier perusal of your plate that you appreciate her cooking as much as I."

"Touché."

His laughter, heard so rarely, sounded like warm honey, squeezing her heart with unmitigated sweetness.

"You wear that contemplative look once more, Lady Charlotte. Dare I wonder if it is smoked trout that has you so entranced?"

"Smoked—? Oh, no. I, er, was wondering about what to do today." She smiled hopefully. "I rather hope Bella wishes for a little jaunt?"

The light in his face fled as his brows knit. "You wish to take her riding?"

Why did he look concerned? "Well, I certainly wasn't planning on inviting her in for tea."

"I'm pleased to hear that." His lips curled to one side.

"But not pleased for me to ride her?"

"It's just . . ." He shook his head impatiently. "You may ride her, of course. She is yours, after all."

She stared at him. "Did you buy Bella for me?"

He nodded.

Her heart filled. How kind! How wonderfully generous—

"I just ask that you ride close to the Abbey. And take a groom, of course."

The warmth in her heart dissipated. "Why must I take a groom? If I stay close to the Abbey I can hardly become lost."

"It is not that."

Her brows rose. Then what was it?

As if sensing her confusion, he gave a small sigh. "I suppose I could escort you."

He supposed he could? "Oh, but I wouldn't want to disturb you from your many important duties." Thank goodness Mama was not here to hear the edge in her voice.

He studied her as if inspecting a new specimen, with a surprised look on his face. "Forgive me. I would be honored if you would accompany me on a ride today, Lady Charlotte."

Her soul rankled under his cool formality and mode of address. Feeling properly chastised for her pettish behavior, she said meekly, refusing to look him in the eye, "Thank you, sir."

He nodded, murmured something about changing into riding dress, and without further ado left her to the scattered remains of her breakfast, and her dignity.

Mama's delight at learning of Charlotte's plans far outweighed the enthusiasm displayed by the duke when she finally arrived at the stables. He ceased his low-voiced conference with the head groom and moved toward her. His smile could only be described as tight.

Her spirits dipped. Why did he seem so eager for her company at times, only to appear to wish her far away at others? Would he prove forever too complex for her to understand?

"Lady Charlotte, may I say you look charming?"

She nodded, unsmiling, perversely pleased to see his face dim when his attempt at gallantry fell flat. If he did not wish to ride with her, then why was he here?

His lips flattened, and he led her to where Bella stood waiting, saddled and ready to go.

He cupped his hands, she placed in her boot, and he boosted her into the saddle, his touch leaving her with a fluttery tremor somewhere in her midsection. Pushing these unwanted feelings aside, she arranged her skirts while speaking gently to Bella, familiarizing her with her voice, all the while conscious that the duke had resumed a similarly quiet conversation with his head groom.

She nudged Bella closer, trying to make it appear she wasn't listening, even as her ears strained to hear what of import was being uttered in the cool, deep tones.

"Stay on the perimeter . . . look out . . ."

Frowning, she met the duke's dark eyes, which flashed with something—annoyance with her? But why? What did he not want her to hear?

Charlotte nudged Bella from the stables. Glancing behind her, she was unsurprised to see Evans also mounting a horse. Her eyes widened. Was that a pistol strapped to his thigh?

"Evans!"

The duke's sharp bark brought a flush to the groom's cheeks and a hasty hiding of the weapon. Unease rippled through her.

He moved beside her now. "Pay no attention to Evans. We've had a spot of poaching in the forest, which is why we shall stay away from there."

She nodded, but the questions continued. Surely the duke had a team of gamekeepers whose job it was to protect the woods from intruders? The way Evans was riding, he seemed more occupying the role of protector, rather than searching the woods for any thieving rascal.

She forced a smile to her lips. "So may we ride to the lake?"

"We can ride any place you choose, my lady."

He said the last with a caress that curled heat through her insides. She tamped it down. "Except the woods."

His expression grew grave. "Except that."

She exhaled. "Very well. The lake it is."

And with a challenging smile and a firm nudge to Bella's belly, she raced him over the hill toward the water's edge.

※

On a normal day, he loved to watch her ride, loved to see her sit so tall and straight in the saddle, moving as one with her Bella. She seemed to revel in time spent away from her mother, able to relax, able to show him those fascinating glimpses of spirit as she had this morning in the breakfast room.

On a normal day, he would delight in wondering what caused her cheeks or smile to bloom, or better yet, in catching the trill of laughter that so enchanted him. He'd never expected she might share a similar sense of dry humor, and that realization would add a layer of sunshine to his soul. On a normal day.

But today was not a normal day. He'd woken too early, his restless night plagued by worry and concerns. Then when she'd suggested riding . . . he groaned.

Charlotte glanced at him, the small pucker in her forehead present since breakfast pushing deeper.

He forced a smile. "Do you approve the view?"

She leaned back, studying the landscape as an artist might examine a painting at Somerset House, steadily, as if appreciating the little nuances and details he'd loved all his life.

"It is a very fair prospect."

He smiled to himself. She sounded like someone quoting an illustrated handbook to a stately home. "And does madam approve the house?"

She glanced at him, amusement quirking her lips. "It possesses a charm both distinguished and warm, the marked symmetry pleasing to the eye."

He chuckled, pleased as she joined his laughter. "I suspect you have read a pictorial guide or two."

"I suspect from *your* comment, sir, that I am not the only one."

"Such wisdom in one so young."

Her head tilted, her blue eyes watched him carefully. "Do you think me so very young?"

He sensed the question was not one for which he could give a glib response. "You are younger than I, of course, but not too young, if you catch my meaning."

"I'm afraid I do not."

He swallowed. "I gather you would . . . understand things that a more innocent young lady might not."

"You do not think me innocent?" Her cheeks mottled.

His chest tightened. How to explain? "I do not think you naive."

Her gaze remained long and cool, and the tightness in his chest eased a fraction only when she nodded and glanced away. "If you do not think me entirely naive, then why will you not tell me why we are being accompanied by your groom?" She pointed to Evans, half-hidden by a tree.

His heart dropped. "I, er . . ."

Her brows rose.

"I explained about the poacher."

She snorted, a sound that made him want to smile, except he felt sure she would be offended. "Yes, you said something about a poacher, but I don't believe you."

He glanced away, thinking desperately of how to explain. He could not admit to the truth, not the whole of it, anyway . . .

"So you *do* think me a child."

His gaze cut to her. "I do not wish to alarm you."

"You think seeing your groom armed and within sight not alarming?"

With her eyebrows pushed up and that cool look on her face, he could see she would make the perfect duchess.

"Well?"

He smiled despite himself. She even had the tone correct; even Cressinda would approve. He gestured to the lake. "Shall we walk?"

"If you promise to explain."

"I promise."

He helped her dismount, warmth shooting through him as he clasped her slender waist to lift her down. He stepped away hurriedly. It would not do to stir up passions before everything was certain.

They walked closer to the lake, leading their horses. "Hartwell has been the unhappy recipient of several odd occurrences lately," he admitted.

"You mean the fire?"

He nodded. "And a road was vandalized. And yesterday's . . . incident."

"The poacher?" Her eyes narrowed.

Guilt speared his heart. "The person who should not have been there, yes."

Tell her this much, yes he would, but he would never admit to what said person had done. There was no reason to frighten her.

Her lips formed a perfect pout. He dragged his gaze away. *Heavenly Father, give me strength.* Hurrying to the water's edge, he studied the rocky ground, before selecting a small stone, and flinging it—one, two, three skips—until it sank into the water.

She studied him for a moment, then, before he realized her intention, she'd bent down and collected a small stone in her black-gloved hand, and with a flick of her wrist released it to spin across the water. One. Two. Three. Four skips. She glanced at him with what could only be called a smirk.

"Somehow I feel that is a skill of which your mother is blissfully unaware."

Her chuckle warmed his heart. "I find it important for Mama to remain oblivious to certain things at times, yes."

"I suppose your brother taught you such things?"

She nodded. "At my grandmother's estate in Salisbury." Her eyes followed a duck's path as it settled onto the water. "Henry never did like it when his stones found the ducks. I don't believe the ducks cared for his throws overly, either," she added thoughtfully.

"You are full of surprises."

"And you are full of mysteries."

"But have I not been led to believe that you are fond of mysteries?"

"Some mysteries, perhaps. But I cannot enjoy feeling like I'm being treated as a child simply because there might be unpalatable truths. It was my understanding that I was to come here to learn if we were compatible." Her cheeks glowed. "I understand you might not appreciate such plain speaking, but I have learned from my cousin just how important that can be. And I cannot subscribe to a relationship when I'm being treated as a child."

"I am not—"

She made an impatient gesture. "You are. We might as well keep skipping stones along the surface for all the truth you reveal. Surely a good marriage cannot exist without getting to know the other person's depths?"

He stared at her. How had such a chit fathomed the inexplicable nature of his ill-fated marriage? She was right. He'd barely known Pamela, had never known her interests, let alone cared about them beyond how they suited his purpose. Fresh remorse twisted within. Perhaps if he had shown more interest, she would not have sought companionship elsewhere. "You speak wisely."

"Astounding, isn't it?"

Again the sardonic edge caught him by surprise. "You have quite a way with words when your mother is not around."

"You disapprove?"

"I'm not sure."

Her lips pursed. Then she sighed. "You are very careful, sir."

"Careful?"

"You give little away. How can I know . . . ?" She swiped her glistening brow. "I've seen those who marry according to rank and duty, without affection, and their marriage is like two horses running side by side yet never properly harnessed. I do not wish to marry merely for duty's sake, simply because an accident of birth made me a marquess's daughter. I wish to enjoy a passionate marriage properly harnessed by love, like that shared by Lavinia and the earl."

He stared at her. Were they really having this conversation?

Her cheeks crimsoned. "I'm sorry. I said too much . . . Oh." She turned, hurrying away.

For a moment he couldn't breathe as the realization of what she was saying finally hit him. Hope lit his heart. She would never have raised this topic had she not felt something.

"Charlotte, please." He hastened after her.

She stilled. "You called me Charlotte."

"You've taken me by surprise." He sighed. "You rightly ascertained I'm not used to such blunt speaking. Let me be equally frank. I have no wish to become attached to someone who will seek romance elsewhere. Having been through it once, I have no desire to repeat the experience. I . . . I have never found it easy to be open with my feelings, but that does not mean I do not feel. I, too, wish for affection within marriage. I understand you might see me as too old or aloof or too serious, but I—"

"Do not wish to be hurt again."

How did she know this? It was like she could read his innermost thoughts. "Yes."

He glanced away, saw Evans hovering at the corner of his peripheral vision. The words wrung from his soul. "I also have no wish for you to be hurt."

"Me?" She glanced from him to Evans then back, eyes wide. "You think someone does not wish us to be betrothed?"

"Perhaps. I do not know. I *do* know I could not stand it if you were harmed."

She stared at him a moment, then nodded decidedly, as a gentleman might buy a horse at Tattersall's. "Thank you."

"For what?"

"For trusting me to cope with the truth."

What was he supposed to say to this extraordinary young lady? "You're welcome?"

She smiled in a way that lit up her face, igniting the dreams of his heart.

On their long walk back, as their conversation touched on everything from poetry to roses to botanical specimens, and they seemed to step ever closer to friendship, he found himself marveling again at how God could have arranged this union between two such different souls, when it seemed as perfect as if he had planned it all himself.

William glanced at the groom, who wore an air of relief as he rode back to the stables.

Perhaps God who arranged all things to work out perfectly might even deliver them from the threat that still unnerved his soul.

CHAPTER TWENTY-SEVEN

A RASPING SOUND tugged Charlotte from sleep. Her gaze flew to where Sarah stood near the windows, newly opened curtains spilling sunlight through the bedchamber. "Good morning."

"Oh! Good morning, my lady." Sarah bobbed a curtsy.

She smiled. No wonder Sarah seemed surprised: her mistress, waking early two days in a row, in a good mood?

"Would you like your hot chocolate now?"

"No, thank you," she said, pushing aside the bedcovers. "I thought I might breakfast again downstairs."

Anticipation fizzed through her, like a skyrocket at Vauxhall Gardens. Last night she had barely managed to sleep, tossing and turning between gladness and chagrin at her behavior. Had she been too bold? But she could not regret honesty. And if it helped the duke realize how much she desired affection . . .

What would he say today? She'd had the impression last night he almost regarded her as a playful kitten, looking at her with that half smile, as if wondering what she might do or say next. She was conscious of a subtle power over him in this; conscious, too, that such power demanded she behave in a manner that would lead to his good.

"Which dress would you like to wear today?" Sarah asked, moving to the wardrobe. "The cream or the green lawn?"

Charlotte peered outside. Not a cloud marred the bowl of vivid blue. "The green lawn should be lighter if this heat continues."

As she succumbed to Sarah's dressing of her person and hair, her thoughts returned to last night. Last night, when the duke had showed her yet another side, laughing, engaging in spirited discussions as they read poetry together while Mama dozed by the fire. Perhaps she had misjudged him, and the serious demeanor he carried was simply a mask he wore to hide his depths. She blushed again, remembering the outlandish things she'd said by the lake, almost like she wasn't speaking but someone else spoke through her. Yet more evidence that he must be good-hearted indeed to put up with such a minx.

As soon as Sarah finished her ministrations, Charlotte hurried down the steps, flitting past the morning room to the breakfast room, to find it—

Empty.

A footfall preceded the butler's entrance. "Good morning, my lady."

"Good morning, Travers."

She shifted, half-poised to leave. Should she stay? Had the duke already eaten? If he hadn't, would he soon? How could she find him without making it look obvious?

"Shall you be dining this morning?"

"I . . . " She bit her lip. Stay? Go?

"His Grace sends his regrets but he was called away on an urgent matter and cannot dine with you this morning."

"Oh." Spirits sinking, she murmured her thanks and blindly filled her plate.

She slumped into a seat that looked out across the rose gardens, before gazing at her plate. Her nose wrinkled. "Ugh." How had kippers landed there?

"Did you say something, my lady?"

She shook her head, carefully scraped the smoked fish to one side, and nibbled on a piece of uncontaminated toasted bread instead, fighting the disappointment of dining alone.

How silly to look forward to being with someone who, until recently, she could not bear to be alone with. Now it seemed she hungered for his presence, to see him smile. The fizzling disappointment was almost like that which she'd experienced when she'd been packed off to Gloucestershire with Lavinia to remove her from Lord Markham's influence. Funny. She hadn't thought about him for the longest time. She wondered how he was.

Propping a hand under her chin, she studied the prospect outside the windows.

The gardens beckoned, the plump heads of red and pink rose bushes swaying gently in the morning breeze, as if begging her to join them. She hurried her toast and tea in a manner sure to displease Mama were she present, and went outside. The gardens were sweet with heavy perfume. She breathed in deeply, then glanced around. There were so many, surely no one would notice if she picked one.

She leaned into a red bloom and was about to break the stem, when a coughed interruption made her jump. Whirling with a smile, she stopped. "Oh!"

The grizzled gardener frowned at her. "You weren't about to take that, were you, miss?"

"Er, this flower, you mean?"

"The rose."

"I know it's a rose. And I don't think the duke would mind, do you? After all"—she swept a hand across the gardens—"he has so many."

"That he does, but only because he don't be picking them all the time."

She fixed him with her sweetest smile. "Forgive me, but he led me to believe that roses needed regular trimming to maintain their flush of flowers."

He coughed. "That may be, but they should only be picked by an expert."

She raised a brow. "An expert picker of flowers?"

"Someone who knows how."

"I know how." Before he could stop her, she'd reached across and broken the dainty stem. "See?"

He closed his jaw, muttering something under his breath. "I see indeed."

She drank in the perfume deeply. "So beautiful. Have a sniff, Mr. . . . ?"

"Callinan, miss."

She shoved the bloom under his nose. "Go on, Mr. Callinan. Is it not very lovely?"

"Aye. The former mistress planted them. She said they were her favorite plants."

For some reason, this information made her squirm inside. "The duke's wife?"

"His mother."

"Oh." The squirming feeling dissipated. Well, if his *mother* had liked them . . . She smiled.

The frost in his face seemed to thaw. "Shall I pick you some, miss?"

"Perhaps in a little while. Tell me, were you responsible for those lovely blooms sent to Hawkesbury House recently?"

"Aye." His brow creased. "His Grace asked me."

Yet further evidence of the duke's kind and thoughtful nature. "My cousin was most appreciative. Now, what is the name of these pinks here?"

The breeze had settled into stillness by the time she and Mr. Callinan had conducted a thorough tour of the roses. She pointed to an apricot rose. "Hawkesbury House has a different variety of these, I believe. Very pretty, with creamy edges, and the most delicate scent."

"Hawkesbury House, you say?" He scratched his chin. "I heard about their roses. Perhaps we could get some here. I'm sure His Grace would not mind."

"His Grace would not mind what?"

The quiet voice spun her around, scattering the flowers she held. "Oh!"

The duke bowed, his manner, his dress, all that was elegant. "Good morning, my lady."

His words, with just the slightest emphasis on the *my*—or was that simply her foolish imagination?—coupled with that intent smile in his eyes, sent a delicious shiver up her spine.

To hide her confusion, she bent to collect her flowers, ducked her head, banging his in the process. "Oh!"

He straightened, rubbing his head in matching action to hers. "Forgive me. I trust you're not hurt?" At her response in the negative, he gave a rueful-looking smile. "How clumsy I am this morning."

Only then did she notice the graze on his hand. She glanced up at him, saw the smile in his eyes disappear, and the gentle shake of his head. She peered past his shoulder and saw a man on horseback. Another guard? Only this man, positioned closer, was not Evans. Fear plucked her heart.

"Perhaps Lady Charlotte, if you have had your fill of the gardens, you might accompany me inside?" He held out an arm, nodded to Callinan. "If you would be so kind as to ensure our guest has a bouquet large enough for her tastes, I'd be grateful."

"Yes, sir." The gardener touched his forehead, nodding as Charlotte thanked him.

When they passed from earshot she said, "How did you hurt yourself?"

He shook his head, his expression grim. "That is nothing to concern yourself with."

"But—"

"Charlotte, is it your intention to argue every time we speak?"

Hurt cramped her chest. She had only intended to show her concern. She withdrew her hand, hurried her steps. Heard his sigh.

"I have no wish to argue with you."

She halted. Waited for him to draw beside her. Glanced up, saw his strained features. Her heart softened. "I wish you would trust me."

"I do." The line creasing his brow lifted, as if he were surprised at that revelation. "I *do*."

He smiled his charming smile, causing her heart to glow. He leaned a little closer. "I just—"

"Charlotte!" She turned to see her mother moving toward them. "There you are. Oh, thank you, sir, for bringing her to us. She can be such a naughty girl, running away without so much as a by-your-leave."

She stiffened as the duke cleared his throat. "Lady Exeter, do you really regard your daughter in such terms?"

"I . . . er, of course not."

"Then why speak so dismissively?"

Mama's smile dimmed. "I . . . well, I know she'll always be safe in *your* company, sir."

"Safe?" He frowned. "What have you heard?"

"I beg your pardon?"

"You spoke as though she might be in danger."

"Charlotte? No. The only danger she has is in running away."

"Mama!"

Charlotte glanced at the duke, whose expression had tightened. He refused to look at her, bowing instead to her mother. "Perhaps you might find sufficient amusement in the conservatory. It is a new addition, and contains a number of plant species from tropical climes. I'm sure Callinan would be happy to point out things," he continued as the gardener drew near, arms filled with flowers.

"Oh! But are you not planning to ride again, Charlotte?" her mother said with a coquettish smile. "After all, you had such an enjoyable time yesterday whilst riding with the duke."

This was said with such a hopeful look at their host Charlotte could only cringe.

And cringe again when he said blandly, "My apologies, but I cannot today. My horse is lame."

"But you have others surely?"

"They are all unfit." Anger flitted across his face then was gone. "I'm afraid riding today is quite out of the question."

"How disappointing."

With a bow and muttered excuses, the duke left them, leaving her to a tour of the conservatory and the gardener's grunted explanations, and her mother's fluster and loudly whispered comments about the duke's peculiar behavior.

⁂

She had to leave.

William hurried back to the stables, determination hounding every step. He had to make her leave. She was not safe. If the person could get at the horses, then they could get at whoever was outside. Which meant the only safe place for her was inside or, better still, far away.

She had to leave.

She was dangerous to his heart. Each time he felt himself begin to trust, a comment would spear his soul, reminding him why it was dangerous to put too much stock in other people. The marchioness's comment about her daughter's inclination to run away had arrowed fear through him. For if they were to wed and she ran away . . .

"Your Grace! Come quick."

William picked up his pace, entering the stables at an undignified trot.

In the far stall, poor Neptune writhed, his hooves thrashing the stable doors as he worked to expel the poison from his system. Emotion clogged William's throat. He swallowed. "How is young Pattinson?"

Evans released a loud breath. "Lucky you were there to get him out in time."

"That wasn't luck, nor any great skill on my part. I think we both know who should be thanked for that particular episode."

"Well, I thank the good Lord above you were here. And I'm sure Pattinson does, too. Well, he will once the swelling goes down."

"Mrs. Bramford was able to help?"

"Aye. She wants him resting. The doctor will doubtless tell the same." Evans eyed his grazed hand. "Her salve will work for you, too."

"And I'll get that seen to as soon as possible."

But he did not want to run the risk of distressing his houseguests more than he could help.

He hastened to the veterinarian, packing up his bag. "Mr. Noyce, thank you for coming."

"We've been able to save them, but whoever stuck that sorghum in with their oats should be strung up."

William jerked a nod. The culprit would be lucky to escape the ire of the stable hands, if he were ever found. "So you're sure there's nothing more we can do?"

"Like I said earlier, sir, there's nothing you can do. We have to let nature run its course. It's just a good thing your men were here early enough to see the problem and get them walking before any of them had sickened too much."

"Thank God for Evans."

"Thank the Almighty for more than that. Young Pattinson has a lot to be thankful for with your quick thinking, Your Grace."

He lifted a shoulder in a half shrug. "I only did what anyone would do. Pattinson didn't know the mare would turn on him like that."

Sorrow panged again. He didn't wish to admit it, but sweet Bella had shown her true colors, proving her unsuitable for Charlotte's use anymore. It was such a shame, when her joy in riding Bella was so evident. But he couldn't run the risk of the horse hurting Charlotte. Couldn't run the risk of anything hurting her.

He reiterated his thanks to Mr. Noyce and his men, and turned back to the Abbey, taking a moment to study the great building. Would it be secure? With so many windows and entrances, someone could get inside quite easily. His heart thudded painfully. Would Charlotte be safe? Was she safe right now? He knew Travers could be trusted to lock up well at night, but should he begin posting guards within as well as without? Or were such musings more fit for a madman? Investigations had proved Wrotham to be on the Continent. If not him, then who? *Heavenly Father, what do I do?*

The prayer hovered unceasingly, as he spent the next couple of hours discussing matters with Hapgood, dictating letters, examining ledgers, checking his calendar to schedule another visit to Barrack, wishing a thousand times he could spend his time with Charlotte instead.

Charlotte. How had the guards he'd thought posted around his heart been knocked asunder by such loveliness?

Charlotte. He groaned. *Heavenly Father, what do I do?*

The burden of a hundred responsibilities and unanswered questions seemed impossible. He slumped over his desk, burying his face in his hands.

CHAPTER TWENTY-EIGHT

IT WAS ONE thing to be invited by their host to visit the conservatory to inspect the hothouse flowers. It was quite another to be made to feel by his sister that Charlotte's company was unwanted, or as Cressinda put it so delicately, "Rather a distraction from his important duties."

Charlotte pushed to her feet, offering a stiff smile to the woman sitting opposite. "If you'll please excuse me?"

"But where are you going, Charlotte?" Mama demanded.

She shot her a look she hoped appeared demure. "Surely a lady may retire momentarily without divulging every detail?"

"Very well, then," Mama said crossly. "Sad mismanagement, somewhere."

Charlotte hurried from the room, cheeks heating. Not that she cared what Cressinda and her foppish husband thought. If only Mama was not *quite* so unbridled in her comments. Sighing, she ascended the great stairs, one hand trailing the smooth wood, one flight, then two, up to visit baby Rose. But when she knocked, the cranky nurse barred the door, saying the child was sleeping. With a sigh, she conceded she would not be granted admittance and went downstairs again.

She paused at the landing, glancing out to where the stable yards were. Why, there was Neptune! He wasn't lame at all! Why had the duke said he was? She leaned against the glass, one hand pressed on either side of her face, and watched the horse kick out violently.

No, definitely not lame. But definitely not well, either. She had never seen any of the duke's horses so agitated. She watched a moment longer as the stable hands struggled to keep him from bolting, the combined efforts of two young men finally enough to constrain him back into the stables.

Her mouth dried. Had something happened to the horses? Who would do such a thing? *Lord, please protect them. Give the duke wisdom.*

Upon descending to the Great Hall, she paused, not anxious to return to the others. Restlessness wove through her, fueling a desire to somehow help. But what could she do? She could not walk the horses—he had stable boys for that. She could not strap on a pistol and chase poachers. But surely there was something she *could* do?

She stopped at the exhibit cases, eyeing the one containing the specimen from the Antipodes. What had the duke called it? A banded wallaby, was it? She strained to remember the inadvertently sad little story he'd mentioned. Something about his father, and a jest she hadn't thought funny. She turned to study the large paintings presiding over the hall. The dark-eyed, dark-haired dukes of Hartington lined up, watching her, dressed in Elizabethan ruffs, austere Jacobean robes, the ornate lacy neckcloths of the Georgian-era seventh and eighth dukes. In each one, the Abbey was positioned in the background. She peered more closely. In each one, she recognized the stag, the family emblem, as she recalled.

Now she remembered. The ratlike little wallaby, with its black stripes and long tail had been a joking gift from the eighth duke to his son as a jest about his height. How cruel! Indignation heated her chest, pricked her eyes. Is that why the duke tried so hard at so many things? Was it an attempt to prove himself? That while he might not bear the height and heft of his predecessors, he wished to show his mind and talents still valuable for something?

Sympathy melded with understanding, tugging at her heartstrings. Poor man. *Dear* man. What could she do?

She sank into a seat and thought very long and very hard for a good many minutes. When she finally rose, purpose lay in her tread as she exited through the side door. She was going to find him and tell him exactly what she thought.

"But miss, he is not here." Evans mopped his brow. "He would have my hide if he knew you were out here. He said on no account—"

"On no account was I to visit the stables, correct?"

He nodded miserably. "The horses ain't well."

"But not lame?"

"One is."

So he hadn't lied completely.

He sighed. "Kicked too hard and hurt her foot."

"Not Bella?"

"Aye. I'm sorry, my lady, but she's proved to have a wicked little temper."

"Surely he is not going to get rid of her?"

Evans glanced at his feet, shuffling, but did not answer.

"He is planning to get rid of her! But why? What made her act in such a way? She's always been such a sweet girl."

"I can't rightly say, my lady."

"Can't say, or won't say?"

Her tone must have been enough like Grandmama's for him to finally meet her gaze. "I think it be best you speak with him."

"Very well." She nearly flounced off when she remembered something else. "The duke. Was he injured earlier?"

His eyebrows shot up.

Heat filled her cheeks, and she hurried on. "I noticed his hand was grazed."

Why she felt she had to explain herself to a servant was something she did *not* want to investigate. How ridiculous!

He shuffled again. "He had to haul out young Pattinson when Bella began kicking him."

"Oh no!"

"He only just got him free before Bella nearly splintered the walls where he'd been."

"Oh my goodness!"

"Aye. Pattinson's been thanking his lucky stars His Grace was there."

"He'd do better to thank the Lord above."

A grin cracked the man's weathered face. "Funny. That's what His Grace said."

She nodded, inordinately pleased to have said something the duke had agreed with. "He is something of a hero, it would seem."

"Aye, that's plenty certain."

Resentment at hearing her Bella was to be disposed of had nearly dissolved by the time she returned to the house. She walked around the east wall, careful to avoid being seen from the conservatory's great glass windows, where she hoped Mama and the others still remained. No doubt Mama had already dispatched a servant to discover why Charlotte was taking so long.

As she rounded the corner, she glanced in at the long window on her left. And stopped. The duke sat in what must be his study, head bowed, clasped in his hands.

Pity wrung her heart. He looked so alone, so sad, so . . . defeated.

Her steps slowed as she made her way through the front entrance and across the checkered floor of the great hall.

"Oh, Lady Charlotte! There you are," Sarah said, hurrying forward. "Your mother is most anxious about you."

"That is hardly new."

"Yes, well." Sarah shivered, glancing over her shoulder. "I've been hearing bad things about this place," she said in a lowered voice.

"What kinds of things?"

"I shouldn't say . . ."

"But you will."

"Oh, my lady! I do not want to be like one of these foolish women in those novels you read, but I can't help thinking this place is cursed."

"Cursed? That's ridiculous. The duke has simply had a run of bad luck, that is all."

Sarah looked doubtful, and Charlotte did not want to stand here all day listening to the silly creature's fears.

"Please inform Mama that I've decided to have a rest."

"But you are not."

But she *was* taking a rest from Mama's continual sniping. Charlotte smiled. "You need only say I told you to inform her that I am." Which would mean Sarah would not technically lie.

"But—"

"Oh, go away, Sarah. Tell her the truth only if she wants to know more."

"But—"

"Now!"

As she watched Sarah retreat, misgivings filled her. How could she ever aspire to be a duchess if her own servants refused to listen? Why did people pay her no heed?

Before she could be questioned by anyone else, she slipped past the stoic footmen, round the corner to where she judged the study to be. A man came out. Mr. Hapgood? She nodded at his murmured greeting, and then pretended interest in the small glass case nearby. A coati, she read on the label. A type of raccoon from Brazil.

She glanced over her shoulder and, judging she was unobserved, stepped forward.

※

A thousand butterflies lit the sky. Red, and white, and pink, and lavender. William kept his eyes closed as the images danced across his vision, the sun picking out the jeweled colors and their softer hues. He breathed in. Out. Forced the whirling thoughts to still.

Be still and know that I am God . . .

Still. Be. God.

He bowed his head, his conscience assailed. How long since he'd sat trying to hear God's voice? He prayed, he questioned, but how long since he'd actually waited for an answer?

Heavenly Father . . .

Despair pressed against him, demanding his attention. His failures soared like scavenging birds arising from their blood-smeared feast. Never good enough. Not strong enough. Not tall enough. Not man enough.

Heavenly Father . . .

Still nothing. No quiet voice. No response. He really should get back to the piles of work demanding attention, but he couldn't. Didn't want to. Had nothing left to offer. No energy. No hope.

Instead, the torturous dream continued.

Her. Smiling at him. Holding out a hand. A hand he pressed to his lips. Causing the strangest of sensations to fill his body, before her face twisted into disapproval and disdain, leaving him bereft, feeling hollowed inside.

Heavenly Father . . .

He breathed in again. Hoping breath would push out fears. In. Out. In. Roses. He could smell roses and lilies now.

Now he could hear music, a soft lilting sound that brought a measure of comfort to his soul. He breathed in again, more deeply, the respite from his pressure too brief.

The music continued, louder now, more insistent. Music? Insistent?

Was he going mad?

He cracked open one eye. Two. Dropped his hands and nearly fell from his chair. Forced his shaky legs to stand. "Charlotte!"

Concern suffused her features as she hurried close. "Oh, sir, what is wrong?"

He shook his head, his hands clenching the sides of the desk. "There is nothing—"

"Oh, please don't treat me as a child."

His previous fatigue peeled away as she moved closer still. He swallowed. "Why are you here?"

Her lips curved. "You wanted me to come. You said so yesterday."

"I mean here, in my study."

"I know it's not quite proper to be here, but I want . . . I want you . . ."

His heart thumped. She wanted him?

"I want you to not despair."

Pain flickered across his chest. She didn't want him. Of course she didn't.

Perhaps it was best if she left. She'd be safer at home. He turned away, eyes smarting. "You should leave."

She did not answer.

"Please, Charlotte. For your own sake. I will speak with your mother, but please leave."

Another long moment, then a soft, "You do not want me?"

He waited for the rest of her sentence. When it did not come, he turned, saw the look of rejection in her eyes. It was all he could do not to crush her to his chest and beg her to stay. He forced his head to shake. "You must not stay. I could not bear it if— if—"

He could not finish, could only watch helplessly as she drew nearer still, an arm's length away.

"You do not wish to marry me?"

"No! That is . . ." His mind raced. How to make her understand? "I cannot hold you to anything. None of this was to your liking, I know. But fool that I am, I dared hope—"

"Hope what, sir?"

He swallowed. "Hope that one day you might not hold me in such dislike, and find it in your heart to like me just a little."

"But I do like you." She did? "Even if you insist on removing Bella."

"You know about that?"

"Yes."

"Then you know someone is trying to harm me. You see, I cannot let you stay, not if it brings you into harm's way, too." He groaned. "I should remove Rose, too."

She moved to where he stood beside his chair, her blue eyes holding him prisoner. "You do this often, don't you? Sacrifice your needs and wants for those of other people." She sighed.

"I . . . I'm afraid I don't understand."

Her mouth opened. Closed. She drew herself up a fraction more. "Do you . . . do you believe we could be happy together?"

"Yes! One day. When this is over—"

"Then I am saying"—she paused, as if collecting her courage—"if . . . if you were inclined to reiterate your offer from before, then . . . then I'm of a mind to accept it."

The last near-cold embers of hope suddenly fanned into flame. Surely she wasn't saying what he thought she was?

Her smile seemed sweetly unsure. "But only if you ask me."

This was not what he'd imagined, not where he'd wished. He'd dreamed of proposing down among the roses, or in the little red pavilion in the Oriental garden. Good heavens, he'd even have settled for the drawing room in Grosvenor Square, but not here. Not among piles of paper, and everything that screamed of his desperation.

He studied her, emotions racing, clashing inside. He *should* say no. He *should* send her on her way. But . . .

He held out a hand. "Come with me?"

She nodded and placed her hand in his.

❧ Chapter Twenty-Nine

Charlotte's heart raced. Her stupid impulsiveness had nearly back-fired, the duke by no means certain to hear her out. She followed along as he strode past the footman, giving no sign when Travers called his name. She only knew the feel of her hand in his made her feel so safe, and wanted, and protected, and gave this sense that whatever obstacles they faced together could be defeated. They walked through the front doors, down the steps, across the close-cropped lawn to the rose garden. In the middle, beside the fountain, he led her to a rustic bench. He gestured to it, and she sank onto it, grateful for the chance to sit, as her legs felt suddenly shaky.

This was it.

She took a deep breath, inhaling the sweet scent of roses. Instead of speaking, the duke pulled out a small knife, and then proceeded to cut three roses. One white. One pink. One red.

He presented the white rose. "Do you know what this symbolizes?"

Of course she did. Every young lady knew the language of flowers. "Innocence."

"And purity. But it can also signify faithlessness and death." For a moment his eyes shuttered then he held out the pink rose. "And this?"

"Friendship."

A fleeting smile. "I seem to remember you once suggested such a thing was necessary for a marriage to succeed." He displayed the red rose. "And this one?"

She swallowed. "Love."

"True love. Deep, abiding love."

The words hung between them, challenging, assuring.

Did she love him? Well, perhaps never in that foolish way with Lord Markham, but she respected and esteemed him. Deeply. Wasn't esteem close enough to love? Memories rose of the love Lavinia shared with Lord Hawkesbury, the affection enhancing something deeper, something more powerful, a commitment to protect and persevere, to seek the best interest of the other, no matter what. A blessing, like she hoped her actions might bring to the duke. Was that enough?

"I know you are innocent." He placed the white rose on the seat, held out the pink. "You said a few minutes ago that you liked me. I hope that means I have your friendship."

Heat flushed her cheeks. "Yes."

He laid down the pink next to the white, still holding the red rose. His dark eyes studied her carefully. "But what I want to know, what I *need* to know is, are your affections engaged elsewhere?"

She swallowed. In choosing the duke she was choosing the better man. Lord Markham was impossible, any thought of him to be ruthlessly quashed. She could do so; she *would* do so. She *had* chosen so when she'd seen the duke's despair through the window and determined to do the one thing she could to help him. This she *could* do. "My affections . . . are only for you."

She held out her hand. He wrapped his fingers around hers, gazed upon her hand like he might a prized treasure. When he next glanced up, his eyes kindled with emotion. "My dearest Charlotte, will you do me the greatest of honors and consent to be my wife?"

Her mouth was suddenly dry. She swallowed. Swallowed again. "I will."

"Truly?" Light filled his eyes.

She nodded.

His charming smile lit his face. "I never dared dream, never dared hope—" He pressed a soft kiss to the back of her hand, another to her palm. "You have made me the happiest of men."

As his head bowed, she was struck by the desire to smooth down his hair. Would he think such a thing terribly forward? But they were now betrothed, after all.

She reached up a hand, stroked the auburn highlights. Heard his breath catch.

"I'm sorry, sir—"

"William. Please call me William."

"I'm sorry, William," her cheeks grew hot, "but it was mussed—"

"Don't apologize, my dearest Charlotte." His lips lifted.

She offered a tentative smile in return.

"Oh, how I love you." He leaned close, closer, and suddenly his lips were on hers, and she was drowning in a dozen sweet sensations that gripped her body. Oh . . .

His arm stole around her back, and he tugged her closer still. His lips were warm, tenderly possessive. Heat kindled deep within. She was kissing him, he was kissing her—

"Charlotte!"

She pulled back hurriedly, bumping noses as she did. She met the amusement in his eyes then saw the storm in her mother's. "Hello, Mama."

"What do you think you are doing?" she snapped, turning to the duke. "I demand you release my daughter immediately."

His smile widened. "Do you refer to my betrothed?"

Betrothed. Charlotte fought the shiver.

Mama gasped. "Really? You are finally, truly engaged?"

William's hand slipped to firmly hold Charlotte's. "Your daughter has consented to be my wife, yes."

He smiled at Charlotte, and the light suffusing his features curled warmth through her, making her so glad she had found courage enough to approach him. Surely the shadows would lift now, and he could be happy.

"Oh, my dear!" Mama tugged Charlotte up into an embrace, before smiling broadly at the duke. "Oh, sir! Forgive me. I just never dreamed you would propose in such a public place."

"Mama, this is hardly Hyde Park."

"It is hardly discreet, either. Why, anyone could have come up that drive and seen you carrying on in such a fashion! How a daughter of mine—"

"Forgive me, madam. I should have been more circumspect, but I got swept away." His smile tugged as his gaze dropped to Charlotte's lips, where she could still feel the taste of his, a combination of hope and honey, coffee and leashed passion.

"Yes, well, I would have thought a man of your experience would have had a little more sense about these things. But never mind—"

"Thank you, madam, I shan't."

"Oh, but this is wondrous news indeed! My heartiest congratulations, sir, and for you, too, Charlotte. I knew you were so pretty for good purpose—oh! We shall have to return to London!"

"I beg your pardon?"

"For Charlotte's wedding clothes, of course. Tell me, when do you think of setting the date?"

The duke murmured something noncommittal, squeezing Charlotte's hand again as Mama's long-cherished plans finally bubbled to the surface. "It should be London, of course. I must write at once . . . marriage settlements already signed . . . satin and lace . . . oh, so happy!"

When Mama finally hurried back to the house, the duke—William!—turned to Charlotte, tenderness in his eyes. "Thank you, my dear. You have made me the happiest man on earth."

Her smile was automatic. But was she the happiest woman? Inside, she felt strangely flat, the triumphant gleam in her mother's eyes at Charlotte's capitulation to her wishes having dispersed the earlier joyous fizzing sensations like a vapor. Perhaps she was not to live by her feelings, but surely love should feel more assured than this?

And when she returned to the house, Sarah's odd reaction only reinforced her unease.

"Well, I'm sure congratulations should be in order, my lady."

But Sarah's doubtful look made believing her good wishes quite impossible.

"Is something wrong, Sarah?"

"No, my lady."

"I don't understand. Back in London you said how good the duke is. Have you changed your opinion?"

"That was before I knew."

"Knew what? What do you mean?"

"The maids, they were talking. Seemed the night his wife was birthing he refused to see her. He refused to acknowledge that child as his until you came along."

"But he believed her to have been unfaithful." Her mind flicked to the white rose.

"God forbid he ever thinks such things about you. They said he was awful angry, with a fiend's own jealous temper." Sarah shook her head. "I don't trust the quiet ones. No, much better to be open-like, like Master Henry. One never doubts where one stands with a man such as he."

Or a man such as Lord Markham. She could almost hear the unspoken words as easily as she could feel the poisonous doubt steal in. She could see the duke's face as he asked her if her affections were elsewhere. Would he continue to believe her? Charlotte pulled her spine straight. "Sarah, you need to stop. I do not want to hear such things about the man I've just pledged to marry."

"Oh, but miss, have you asked him about the duel?"

What?

"Aye, now you look at me like that. One of Lord Ware's maids heard him talking. Seems Lord Ware was *at* the duel—"

"No."

"Yes! Seems the duke called Wrotham out but he denied it so they met at Bishoplea. The duke wounded him then forced him to leave for France. They say he's a crack shot at Manton's."

The *duke* a crack shot at Manton's shooting gallery? Where Henry liked to boast about shooting wafers? "You must be mistaken."

"Am I? You should ask His Grace about it. Or at the very least, ask Lord Ware."

Something cold rippled over her soul. Sarah sounded so certain.

No. She shook her head, refusing to believe it.

Refused to believe he was anything but the kind man she had always seen.

Refused to believe scurrilous rumors, scandalous lies, even if the people had known him for so much longer, even if he'd once admitted to his temper being the worst of his faults, even if—

No! She *refused* to think badly of him.

Her eyes filled with tears. Who was this man she'd agreed to marry?

Oh, what had she done?

CHAPTER THIRTY

THE HOPE FILLING his heart leaked out the next day when he saw the way Charlotte barely looked at him. Gone was the impudent chit who had entranced him into proposing, leaving instead a mere shadow of such a girl. He wondered what her mother had said to her last night. Or had it been his kiss that frightened her so? His heart panged. He best master his desire and give her no reason to cry off.

From across the breakfast table, the marchioness glanced from him to Charlotte's averted eyes, before smiling broadly at him. "Hartington, I'm afraid we must return as soon as possible."

"Of course." He inclined his head. "I shall arrange for the carriage to be at your disposal. Will tomorrow be convenient?"

"This afternoon would be preferable."

He blinked. "Of course."

"Thank you."

"I . . . er, trust that nothing has occurred to make you wish to speed your departure?"

"No, no, not at all," she said, smiling in an overly bright manner. "Charlotte is merely anxious to return to London for her fittings."

He glanced at Charlotte. She still avoided his eyes. He fought to overcome the disappointment. Perhaps it would be best if they were in London. She would be safe, and he would have time—*please God*—to learn the truth about the mysterious happenings at the Abbey.

"Of course!"

He glanced up to see the marchioness clap her hands.

"We shall have a party to celebrate." She smiled at him. "I am sure you would not object to a short visit in the next few weeks to celebrate such an auspicious event?"

Any doubts about the marchioness's intentions fled. "Of course not."

"Excellent! Let's see, we should have a ball, and, perhaps a dinner, exclusive of course, for only family, and a few special guests, such as the Seftons, and Castlereaghs, and . . ."

HEAVEN HELP HIM.

Evening shadows cast by the flickering candles only seemed to reinforce his loneliness.

The carriage had left hours ago, taking a piece of his heart with it. He was glad Charlotte was safe. But now she was gone.

The Abbey felt too big, too grand, too . . . lonely.

He shivered. The creakings and sounds of the house had never really unsettled him before. They had long been a part of the Abbey as much as the magnificent staircase, and his scientific mind had long-ago known of the settling of bricks and old timbers and foundations. But now the sounds seemed ominous, a portent of doom.

"I'm being ridiculous," he muttered to the room.

Flames glowed in the fireplace, gleaming gold as he swirled the yet-untasted brandy. He'd wanted a drink tonight, something to dull the pain of her departure, but the smell had been enough for his stomach to resist so far. His nose wrinkled—he'd lost the taste for such things—and he placed the glass back down as he thought of his betrothed.

His betrothed! So vibrant, so compassionate, her buoyant spirit the perfect counterpoint to his more serious ways, their shared faith and humor and mutual interest in art, botany, Wordsworth, and so many things surprising yet reassuring. And soon to be his! Excitement flickered, sputtering as doubts stole in, like the drafts whistling past the window frame.

Would Charlotte really marry him? Did she even want to? She seemed so uncertain at times. Was that her mother's influence, or her own doubts? Did she still hold affection for that Fanshawe fellow? For the Markham man? Would she prove faithful?

His heart clenched. "Heavenly Father, help me to trust."

The word seemed to soak into the old walls: trust. He had to trust both God and Charlotte. Trust that God truly did have good plans as promised in the Bible, and trust that Charlotte would learn to love him, and fully give him her heart, just as he had given his.

"Heavenly Father, help me trust."

A measure of peace stole into his soul. In the quiet he heard the faintest echo of a verse read at his wedding years ago: *"Charity . . . beareth all things, believeth all things, hopeth all things, endureth all things."*

The challenge rose before him, like a wavering flame. If he claimed to love, he would need to trust. "God, help me."

❧

London
One week later

"Oh, Charlotte, you look beautiful!"

"Tres magnifique!" Madame Lisette confirmed, in an accent that did not sound entirely French.

As the dressmaker bent to fiddle with the hem, Charlotte's attention returned to her reflection, unable to quite believe the exquisite picture presented was truly she. The ivory satin gown, cut square and low at the bodice, lay beneath an overdress of white spider-gauze delicately embroidered with silver roses. The short sleeves were lavishly trimmed with point Brussels lace, and the silk skirt possessed three tiers of ruffles cascading to the floor. The most beautiful dress she had ever seen, and far, far lovelier than that ridiculous court dress of so many months ago.

"Mademoiselle approves?"

"I . . . of course, yes."

Mama frowned at Charlotte, out of sight of the mantua-maker. "You look very lovely. I am sure the *duke* will approve."

The heavy emphasis on her future husband's title caused a twinge across her chest, but only seemed to make Madame Lisette glow with glee. "Of course! The beautiful maiden with the oh-so-sad duke. Ah, but he is rich, *non?"*

"One of the richest in the kingdom," Mama said proudly.

Before many more minutes had passed, they'd exited the shop and crossed the freshly swept street. Charlotte gave the street-sweeper urchin a coin before noting two figures approaching. Her heart sank. Lady Winpoole and her daughter, Clara.

"Ah, Lady Exeter."

"Lady Winpoole."

The mothers exchanged stiff curtsies, as Charlotte did with Clara.

Lady Winpoole turned to Charlotte. "I understand I'm to wish you happy." Her cold eyes and smile did not lend sincerity to her words. "When is the happy event?"

"Soon. We shall celebrate the announcement with a ball," Mama said, in a way that left no room for speculation that the Winpooles might expect to receive an invitation.

Lady Winpoole's face seemed to stiffen even more.

As the two mothers engaged in a volley of icy politenesses, Clara moved a little closer. "I am pleased to hear your news, Lady Charlotte."

"Thank you." She studied the older girl who had endured several seasons now. The hard edge seemed eroded from the polished young lady she'd first met nearly a year ago. "How was your trip north?"

"Oh, we did not make it so far, after all." Clara's cheeks flushed.

Her chest heated. So Aunt Patience *had* been right about the dowager's wicked scheme.

"I was wondering, Lady Charlotte, how does your cousin? I . . . am sorry about her situation."

The words, uttered in a tone without the slightest hint of falseness, accompanied as they were by Clara's drawn features, compelled Charlotte to cautiously own the truth. "Lavinia is . . . as well as could be expected."

Clara nodded, they soon parted, freeing Charlotte to follow in Mama's wake and reflect on her cousin's words from yesterday.

The earl and Lavinia had visited, calling in on their return to Lincolnshire, having spent time at St. Hampton Heath. The roses had returned to Lavinia's cheeks, her kindly interest in others undaunted as ever. But occasionally Charlotte had caught a wistful look, which saddened her and renewed her wish for her cousin to find joy and peace again. Lavinia had been all delight at Charlotte's betrothal, all happy acceptance to delay their return north to attend the upcoming dinner and ball to celebrate the engagement. It was only later, when Father, Mama, and the earl were firmly engaged in conversation, that her cousin had asked the question that caused sleep to elude her last night.

"Charlotte, please forgive my temerity in asking such a question, but do you love him?"

"Of course," she'd managed to say in a light tone.

"Of course?"

"Yes!" she said impatiently. "Yes. No. Oh, I don't know."

"You do not know?"

An eyebrow rose, prompting further honesty. "I felt sorry for him."

Lavinia blinked. "You're marrying him because of pity?"

"No! There are many other reasons."

"Keeping your mother happy should not be one of them."

"I think he is a good man. He wishes to marry me," Charlotte said, adding quietly, "he says he loves me."

Lavinia nodded, biting her bottom lip.

Mortification washed over her. "You don't think I'm good enough for him, do you?"

"Of course I don't think that. But he's been hurt, and if he's unsure of your affections—"

But she had kissed him—had even enjoyed it! Surely that was proof?

"—might struggle to trust you." Lavinia opened her mouth as if to say more, then seemed to think better of it, and closed her lips.

"What were you going to say?"

"I . . . forgive me for such an impertinence, but I want you to be certain in your choice."

Choice? For one glorious moment she'd thought she had decided, thought she could make him happy, and even be happy herself, but Sarah's silly speculations had fed doubts most toxic. She'd tried to talk to Henry, but he'd dismissed her, saying something about a husband's natural right to jealousy, and that if she behaved as she ought there'd be no need to worry. His words only fueled her anxiety, and her resolve to speak with William when next they met—if she could ever decide what to say.

Charlotte's thoughts returned to the present as she neared the carriage and Mama issued instructions to Ellen and Sarah about purchases still to be made. A footman handed them in, along with their packages. "Now, mind you only purchase the best."

The maids murmured assent, then continued their journey. Mama settled against the cushions. "As for us, we'll visit Gunter's for a restorative ice. Such excitement is quite wearying."

"Yes, Mama."

Mama's brows drew down. "I was concerned back at Madame Lisette's. Did you not like the gown?"

"It is very lovely."

"Well it should be, seeing as she's charging so much. I simply did not understand your lack of enthusiasm."

Charlotte pasted on a smile. "Forgive me. I'm a little tired."

"Yes, well, we have been a trifle busy this past week, I suppose. It might do you good to have a rest this afternoon. We don't want those roses lost," she said, stroking Charlotte's cheek.

For some reason her mother's uncharacteristic caress filled her with tears, forcing her to pretend interest in the ribbons of her reticule until she had sufficiently blinked away the emotion.

"No doubt you are missing him," Mama said.

"Missing whom?"

"Why, the duke of course!" Her eyes narrowed. "Who else could you think I meant?"

"No one," she said, forcing her lips to smile and her uneasy thoughts back to her betrothed.

❧ Chapter Thirty-One

Grosvenor Square
September 14

THE ROOM GLITTERED with a thousand points of shiny light, the bright glow from the chandelier above glinting off heavily beaded gowns, tiaras, and the silver epergne centering the dining table.

Charlotte glanced up to meet the dark gaze of the duke—no, *William*. She smiled, but the nerves tripping inside soon lowered her gaze to her plate. Ever since waking this morning, her stomach had been gnarled with knots, refusing even now to let her eat beyond the merest mouthful, forcing her to move the food around on her plate.

She'd half hoped the duke's arrival earlier would calm her nerves, but his careful, quiet conversation had only heightened her tension. There had been little of the lover about him, certainly no kiss, nor anything else that indicated he held any deep affection for her. Was he having second thoughts? Perhaps he did not trust her. She'd struggled to act normally, as other questions loomed inside. What was she to say? "Is it true you are a crack shot at Manton's? Could you tell me about the duel with your wife's lover?" For once she had been almost glad for her mother's intrusion, her gay insistence that they join the new arrivals, "For we cannot have tongues wag!"

Charlotte had caught the way he'd stiffened, and his polite smile, a troubling smile that did not meet his eyes. Was he also concerned about what tonight's announcement would bring? More disquieting was how such action elicited the memory of Sarah's words. Was the duke quiet by nature or design? And if by design, what was he *not* saying?

An hour later, she stood in the receiving line, cheeks sore from smiles as the cream of society came to pay their respects. From this position, between Mama and William, her nerves had reached fever pitch, her pulse a frantic patter in her veins. She drew in a desperate breath.

"Lady Charlotte?"

The quiet voice drew her attention, the duke's hand on her elbow providing support and comfort. She drew in another breath, caught the slightest tang of bergamot. She steadied, heart calming, and eased a fraction closer to his side.

"Charlotte," her mother whispered, still managing to sound shrill. "Remember, eyes are watching." In a louder voice she said, "Ah, Lady Buckington. How wonderful of you to visit."

When the countess had passed, Mama murmured, "You should have eaten more."

Of course she should have. But it was not the lack of food that filled her with trepidation.

Soon the strains of the musicians led to their release from the reception line. William captured her hand in his and led her in the first set.

Faces and gowns blurred into glimmering indistinction. She forced herself to focus on her betrothed. Dark slashing brows bade her glance away.

She caught Henry's frown. Caught Lavinia's concerned look. Around her the noise only increased. She felt her smile slip; she hitched it back up. She glanced back at the duke. He was speaking, but she could scarcely hear him over the musicians and the rushing in her ears. She forced herself to concentrate, to lean in to hear his words.

"Appear to be a trifle unwell."

Who did? Oh. Judging from the serious look in his eyes the duke referred to her. She swallowed, cheek muscles aching from her pose. "I am quite well."

He nodded slowly, as if disbelieving, so the next half hour was spent forcing herself to laugh and talk, until a comment about Lord Ware's garish waistcoat made him laugh aloud and her smile real. He *did* have a nice laugh, she thought, eyeing his smile lines and the warm sparkle in his eyes with approval—even if he did not laugh terribly often.

William's partnering soon gave way to the Duke of Sussex—high honor indeed, Mama said, as he did not appear at every young lady's ball—followed by a host of other gentlemen.

By the time the supper bell was rung, she was very happy to escape the crowd, but her nerves still did not permit her to eat more than a mouthful.

"Charlotte?" William moved near. "Is there something I can get for you?"

"I . . . I feel a little warm."

"Would you care to go to the terrace? I'm sure your mother would have no objection."

Was this a belated attempt to show his affection? Or was he simply being kind?

She accepted his hand as he murmured excuses to her mother. Once outside, the cool air seemed to knock sense into her, and she drank in great drafts. Slowly the nerves jangling through her system calmed. She was making the right choice. She was! Wasn't she?

"Forgive me, Charlotte, but you still seem a little pale. Do you wish for a drink? Perhaps some lemonade?"

She nodded. She wasn't thirsty, but if she could be by herself for a moment—if she could only think!—perhaps clarity would come. She grasped at the excuse like a lifeline. "Yes, please."

"I should not leave you on your own." His eyes held a slight frown.

"But I would relish it! Oh! I'm sorry. Not that I don't appreciate your company." As his lips curled to one side, she rushed on. "It is just I have been overwhelmed by all, by all . . . this." She lifted a hand, gesturing helplessly.

"I understand," he said, in a tone that suggested he really did. "But the efforts have been worthwhile. If I may say so, you do look truly beautiful."

She fought the spurt of irritation. *If* he may say so? As her husband-to-be, wasn't he *supposed* to say so? Why had he waited until now before saying something? The other men she had danced with tonight—why, even Henry!—had barely ceased in their compliments on her gown, her hair, her beauty. Was it too much to ask for the man she was supposed to marry to say something?

With a bow he was gone, her smile faded, and she rubbed her sore cheeks.

For a few precious moments she savored the solitude, savored the fresh night air. She exhaled, praying for the internal clamor to cease, when awareness prickled around her and within. Someone else was here. Her pulse accelerated. Had those threatening the duke come for her, too?

"Excuse me, m'lady."

She jumped, turning wildly, to see a footman wearing the Exeter livery. "Yes?"

"A . . . package has arrived for you."

"Oh! Is it a gift?"

He inclined his head. "If you would come with me?"

She frowned, following regardless. Why would Mama insist on such a thing now of all times?

Upon reaching the corner of the garden where the light was most dim, he stopped. "I'm told this is something you'd prefer above all." He stepped back into the shadows, as another man stepped forward.

She blinked. Blinked again, as the rushing in her ears returned, accompanied by a dizzying sensation. "You!"

Dark blue eyes flashed.

"Yes, only I."

"What . . . what are you doing here?"

"I had to see you." Lord Markham gave a low, bitter-sounding laugh. "I know you enjoyed my company in the past."

Chagrin writhed within. Her attentions to him *had* been a trifle marked. "Is it true? You chose Hartington?"

"I—"

"How could you?"

She swallowed. "It was Mama and Father's doing."

"You could've said no!"

"I—no. It was never like that."

"It is always like that." He drew near. "Why couldn't you wait for me?"

Before she knew what had happened, his arms were around her, her lips were under his.

She froze for an instant, before wriggling and straining, pushing him away frantically. She pivoted her head, dragging her lips away from his hot, insistent mouth. "My lord, please—"

"I love you, darling Charlotte. Can't you see how much you mean to me?"

Dazed, she shrank away, even as he pressed his lips to her cheek, scratching her with his unshaven chin. "I—"

"Good God, say you will not marry him." His breath was hot on her neck. "Say you love only me!" His ardent eyes glittered in the darkness.

"I love—"

"Markham! Get your hands off my daughter!"

Mama's low-pitched voice, so unlike her usual intonation, managed to pry his arms away. She stumbled to her mother's side, shaking, but Mama refused to look at her. "You wicked villain! How dare you?"

"Lady Ex—"

"Do not speak to me, and do not *ever* attempt to contact my daughter. If you do, I'll ensure my husband knows of the mischief you have tried to cause, and *he* will ensure you will hang. Do you understand me?"

"Yes."

"Now go!"

When his shadow had melded with the dark and they were sure he no longer remained, Mama turned, clutching Charlotte's arm with a pinching grip.

"Mama, I did not know—"

"How you could treat the duke in such fashion I do not know."

"But—"

"Give me no excuses! Your conduct is appalling! How you could behave so—I am so ashamed I do not know where to begin!"

"But Mama—"

"You will go inside and act like nothing happened," she said grimly. "If you breathe a word of this to anyone, the duke will call things off and you will die a lonely spinster. Is that what you wish?"

"No, Mama."

"Then return and behave as if nothing happened." Iron underpinned her mother's voice. "Do you understand?"

"Yes, Mama."

They returned to the ballroom, only to immediately encounter the duke. "Ah, Lady Exeter, I see you found her at last."

Charlotte attempted to smile. Her cheeks remained frozen, her heart numb. How could Lord Markham profess his love and then treat her so? His love was neither patient, nor kind, nor unselfish, though it seemed to persevere—

"Please forgive my daughter, sir. She's a trifle tired."

"I should not have left you." He gave Charlotte a glass of lemonade and an apologetic smile. "Such a crush of well-wishers."

She felt as fragile as crystal, like she might shatter at any moment. She prayed away the tears, prayed the smile would appear genuine enough. "Th–thank you." The fizzing liquid trickled down her throat.

He glanced at her mother, a faint frown between his brows.

He had been looking for her? Had he seen her in that wicked embrace? Oh, what would he do if he ever learned what Lord Markham had done? She felt herself sway.

He caught her, half leading, half supporting her to a couch. "My dear."

The quiet concern pricked her heart anew, drawing heat to her eyes. Why couldn't he approach her with just an ounce of Lord Markham's passion?

Her mother fluttered a fan, cooling her cheeks, whilst murmuring something about hartshorn and smelling salts. Charlotte closed her eyes, drawing welcome reprieve from the cacophony of sounds and light. Her mind formed a barely coherent prayer: *Lord, help me* . . .

"You must excuse her . . . so busy . . . hardly eaten a thing all day . . . perhaps another visit to the country . . . oh, yes, Charlotte loves hunting . . . thank you, sir, that would be *very* kind . . ."

She pried her eyes open, to see the duke standing next to her mother, the pair of them all outward solicitude, but both sets of eyes holding matching frowns.

❧

Hartwell House
Hanover Square, London

William studied the ceiling, shadowed in the dim light of dawn. Something had happened. He could tell by the way mother and daughter did not look each other—or him—in the eye. He prayed Charlotte had no second thoughts. Now their announcement was published in *The Times* he had no wish for further speculation. His offer to have them stay was mere guise for his real intention: more time with her. But still he sensed she would not care for his attentions, would shy away from his affections. After all, hadn't his betrothal kiss frightened her, making her timid with him later?

But part of him was growing greedy for her presence, greedy for the sunlight she brought into his world. Greedy for the hope of a future.

He rolled over in his bed, remembering how dignified and beautiful she was tonight, remembering her quick wit and their shared laughter, remembering the swell of her lips, remembering the curve of her lovely form in that gown.

Heavenly Father, help me.

He wanted her. Oh, how desperately he wanted her.

And how he wanted to believe that one day she would want him, too.

✺ Chapter Thirty-Two

Hartwell, Northamptonshire
September 19

CHARLOTTE SWALLOWED A yawn as the carriage slowed through the village of Hartwell. The journey had seemed interminable, the knowledge they neared their destination sweet relief. She glanced out the window, past Henry who rode alongside, to study the thatched cottages and other stone buildings rolling by, the neat hedges, their leaves gilded in the afternoon sun, the medieval church. All owned by the duke. All hers to share as soon as she became his duchess. Her heart panged.

She glanced across to where Father dozed and Mama glared, the frown in her eyes far more perceptible these days. The frost evident since that terrible night five days ago had grown icier, as if she could not wait for Charlotte to finally marry and be off her hands. She still refused to listen to Charlotte's pleas of innocence. It had grown to the point where Mama seemed to barely speak without snapping at her, something that had caused Henry to remark in surprise more than once, and had led him to insist upon accompanying them to Hartwell Abbey. Had led him also to attempt to speak with her, but her embarrassment had been so great she could utter nothing save some incoherencies about pre-wedding nerves.

For the wedding date had been set. Four weeks hence she would be married from Hartwell's tiny Norman church. She was here ostensibly for the hunting, but everyone knew it was to be much more. The banns were being posted this Sunday.

The carriage slowed to a walking pace.

Through the open window, her eyes met those of a woman dressed in black. Charlotte frowned. Had they met before? Nonsensical, but still, she appeared somewhat familiar.

The woman edged forward. Now that she was closer, Charlotte could see the grooves etched on her face. "Pardon me, my lady, but are you to be the new duchess?"

She nodded, as her mother snapped, "Oh, don't speak to the riffraff, Charlotte!"

Cheeks aflame, she caught the woman's glare, then returned her gaze to her lap. The duke's ring gleamed from her finger. She turned it over, studying the facets of the sapphire as the carriage jerked back into motion. He said it had been his grandmother's, that the blue stone reminded him of Charlotte's eyes.

"I trust I shall not have to remind you of your obligations?"

"No, Mama."

"You will *not* do anything to jeopardize your future with him."

Was this a statement or a question? She murmured, "Of course not."

She knew what was expected. Had known her family's expectations all her life. She would simply have to show the duke that he was right to choose her as his bride and trust God to help her love him and work this out for good—and trust this was not some gigantic mistake.

❧

"And this is called a hellebore, though some call it a winter rose. It grows in the foothills of the Himalayas."

She nodded, but otherwise said nothing, her marked look of disinterest as plain as his sinking hopes. William tried to reason with himself. Perhaps she was merely tired from a day's long travel. Or perhaps showing off the new acquisitions in the hothouses was a ridiculous idea, even though he'd thought the exotic blooms would prove to her taste.

He trailed after her, watching as she briefly examined the plants. The arrival of his London guests had filled him with anticipation, but his spirits had dipped when he saw his intended, wan and weary, as though drained by something other than travel. Rain showers had reduced his hopes for a romantic stroll through the gardens to a visit to the greenhouses to see the flowering camellias and hellebores. But what would he know? How could he have hoped her previous all-too-brief visit enough time in which to learn to please her?

She glanced over her shoulder. He forced his lips up. "I trust I've not hugely bored you."

"I am not bored." Her forehead creased. "Did I give that impression?"

"You did not give an impression of great enthusiasm, shall we say."

Her smile flashed, then her expression took on a pensive note again. "I think your flowers are lovely, sir. Thank you for showing them to me."

She pointed to his table, where an array of beakers held a variety of concoctions Callinan used for the plants. "What are these?"

He explained a little about his formulas, the distilling process, how plants held a range of special qualities that made them useful for everything from fertilizer to medicine. He pointed to the glass containers, whose contents were locked away each night. "This contains arsenic, this one cherry-laurel water."

"What a pretty name."

"But not a pretty drink."

"No?"

"I distill it for medicinal purposes. In tiny doses it helps suppress asthma, but in larger quantities it would make one very sick."

"How sick?"

"Deadly sick."

She nodded, eyed it carefully, then looked back at the house, as if she could not wait to return.

Where had the vivid Charlotte gone? What had happened? Was he that dull she could not bear his company? Could he ask that? Of course not! He glanced around, looking for something, anything that might hold her interest. Plucked a delicate blue orchid. "For you, my lady."

A wisp of a smile appeared. Disappeared. "Thank you."

"It matches your ring *and* your eyes."

Those eyes met his. Rimmed with doubt? Fear? Guilt? Or was it just nerves?

As they walked back across the graveled path he found himself growing more desperate. He wanted her to enjoy her time, but what had she enjoyed last time?

Suddenly it came to him. "I hope you will find time to honor Rose with a visit."

Her face lit. "Of course I will."

But those brief minutes he was privileged to accompany her as she played with his daughter before the dinner gong were only too short. It was perhaps fortunate he had several others to stay, including his sister and Lord Ware, as his betrothed barely looked at him, let alone found a smile to cast his way.

Throughout the evening meal and conversation, he found his own spirits waning. While it was good to see his staff were all solicitude toward her, now they knew her as his intended bride, the cynical part of him could not help wonder if their interest was self-motivated, and they were doing their best to make sure their attentions did not pass unnoticed. Charlotte seemed so tired, pale, with shadows under her eyes. Any attempt on his part to talk with her was quickly interrupted by her overzealous Mama, so he had yet to ascertain if it were illness or some other malady that made her appear so. He could only hope and pray a refreshing sleep would see her health and spirits return.

The next day

"Lady Charlotte, may I have a word?"

Charlotte glanced up. Judging from the look on Cressinda's face she doubted it would be a single word. Fighting the trickle of fear, she snapped shut *The Castle of Otranto* and nodded, gesturing to the space beside her on the garden bench.

"Thank you, I prefer to stand."

Oh dear. Charlotte summoned up a smile. They were to be sisters after all. And it wasn't as if William would permit his sister to *eat* her. "How may I help you, Lady Ware?"

"What you can do, my dear, is to start telling the truth."

She blinked.

"Oh, don't play innocent with me. You were seen."

"I beg your pardon?"

For a moment, something like a snarl swept across the older woman's face. "How can you pretend to love my brother when you kissed another man?"

She felt hot. Cold. Hot again.

"You do not deny it—"

"No! It wasn't like that!"

"Of course it was." She eyed the ring. "It sickens me to see you wear my grandmother's ring. How dare you? I've always known you were like Pamela, would play William for a fool. He's always been too trusting, too naive, better at understanding science books than people. He spent half a lifetime trying to win our parents' approval, only to carry on with their wishes even when they were dead, and it was obvious what a sad mistake such a marriage would be." Lady Ware shook her head. "He's always been too mild for his own good, would never hurt a spider."

"But he dueled—"

"Well of course he did! Society had spent long enough sniggering behind his back, and the family honor demanded he sacrifice personal scruples, yet here he is again, saddled with you." She eyed Charlotte with an expression close to loathing. "Such gall! You do not love him."

Her senses began to swim. She reeled in the lightheadedness, forced herself to focus. "No," she whispered. "You have it wrong."

"Love? Pah! You cannot know the meaning of the word!"

But she did! Love was patient, and kind, and long-suffering—

"Can you deny you kissed Lord Markham?"

❧

William stilled. Heard no denial from outside the library windows. The shame slithering into his soul at his sister's earlier words gave way to a wrenching pain. Hope dissolved in the continued silence. Prayers about trust seemed to crumple, melting like the first fall of snow.

Charlotte did not love him. She had never loved him. She would always love another.

His hands clenched.

❧

Hartington. Markham. Hartwell. Heartsick. Other images interspersed her dreams. Cressinda's venomous expression. The duke's averted gaze at dinner. Pistols fired on a dark night. The castle of horror—

Charlotte woke with a gasp. Was it just a dream? Or had she really heard that creak? She lay still, eyes wide open, ears straining, heart thumping painfully in her chest. The noise came again. A creak, followed by the slightest squeak, as if weight moved from one space to the next.

Dear God . . .

Her prayer was mere breath, then there was a wheeze and a thud, and a patter of something like feet.

"Sarah!"

She hadn't meant her voice to sound so shrill. Her maid raced into the room, half-drowsed, but fully anxious, holding a lit candle. "What is it, my lady?"

Charlotte huddled against the bedhead, glancing around the room frantically as her pulse beat a wild tattoo. "Were you in here?"

"I beg your pardon?"

"Were you here, in my room, a minute or so ago?"

"Of course not."

Coldness crept along her spine.

Her maid frowned. "Do you think you heard someone?"

Charlotte nodded, but was she sure? Had it been a dream? If she had heard someone, where would they be? Under her bed?

She screamed, jumping off, pointing to the bedclothes.

"Shh, shh." Sarah patted her back. "There's no need to be frightened."

She shuddered, wishing she could beg for Sarah to search under the bed, knowing such a request might be made known below stairs, and any respect the staff here held for her would evaporate completely.

Girding up her courage, and with another muttered prayer, she crept to the side of the bed, flinging up the heavily tasseled brocade valance.

Nothing.

She exhaled. Forced herself to laugh. Met Sarah's anxious expression with a strained smile. "I must have heard a mouse."

"I've never known you to be bothered by a mouse, my lady."

"I suspect it's something to do with staying in such an old house. One must expect creeping things."

"Especially when one devours the kind of novels as you do. Did you imagine a ghost had come to visit? Not that such a place as this might possess such things, and all."

Her skin tingled, but she refused to let Sarah see her fear, instead allowing the maid to guide her to bed and prop another pillow behind her back.

"Have a drink of water, and then you can lie back down and dream of far more pleasant things." Sarah moved to the small table where a jug of water and glass were positioned ready for guests. She poured two fingers worth into the glass, then handed it to Charlotte.

She tasted it, made a face. "Ugh."

"Come. I know you don't prefer water. But they say Hartwell water is direct from a spring underground."

Charlotte coughed. They might say that, but it tasted like it should have stayed there.

"Now, off to sleep with you," Sarah said, taking the glass. "You best be getting your beauty sleep. Just think on pleasant things."

Charlotte closed her eyes obediently, glad the sudden vision blurriness ceased. As the liquid stung her throat, her maid's words reminded her of the letter she'd found earlier, definitely not a pleasant thought.

Her name, in a script unknown, scrawled across a paper propped upon the dressing table. She—and Sarah—had assumed it was from the duke, so she'd waited until her maid had exited before opening and reading.

But it was not.

It was from Lord Markham. Wishing to know if this were the end, or if she would run away and marry him. She'd nearly flung it in the fire but had instead stowed it in her Bible, knowing it was the one place she could be sure Sarah would not search in her ever-assiduous duties. The questions raged, burning through her brain. How had the letter arrived here? Who had placed it here? Did the duke employ someone who could be bribed by Markham to do such a thing? Was it a test from Cressinda? Was she even safe? What would the duke say should he learn of such a thing? Why, he would be horrified!

Her heart stung, her throat constricted, and a pain began in her temple. She had no wish to hurt the duke. He had been misused by his first wife and she didn't want him to suffer that way again. Her lips burned at recollection of the kiss Markham had forced upon her, nothing like William's tender passion that excited her senses. But it was more than that. She loved watching him with Rose, and could well imagine him always the devoted father, devoted husband.

Charlotte twisted to her side, working to ease her discomfort. Husband? No. Yes? *Heavenly Father?* Did she love him? Could she be patient with his reserve? Share his hope for improving life for others? Enjoy a future built around a mutual love for God? Yes? No, yes. With certainty, yes.

The fire in her head now spread through her chest like a vise.

She coughed. Nothing happened. Tried to speak. Her throat was clamped. She couldn't breathe. Couldn't breathe! The room faded to black.

❧ Chapter Thirty-Three

William drew in a deep breath, working to keep the anger at bay, as he eyed the drawing room's other occupants. "I repeat: I do not like to be made a fool. If you have information pertinent to my engagement then I wish to know immediately!"

"Oh, but William—"

"Cressinda, I heard you accuse Charlotte this afternoon!"

His sister flushed. "Perhaps you should ask Lady Exeter."

William eyed the pale marchioness seated beside her husband and son, whose airs of confusion suggested William wasn't the only one who had lived too long in the dark. Outside, the night wind stirred ivy to scrape against the windows. "Madam? Am I to understand something has happened between Lord Markham and your daughter?"

"Oh, sir, I'm sure it's nothing but a silly misunderstanding." She gave an artificial-sounding laugh. "You must not credit every bit of tittle-tattle."

"I am not. I merely ask about the veracity of *this* particular piece of speculation."

"What is this all about?" Lord Exeter frowned, looking between them. "I thought Markham dealt with months ago."

"Exactly so," his wife said, nodding desperately. "Perhaps you could speak with Charlotte tomorrow. Such a shame she retired so early—"

"I wish to know *now* if the marriage should be called off."

"Oh no, no, sir! She'd be a fool not to choose you! As it is, she denied planning to meet him—"

"Where? When?"

Her gaze dropped. "In London, on the night of . . . the night—"

"The night of our engagement ball." At her nod he slumped in his seat.

"What?" exclaimed Exeter. "Constance, I cannot believe—"

"Duke, Charlotte assures me it was all Markham's doing!" Lady Exeter said frantically.

"Enough." He held up a hand. "I cannot stand to hear another—"

A commotion, then a knock, drew their attention to the drawing room doors, which were immediately flung open by a footman. "Pardon the intrusion, sir, but it's the young lady."

"Charlotte?" His chest cramped. "What has happened?"

"She's extremely ill."

"What?" Lady Exeter paled. "Not my dear Charlotte!"

"Her maid wishes a doctor to be called immediately."

"Of course. Hurry." He nodded a dismissal.

"I should go, see what my darling daughter needs—"

"Mama, no," said Henry, catching William's eye, as he gently pushed his mother back in her seat. "You know you can never abide illness."

She allowed herself to be persuaded to remain, to be comforted—or admonished—by her husband, releasing William and Henry to hurry upstairs.

Travers hastened toward them. "I'm sorry, sir, but Lady Charlotte is in a sad way. Her maid thinks it might be poison."

"How can this be?" He pushed into the room to see a scene reminiscent of his nightmares. Charlotte—*his* Charlotte—lay curled on the bed, long unbound strands of golden hair spread wildly about, while her teary-eyed maid gently slapped her face. "Wake up! Wake up, my lady!"

Oh, dear God . . .

He rushed to her side, felt her wrists for a pulse, found a thready beat. "What has been done for her?"

The maid turned a tearstained face to him. "I found her like this. She woke me not half an hour ago, and was complaining of hearing things, but I thought she'd been dreaming. I told her to have a drink of water—"

"What water?"

She pointed to the glass. He dashed it up, sniffed. Felt himself sway. "Oh, dear God!"

"What is it?"

He gently pulled down Charlotte's bottom lip, and sniffed. The same bitter almond scent tickled his nose. "Henry, help me turn her on her side."

"What are you doing?"

"I think she drank cherry-laurel water."

"What?"

"It is lethal when taken in large enough quantities." Henry helped him reposition her. "How much did she have?" William barked at the maid.

"I don't know!"

"A swallow? A glassful? How much?"

"I don't know— I— Not too much. She doesn't like water, sir."

His heartbeat grew frantic. "She must wake and expel the poison before it travels farther in her body."

As her brother slapped her face far more vigorously than her maid had done, Jensen rushed in, holding a spoon and small bowl. "I've brought mustard and warm water. When I heard it might be poison—"

"Give it here." William's hand shook as he took the teaspoon and directed it to her mouth. "Henry, help her sit upright, and open her mouth. Get some ammonia!" he snapped at her maid, who scurried out.

"She won't open," Henry said desperately.

"Force her to! Do you want your sister to die?"

Recriminations rushed over him. Oh, why had he shown her his poisons? Why hadn't he realized the depths of her despair? *Heavenly Father, make her live, make her live!*

Henry forced open her lips, allowing William to shove in a spoonful, hear her choke. "Good!"

The maid rushed back with a small bottle. "Quick! Wave it under her nose. She needs to wake; she needs the poison out."

As Henry continued clutching his sister's shoulders, the maid waved the bottle of ammonia under her nose. Again a choking sound, then heavy-lidded eyes fluttered open. Blue eyes glanced at him, she seemed to withdraw, but he forced in another spoonful of mustard-laced warm water.

"You will not die, do you hear me?"

She blinked. Coughed. Spluttered. Tried to pull away.

He chased her with the spoon. Another spoonful pushed in. "You will *not* die!"

She coughed, then gave a kind of heaving breath, before retching.

"Excuse me, your Grace." The maid bustled him out of the way, holding the bowl as her mistress coughed and upended the contents of her stomach.

William backed away, prayers chasing fears. "Jensen, get coffee. And brandy!"

As the maids hurried to help, Henry shifted from the bed to stand beside him. "I don't understand."

He could say nothing. He wished he didn't understand. But he did, and the fact made him want to weep.

She would rather choose death by poison than marriage to him.

Dr. Lansbury found William and Henry later, holed up in the billiards room with Exeter and Ware, trying to play a clumsy game while their hearts paced more frantically than their fears. At the news of her daughter's brush with death, the marchioness had collapsed into hysteria, necessitating her maid's strenuous efforts to calm, before a strong sedative had settled her to sleep. Jensen had sent down a message a quarter hour earlier to say Charlotte was improving, but it had not alleviated their fears. Some form of order and control was necessary, otherwise their pacing threatened to send them all mad.

"How is she?"

Lansbury shook his head. "I don't like to say. I've given her a dose of iron and soda to help balance the system, but this does not always prove effective."

Henry ran a hand through his rumpled hair. "Why aren't you still up there?"

"The maids are up there now, caring for her. I cannot do much until we see how the medicine takes effect."

William cleared his throat. "And you think it was the cherry-laurel water?"

"Aye, I do." The doctor's gaze narrowed. "How a young lady came to be in possession of such a thing I do not know. It's a good thing you knew what to do, sir." He bowed and exited the room.

Recrimination swirled within. "I showed her the cherry-laurel water today."

Exeter's eyes flashed. "Then *you* are responsible!"

"I did not give it to her! I told her it was harmful. I thought it locked away."

"But . . . but why did she have it?"

"I don't know."

"You don't think . . . ?" Henry's voice quavered. He pressed his lips together, but his chin trembled. After a moment, he said, "She would not wish to harm herself."

"Of course not." Was that a lie?

"No." The younger man's voice sounded firmer now, more assured. "No, she *wouldn't*. And I cannot believe Sarah would hurt her. She loves Charlotte."

William's lips twisted. She wasn't the only one. Despite the painful revelations from the earlier interview, the past hour had confirmed his love may be bowed but not broken. He'd set her free to marry Markham if she so wished. If she only lived.

"So who *is* responsible? I want them found and punished!" cried Charlotte's father.

"You don't think Wrotham?" Ware murmured, in an aside.

"No." The last missive concerning that man's whereabouts had him on a boat to America.

Gradually, the panic besieging William's heart eased to a dull roar. If Exeter was right and someone had poisoned Charlotte, then perhaps she was not disinclined to marrying him, after all. Could he have been wrong about other things, too? *Heavenly Father?*

He stilled. Listened. A wisp of memory begged recollection. What was it? "Sarah."

Henry looked at him with narrowed gaze. "No, I told you. She adores my sister."

"Remember? She said something about Charlotte hearing something, waking."

"That is nonsense."

"Not necessarily." He gestured to the ancient walls. "These past months we've had a number of strange happenings."

"The fire." Exeter nodded.

"Amongst other things. When she stayed before, Charlotte mentioned having seen a strange person on the premises. I did not believe her at the time, but later . . ." Other memories flickered, surfaced, firmed. "I saw someone, too."

"Who?"

He strove to remember, but the image remained indistinct. "I cannot say."

"A man? Woman?"

"I . . . I do not recall."

"You think someone wants to harm Charlotte."

"I think someone wants to harm me, by any means possible."

"But why?"

Suddenly a name and image solidified, as a very good reason planted certainty in his soul. "Because she wants me punished for wishing to marry again."

"She?"

"Yes, she."

"But who?"

A vision of a curse, of a woman driven mad with grief, wavered then formed before him. What had she said? She would make him sorry? He shuddered. Well, she certainly had.

"Hartington?" Henry shook his arm. "You look as though you've seen a ghost."

Perhaps he had. He rubbed a hand over his face, wishing the late hour hadn't made him so weary he could barely think through such fogginess. Ghosts? Death? Curses? He shook his head, as if the action could shake free the darkness encroaching his wavering faith.

Heavenly Father, help me see.

Like mist lifting for a sunny day, his soul's torment suddenly eased. His God was greater than the fears, greater than evil intent. The God who loved him, who loved Charlotte, did not want to see harm but had plans for good and not for evil, to give them hope and a future.

Truth firmed in his soul, giving courage, giving strength.

"We need to pray."

Henry flushed. "Fact is, I have been."

"So have I. But we need to pray here, right now." Without waiting for embarrassed assent, he closed his eyes, and declared, "Heavenly Father, I thank You that You are in control, that You are a good God who loves Your children." Conviction solidified, his heart weighty with truth, and a certainty he was being heard beyond the billiard room's four walls. "Heal Charlotte, heal her completely, Lord, and protect us from the attacks of the evil one. In the name of Your Son, by whose stripes we are healed, amen."

"Amen," the others echoed faintly, gazing at William in fascinated interest.

He felt a burn creep across his cheeks, but his faith was not negotiable, and he stared back. This moment called for conviction not hesitation.

Exeter's cheeks flushed. "I . . . er, thank you."

"Don't thank me. Thank God she still lives, and pray she sees morning."

So tired. Heaviness pressed upon her limbs. It hurt to breathe. Hurt to swallow. She could barely move. Charlotte lifted her lashes. A blurry figure. Sarah. Sitting by the window, her lips moving as if in prayer. She closed her eyes. Thoughts whirled around her brain, a clamor of confusion and nightmare, the thumping in her head echoed in a distant sound. Such odd dreams! Ghosts. Secrets. The duke. A kiss. Tenderness in dark eyes. Passageways. Pain. Life. Loss. Hope. Future. Marriage. Love. Yes?

Yes.

Darkness drew her down.

Ӂ

When she next awoke it was to see sunlight streaming through her window, and a strange man sitting beside her bed. Mama was there, wringing her handkerchief, chattering like a nervous bird to the unknown man. She finally glanced in Charlotte's direction, her wearying stream of prattle coming to an abrupt halt. "Oh, Charlotte! You are awake! Oh, Doctor! She's awake!"

"Now, Lady Exeter," the man—a doctor?—said cautioningly.

"Oh, my darling! I thought I'd lost you!"

Charlotte tried to speak. Coughed instead.

"Here, have some water."

Instincts recoiling, she drew back, shaking her head.

"It is safe, my lady," Sarah assured, taking a sip, before helping Charlotte. "See?"

She swallowed. The thirst subsided fractionally. "What . . ." Her voice grated like a creaking door. "What happened?"

"You've been unwell," Mama said, with a sharp look at the doctor, "but Dr. Lansbury here says you're getting better now."

The doctor nodded. "You were quite sick, my lady, but it seems you're on the mend."

"I . . . I dreamed such strange and frightening things."

"That was not a—"

"Thank you, Lady Exeter," the doctor said, frowning at Mama.

Her mother pouted, but said nothing more.

From far away came a faint hammering sound, pressing against the ache pounding her head. "That noise . . ."

"The duke." Mama's forehead wrinkled. "Is it too loud? Shall I tell them to cease?"

She shook her head. Pain ricocheted. She winced.

"Oh, my dearest girl! What is it?"

She studied her mother, whose puffy eyes told of tears and turmoil, yet the anxious strain within them spoke more deeply of her love and concern. Tears heated her eyes. How long had she dreamed to see Mama's love?

"Oh, Charlotte! I could not bear for you to leave us. Not my darling girl. Not my sweet angel. Not my—"

"Come now, Lady Exeter," calmed the doctor. "No need to become worked up."

"Oh, but I love her," Mama turned to her, smiling through her tears. "I love you, dearest."

"I love you, too, Mama."

Her mother clasped her hand, speaking soothingly, until the doctor murmured she should leave. "Do not be upset, my dear. Your father will wish to see you, and I shall return after your rest."

Charlotte's lips twitched, but she simply said, "Thank you, Mama."

When her parent had exited, Charlotte eyed the doctor and Sarah, standing nervously behind. "What happened?" she whispered, to avoid aggravating her throat. "Why is Mama acting so peculiarly?"

The doctor sighed, while Sarah clasped her hands. "Something happened three nights ago." The doctor frowned. "You do not remember?"

"No."

"Oh, my lady! Such a terrible night! We thought you were—" Sarah stopped.

"You thought I was. . . ?"

Sarah gulped. "You were so still, see. And none of us knew quite what to do. It wasn't until the duke came in—"

"The duke was here?"

"Yes. Oh, don't look like that, my lady. He's *such* a good man. Nothing inappropriate happened."

Heat swept through her body. "He saw me in my nightgown?"

"Yes, but—"

"Oh!" She covered her face with her hands. How embarrassing!

"Please don't be upset. It's just that you were so unwell, and he needed to know—"

"What I looked like in my nightwear?" Never would she have picked him as such a man!

"He came to help you, Lady Charlotte," the doctor said calmly, his voice settling her fractionally. "As your maid said, nothing untoward happened. I believe he maintained the strictest notions of propriety. In fact, if not for him . . ."

At the doctor's uncomfortable look, she pressed. "What did he do?"

"He saved your life, my lady."

What? Charlotte glanced at the doctor, who nodded his confirmation. "I don't understand."

In a few words, the doctor explained, leaving her internally cringing, yet with an immeasurable sense of gratitude. "His Grace did that for me?"

"Yes." The doctor took her pulse, frowned. "Now, I don't like to see you getting excited. I want you to try to rest some more."

"Rest. Yes."

She closed her eyes obediently, listening as the doctor issued instructions to Sarah, before hearing the door open, then close. She peeked to see Sarah drawing close the curtains.

"Sarah."

Her maid jumped. "Oh, my lady, you gave me such a start! I thought you were asleep."

"I will soon, but first I wish you to do something for me."

"Of course."

Charlotte swallowed, then issued her instructions.

※

Another fruitless day.

William slumped into his chair, the desk piled high with papers, and closed his eyes. What could he do? He'd thought he'd know more by now, but there had been no news. His men's search for the nighttime intruder had failed to turn up a single lead, save for the discovery of several tiny rooms the Abbey had finally divulged, necessitating their being nailed shut in recent days. And while he had his suspicions, indeed had shared such suspicions with Jensen and Ware, he rather doubted anyone's ability to do anything but respond belatedly to any upcoming crisis. William sensed this situation was only set to accelerate further.

Father, help us.

He stilled his mind, waiting for the peace of God to fill him, but the questions and fears refused to be silent. His letter to Bow Street, requesting information pertaining to a certain individual had not yet been answered. He sighed, turning back to the letters requiring attention. Missives from Mr. McAdam, from Hawkesbury, from Barrack's caregivers, from the Duke of Sussex could wait a day or so. He read a letter from the man tasked with ascertaining Wrotham's whereabouts. Relief filled him; he'd arrived in New York. He quickly scrawled a response, then another to the letter from Bethlem. The board of trustees would simply have to meet without him. He dared not leave the Abbey, not with matters still in such a perilous state.

He leaned back in his seat, shifting to gaze out the window. Near the boundary he could see a number of workmen ostensibly digging a new garden, their movements thin disguise for their real purpose: protection. But what to do now? How could he move forward, when he always seemed a step behind his adversary? Clearly it behooved him to remove Charlotte from the Abbey to a safe location, but how could he be sure where that would be? Surely any new location would soon be discovered; after all, servants talked, innkeepers talked, other travellers talked. No, between the marquess, Henry, and himself, they had determined she was safest staying here, at least for a little while. But what then? What should he do?

A scratching sounded at the door, and he called for admittance. Surprise filled him at the sight of the maid, Sarah. "Yes?"

"Pardon me, Your Grace." Her eyes were large, her voice quavery.

His insides churned. Surely Charlotte hadn't worsened. "How is your mistress?"

"Awake now, sir, thank you. She seems a little better."

Relief flooded his chest. "Thank God."

"Aye, sir, that I do."

She was a praying girl? Good. Charlotte needed all the prayers she could get. "What can I do for you, Sarah?"

She blushed. "'Tis not for me, sir, but for my lady. She be asking to speak with you."

"Now?"

"If it's not inconvenient, sir."

"Very well."

Two minutes later he crossed the threshold into the room of his nightmares, halting at the sight of Charlotte lying in bed, bleary-eyed, weary and wan.

He acknowledged Lord Exeter, sitting on a low chair beside her bed, a book opened as if he'd been reading to her. Her father nodded and rose to remove to a position near the window, from which he assumed a fixed perusal of the grounds. Conscious of the impropriety of being in her room, William remained near the door, and bowed. "Good afternoon, my lady."

"Good afternoon, sir." Her voice was too soft, her cheeks too pale.

"How are you feeling?"

"Better, thank you."

"I'm glad." He paused. Why was he here? What did she wish to say?

"My father visited"—her eyes seemed tinged with apology—"with a volume of Wordsworth's. Remember our discussion on his merits?"

Pain slivered through him at the memory of their firelit laughter-filled discussion weeks ago. A lifetime ago. Back when he'd dared believe romance might be possible for him after all. Had she been pretending to agree with him all this time? He jerked a nod. "I'd rather you recall three nights ago."

A look of surprised hurt filled her face.

He pressed on, ignoring the twinge of conscience. "Do you remember *anything* about that night?"

"I . . ." She closed her eyes, but the furrowed brow spoke of concentration. "No."

She *could* not remember, or *would* not remember? He smiled grimly. "Ah, well. I told you our Abbey had many secrets, remember?"

"I remember." Dull eyes sparked. "Perhaps your Abbey holds ghosts after all."

"Perhaps."

A delicate blush transfused her face. "Sir, I . . . I understand that I owe you my life."

He stepped forward then checked himself. "No, that is . . . no. You owe me nothing."

"That is not what others say."

Dismay chased the suspicion creeping through him. Surely she wasn't now going to admit she loved him, out of some misguided sense of obligation? "Lady Charlotte—"

"Sir, I—"

"Please continue," he gestured, bracing internally.

Blue eyes fixed on his, unwavering. "I cannot begin to thank you. I thought what happened but a nightmare and did not dream I lay so close to death. In those moments, I . . ."

Here it comes, he thought miserably.

"In those moments I realized how much I wished to live, and live with you as your wife."

She paused for breath, and he felt the anger spurt again. What about Lord Markham? He glanced at her father then back at her, keeping his voice low. "We shall discuss such matters later when the doctor and your parents believe you well enough."

As soon as he spoke he regretted his tone, her glistening eyes wrenching pain in his chest. But now was not the time to discuss their future, not with the villain still to be found, not with so much uncertainty, not with all his doubts.

She closed her eyes and grimaced, lifting a hand to her head.

"Charlotte?" William hurried to her side.

Lord Exeter turned, stepped closer. "Charlotte? Shall I send for Dr. Lansbury?"

She rubbed her forehead. "Please."

As her father exited the room, she licked her lips, leaving him transfixed by the movement. "I'm so thirsty."

Sarah retrieved a glass, then assisted Charlotte as she carefully sipped. When she turned her head away, indicating she'd had enough, she caught his hand, and gingerly pressed it to her lips. "Thank you, William."

Heat throbbed at the site of her caress. Twin moonlit oceans beckoned him with light and promise. But he could not yet trust, could not yet believe. Pulse racing, he gently removed his hand and forced his steps away, offering another bow, followed by muttered excuses that he must away.

He returned to his study and sank down at his desk once more, as images and questions continued.

Charlotte. Bewitching as always, beguiling as ever. Holding his hopes prisoner and his dreams captive. The captivating Lady Charlotte. How he wished their vows were said and he could hold her in the way he imagined. A savage pang twisted his heart. How he *wished* he'd never heard anything Cressinda had said. How could Charlotte look at him like that, speak such sweet words, if she loved another?

He groaned, sank his hands into his hair, as hope battled hurt.

What was he to do?

❧ Chapter Thirty-Five

Four days later

WHAT COULD SHE do to show him he could trust her?

The duke now knew about Markham—Mama had admitted as much—his mistrust obvious in the way he refused to meet her eyes, save that one time in her bedchamber. His short answers, the disappearance of any tenderness, merely confirmed it.

He did not love her. He did not trust her.

Heat pricked the back of her eyes.

Oh, wretched woman his first wife had been, scarring him to such a degree that he struggled to believe any woman now! Her vision blurred; her bottom lip trembled. How could he decide not to love her, when she'd finally realized just how much she cared? She knew now that she loved him, this deep certainty within, a blend of warm affection and high esteem. Coupled with the awareness that throbbed whenever they met, it only underlined her conviction that she would never meet his equal. What could she do to show him she truly meant it when she said she looked forward to being his wife?

A shiver ran through her at the memory of his kiss. While her feelings for William might never excite the same depths of heady passion once induced by Lord Markham, his kiss, his hug, now only made her hungry for more. Her midsection fluttered. William might never wish to read Byron by firelight, but he *was* someone who would both know how to light a fire and ensure his every tenant be warmed sufficiently. And in a marriage, wasn't kindness and forbearance to be preferred to romantic sensibility?

That is if they were to be married at all. Even Mama seemed to have her doubts, despite plowing through preparations in a frenzied way, as if determined to complete arrangements before something could prevent them. No. Despite her having undergone an experience worthy of a gothic heroine—something that should have most gentlemen declaring undying love—the duke had said nothing. Surely if he truly cared, he would have said something? Her soul writhed. Except wasn't she trying now to not be so self-centered? *Lord, forgive me my selfishness. Help me be a blessing to William. How can I show him how much he means to me?*

She glanced out the window. The rose gardens beckoned, the past few days of warm cloudless skies lifting their scent. "Sarah, please find my parasol."

"Oh, but the doctor says you must be careful not to exert yourself."

"And I will be. But I cannot stay inside a moment longer."

Ignoring further protest, Charlotte hurried into her pelisse. She needed to get downstairs before her mother made her afternoon ascent to the sickroom.

Within twenty minutes they had achieved the rose gardens, the only notice they'd attracted was from Henry, who happened upon them in the hall, and offered his arm amid concerned cautionings. His arm she was glad to accept; his chiding less so. As sunlight bathed her face, she gloried in drinking in fresh air, the feeling of freedom at finally escaping her room.

"Lady Charlotte."

A rush of gladness filled her at the voice. She turned.

And met the duke's black gaze. Her heart chilled. "Sir."

There was an exchange of bow and curtsy. She compelled her lips to remain tilted. "Is it not a glorious day?"

"I thought you knew to stay inside."

"Oh, but—"

"Featherington, I'm disappointed you condone this behavior."

The duke's words apparently nettled Henry as they did her, but while her brother resorted to flushing, she could not be so circumspect. "I do not wish to be caged like a prisoner."

"No?" The dark brows lifted. "What *do* you wish for?"

What had upset him? Why did his words hold a faintly ominous tone?

She released her brother's arm and moved closer, forcing herself to smile playfully. "Surely you know the answer to that, sir?"

He stepped back, eyes unsmiling, refusing to play her game. "I'm afraid I do not." He turned and walked away.

Leaving her aching, bereft, and fighting tears.

⁂

Twilight shadows stretched deep across the study. He should get dressed for dinner, but couldn't be bothered moving. He was a fool. A sentimental fool. Deceived by a fair face and sunny humor. Misled by a broken heart and foolish dreams. Hadn't her flirtatious ways in the garden this afternoon only revealed the truth?

"The post, Your Grace," Travers said, holding out a silver salver.

He collected the letters, ripped open the one from London, scanned the contents. Let out a long breath. Markham had not been seen for weeks. The doubts roared again, dragon-like, spewing fire across his soul. A scratching came at the study door then it opened. "What now?"

The footman's eyes widened. "Pardon the intrusion, sir, but have you seen the young lady?"

"What?"

"Sarah, the maid, says Lady Charlotte is nowhere to be found."

Fear arrowed within. He pushed to his feet. Went upstairs. Found it only too true, as he met the hand-wringing maid and mother.

"Oh, dear Duke. Tell me you know where she is!"

"I have not seen her for several hours."

"She was resting after her walk," Sarah averred. "I only left her for a few minutes."

"Evans said—oh, Hartington, I did not see you there." Henry pushed into the room past the servants. "Evans said no horses have been taken, and the footmen have found no trace of her downstairs."

"The attics?"

"They are searching now."

His heart twisted. Surely she hadn't run off?

"Oh!"

He spun on his heel, facing her frightened-looking maid who held a piece of paper.

"What is that?" The marchioness snatched it from her hands, reading it before stumbling to a chair. "Oh, no! The stupid, *foolish* girl!"

Pulse thudding with trepidation, William held out a hand, and the white-faced Henry passed the letter to him. "I'm sorry, Hartington."

He scanned the letter, his hopes dropping. "Where did you find this?"

"In her Bible." The maid gestured to the book, opened at first Corinthians chapter thirteen.

He studied the underlined verses, ones to do with love being patient, trusting, hoping always. How love never failed.

His heart wrenched. Clearly she had twisted such words to justify her feelings for Markham. He clenched his hands.

"The simpleton!" The marchioness moaned. "I told her Markham would never come up to scratch."

William slowly exhaled, tamping down the anger as he turned to her. "You said Charlotte denied it."

"She said it was all *his* doing. You must believe me!"

"I confess, madam, I find it hard to believe anything you say." He eyed the maid, cowering in the corner. "Were you aware of your mistress's affections?"

"Sir, she might have loved him once—"

But she had never loved William.

"But she did no more, I'm certain. Besides, she was so weak she could barely stand after our walk. And how could she leave without anyone noticing?"

"Enough." He strode away, the heat blazing across his chest and eyes begging release.

"Sir." Henry clasped his arm, looking terribly young at this moment. "I cannot believe Lottie would do this."

"No? Unfortunately, I can."

Shaking off Henry's hand, he spun and left, mortification chasing his heels.

❧ Chapter Thirty-Six

After the wild and dangerous imaginings of the past week, this dream was far more delightful. She was being carried, the scent of sandalwood tickling her senses as sweet murmurs filled her ear. "Dearest love, we shall soon be there. Do not worry."

She smiled in her sleep. Why should she be anxious? She was safe, held in the arms of the man she loved, whose soft words and dulcet tones assured her he felt the same.

"I love you, my darling."

She sighed, snuggling closer. "I love you, too."

Warm lips touched her brow, touched her cheek, touched her lips, tasting of—

Her eyes opened. She gasped. "You!"

Lord Markham smiled, teeth glinting in the moonlight. "Of course it is I."

Was this delusion? Cool night air nipped at her cheeks. She glanced up at the canopy of twisting branches, then down at her gown, now covered in a man's black driving coat. "What are you doing?"

"Rescuing you, my love."

"No." She struggled for release. "Let me go."

"We shall both go, my dear." He chuckled. "Can you guess where?"

Charlotte stared at him. *Dear God, no . . .*

"Scotland, my love. Tomorrow we'll be husband and wife."

"What?" She wriggled more strenuously. His arms tightened. "Are you mad?"

He laughed. "Mad with love, *my* lady."

His emphasis sounded possessive, with nothing of the duke's respectful caress.

"Ah, here we are. Your chariot awaits."

She twisted, writhing even more violently as she saw the carriage. "No! This is wrong. You cannot take me—"

"Ah, but you are mistaken, for this is right, and I do take you."

The door opened, and she was pushed inside. She scrambled to open the door opposite, but was barred by an outstretched arm. Turning, she faced a woman dressed in black, who eyed her with the malevolent glare she recognized from the village before. Charlotte shrank against the seat as Markham pounded the padded ceiling and the vehicle began to move. "Oh, stop, please stop!"

"Hold your tongue," the woman said, in heavily accented English, before spewing forth a volley of French Charlotte was pretty certain were blasphemies.

Fear rushed up her spine. "Who are you?"

"I serve Her Grace."

"Who?" She wriggled from Markham's hands, to no avail. "My lord, please stop!"

"But I cannot! To not have you in my arms again after so long is more than I can bear."

She struggled as his hand crept to her waist then climbed higher. "Please stop!"

"Markham!" The woman's whiplike voice finally stilled his hands, which he brought to rest on Charlotte's thigh.

She shuddered, tears clogging her eyes and throat. But she could not yield to crying. She had to think. Had to think! *Lord, help me!*

Dredging up a smile, she picked up his hand and held it firmly to the seat. "Not now." Not ever.

"You are not worthy!" The woman hissed, before releasing another volley of invectives.

Ice ran through her veins. "Worthy of what?"

"You'll never take her place!"

"*Whose* place?"

"The Duchess of Hartington." She shook her head. "You'll never mother her child!"

"But Pamela is dead!"

Crack!

Pain splintered up her cheek as her face was knocked to the side. A rushing filled her ears, muffling Markham's angry protests. Now the tears leaked. She touched her cheek. Saw blood. Her vision hazed in and out as a torrent of words flowed between the others.

"Maria! How dare you strike her?"

"Pah! She's nothing but a strumpet, pretending to love you, pretending to love that fool duke. Can't you see she does not love you?"

"That is not true." Lord Markham turned to her. "Tell her it isn't true!"

"I . . ." Charlotte glanced between them, terror rising within. What should she do? She pretended to swoon.

"Now look!"

"She pretends. See?"

A savage pinch almost released a scream, but she kept her teeth clenched, her limbs motionless.

"Maria, stop! I won't let you hurt her!"

"You are such a weakling, like that fool Rogerson, like Exeter's stupid footman, like all men. So easy to manipulate. You see a pretty face, and your brain forgets to work. But what do you really know? She plays you for a fool!"

Charlotte kept still, forbidding the luxury of a single movement. She had to escape. They were as mad as each other. But what could she do? What could she do? *Oh, God, please help!*

❦

Faith wrestled fears. Hope grappled shame. Love struggled to believe.

After a desperate hour's search revealed nothing, his guests and servants regrouped in the Great Hall. He could barely look at them, knowing he'd see pity in their eyes, resignation in his sister's. He'd had enough of pity. And yes, he despised his weakness, falling for another pretty face without character. Did a bigger fool exist on earth than him? Torturous thoughts kept him searching, kept him moving, otherwise he'd be tempted to curl up and hide and never see another soul again.

A sound drew their attention to the landing. Henry. Listening to the maid. Holding that wretched letter. "Sir, you should hear this."

A minute later, Sarah stood tearfully before him, explaining more about the night her mistress had been poisoned. "I just realized, it's the letter that was on her bed the night she was poisoned. I thought you wrote it, sir—"

"Why would I do such a fool thing?"

"But don't you see? It must've been *him* in her room! The night she nearly died!"

Something cold swept across his soul. "You think he wants her dead?" Not his Charlotte.

"I don't know, but I cannot think she went with him willingly." She sobbed. "Please sir, she said she heard noises that night."

Yes, she had. Had he wronged her, after all? Hope propelled his feet up the stairs to the bedchamber, trailed by Henry and the others. "Where did she think she heard the noise?"

The maid pointed to the wall near the window. "I think she heard it around there."

He took a step back, frowning as he examined the wainscoting.

"Hartington? What is it?"

William briefly explained his suspicions to Henry. "I'm hopeful tonight the Abbey might give up more of her secrets. Now, does anything look odd to you?"

They studied the east wall. It was in two sections, the upper consisting of quite plain wooden panels; the lower tier's panels marked with scrollwork and four pilasters. About chest height stretched a frieze of intricately carved pears and apples, entwined with roses and the harts of his family emblem. He began knocking on the wall.

"Sir?" Jensen said. "What are you doing?"

"Searching for a secret passage."

Henry, Ware, and Jensen joined in with tapping, until a hollow sound emanated from the panel closest to the window. "Here!"

William gripped each piece of fruit, twisting, pressing within. Finally one shifted. With a click of the carved wooden rose, the door spun open silently, as if recently oiled, into blackness. "Voila!"

As the others rejoiced, Jensen ran to get a lamp.

"This room used to be the master, remember?" Cressinda said from the door. "Mother didn't like that it connected to outside, and reorganized the bedchambers when you were a boy."

"I don't recall."

She frowned. "But how would Charlotte know about such things?"

"Perhaps she didn't." He sent her an even look.

His sister's mouth formed an O, her look of sympathy sending a burn to his throat.

Jensen returned, the lamplight revealing the passageway's recent use, the long stringy remains from the destruction of spiderwebs.

"Sir, look!" Jensen pointed to footmarks. Large boot prints in dust, such as might belong to a man. And small boot prints, such as those belonging to— "A woman passed through here."

His heart sank. So she had gone willingly?

"Your Grace!" Sarah's anxious face loomed behind him. "They don't be my lady's. Her foot is bigger." She retrieved a boot he recognized as Charlotte's and placed it next to the mark. It was bigger, by at least an inch.

"Then . . ."

"She was carried, sir."

Dear God! One guess by whom.

❧ Chapter Thirty-Seven

Charlotte peered beneath her lashes. The carriage was picking up pace, pulling farther away. If she did not escape soon, she'd be hard-pressed to ever find her way home to the Abbey. But what could she do? *Oh, Lord, help me!*

Snatches of a plan shimmered into being. She sighed, fluttered her lashes. "Oh!"

"Darling!" Markham's hands lifted her up. She fought the shudder, tried to act pleased. "She did not mean it, you know," hot breath whispered in her ear. "But these French, you know how they can be."

"I feel so wretched." She groaned, clasping her head. "Ever since the poison . . ."

"The poison?"

At the frown in his voice, she glanced up, glad to see a matching scowl on his face. She pointed at the woman seated opposite. "She poisoned me. I nearly died!"

He growled something before demanding to know if this was true. Maria at first tried denial, but it was apparent Lord Markham did not believe her. "You could have killed her!"

"Pah! She did not have enough for that—"

With a curse, Markham leapt at the woman, leaving Charlotte free. As the two wrestled, she saw the woman reach under the cushion, drawing out a pistol. Horror bade her to freeze, but she had no time. She leapt at the door, pressed down the latch, the momentum swinging her outside to tumble down onto the road, just as an almighty bang came from within the carriage.

There was a shout, and the horses whinnied and took off at a canter. Sobbing, Charlotte pushed to her feet, but her knee buckled and she fell. Gravel bit into her skin.

Pushing up onto her hands, she half crawled, half limped to the side of the road. She could not stay; they would return. She must hide in the woods. She stumbled into the black forest, thankful for moonlight, but knowing the very thing that aided her would also aid her abductors. She must flee into darkness. "God, help me!"

❧

"Your Grace! We heard a gunshot."

William stumbled from the cellars, the mystery passageway's terminus, into the pools of pale light on the grass afforded by the Abbey's windows. "Where?"

"In the woods. Pattinson just got in, said it happened not more than ten minutes ago."

His mouth dried. For ten minutes she might have been lying injured . . . or worse.

"Evans, go saddle Neptune. Jensen, get the others, divide up. We must find her."

He raced to the gunroom, selected a pistol, his pulse thundering as the last of his doubts tumbled. If a gun had been deemed necessary, surely Charlotte had not gone willingly after all.

❧

The trees were too big and dark, the night air filled with a hundred noises she did not wish to know. Desperate to return to the Abbey, she stayed along the edge of the road, ears straining for the faintest sound to indicate her pursuers neared.

Fear rippled through her. A stitch tormented her left side. Her mouth tasted of blood and dread. She had to get home. Had to get home!

To think she now counted the Abbey as her home! A broken chuckle escaped, quickly smothered in a sob. Not that the duke wished for it. His attitude was very clear. He no longer wanted her. But she did not want the man who professed he did. She tripped over a branch, tumbling into mud. Shuddered out a quiet moan. What would her life be now? Would the duke cry off, the scandal ensuring she be sent to live with an obscure relation, like poor Maria Bertram from *Mansfield Park*?

Oh, if only she had told the duke how much she cared! If only she had shown him that she loved him. Her eyes filled, spilled. If only he believed her . . .

A faint sound arrested her tears. A horse. She froze. Had they returned on horseback?

She pushed to her hands and knees, palms stinging with a thousand cuts. With a stifled sob she rushed back to the cover of the trees, stumbling through thickets and stubby trees.

Now the breeze carried a faint voice. "Charlotte!"

She pressed on, blood pulsing in her ears. She would *not* go to Scotland. She would *not* be forced to marry someone for whom she could not care. She would not!

A large rock loomed in front of her. She hurried forward, its very bulk providing assurance. As she huddled in the dark, she heard another voice, a much, much fainter voice, calling her to be still, to wait, to trust God.

She closed her eyes. *Lord, forgive me for not trusting. Help me believe Your plans are good. Help me trust Your promises, no matter what tonight brings.*

Gradually the voice calling faded, and her heart's wicked pace dropped to a mere gallop. She breathed in, wrapping her arms around her knees, wishing she still had the dark cloak to hide beneath. But she'd left that in the carriage. The carriage! Had Lord Markham been hurt? She did not care for him, but—*Lord, please don't let him be injured.* She shivered. How could she have ever thought herself in love with him? His actions tonight had proved his love selfish, whereas the duke . . .

Her eyes filled again, only to drip down her cheeks. How many times had William proved his affection? His recent actions she'd forgive, knowing they'd come from a place of hurt. But over and over he'd shown himself the better man, the wiser man, the kind, unselfish man. The man she loved, the man she wished she could call husband.

Dear God, help him give me a second chance.

No sooner had the prayer escaped her heart than a twig cracked.
She spun around.
And screamed.

CHAPTER THIRTY-EIGHT

THE SCREAM PEBBLED his skin. Charlotte!

William gestured to Henry and slipped from Neptune's back, tying his reins loosely around a branch. He ventured into the woods, pausing every so often as his ears sought to hear the noise again. There!

Two voices. He stepped closer, uncomfortably aware that he was not protected from behind, hoping Henry had understood his silent message to get help.

Another step. Another.

A twig cracked. He bit back a curse. Pressed on. Ahead, a large boulder was dimly visible in the waning moonlight. He crept closer, closer. Another step . . .

"Your Grace."

He spun around to see the figure holding a pistol aimed at his heart.

Nausea swished through his stomach at the sight of the bedraggled figure huddled beside her. "Charlotte! Thank God. Are you hurt?"

She shook her head. He took a step forward.

"Get back!" Maria hissed, waving the gun at him, before training it on the frightened girl.

He froze. "Maria, your argument is with me. Release her, please."

"No! You cannot have her, not when you took away Madam."

"I didn't take Pamela away. She died."

"No!" she screamed. "She cannot be dead! They said the baby died, but she lives. How do I know Madam does not also?"

"Because she is buried in the cemetery not a mile away."

"You lie!" Beside her, Charlotte's tears fell unchecked.

"Maria, please let Charlotte go," he begged.

"No. I've seen the way you look at her, like you used to with Madam. He would have abandoned you too, you know," she hissed at Charlotte.

"I abandoned nobody." William stepped forward, thankful he drew the maid's attention—and weapon—back to himself.

Maria spat another curse, pointed a sticklike finger at Charlotte. "She must be gotten rid of. I promised Madam to keep her child safe from this one."

"So you poisoned her."

"Yes."

"And Lord Markham?"

"Such a fool. So easily persuaded." She cackled.

"Where is he now?"

"Who knows?" The maid shrugged. "Probably bleeding to death where I left him."

Charlotte gasped, hand over mouth.

"Yes, I shot your lover—"

"He was not my lover!" Charlotte turned pleading eyes to him. "He came to London and tried to kiss me. Mama saw, but she thought I arranged it. But I didn't. I promise you I didn't!"

"She lies!" Maria said.

"No! And then he wrote a letter begging me to run away, which I wouldn't do. He took me when I was asleep. I had to escape, I didn't know"—she hiccuped—"I didn't know what he would do!"

"*Pauvre enfant*," Maria mocked. "She has always loved him."

"No! How could I?" Charlotte's blue eyes widened. "He is nothing compared to you!"

He snorted. "Because I am a duke?"

A sob escaped her. "Because you are good, and faithful, and not self-seeking—"

"He will leave you, like he did my mistress!" Maria cried.

"I did not abandon Pamela," William said. "She abandoned me for Wrotham and a host of other men."

"Could you blame her for wanting more? Wanting more than your coldness, than your plants, than that oh-so-ugly house, than an oh-so-ugly husb—?"

"Stop!" Charlotte gasped, tottering to her feet. "Do not say such things."

Her words, leaping to his defense, trickled hope into his heart. If only he could be sure that her escape was not only from Maria, but from her handsome Markham as well.

The sound of the pistol cocking snapped his attention to the maid, her weapon pointed at Charlotte's chest. "Maria! Stop." William drew out his pistol, readying to aim. "I do not want to shoot you."

She gave a hysteria-laden laugh. "You! You think yourself so clever, but you are an *imbecile*! I'm not afraid—"

His finger twitched.

Bang!

Maria staggered, looked at the blood staining her gown, then at him. "I hate you." She spat another curse in French, then redirected the gun.

"Lord Markham!"

At the sound of Charlotte's voice, the pistol cracked.

Fire grazed his left arm. William stumbled to one knee, clutching his shirt through which seeped the unsettling sight of blood. In his periphery he caught the sight of Charlotte's handsome beau rush toward her, saw her face light, saw him claim her lips with his, heard the shouts and moans of chaos.

And he toppled to the ground, conscious of nothing but his complete and utter failure.

❧

"Get off me!" Charlotte pushed at Lord Markham, straining away from his scalding touch.

"Charlotte! Charlotte, my love—"

"I am not your love!"

A moment later the pressure released. "Sorry, Lottie," Henry muttered, arms pinning Markham from behind. "He got away from us."

Us. Heart racing, she glanced at the other rescuers: Evans jerking a bloodied Maria to her feet, Jensen and Lord Ware kneeling beside the duke, lying on the ground.

"William!" She crawled to his side as the valet pulled up a sleeve, caked with blood. "Oh, tell me he isn't dead!"

"He's breathing," Jensen muttered. "But bleeding heavily." He tugged off the duke's neckcloth, folded it, then held the padded fabric against the wound.

She inched closer, smoothed the duke's rumpled hair. "Oh, William . . ."

"Lady Charlotte," began Lord Ware, "you really should not be here."

"Of course I should!" she snapped. "He's soon to be my husband."

The duke stirred, the thickly lashed eyelids lifting. Pain filled the darkness of his eyes. "Charlotte . . ."

"Yes, my dearest?"

"Now sir," his valet said, "this might hurt a little."

He winced as Jensen wrapped another neckcloth around the wound and pulled it tight.

"Come, Hartington," said Ware. "Thought Manton's star would prove a better shot than that. Only winged her."

"Only intended to." William's smile flickered.

"You're Manton's star shooter?"

Ware chuckled behind her. "Only his best."

Charlotte bit her lip, before finally asking, "Were you really in a duel?"

William's lips flattened. "Much to my shame. I let pride overrule good sense and called out Wrotham."

She swallowed. Dared anyway. "Rose's father?"

"Perhaps." He shrugged. Winced.

"Sir," Jensen said, "please don't move."

Ignoring him, William grasped her hand. "I cannot know for sure. My wife was never discreet with her favors, shall we say."

"I'm so sorry."

"So was I, for a very long time. Until I met you." He smiled.

Her breath caught. What a wonderful, passionate, handsome man he was.

"Still, dueling was a stupid thing," he muttered.

"It was a necessary thing. Wrotham was an utter scoundrel," Ware said. "Always thought you went too easy on him, Hartington. Some men deserve to be put out of everyone's misery."

"Where's Markham?"

"Henry's got him now. Oh, I wish I'd never met him!"

"But I love you!" shouted Lord Markham from behind her.

"Shut up," snarled Henry, as Ware staggered to his aid.

"Love?" Charlotte shivered. "You never really loved me." Not like William. Who loved her so selflessly. "I know now I *never* truly loved you."

"She knows nothing!" Maria screeched. "She's nothing but a silly, stupid girl—"

Evans clamped a hand over her mouth and dragged her away.

Charlotte's attention returned to the man Jensen had assisted to a sitting position, the man who watched her so intently. "She's wrong. I know that love is more than just a feeling, more than just emotion." She thought back to Lavinia and her earl. Swallowed. "Real love perseveres through the hard times, never giving up. True love trusts."

The duke's eyes flickered. "Trust."

His whisper swirled between them. Oh, if he could only learn to trust her again!

She bent closer, fixed her gaze on William's dark, dark eyes. "There is no choice between you. Markham was a foolish fancy, but you're the substance of my dreams. Oh, if only you could believe me!"

"I do believe you."

"I didn't realize what would happen. I only want you."

"I believe you," the quiet voice said again.

"I'm so sorry, I didn't know—" She paused as his words sank into consciousness. "You believe me?"

"I love you."

The words from Scripture sang in her memory. "Beareth all things, believeth all things, hopeth all things, endureth all things . . ."

"I love you, too." A rush of assurance warmed her insides. She *would* believe, she *would* hope, she *would* endure. The God of love would help her. "Oh, William, I love you so very much."

By the pale thin moonlight she saw his smile, saw his eyes light, and she pressed into his arms, her lips finding his. Pleasure tingled in their touch, curling heat in her midsection as he returned her affection fervently. How wrong she had been. *Here* was passion, passion that fueled hope, igniting dreams.

Faintly she heard the sounds of protest from her brother and the man he held, but she did not care. She cared only for the man *she* held, whose arm had stolen around her back, pulling her to him, as his lips became more urgent—

"Ahem!"

She glanced up. Saw the stunned expressions. Drew back. Her cheeks heated. "Forgive me, William. Your arm."

He grinned. "I wasn't thinking of my arm just now." And he pulled her into another embrace.

"Lady Charlotte, you'll be doing the man an injury," Ware called.

William's arm tightened around her, his lips finally drawing away. "Go find your own wife, Ware, and see if you can sweeten her into acceptance of my new bride. I thoroughly recommend this method." And he kissed Charlotte again.

"Charlotte, no!"

With a wail, Lord Markham was led away, following the hysterics of the black-clothed maid. Charlotte turned her head away, buried her face in the duke's shoulder, smelled his scent of bergamot and honor, and drew in a deep, reassuring breath.

"Oh, William."

"Yes, my darling?"

"I know you do not care for London, but if possible, could we please live *quietly* in the country?"

And the joy in his laughter chased out the last of her fears.

 Epilogue

Hartwell Abbey
April 1845

CHARLOTTE LAUGHED, TICKLING little Rose's bare feet as she crawled across the blanket. The sun was shining, the day warm enough to sway Mrs. Bramford and Nanny to the benefits of a picnic, and her husband to take a more substantial break from his latest scientific plans. He looked so cheerful these days, so much younger, the light in his eyes rarely dimming, save when he returned from his visits to Bethlem and reported on poor Maria's condition or heard news of wretched Lord Markham and Rogerson, soon to face transportation to Van Diemen's Land.

A shadow crossed her mind at how easily she'd been led astray. How childish to have thought love was something that happened to her rather than something she could learn to cultivate. She knew William would keep her heart safe, but more importantly, she'd determined not to permit anything to hinder her love for him—no offense, no unforgiveness—as she sought to put him first. And the more she strove to bless him, to be a blessing for him, the more she found her affection growing. Learning to appreciate his many kindnesses had only increased her esteem for him, had only made her realize just how much she had for which to thank God. For without Him, this joyous, precious life would never have been possible.

She drew in a deep breath of rose-scented air and smiled, her heart singing unto heaven.

❧

William watched his wife, his wife so full of love and affection as she played with their daughter. He'd never dared dream to feel so happy, to know Charlotte was as content as he. All doubts had fled, his trust renewed, her manner warm and playful with him, her look and tone becoming frosty and most duchess-like whenever somebody tried to take a liberty.

Not that there was much chance of that. They barely left Hartwell, Charlotte declaring no place was nicer—especially now the tunnels were all blocked up. The priest holes were kept open, at her insistence—and that of Henry's—ostensibly "for Rose's sake" they said, but William suspected it was more for their own amusement, just as he and Cressinda had also found such things diverting in younger days. Cressinda had not visited *quite* so often in recent months, William's quiet word with Ware about controlling his wife's tongue seemingly doing the trick, just as it had with Lord and Lady Exeter. The marchioness's overbearing presence was such that he couldn't bring himself to issue invitations beyond the barest necessity.

His wife's blue eyes caught his, and she smiled at him, that secret smile hinting at the arrival they both hoped would join them before another Michaelmas had passed. Joy sparked anew in his chest.

God was good. His plans were good. He was faithful. Together they would trust Him.

Author's Note

Vauxhall Gardens, which so delighted Charlotte, was one of London's chief places of pleasure beginning in the 1660s. The gardens were privately owned, cost a shilling entry fee, and were situated just south of Westminster—behind the present-day location of Britain's Secret Intelligence Service, MI6! They were much as described here, with entry via boat across the Thames, and filled with twinkling lanterns, musicians, and twisting paths amid trees perfect for clandestine rendezvous.

John Loudon McAdam was a Scottish engineer, whose signature smooth coating for roads became the precursor for what is known as tarmac today. He lived in Bristol in the early 1800s, and made a number of proposals to Parliament about the benefits of his method of road construction. I like to think that the scientific, progressive Duke of Hartington would be keen to adopt his methods, hence his inclusion in this novel.

While Hartwell Abbey is completely fictional, I have based some of its design and features on the magnificent Woburn Abbey in Bedfordshire, including the twenty-four views of Venice painted by Canaletto.

In 1814, London was filled with relief that the long-running war with Napoleon was over. This led to the Prince Regent sponsoring a number of celebrations: the parade of Coalition Allies on June 20, the ball at Carlton House on July 21, and celebrations in various parks on August 1, which involved a number of high-priced extravaganzas, such as a balloon ascent in Green Park, reenactments of Nelson's victory on the Serpentine, and the building (and unfortunate accidental burning) of a seven-story Chinese pagoda in St. James's Park. (History tells us these celebrations were a trifle premature, as Napoleon made one final push before the Battle of Waterloo in 1815 finally sealed his fate, but we all benefit from hindsight, don't we?)

On a far more personal note, Lavinia's experience with miscarriage is another blend of fact and fiction. In 2001, after four years of marriage, my husband and I were thrilled to learn I was expecting. I still remember waking before dawn only a few weeks later, knowing something was wrong. In those cold, dark hours as I watched a precious life ebb away, I felt myself challenged: I had praised God in church only the day before; could I still praise God even when my world tumbled apart?

The Bible doesn't promise a life of roses, but God does promise to be with us, that nothing can separate us from His love. My challenge in those dark hours was whether I would blame God or actively trust Him by doing what He says. I chose to "put on the garment of praise for the spirit of heaviness" as described in Isaiah 61. Like Lavinia, I was desperately sad, but in those days and weeks afterward, I felt the depths of sorrow were eased by this decision to sing by faith.

At times the Bible may seem full of contradictions: love your enemies, do good to those who persecute you, rejoice in times of trouble. They're easy phrases to say, so much harder to do.

I hope that no matter what situation you might be facing that you'll be encouraged to turn to God, not away, and allow Him to ease your burdens and heal your pain. In the words of a former pastor of mine: our God loves us, His plans are good, and we can trust Him.

God has proved this in my life; God will prove it in yours, too.

ℛ Acknowledgments

THANK YOU, GOD, for this gift of creativity, and the amazing opportunity to express it. Thank You for demonstrating the ultimate in sacrificial love through Jesus Christ.

Thank you, Joshua, for your love and encouragement. I appreciate you more than you know.

Thank you, Caitlin, Jackson, Asher, and Tim—I'm so proud of each of you, and so thankful you understand why Mummy spends so much time in imaginary worlds.

To my family, church family, and friends, whose support I've needed when I felt like giving up—thank you. Big thanks to Roslyn and Jacqueline, for being patient in reading through so many of my manuscripts, and to Kim, for believing in me even when I didn't believe this dream could come true.

Thank you, Tamela Hancock Murray, my agent, for helping this little Australian negotiate the big wide American market.

Thank you to the authors who have endorsed, encouraged, and opened doors along the way. Carrie Turansky, Dawn Crandall, Julianna Deering, Angela K Couch, Kara Isaac, Rita Stella Galieh, and Narelle Atkins, you are a blessing.

To the Ladies of Influence and Ladies Who Launch—your support and encouragement is gold!

To the great team at Kregel: Noelle and Katherine, Joel, Steve, my editors Janyre, Becky, and especially Dawn Anderson, thank you for making Lady Charlotte look pretty and read better.

Finally, thank you to my readers. A novel is merely words on a page until someone reads them. Thanks for helping spread the love for Miss Ellison. I hope you enjoyed Charlotte's story, too.

God bless you.

Visit carolynmillerauthor.com for a book club discussion guide and more about upcoming titles.

REGENCY BRIDES
A LEGACY of GRACE
BOOK 3

The
DISHONORABLE
MISS
DELANCEY

REGENCY BRIDES
A LEGACY of GRACE

CAROLYN MILLER